What will we encounter when we escape Earth's boundaries to reach other worlds, other solar systems, perhaps even other galaxies? How will we defend ourselves from unknown perils, hostile aliens, and dangerous environments? Who will we forge alliances with, and who will they be against? These are some of the questions tackled in thirteen original tales that will remind readers of science fiction's golden age even as they take us into the farthest future. . . .

"Procession to Var"—The Guardian had been left by the Great Ones to protect all they had left behind, but were the strangers who'd come the enemy or some part of the Great Ones themselves?

"That Doggone Vnorpt"—How do you bounce an alien out of your bar, when he could eat you by accident, wasn't harmed by blasterfire, and couldn't take even the most obvious hint?

"The Silver Flame"—What were you supposed to do when the small artifact you were supposed to convey turned out to be both alive and dangerous?

"A Time to Dream"—They thought him a doddering old fool dreaming away the last years of his life. But time and space were funny things, and when the call to battle came from the Earth Protection League he knew he would not fail to meet the challenge. . . .

GUARDSMEN OF TOMORROW

More Imagination-Expanding Anthologies Brought to You by DAW:

FAR FRONTIERS *Edited by Martin H. Greenberg and Larry Segriff.* Thirteen of today's top authors—including Robert J. Sawyer, Alan Dean Foster, Kristine Kathryn Rusch, Lawrence Watt-Evans, Julie E. Czerneda, and Andre Norton—blaze new pathways to worlds beyond imagining from: a civilization of humans living in a Dyson sphere to whom the idea of living on a planet is pure mythology . . . to an ancient man so obsessed with an alien legend that he will risk ship and crew in the Void in the hopes of proving it true . . . to the story of the last free segments of "humanity," forced to retreat to the very edge of the galaxy—in the hope of finding a way to save themselves when there is nowhere left to run. . . .

STAR COLONIES *Edited by Martin H. Greenberg and John Helfers.* From the time the first Homo sapiens looked up at the night sky, the stars were there, sparkling, tempting us to reach out and seize them. Though humankind's push for the stars has at times slowed and stalled, there are still those who dare to dream, who work to build the bridge between the Earth and the universe. But while the scientists are still struggling to achieve this goal, science fiction writers have already found many ways to master space and time. Join Robert J. Sawyer, Jack Williamson, Alan Dean Foster, Allen Steele, Robert Charles Wilson, Pamela Sargent, Mike Resnick, Kristine Kathryn Rusch, and their fellow explorers on these never before taken journeys to distant stars.

MY FAVORITE SCIENCE FICTION STORY *Edited by Martin H. Greenberg.* Here are seventeen of the most memorable stories in the genre—written by such greats as: Theodore Sturgeon, C. M. Kornbluth, Gordon R. Dickson, Robert Sheckley, Lester Del Rey, James Blish, and Roger Zelazny—each one personally selected by a well-known writer—among them: Arthur C. Clarke, Joe Haldeman, Harry Turtledove, Frederik Pohl, Greg Bear, Lois McMaster Bujold, and Anne McCaffrey—and each prefaced by that writer's explanation of his or her choice. Here's your chance to enjoy familiar favorites, and perhaps to discover some wonderful treasures. In each case, you'll have the opportunity to see the story from the perspective of a master of the field.

GUARDSMEN
OF TOMORROW

EDITED BY
MARTIN H. GREENBERG
AND
LARRY SEGRIFF

DAW BOOKS, INC.
DONALD A. WOLLHEIM, FOUNDER
375 Hudson Street, New York, NY 10014
ELIZABETH R. WOLLHEIM
SHEILA E. GILBERT
PUBLISHERS

ACKNOWLEDGMENTS

Introduction © 2000 by Larry Segriff.

A Show of Force © 2000 by William H. Keith, Jr.

Blindfold © 2000 by Robin Wayne Bailey.

Wiping Out © 2000 by Robert J. Sawyer.

Smart Weapon © 2000 by Paul Levinson.

Procession to Var © 2000 by Andre Norton.

The Gemini Twins © 2000 by Paul Dellinger.

That Doggone Vnorpt © 2000 by Nathan Archer.

The Silver Flame © 2000 by Josepha Sherman.

Stardust © 2000 by Jean Rabe.

Keeping Score © 2000 by Michael A. Stackpole.

Alliances © 2000 by Kristine Kathryn Rusch.

A Time to Dream © 2000 by Dean Wesley Smith.

Endpoint Insurance © 2000 by Jane Lindskold.

CONTENTS

INTRODUCTION

by Larry Segriff

Adventure stories. FTL ships rocketing through space; the Space Guard keeping vessels safe from pirates; ray guns, BEMs, and damsels in distress. These are the stories I grew up on, and these are among the stories I still like to read.

Robert Heinlein. Isaac Asimov. E. E. "Doc" Smith. And, of course, Andre Norton. These are some of the people whose work I devoured growing up—and, in Andre's case, whose new books I eagerly look forward to.

Space opera has changed a lot since the Golden Years of SF. The laws of science are followed more rigorously, for example ("modern" spaceships don't bank when they turn), and the people in the stories tend to be more well-rounded, and even more flawed . . . more human, if you will. But the heart of space opera—the rousing sense of adventure, the strong pacing, the exotic settings, the larger-than-life issues—these haven't changed. Or, if they've changed at all, they've only gotten better . . . as the stories in this anthology prove.

So sit back, turn the page, and enjoy . . . but before you do, you might want to buckle your seat belt, 'cause it's going to be a wild ride.

INTRODUCTION

A SHOW OF FORCE

by *William H. Keith, Jr.*

William H. Keith is the author of over fifty novels, divided more or less equally between science fiction and military technothrillers. While most of his SF is written under his own name, he writes the military novels under a variety of pseudonyms. His most recent work is *Europa Strike*, third in a planned series of military science fiction novels written under the pseudonym Ian Douglas.

"Watch your helm, Mr. Sotheby," Captain Fifth-Rank Greydon Hazzard said quietly. "Put a dent in that thing up ahead and they're going to be taking it out of your pay for the next ten thousand years objective."

"Aye, sir. We're at fifty-three meters per second, in approach."

Hazzard could sense the drift of the ship, the tug of gravity, the caress of the photon breeze, the shrill, insistent drag of the interlocking magnetic fields of planet, star, and galaxy. The frigate *Indeterminacy* was edging gently toward the orbital moorings, primary sails folded, her impetus coming now entirely from way sails and jigs, her secondary drive barely ticking over.

Jacked into the virtual display of the shipnet, Hazzard was immersed in the data feed, with a crystalline, all-round view of the approach, just as though he were perched out on the fifty-meter thrust of the ship's dorsal flying jib spar. The sprawl of Tribaltren Station spread across star-limned blackness dead ahead, the nearest bastions and field guide towers now just ten kilometers distant, dark and monolithic against the soft, liquid-light glow of the Milky Way.

The moorings about the station were crowded with other vessels, and there was heavy traffic in the approach and departure lanes. The steady wink of IFF netbeacons and shipboard running lights crawling across three dimensions would have been a bewildering tangle of confusion to any observer not equipped with an AI that could make sense of the chaos and feed it in manageable chunks to the bridge.

"Approach Control signals we're clear for Bay 12," the comm officer of the watch announced. That would be Midshipman cy-Tomlin. Bright kid. Steady, with a streak of laziness that watch-and-watch for a few subjective months would cure. And of course, with the cy-enhancements, he was of the Chosen and destined to go far in Union service.

"Very well. I see it." Text and flickering symbols overlaid sections of Hazzard's view of the sensory feedscape around the vessel. He could see the steadily incoming trickle of navigational data both from the *Indy*'s helm and from Tribaltren Station Approach Control, see the traffic sites of other ships in the moorings, see the readouts for all departments and decks of his own ship. All of that information played across his brain, instantly accessible, but his responsibility was the whole, not any given part. He held back, aware of the rhythm of ship operations, giving orders when needed, but letting his people do their jobs. *Indy*'s officer complement was a good one, well trained and experienced. Her crew, like most crews in the fleet, was a mélage of gutter sweepings, metplex gangers, and pressed c-men, but, by the Goddess, they were *his* sweepings, gangers, and c-men, and he was proud of how they'd shaken out over the past three months subjective.

He took a moment to check crew deployment on the

Indy's starboard foremast, a constellation of golden stars, each light representing in netgraphic clarity the position of a sailhandler maintaining the delicate set and trim of the 2,000-ton frigate's spacesails. At the moment, only the foreways'ls were set, giving the ship just enough of a vector that she could maintain way.

The image of Tommis Pardoe, *Indeterminacy*'s First Lieutenant, materialized to the right of Hazzard's viewpoint. "A good deployment, First," he said. "The new hands shaped up well." *Indy* had been on blockade duty off Danibar, three months subjective pacing back and forth at near-*c*, which had translated to almost two years of tau minus.

"Thank you, Captain." He sounded worried.

"Problem, First?"

"Just wondering what the urgency is, sir. The dispatch calling us in to Tribaltren was still smoking when it came across the comm station. 'Report immediately,' it said. Where's the war?"

"All around us, Tom. We'll find out in a few hours which particular part of the war is so urgent."

"I suppose so, sir. But it's not like they don't have plenty of assets right here in port."

His senior lieutenant had a point. Closer in to the mooring station roads, the ship traffic ahead resembled a swarm of angry stingflies, everything from service bugs, LO coasters, and single-sailed planetary luggers to huge three-decker first-rates.

An alert klaxon sounded through the shipnet. "Bridge, port lookout! We have a collision alert. Incoming at port high at two-zero-three plus one nine!"

Hazzard spun his point of view, looking off *Indy*'s port beam. A ship moved athwart the blue-white crescent of Tribaltren IV.

"Mass reading! Ninety-eight thousand tons, range 705 kilometers. It's a first-rater. . . . *Goddess!*"

That last exclamation accompanied the deployment of a dozen sails, spreading across the first-rater's yards. She was huge and blunt-prowed, a five-hundred-meter dagger shape carrying several square kilometers of mesh sail, a Galactic Union ship of the line. On *Indeterminacy*'s sensory feeds, she was painted a patchwork red and black, with white trim highlighting the lines of sealed firing ports along her three gundecks. The G.U. flag materialized across her foreways'ls as their surface displays altered. A second emblem shimmered into visibility beneath the first, a family crest in red, gold, and black.

"She's the *Victor*, Captain," Lieutenant Pardoe observed. "One-oh-two. Captain First-Rank Arren Sullivese, commanding. She's flying Admiral Starlord cy-Dennever's flag."

"She's closing, Captain," the helm watch called. "Oblique approach at one point one kilometer per second! Looks like she's trying to cut us off at the moorings."

"Damn it," cy-Tomlin said, "*we* have right-of-way."

Hazzard scowled, the expression safely hidden within the anonymity of the shipnet. *Victor* had been on normal approach, her velocity a bit high for that approach corridor. As soon as her helm AIs had identified a collision danger with the frigate *Indeterminacy*, though, *Victor*'s captain had crowded on more sail, hoping to pass the *Indy*'s prow, rather than slowing in order to pass astern.

Technically, *Victor* should back down and allow the *Indeterminacy* to proceed; vessels to port and zenith always had right-of-way over ships to starboard and nadir. However . . .

"You feel big enough to argue with him, Tomlin?" Hazzard said gently. "Maneuvering! Back full!" In any case, *Victor* was the burdened vessel right now . . . burdened with too much mass and too much speed in a claustrophobically narrow volume of space. First-raters had all the maneuvering finesse of a Thaldessian bloaterslug, especially when compared to the nimble sail-handling elegance of a frigate. It made more sense for the tiny *Indeterminacy* to defer to the drifting mountain of the *Victor*. "Bring us to zero closure with the station!"

"Maneuvering back full, aye, sir!"

"Spread more sail! Deploy main tops'ls, port, starboard, and dorsal!"

"Loosing main tops'ls, aye!"

Like all trihull lightjammers, *Indy* possessed three sets of masts and field-guide spars, canted out and forward from port, starboard, and dorsal fairings, mizzen and main masts astern of the gundecks, foremasts well forward, nine masts in all, not counting the trinity of bowsprits reaching far out ahead of her prow dome.

Sails unfurled, popping taut under the snap of static fields. Their leading faces shimmered, then went mirror-silver as their trailing surfaces dulled to black, perfectly reflecting the star-misted black of space and the red-brown, black, and gray battlements of Tribaltren Station ahead. As yards pivoted, the reflective surfaces of the sails caught the light of Tribaltren's sun, as the mesh beneath the adaptive surface display grabbed hold of the local magnetic fields. The total energy striking the sails from forward was equivalent to less than a ten-thousandth of a gravity, and yet . . .

"Drive room! Emergency maneuvering! Cut in the main drive!"

Vector drive fields amplified any acceleration, however minute, drawing on the literally inexhaustible energy of quantum space through a singularity-induced Cashimir cascade to augment the ship's vector or, as in this case, to arrest *Indeterminacy*'s forward momentum. Since everything within the field was affected uniformly, there was no sensation of deceleration as the *Indy* slowed sharply. A two-thousand-ton vessel moving with a relative closure rate of over fifty meters per second could *not* stop on the proverbial tenth-credit piece. Still, the *Indeterminacy* slowed rapidly as the *Victor* loomed huge to port.

"Incoming signal from Approach Control," cy-Tomlin said.

"I should think so. Let's hear it."

" 'Slow to full stop and yield to incoming traffic.' "

"Already in hand, Mid. Acknowledge."

"Aye, sir."

"Too little and too scrabbing late," Pardoe muttered. "What are those people playing at over there?"

Hazzard didn't know if he was complaining about Approach Control's tardiness or the heels-in maneuver *Victor* was attempting to pull off. The *Victor* was still two kilometers off *Indy*'s port beam, but through the magnification inherent in the ship optical sensory feed, the immense vessel loomed like a passing cliff face, with sponsons, barbettes, field projector arrays, and fairings turning hull metal into a landscape of faceted surfaces and complex topographies, with masts like forest giants, with gun ports grinning down her gundeck modules like bared teeth.

"Now," Pardoe said, "just so long as he doesn't—"

A shudder rolled through the *Indeterminacy*, a long, crunching lurch that seemed to rack the brain and twist the stomach. For a jarring few seconds, Hazzard's linkfeed was interrupted; he was plunged into blackness and, for just an instant, was back on his jackrack, hot, drenched with sweat, as other command deck personnel shouted and screamed in the echoing close darkness around him.

Then the feed came back on-line. Still queasy—he hated field interface transits—he scanned the cascade of data on his visual field. There were reports of disorientation, jacker shock, and obvious confusion . . . but no damage, thank the Goddess, and no link dissociations.

"*Damn* them!" cy-Tomlin's voice said.

"As you were, Mid," Pardoe warned. But his own voice was barely under control. *Victor* had popped her drive field to further slow her lumbering mass just as she cut across the *Indy*'s bow. Vector drive fields worked on the fabric of space-time, a true space drive; a kind of curdling of bent space rippled along the interface between the inside of a deployed VDF and what lay outside. Though not dangerous if encountered at low speeds, it was disorienting and could damage delicate electronics. At high relative velocities, it could generate disruption enough to shred the largest vessel into scattered debris.

"Signal, *Victor* to *Indeterminacy*." Cy-Tomlin reported. "'Ware our wake!"

"The bastards did that on purpose!" Sotheby said.

"I very much doubt that, Lieutenant," he replied. "They were already moving too fast, and spreading that extra sail moved them faster. They had to drag their fields to decelerate in time." Still, it did seem to be a calculated insult. As *Indy* came to a near-dead stop, *Victor* drifted across her bow a scant half kilometer distant, making for Mooring Bay 16. Cooling vanes like squared-off wings, the vast reach of her sails, shimmering as they fought to slow the behemoth, and the deadly complexity of the first-rater's aft maneuvering drive venturis passed slowly, a moving mountain. *Indeterminacy* rocked and shuddered again with the passing of the big ship's wake, and then the way ahead was clear once more.

Hazzard let out a slow breath. Things could have worked out *much* worse. "Let's have the extra sail in now, Mr. Pardoe. Set sail for ahead, maneuvering dead slow."

"Furling all main tops'ls, Captain. Set sail for ahead, maneuver dead slow."

"What do you think, Captain?" Pardoe said on their private link. "Was Sullivese trying to be flashy for the admiral's benefit? Or was he just being incompetent?"

"Arren is *not* incompetent," Hazzard replied, a bit more sharply than he'd intended. Sometimes, Pardoe spoke his mind a little too freely. "Maybe they're just in a hurry."

"Aye, sir. And maybe some cyberenhanced Starlords think they're just a rung or two higher up the Darwin ladder than the rest of us."

Hazzard said nothing. Pardoe's bitter aside had struck just a little too close abeam. Their blockade deployment at Danibar had been cut short by the arrival of dispatches requiring *Indeterminacy* to make for Tribaltren Station with all due haste and for Greydon Hazzard to report to the Port Admiral's office immediately upon docking. With so many other vessels available within a few days' travel of Tribaltren, why had the *Indy* been called in?

Immediately, fortunately, was a flexible term in the Galactic Union Navy, however. There was the routine of seeing to it that the ship was safely docked, of course. Most of the minutiae could be properly left to his First Lieutenant, but there were reports to electronically sign and a grumpy Port Disbursement Officer to cajole into giving an upcheck to the purser's request for new condenser tubes for the galley's stasis units.

And, perhaps more immediate, he needed to get presentable first. One did not visit a two-star admiral in shipboard skins. When he chose to make himself visible on the shipnet, of course, his icon could take on any appearance he chose . . . which meant in uniform. When he came fully awake on the jackrack, however, the crisp and spotless Navy blacks were gone. In their place were gray skins soaked with sweat, and all the usual accoutrements for waste absorption, cooling, and nutrient tubes. A jackrack technician helped him unplug, took his helmet with its forest of electronic feeds and cables, and stood by as he swung his feet onto the steel grillwork of the deck.

Forty minutes later, freshly showered with the last of this deciyear's personal water ration, Hazzard was clad in his one decent set of dress black-and-golds, complete with shoulder half-cloak, visored cap, medals and decorations, and his personal computer woven into the left arm of his jacket, from shoulder to wrist, in closely worked patterns of what looked like liquid gold.

"You loog good, zur," Cadlud, his steward remarked, brushing his uniform with a static cleaner. The Irdikad hovered over him as it worked, its single eye in an elephantine head studying his uniform in minute inspection as all three tentacles twitched the fall of his cloak into perfect line. "Zhip-zhape ond sqvared avay."

"Thank you, Cadlud. I just hope the admiral thinks the same."

A launch took him from the *Indy*, now moored alongside the towering bulk of the station, across to one of the turreted tower complexes extending above the main body of the twelve-kilometer-wide facility.

The Port Admiral's office was decorated in Late Jingivid Imperial, all mirrors and black trim in a jarring cacophony of light and reflections. Admiral Dalim cy-Koenin was a blunt, bullet-headed man with a no-nonsense attitude and little patience for protocol. Hazzard wondered, in fact, how the man had managed to survive politically long enough to be awarded two stars. Cy-Koenin's implants encased parts of his head and were visible on the backs of his hands and extending down each finger to the tip.

Well, that, as much as anything else, explained his rank and considerable power.

"You're late" was the way he greeted Hazzard, as the office door dilated and the ship captain stepped between the Marine sentries and into cy-Koenin's inner sanctum.

"Yes, sir," he replied. Hazzard was familiar enough with the ways of admirals to know that excuses were neither desired nor appropriate.

Wall screens displayed deep space—not the view from Tribaltren, but someplace closer in toward the Galactic Core, teeming with orange suns and the mingled, softer glows of pale nebulae. The mirrors, black trim, and star projections made it difficult to see where the walls of the room really were. Hazzard wondered if he could even find the door again.

Another man was in the room, reclining in a black synthliquid chair. Lean, hard, and angular, his face was faceted as though carved from obsidian. Both eyes were covered by a sensor array implant, and he was, if anything, more heavily intertwined with hardware than the Port Admiral. "Admiral," cy-Koenin said, "this is the young man I was telling you about. Captain Hazzard, Admiral Starlord cy-Dennever."

Hazzard inclined his head, as courtesy required. "My lord."

Cy-Dennever looked him over coldly. "A noncy? My dear Dal, you *are* joking, I trust."

Noncy. Non-cybernetically augmented. *That* again . . .

"I believe you will find me up to any task required of me, my lord."

He sniffed and continued to address cy-Koenin, pointedly ignoring Hazzard. "I specifically require a frigate captain capable of leading my in-system squadron and with a master's understanding of the Ordiku Anarchate and the political situation there. A noncy simply will not do."

"Captain Hazzard is what's available, Admiral," cy-Koenin replied. "And he has personal knowledge of Kaden. Don't you, Hazzard?"

"Yes, sir. I was an assistant diplomatic naval attaché to the Anarchate home world for a year. My steward is Irdikad, in fact."

Cy-Dennever gave him another look, harder this time. "And how long ago was this?"

"Oh, about eight years subjective, my lord."

"How long objective? Things *do* change groundside while we're on highspace approach. Or hadn't you noticed?"

Hazzard had to consult his PC. He'd minused some subjective with this latest deployment at Danibar. How much? Nearly two years, this time.

"Nineteen years objective, sir."

"Nineteen years. Well, you'll find the political situation within the Anarchate radically transformed. I'm not so sure you will be of any use to me."

"Their politics may have changed, my lord, but I doubt that the Irdikad have. They're solitary, traditional, meticulous, a bit stuffy, even stubborn at times. They are also unflinchingly loyal." He smiled. "Despite their interest in tradition—their recorded history goes back something like nine thousand years—they respect, you might even say *revere*, madness. Insanity is rare, but it's granted a special status in their culture, maybe to avoid the problems of stagnation."

"Ahem, yes," cy-Dennever said. "All very amusing, I'm sure. But the facts of the matter are that the Anarchate is now in negotiations with the P'aaseni Orthodoxate. The Ministry of Political Intelligence assures me that a decision by the Anarchate is imminent, perhaps within the next ten days, and that Orthodoxate ships will almost certainly deploy before then to, um, convince the Irdikad to come along."

"The Irdikad volume is small, but strategically placed," cy-Koenin added. "They have a fleet . . . a small one, true, but one capable of causing some considerable inconvenience should we extend our operations in that quarter. Lord cy-Dennever's orders are to present a show of force at the Anarchate capital."

"Exactly. My squadron has firepower sufficient to convince the Irdikads that joining with the Doxies would *not* be in their best interests."

"I should think their best interests would be obvious," Hazzard said. "The Orthodoxate is anthropocentric. Rather virulently so, in fact. The Irdikads would be reduced to slave status or worse."

"Obviously." Cy-Dennever sniffed. "And obviously, too, the Doxies are on their best behavior until the Anarchate planetary defense batteries are safely in their hands. Remember, most Irdikad dealings have been with the Union so far. They are a simple people. To them, all humans are the same. Planetary genocide by what they consider to be an honorable and *civilized* species is probably utterly beyond their comprehension."

Hazzard held his peace at the patronizing nonsense of "a simple people." The man acted like he was a few genes short of a full chromosome.

If cy-Dennever represented *Homo sapiens superioris*, though, as his kind so often claimed, maybe he simply wasn't done evolving yet.

"The question of Anarchate neutrality is in the hands of the diplomats," cy-Koenin said. "Your mission, Captain Hazzard, will be to take command of the in-system squadron, as a part of Admiral cy-Dennever's diplomatic show of force."

Hazzard digested this. The in-system squadron would be the mission's cutting edge, of course, patrolling within a few million kilometers of the Anarchate home world. Admiral cy-Dennever would have the heavies, the main squadron's ship of the line out on the fringes of the Kaden system, accelerating back and forth at near-*c* so as to be ready for a near-immediate jump in-system at need. "Aye, sir," he said.

"It is vital, absolutely *vital*," cy-Dennever put in, "that you not fire on Irdikad assets. Enemy vessels, of course . . . but under no circumstances will you fire on the locals, even if you are provoked."

"You're saying, my lord, that we can't shoot even if they shoot at us first?"

"Well done! That is *precisely* what I am saying. These negotiations are too delicate, and too much is at stake to risk . . ." He stopped and looked at cy-Koenin. "Are you certain there are no augmented frigate captains available? I can't be expected to trust a mere biological's reflexes or instincts in a situation this precarious! He doesn't even have the hardwiring to handle his ship properly! His vessel very nearly fouled mine during our approach a few hours ago!"

Cy-Koenin glanced at Hazzard, then looked hard at cy-Dennever, saying nothing outwardly. Hazzard decided the two must have shifted to a telepathic exchange, one he was not privy to. Micro-radio transceivers implanted in their skulls allowed Starlords to converse privately, in much the same way that Hazzard could open a private channel to Pardoe when they both were on-line.

At last, cy-Dennever sighed and looked away. "Very well. But you are responsible, sir, if this goes wrong!"

"Of course, cy-Dennever," cy-Koenin replied.

"What ships will I command?" Hazzard asked.

"Besides *Indeterminacy*," cy-Koenin said, "there is *Decider*, a frigate of thirty-three guns, Captain-sixth Bellemew. The other vessels are smaller . . . *Swift*, twenty-seven; *Fire Angel* and *Ferocious*, both twenty-one; and *Uriel*, of eighteen guns. All five are already on-station or will be by the time you arrive. Four line battleships will be on blockade station out-system within two days objective. Admiral cy-Dennever's *Victor* will bring that to five, under his flag. Your full operational orders will be transmitted to your ship. You are clear for departure as soon as you complete taking on necessary stores and provisions."

"Aye, aye, my lord."

"Should be an easy deployment, Greydon," cy-Koenin added, dropping into less formal speech. "The Irdikad aren't hostile, and they won't pick a fight with one of our line battle squadrons!"

"Clarification," cy-Dennever said. "They're not hostile *yet*."

"Mm," cy-Koenin said. "As always, minus-tau is against us. We need you at Kaden as quickly as possible. Assume one day for refit, five days for the trans-*c* jump to Kaden. You will have a three-day margin, some of which will be lost to minus-tau."

"Tau is of the essence, you might say," cy-Dennever added, smirking at his own joke.

"Admiral cy-Dennever will be there in *Victor* within five days more," cy-Koenin went on, ignoring him. "It will be up to you to assess the situation when you arrive, and to report to Admiral cy-Farrol, currently in command of the Kaden Squadron. You will have dispatches and orders to deliver to him."

"Aye, my lord."

"Dismissed, Captain Hazzard. Inform me when your vessel is fit for space."

"Aye, aye, sir."

As he left, the two Starlords were arguing in low but nova-hot tones.

Twenty-one hours later, *Indeterminacy* boosted for c and the jump to Kaden, the Anarchate capital, without even time enough for Hazzard to visit Cynthea, his portwife at Tribaltren. Though the *Indy* cast off from the station at almost the same moment as the *Victor*, the frigate, with far less mass to boost, accelerated more quickly. Within another hour, the *Indy* was tacking on nines to her ninety-nine percent of light speed, as the universe, crowded forward by the distortions of relativistic travel, took on the appearance of a ring of frosty light encircling the prow, and objective hours in the universe outside passed like minutes to the men and women crowded within the frigate's steel and duraplast hull.

A vessel's spacesails could ride the almost nonexistent currents of light, gravity, and magnetic flux, while her Cashimir cascade array boosted milli-G accelerations to accelerations measured in kilogravities. As the ship crowded c, a phantasm seeming to recede like Xeno's Paradox the harder the ship boosted, space around the vessel turned strange, warped by the starship's own pyramiding relativistic mass. A command from the bridge, and the trans-c primaries engaged, kicking her into highspace where they devoured light-years by the handful.

But star travel came with a cost. Each time a ship approached the pace of light before engaging her highspace drives, relativistic effects invoked the steadily mounting curse of minus-tau. Three minutes subjective at 99.9 percent of the speed of light translated as almost an hour objective; sixteen weeks on patrol at .95 c saw the passage of over a year. C-duty, as it was called, carried c-men and of-

ficers alike into the future, sundering the bonds of family
and friends left behind.

It made for tighter bonding among the men and women
serving aboard for, after accumulating a minus-tau of a scant
few decades objective, they had few ties left to the planet-
lubber populations of world surfaces. Others within the crew
became family. . . .

Greydon Hazzard, though, had no one aboard. As captain, he was expected to stand apart, to command without
seeming to have favorites or cliques. It made for a painfully
lonely life, one marked by periods of watch and watch . . .
and the inexpressibly vast deeps of emptiness between the
sundered suns.

"Tell me about your world, Cadlud. Tell me about your
people."

They sat in Hazzard's day cabin, a tiny office aft of the
gun decks. Or, rather, Hazzard sat behind his desk, while
Cadlud squatted in a bulky huddle in the center of the deck.
Irdikad were humanoid, more or less, if massive, blunt, and
elephantine to human sensibilities. Each shoulder sprouted
a heavy tentacle with a graceful, sinuous tip; a third grew
from the face, above the inverted-V slash of a mouth and
beneath the single, slit-pupiled eye. Most Irdikad wore ornate robes with patterns expressing individual tastes and
artistry, but Cadlud generally went naked aboard ship. *Indeterminacy*'s crew spaces were warmer than he was used
to, and his species seemed never to have developed nudity
taboos . . . quite possibly because their genitals were located
in their central arm, and sex for them was the equivalent
of a casual handshake.

"My people are my people," the Irdikad said with stolid
indifference. The tips of his tentacles twitched to some emotion beyond human ken. "There is little to zay."

"Well . . . you could tell me why they're interested in

joining with the Orthodoxate. The Doxies and their allies are all human, or human-derived. Some of them hate non-humans, have vowed to eradicate them across the Galaxy. Why would any nonhuman civilization join such an alliance as that?"

Cadlud stared at him for a long moment with that liquid, glittering eye. "Zur, many humans, they make miztaig. Think all Irdikad are zame, *think* zame. Not zo."

"I know your culture is focused on the individual . . . "

"And that azzumes we have zingle, uniform culture. Not zo."

"I remember." His months as Naval attaché to the Irdikad home world had been confusing at best, bewildering at worst. Each region, each continent, each valley seemed to have its own language, its own religion and gods, its own festivals, its own philosophies. "I remember too well! When I was there, no one paid attention to anyone else, and it was a miracle if anything got done. Seemed like an exercise in chaos theory as applied to social studies."

A shrug, an enigmatic slight lift of all three tentacles. "It worgs. For us, anyway."

"But why would your people embrace the Alliance? It doesn't make any sense!"

For nearly twenty years now, objective, the Galactic Union had been in a standoff with the Grand Association of Humankind—a revolutionary jihad sweeping through vast sections of the Galaxy, tracking down and killing all cybernetically or genetically enhanced humans . . . and often nonhuman beings as well, for no better reason than that they were *different*. Four years ago objective, the Association had struck a formal alliance with the P'aaseni Orthodoxate, a very old human empire seeking to define what was truly human. The Alliance of the two, founded at the Treaty of Garth, promised real trouble for the beleaguered Galactic

Union . . . and for every sentient species in a vast and war-
torn Galaxy.

"My people, zur, have been here for a long, long time.
Perhaps they grew bored."

"What? You'd risk extinction because you're bored?
That's crazy!"

"Yes?" The single eye watched him steadily, as if waiting for him to make his point. "Remember that we have no
government, as you use term. No rules. We use . . . guidelines, only. And do what zeems best."

Irdikad behavior seemed insane to humans more often
than not, but it was consistent and it was sane within the
context of their society . . . correction, *societies*. With a
recorded history going back at least nine thousand years,
Irdikad civilization was static, even stagnant, almost as
though all the good, new ideas had long ago been thought
of, acted upon, and forgotten. They were a study in con-
trasts. They prized originality and spontaneity, but during
his entire tour on Kaden, Hazzard had seen little variance
among the natives, save in their dress, which ranged from
none at all to costumes of indescribably complex and bizarre
design. *A herd of blandgroth* was how the Union Ambas-
sador had described them, sheeplike followers of fashion,
adopting the philosophy, the religion, the attitude of the moment. It was the same problem faced by human gangers in
the big metroplexes, tattooing lightshow art onto their bodies, grafting on biomechanical prostheses, growing animal
heads, downloading minds to fantasy bodies, all in the name
of being *different* . . . and in the end, losing their individu-
ality to a group where everyone was the same because everyone was bizarrely different.

The one truly distinct social group on Kaden was the
military, which by definition required a measure of uniform-
ity. The military . . .

Irdikad society also respected strength, an obvious out-growth of a society where individualism ruled.

"Tell me about the Anarchate's military, Cadlud."

Again a shrug. "They are . . . crazy. And strong. And therefore respected. They control the planetary defense batteries and the Vleet, but you know this."

"Yes. I remember." The Union had long been courting the Anarchate, seeking to win their help against the Alliance. The military had been the world's single loudest, most unified voice, and it had been dead set against *any* alliance, with anybody.

What had changed?

"I don't believe anyone would risk extinction simply because they were bored, Cadlud," Hazzard said at last. "There's more to this. I just wish I knew what it was."

"You would be zurprized, zur," the Irdikad replied, "at how tedious *zameness* can be."

At her best trans-*c* pseudovelocity, *Indeterminacy* crossed the nearly eight hundred light-years between Tribaltren and Kaden in five days, an extra-spatial time frame fortunately beyond the reach of Einstein and not subject to the grasp of minus-tau. At a meticulously calculated moment, she dropped from highspace in a burst of blue-shifted photons and a crawling, twisting effect as local space momentarily assumed the topological characteristics of a Klein bottle. Hazzard, occupying the image virspace of the shipnet, grimaced at the crawl and wrench as the *Indy*'s acceleration field expanded, seizing hold of the space-time fabric as the familiar rules of physics once again took hold.

The literal bending of space at the field interface with the S-T continuum was not harmful of itself. All space is curved slightly—the effect is called gravity—and since the effect is uniform, the fact that a straight line isn't is never noticed. When the effect is sharply localized, however, and moving quickly, there is some inevitable dislocation. At low velocities, the deployment of the acceleration field was noticeable as a distinct queasiness; at high speeds, matter, from ship's hull to electronic circuitry to human neurons, could be sharply disrupted and even destroyed.

Needless to say, the field was deployed slowly. As usual, as the nausea twisted in his stomach, Hazzard wondered if the jackrack crews were going to have to clean up his inert body.

The *Indy* had emerged with the same velocity she'd carried upon entering highspace, a fraction of a percent below light speed itself. At Hazzard's command, sails unfurled, snapping into place, shimmering with the field effect distortions twisting time and space. The sensory feedscape showed the universe turned strange, with all of the sky compressed into a cold ring of light ahead of the ship as she plunged forward into darkness. As always, the computers handling sensory input corrected the image, eliminating the visual distortion effects of near-*c* travel.

Now, with a saner sky, an orange beacon glowed dead ahead. Here, light-centuries above the Galactic Plane, the Galaxy was a vast pinwheel of pale, pale silver-white light viewed not quite edge-on. The result was a sky divided in twain, to one side a vast, softly glowing wall of stars spread out in a distinctly spiral panorama, the Galactic Core in the far distance, swollen and gold-hued, a fuzz of myriad suns rising above the dark blots and smears of nebulae; opposite, the sky was empty, save for the scattered, solitary stars here at the Verge . . . and the inconceivably distant smudges of radiance representing other galaxies adrift on the Ocean of Ultimate Night.

Closer, much closer at hand, an orange sun glowed cool and ancient, and worlds shone in darkness. Kaden was the second world of four, tucked in close enough to the K4 primary that it enjoyed cool but not frigid climes along its equator.

Indeterminacy had emerged nearly half a light-hour from Kaden. Dumping velocity in space-twisting torrents of bleed-off energy, the frigate dropped toward the orange-lit world, six hundred million kilometers distant.

Through the magnification of the sensory inputs, ice caps gleamed in the orange light, together encompassing nearly half of the world's rugged surface. Hazzard opened a display showing a computer-generated image of the world, slowly rotating, as the actual planet swiftly grew from an isolated point of light to a tiny crescent, to a living world, a scimitar of white and silver and orange bowed away from its sun, with three small moons in attendance.

Indy's sensor arrays were also sampling the flood of electronic and laser signals crisscrossing the system, noting the time-lagged positions and vectors of spacecraft, identifying threats.

Out-system, in the comet-haunted deeps two light-days out, were the four ships of the line of the Union show of force, led by the old seventy-five-gun *Trimirage*, keeping blockade station as they awaited the arrival of the *Victor*. Their field-distortion wakes, generated as they cruised close to c, were distinctly visible against the night as crisp, blue cones of light in line-ahead formation.

Blockading a star system required careful timing and reliance on the physics of highspace. Clearly, it was impossible to englobe an entire planetary system in order to intercept vessels that might leave at any time, on any heading. By having a blockading squadron cruise back and forth at near-c velocities, however, the ships were able to drop into highspace with a few minutes' warning and reappear within seconds anywhere in-system they needed to be. The

problem, of course, was that the light informing the blockade that enemy units were in motion in-system took hours
or days to reach the blockade station. That was why light-
rates—frigates and lesser craft—were used in-system to provide early warning and to carry information out to the battle
line at trans-c velocities. Even at usual planetary velocities,
they could accelerate to c within an hour or so. Larger vessels, the big ships of the line, took a lot longer to reach
near-c, and so were vulnerable to intercepts by the blockading squadron.

There were numerous vessels in-system, close by Kaden
itself. "I've got radio transmissions, Captain," cy-Tomlin
announced. "Military bands, VHF through UHF." Hazzard
could see the transmission point sources on his panorama.
Four showed friendly IFF signatures, and the data tags beside each vessel identified them further as *Decider*, *Swift*,
Fire Angel, and *Ferocious*. Close beside them were other
targets, six of them, these showing red on *Indeterminacy*'s
visual display. At Hazzard's triggering thought, schematics
of each vessel appeared to one side, together with lists of
stats showing mass, acceleration, vector data, and range.
The situation unfolding there was . . . make it twenty minutes old, now, as *Indy* closed with them. Thanks to the
speed-of-light time lag, they were looking that far into the
past, watching the maneuvers unfold with bewildering apparent speed. Fortunately, their absolute velocities were low
enough that they didn't appear to be moving anywhere fast.

"Six hostiles, Captain," Lieutenant Pardoe announced, as
additional schematics drew themselves on the feedscape—
ornate hulls, curved masts, triple gundecks set far back on
the spine. "They look like P'aaseni. Two ships of the line . . .
seventy-twos or seventy-fives, four frigates."

A fifth point transmission was closer, climbing out of
the system, high above the plane of the ecliptic on a bear-

ing straight for the out-system blockades, broadcasting on an emergency band. That would be little *Uriel*, accelerating clear of what obviously was a major squadron action. Four of her masts were missing, though, and her spread of sail was ragged, putting a sharp limit on her ability to hump Gs.

Time passed, achingly slow. The battle ahead was unfolding slowly, the Union ships apparently trying to maneuver clear of incoming Orthodoxate ships. Subjective time crawled, while the universe outside *Indy*'s isolated space-time reference point seemed to race along. And it would take time—another forty minutes yet—to decelerate to battle speed.

"Communication coming in from the *Uriel*, Captain," cy-Tomlin said.

"Let's hear it, please."

". . . attack by Orthodoxate ships. We are heavily outgunned, and planetside defense batteries on Kaden have opened fire, causing severe damage. *Indeterminacy*, please acknowledge." There was a long pause. At this range, there could be no true conversation due to the speed of light time lag. The message would begin playing again in just a . . .

"*Indeterminacy*, this is *Uriel*, Lieutenant Lasely in command. The in-system squadron has been trapped and is under attack. We were lured in close to Kaden by a request for real-time communications from the Kaden Military Council. It was a trap. Six Orthodoxate ships jumped in-system and attacked, just after we were taken under heavy fire from the planetary defense batteries."

As the message played itself through, Hazzard checked range, vector, and time lag. *Uriel* was eight light-minutes away, and sixteen had passed since their emergence from highspace. The sloop must have begun broadcasting as soon as they'd become aware of the *Indy*'s arrival.

Uriel was clearly making for the line ships two light-days out but was still moving at only about half the speed of light. With the damage she'd suffered to her rigging, though, it would be another hour, at least, before she would be able to engage her trans-*c* drive and make the jump to the blockade point.

Mentally, Hazzard engaged a side communications band, one linking him not with other men and women strung together in the shipnet, but to an ordinary radio in his physical quarters, deep in the bowels of the ship. "Cadlud? This is the captain. Are you there?"

"I am here, zur."

"Ever hear of something called the Kaden Military Council?"

"No, zur. It zounds . . . most un-Irdikad."

"It does to me, too. It also sounds like they're making decisions for your world's government."

"Kaden does not have a world government," Cadlud reminded him. "Guidelines, zur, not rules."

"Thank you, Cadlud." He broke the link.

A cyberenhanced starlord, he thought, might have been able to tap directly into local communications and informational channels, might have accessed ocean-deep volumes of material on the current political situation on Kaden. He trusted, however, his own intuition, and the observations of his steward.

Hazzard studied the tactical display spreading out before him against the visual field of his mind. The other four Union ships were closely engaged with the P'aaseni squadron half a million kilometers past the crescent of Kaden. An hour before *Uriel* could summon help from *Trimirage* and her consorts . . . a little less, possibly, if *Indeterminacy* began accelerating to *c* and made the jump to the blockade point herself. The Union in-system squadron was in serious trouble, though. Pounded by the P'aaseni heavies and by Anarchate planetary defense batteries, *Fire Angel* was a mass of fiercely radiating wreckage drifting down the walls of Kaden's gravity well, and *Decider* appeared to be crippled. *Ferocious* and *Swift* were both still firing, but their life span could only be measured now in minutes, unless they were able to win clear.

At the moment, *Indeterminacy* was moving at just under .9 c, and still slowing; at that velocity, twenty-five seconds of shipboard time translated as almost a minute in the outside universe, and so the battle appeared to be evolving at breakneck speed as the Union frigate plowed through the photons revealing the conflict ahead. Add to that the fact that thanks to c-lag, he was still seeing things as they *had* been, fourteen . . . no, make it thirteen minutes ago. He had to decide *quickly*. . . .

He shifted his attention to a global display of Kaden, with the locations of known planetary defense batteries plotted as gleaming yellow sparks scattered along the equator. As on most technic worlds throughout this sector of the galaxy, the locals had been beefing up their PDS against the possibility that they would be dragged into the spreading war between Union and Alliance. There. The eight or ten Planetary Defense System emplacements stretched along the Dalacradak Peninsula were likely the ones firing on the Union squadron.

Hazzard was uncomfortably aware of his orders, specific to the point of anality, forbidding him from opening fire on any Kaden military facilities even in self-defense.

Planetary defense batteries tended to be immense fortresses, buried, for the most part, under kilometers of bedrock, with only the surface turrets mounting the massive singularity cannon visible on the surface. A return bombardment from space, with the throw-mass possible for a frigate like *Indeterminacy*, might damage some of those batteries, but it wouldn't knock them out . . . not before the *Indy* herself was smashed into blue-hot fragments.

But there might be another way. . . .

Range to the battle was now eleven light-minutes. The light announcing *Indy*'s arrival in-system still hadn't reached Kaden but would in another . . . make it ninety-five seconds. He reached out through the ship's senses, trying to feel the accelerated flow of the situation, to guess what was actually happening *now*.

"Captain?" Pardoe said, perhaps wondering if Hazzard had his mind on the situation at hand. "Shall I order more sail and a shift to acceleration, Captain?" Clearly, fleeing for the safety of the out-system station—and giving warning to the heavies—was where duty lay.

Or . . .

"Affirmative," Hazzard snapped. "Have all hands prepare for hopskip."

"A microjump?. . . We're not going to warn the squadron, sir?"

"If we do, Bellemew and the inshore squadron are dead. *Uriel* can warn the fleet. And maybe we can make a difference down there." Speaking quickly and with a calm he could not feel, Hazzard described what he was planning.

Pardoe hesitated only a moment before giving a sharpedged "Aye, sir."

"Let's go to battle stations, if you please, Mr. Pardoe. We will be engaging within a few minutes."

Under the frantic urgings of rigging rats and spiders teleoperated by *Indy*'s *c*-men, jacked in from their racks deep within the ship's hull, the frigate's sails transfigured, top and t'gallant sails unfolding, sail surfaces turning from silver to black forward, and swinging on the yards to set the ship accelerating toward the battle, instead of slowing down.

Minutes crawled as she built back her velocity, reaching toward the speed of light as her primary drive compounded the minute accelerations of photon flux and magnetic field into near-*c* jamming. Ahead, a fuzzy, hard-to-look-at sphere the color of the back of one's eyelids began condensing out of empty space, the singularity created and focused by *Indeterminacy*'s fast-increasing relativistic mass. At velocities above .99 *c*, the singularity became a doorway for the ship into trans-*c*.

"*Indeterminacy* ready for microtransition," Ishiwara, the drive engineer, reported.

"Strike the sails," Hazzard ordered. "Stand by for transit!"

The crescent of Kaden swelled rapidly ahead as the frigate's sails collapsed and furled. By now, even with light's snail-pace crawl, the P'aaseni squadron had noted the frigate's initial arrival, and their ships were redeploying to intercept this new threat. They wouldn't know yet, however, that the *Indy* was coming to meet them.

"Helm, we're feeding you transit course corrections."

"Aye, sir. Got 'em."

"Sails furled," Pardoe said. "Vessel ready in all respects for transit."

"Punch it!"

Indeterminacy dropped into the singularity, in a sense swallowing herself whole. At the last moment, the helm used the singularity's intense gravity to bend the frigate's course slightly, adjusting her heading as she dropped into utter strangeness . . .

. . . and reemerged, a fractional blink of an eye later.

A scant light-minute ahead, huge in the magnified display, Kaden hung in orange, ice-capped splendor. Hazzard's commands crackled through the shipnet. "Deploy full sail! All back! Ishi, dump V into the drive fields! . . ."

Like the *Victor* at Tribaltren Station, the *Indeterminacy* was now barreling into the fray with far too much velocity. Much could be dumped as energy fed directly into the drive fields, expanding them across well over a hundred kilometers of empty space where it could actually be applied to braking the ship's headlong plunge forward. Still, V could be translated into energy only so quickly. By the time they neared Kaden, they would still be moving too quickly to engage the enemy vessels.

"Mr. Ishiwara," Hazzard said. "I want you to stand by on the drive controls. We're going to pop our fields out full as we round the planet."

"The fields are already extended all the way, Captain." The larger the volume of *Indeterminacy*'s space-warping wake, the more velocity could be safely dumped.

"I know. We're going to pull an anchor drag."

He heard the pause, as loud as a shout, as the engineer digested this. "Sir . . ."

"Do it. Planetary encounter in . . . twenty-eight seconds, now."

"Aye, aye, sir."

Hazzard took a last look at the *Indy*'s alignment with the fast-growing planet and the squadron battle ahead. This was going to be *damned* tight. . . .

"Strike all sails," he ordered. "*Smartly* now! Helm . . . you're on thrusters, now. Hang on to her! She's going to buck!"

Swiftly, as rats and spiders swarmed through the rigging, *Indeterminacy*'s spread of sails collapsed, folded, and vanished, furling into their storage lockers on mast and spar.

"All hands below!" Hazzard ordered. He didn't want to lose anyone with this maneuver . . . though that was a fairly forlorn hope. What he was trying to do was not exactly recommended in *Yardley's Book of C-Manship*. "Set ship for close passage!"

Constellations of points of light flowed down the rigging and masts, vanishing into *Indy*'s below-deck spaces. Slowly, now, the yards were folding, the masts telescoping down their own lengths, truncating themselves to reduce the possibility of crippling damage from tidal effects or—don't think about the possibility!—drive field failure.

There wasn't time for a full close-passage deployment. They were going to take some damage here, in another few seconds. The question was . . . how much?

As *Indeterminacy* had approached Kaden over the course of the past few minutes, the ship's display computers had been steadily recalculating magnification factors and redisplaying the view forward. Hazzard noted with a small kick of surprise that the magnification factor was down to one, that the planet now filling his mental view ahead was as it really was outside the all-too-thin walls of *Indeterminacy*'s hull. They were crossing the terminator now, swinging low across the white and orange curve of the world into dayside. He could sense the growing tug of gravity . . . though far, far too weak to capture the frigate at her current velocity of over ten percent of the speed of light itself.

Ahead, close along the equator, just south of the motionlessly sprawled swirl of a tropical storm, lay the ragged, mountainous thrust of the Dalacradak Peninsula, thrusting out from the eastern coast of Alekred and into the violet-blue, cloud-dappled reaches of the Zurkeded Ocean like a Valosian scimitar, straight at the hilt, wickedly curved at the tip, Cape Zhadurg. Goddess! He could *see* the big guns of the PDS firing up ahead, each discharge like a straight-line bolt of lightning stabbing into space from the wrinkled, snow-capped barrenness of the mountains as they smoothly rolled over the horizon and into view.

"Captain?" It was cy-Tomlin, the bridge team's Starlord-

in-training. "We're not supposed to fire on the Irdikads!"
He sounded outraged. "*Especially* not their planet!"

"As you were, Mid," Pardoe said.

"I'm not about to fire on them," Hazzard explained gently. "I'm about to make a mistake. . . ."

"Sir?"

Hazzard smiled to himself. Starlords might have all the advantages with their hardwired personal technology, but they were hampered, sometimes, by an almost desperate need to play by the rules.

Rules that, sometimes, could be bent. . . .

"Altitude three hundred two kilometers," the helmsman reported. "Now two fifty-five kilometers. One hundred eighty-one . . . One hundred seven . . ."

"I can read the altitude data, Mr. Sotheby, thank you. Bring us up just a bit, plus zero-two."

Maneuvering thrusters, fueled by water from the ship's forward tank, imparted a scant few kilos of thrust, amplified by the drives. Hazzard was completely focused now on the dance of numbers—*Indeterminacy*'s heading, altitude, dwindling velocity . . .

Ahead, almost below now, the big guns kept firing, hurling pinpoints of dazzling sunlight into the tangle of starsailing vessels ahead. *Decider* had just taken several more hits, as microsingularities from both the planet and the P'aaseni smashed through drive barriers, sails, and hull with equal ease, savaging armor plate, splintering bulwarks, slashing through the deep-buried vitals of a dying ship.

"Captain!" Ishiwara's voice said. "We're dragging upper atmosphere. Contact with the surface in five seconds . . . four . . ."

"All hands!" Pardoe called. "Brace for impact!"

Even empty space has substance, on the quantum level, the eleven-dimensional structure of emptiness sometimes called the fabric of space-time, the stuff a starship's drive fields grab hold of during maneuvers and acceleration. Now, though, the interface surface of *Indeterminacy*'s drive field was intersecting solid rock as the frigate hurtled low across the Kadenese surface. At low velocity, space would bend, gravity-like, with no noticeable effect. At several percent of the speed of light, *Indy*'s current velocity, the fringe effects of a drive field dragging through unyielding rock . . .

There were . . . effects.

Indeterminacy slowed, first of all, decelerating sharply and for free at tens of thousands of gravities, though the drive field kept the velocity change uniform and unfelt aboard . . . fortunately for the men and women belowdecks.

On the surface, solid rock flexed . . . warped . . . then snapped as stress points were reached and surpassed.

The interface shock wave dragged along the Dalacradak Peninsula well astern of the hurtling starship, visible from space as a frothy white V arrowing across land and sea alike. The south face of Gadeddej Mountain shuddered, shouldering slightly skyward, then collapsed, a thundering, booming detonation of rock avalanching into the Drudep Valley below, carrying with it the bristling array of deep-space sensor antenna and wave guide towers mounted there.

The shock wave boomed across Egezhur Bay, slammed into the Drugid Cliffs, and hit the Razurig defense facility like an oncoming storm wall straight from the depths of hell. The main gun turret, its muzzle cocked at a point in the sky above the eastern horizon, tipped crazily, spun, then shredded under the impact of fast-moving discontinuous space. The military garrison town of Krebur vanished as buildings shook themselves to pieces in the seismic quake rolling along behind the storm front. Mount Gadez, long dormant, awakened as its lava plug shattered and long-pent energies deep within the crust were catastrophically released.

The close passage, as *Indeterminacy*'s wake lightly brushed the planet's surface, lasted less than three seconds. As the frigate arrowed now back into the interplanetary depths of the Kaden system, the planet receding astern showed evidence of the ferocity of that encounter. The shock wave continued to ripple east across the Zurkeded Ocean, though with fast-fading force. Storm clouds were gathering in white-swirling fury above the peninsula, and Mount Gadez glowed in the depths of its fast-expanding cloud of dark gray volcanic ash.

And every one of the planetary defense batteries on the Dalacradak Peninsula, from Razurig to Cape Zhadurg, was silent now, lost in the pall of the gathering storm.

Aboard the *Indeterminacy*, all was darkness, chaos, and confusion. Despite the insulating effects of the drive fields, the shock of the planetary close encounter had wracked and twisted the frigate, knocking vital systems off-line, including the shipnet itself. Hazzard blinked into a smoky darkness filled with screams and yells and the intermittent flare of small electrical fires. Circuit breakers had tripped, knocking whole ship sections off the power grid; in some places, power feeds had arced, melting circuits and fuses and setting fires. Damage control robots swarmed like spidery hands, weird shadows against the flames, and Hazzard caught the acrid stink of burning insulation and fire-smothering kaon gas.

Terror clawed at the back of his brain, but he fought down both the panic and the urge to unstrap from his jack-rack. Either full power would be restored in a moment . . . or the *Indeterminacy*, blind and helpless, would drift into the squadron melee, a crippled target. Either way, there was nothing he could do at the moment to change things, nothing to do but wait and pray that automated DC systems would bring the ship back to life.

It was always the waiting that was the worst.

At least he had awakened. In ship-to-ship combat, between vessels crewed by the disembodied uploads of men and women into the machines that handled the sails and fired the guns, the danger was not so much outright death, though that possibility was real enough, as it was the possibility that the data linkages between your mind within a machine and your comatose body might be abruptly broken. In one sense, your mind did not actually leave your body; the remote spider or rigging rat crawler was no more than an extension of your sensory organs, not of your brain.

Still, too many minds were destroyed when the machinery failed, in the crippling trauma of dissociation. When the shipnet had gone off-line, most of the officers and crew had reawakened on their jackracks. *Most . . .*

Hazzard, like most *c*-men, dreaded insanity more than outright death.

At least this time, he'd come through okay. But next time—

Light, life, motion, sensation flooded his brain, replacing the fire-shot blackness of the jackrack deck as the shipnet came back on-line. The damage . . . the damage was bad, though arguably not as bad as it could have been. *Indeterminacy* was in a slow tumble, falling away from Kaden's orange-and-white disk at 29,000 kph—a slow-drifting crawl by interplanetary standards. Her dorsal fore and mainmasts, her port mizzen, her starboard mizzen, main, and foremasts were gone, snapped off by the violence of their close passage. Wreckage—the shards and tangle of splintered masts and shredded rigging—trailed alongside, threatening to further cripple the vessel as her spin fouled the remaining masts and spars.

"Get that wreckage cut away!" he yelled into the confusion of the net. "Helm! Get this tumble under control!"

Ahead, less than a hundred thousand kilometers distant now, four ornately decorated P'aaseni warships were moving into line-ahead for an intercept, the lead vessel the *Gilaadessera*, a seventy-five-gun ship of the line. Her sails spread slowly, catching the outwind of the local sun, their lead surfaces adazzle in shifting, light show display. It was a race now, between those oncoming warships and *Indeterminacy*'s damage control parties, ship handlers, and machines.

Hazzard glanced astern, at the slowly receding, slowly tumbling disk of the planet. "Make a signal to Kaden," he told cy-Tomlin. "Put it in all of their major dialects. Tell them . . . tell them, 'Sorry for the miscalculation. I guess we cut that one too close!' "

"Do you think they'll believe our brushing them that way was an *accident?*" Pardoe asked.

Hazzard gave a mental shrug. "It gives both sides a bit of something to save face with," he replied. "And at least we stopped those damned guns!"

"I hope the Admiralty sees it that way, sir."

"Skek the Admiralty!" The curse was more bitter than he'd intended. "They're not here!"

Bursts of plasma from *Indy*'s maneuvering thrusters slowed, then arrested the ship's spin. A large tangle of wreckage—remnants of the entire starboard mast array—broke free a moment later, imparting a slight yaw to port.

"Helm! Don't correct that!" Hazzard snapped. "Let them think we're still helpless!"

The port yaw was turning the *Indy* relative to the oncoming enemy line, bringing her dorsal gun deck around.

Naval tactics were dictated by the physics of ship handling and the nature of ship design. Vast arrays of sails and rigging forward and astern meant that a warship's guns—all but her relatively small bow and stern chasers—faced outward, abeam. The wooden warships that had sailed the oceans of ancient Earth four thousand years before had adopted tactics quite similar to these, shaped by the cold hand of physics.

"Port roll," Hazzard ordered. "Dorsal guns, run out! Fire as you bear!"

In those long-vanished sailing vessels at the dawn of history, shipboard guns had used charges of exploding chemical powder to impel spherical lumps of inert metal across hundreds of meters of open sea. Aboard *Indeterminacy*, guns used magnetic fields to launch artificially generated micro-singularities across far greater gulfs of empty space. *Indy*'s largest guns were 32s, each accelerating a thirty-two-kilogram mass, compressed to a volume rivaling that of a single proton, to a velocity of nearly twenty percent of c.

Along the checkered surface of *Indeterminacy*'s dorsal gun deck, hatches swung open and the blunt, black muzzles of the singularity launchers snubbed forth. They fired, the massive, rippling broadside slamming the frigate sideways in hammering recoil, the dead hand of Isaac Newton rocking them back in all the fury of his Third Law. *Indy*'s drive fields absorbed much of the recoil, and the massive shock absorbers housing each of her guns dissipated much of the rest. Still, the effect of a broadside on those aboard the vessel was one of jolting, thundering power barely contained by the drive fields.

Hazzard felt the lurch and rumble, driven to the core of his being.

Indy's first broadside struck home.

"Maintain port roll!" he called. "Starboard deck, roll out! Fire as you bear!"

A ship's drive field could be fluttered, distorting space enough to bend laser and particle beams safely clear of the vessel . . . or to crumple and shred the electronics of any missile, or the fusing of an incoming explosive warhead. Microsingularities, however, smaller than an atomic nucleus and moving at velocities only slightly less than relativistic, tended to slide through a field's fringe interference effect, and the damage they wreaked on the target came not from exploding warheads, but from the simple kinetic destruction wrought by high-velocity mass.

Like the shipboard guns of an earlier era, *Indeterminacy's* singularity cannon pounded away at the lead P'aaseni ship, puncturing main courses, jibs, and tops'ls, slamming home into her ornately painted prow. Where most Union warship prows were broad, flattened domes, fifty meters or more across, P'aaseni vessels bore clusters of twelve spherical water tanks, held together by gilded frames that gave them the look of bizarre baskets of fruit. Each impact blew glittering bits of hull metal, basket loads of scrap, and gushing white plumes of escaping steam, crystallizing almost at once into frost-gleaming clouds of ice-fog. Every starship carried a small lake in its prow storage tank—water for the crew's use, for use as fuel in the fusion reactors, and reaction mass for the thrusters. Storing the water in a prow tank provided protection from particulate radiation when the ship was at near-c velocities.

Indeterminacy's broadside had holed at least half of *Gilaadessera's* tanks. Water exposed to hard vacuum expanded quickly, turning to steam . . . then condensed almost immediately into ice crystals. In another moment, *Gilaadessera* was wreathed in fog as water gushed from savage rents in the storage tanks. As *Indy's* second broadside tore into the enemy vessel, high-speed microsingularity rounds scratched dazzling blue threads of light through the ice-fog.

More debris spilled into space, mixed with the gush of frozen atmosphere. The *Gilaadessera* was hurt, and badly.

Indeterminacy continued her roll, bringing her port side guns to bear, loosing a third broadside with devastating accuracy. One of *Gilaadessera*'s bowsprits and foremasts collapsed in a tangle of broken spars and whiplashing, severed rigging. A moment later, the main mast on that side followed, crumpling under the deadly barrage.

But the big P'aaseni vessel was yawing now to bring her own guns to bear. Worse, the three light rates in her van were moving past her now, accelerating beyond her debris cloud, angling for a clear shot. They would pass astern of the *Indeterminacy* within another two minutes.

And the *Indy* had fired all three broadsides. It took time to reload; the power requirements for readying a singularity and launching it at the target were enormous, and a naval gun could simply not cycle faster than a shot every three or four minutes. All guns were being reloaded, but it would be another two minutes before the dorsal gun deck was ready for another broadside.

And in that time . . .

"For what we are about to receive," Tommis Pardoe said, speaking an ironic prayer from the days of wooden ships on water oceans, "may we be truly thankful. . . ."

"Not bad, all in all," Sotheby added. "Three broadsides, and not a shot in reply!" He sobered. "Too bad we're half crippled, though, or we could keep the dance going!"

Hazzard ignored the byplay. "Helm! Bring us right fifteen degrees, down minus five," he said. "Take us in closer!" If they could swing beneath the enormous *Gilaadessera*'s shattered prow, they could continue to pound the line battle-

ship and perhaps find some protection from her consorts'
fire.

The ship of the line began firing as soon as the first of
the guns on her port gun deck could be brought to bear.
Holes, neat punctures, appeared in *Indy*'s portside forecourse
and mains'l, which were still just in the process of de-
ploying. A jarring shudder ran through the shipnet imagery
as singularities slammed into the ship's hull, smashing
through her prow. Her dorsal bowsprit shattered under an
impact, debris spinning back, colliding with rigging, knocking off a port main spar.

More hits, more shudders. *Indeterminacy* lurched to
port, tumbling again. Sotheby was firing the maneuvering
thrusters almost constantly now, fighting the ship, trying
to maintain both control and way. The frigate continued
drifting ahead, her straight-line course carrying her along
just slightly faster than the ponderous *Gilaadessera* could
turn. As *Indy*'s gun decks reported ready to fire one after
the other, Hazzard ordered all decks to commence general firing.

More rounds struck home, sending deck-wrenching shudders through the Union vessel, and now some of the rounds
were coming from the stern quarter, as the lead P'aaseni
frigate cleared the *Gilaadessera* and brought her guns to
bear. One of *Indy*'s stern cooling vanes tore free, fluttering
away into night end over end. Her dorsal mizzen shuddered,
twisted in its mounting, and then tore free, the shriek of
shredding metal echoing through the frigate's manned
spaces, loudly enough that the sound crossed the jacking
barrier and was heard by the men within the virtual environment of the shipnet. A scattering of golden sparks—teleoperated spiders bearing the minds of *Indy*'s dorsal mizzen
sail handlers—spilled into emptiness.

Goddess, bring their minds back safely. . . .

There was nothing to be done beyond the minor comfort of prayer, and no time even for that. Seven rounds slammed into the gun deck section, ripping out bulkheads, upending guns.

Ferocious and *Swift* were attempting to join *Indeterminacy* now, though they were badly damaged. The *Swift* bore only three masts now, one on each deck, while little *Ferocious* had only a single foremast left, thrusting out from her starboard deck with a single tops'l filled.

The remaining two enemy ships appeared to be concentrating on the crippled *Decider*, closing with her in order to board.

"Make to *Ferocious* and *Swift*," Hazzard said. "Tell them to bear clear and make for the out-system rendezvous."

A moment later—"*Ferocious* and *Swift* both say they're too badly damaged for transit, Captain. Both say they're going to stay and fight it out."

Damn. *Indeterminacy*'s sacrifice was going to be in vain. He'd hoped that by making the microjump, he could distract the P'aaseni forces long enough for *Decider*, *Swift*, and *Ferocious*, at least, to make their escape. *Fire Angel*, he saw, was beyond hope, her hull wrecked and glowing with savage, blue-white heat.

And it now appeared as though all three ships, and *Indeterminacy* as well, were going to be in a similar condition within the next few minutes.

Indeterminacy loosed a long, rippling broadside from her dorsal guns, round after round slamming into the inert hulk of the huge *Gilaadessera*, her leaking, fog-wreathed prow now less than three hundred kilometers abeam. *Indy*'s portside guns were engaging the *Thaspasin*, a thirty-three-gun P'aaseni frigate, while her starboard guns dueled with the ship of the line crowded up alongside the *Decider*.

Another broadside struck home aboard the Union frigate.

Her port foremast was snapped in two, halfway out, and tumbled away, cordage spinning. She could barely crowd on enough sail to maintain acceleration, now, and she was in immediate danger of losing all maneuvering way.

"Captain, port lookout. I think . . . I think they're getting ready to board. I see boarding pods on their foredeck."

Pardoe's shipnet image looked at him, the man's long face drawn and tight. "It was a good run, sir. I didn't think we'd make it this far."

"I'd hoped to give the squadron a chance to escape," he said. "I guess I miscalculated after all."

He was facing that bitterest of moments in any ship captain's career, the moment when he knows he can fight no longer and must surrender to an overwhelmingly more powerful foe.

"Bridge! Dorsal lookout! Highspace entry point forming, at one-three-eight, plus two-five! We have incoming vessels!"

Goddess! More P'aaseni? . . .

"Sir! It's *Valorous!* And *Trimirage!* And the rest of the out-system squadron!"

"It's the goddamn cavalry to the rescue!" Pardoe shouted. "It's a skekking miracle! . . ."

"Not a miracle," Hazzard replied, trying to keep his voice from breaking. "*Not* a miracle. Just very, *very* good timing . . ."

". . . it is the judgment of this court, furthermore, that Captain Fifth-Rank Greydon Hazzard acted at all times within the very best traditions of the naval service, rendering timely assistance to four smaller embattled friendly vessels and almost certainly preventing their destruction or capture by the enemy.

"This court of inquiry finds him not guilty of criminal negligence and urges his immediate restoration to command." Admiral-Fourth Howard looked up from his computer display. "Congratulations, Captain."

"Thank you, my lord."

The court of inquiry would have been necessary even if Admiral cy-Dennever hadn't filed charges against Hazzard in the wake of the Battle of Kaden, as it was being called now. After the fight, and the surrender of the *Gilaadessera* and two of her consorts, *Indeterminacy* had barely been able to make it to light speed for a long, heart-in-the-throat highspace jump back to Tribaltren. She would be in spacedock undergoing repairs for at least the next six months. Twenty-five of her crew of three hundred were dead, another fourteen mindless, helpless dissociates.

A hell of a butcher's bill to pay. Poor cy-Tomlin. He was one of the dissociates, the circuitry projecting his mind into the shipnet burned out during the final, savage enemy broadside. The poor kid had never had a chance.

Hazzard knew he'd done it to save the other ships. That didn't make the loss any easier to bear. The loss of his own was like a small piece of himself dying.

A bell rang. "These proceedings are completed. Dismissed."

Hazzard straightened to attention as the three admirals behind the imposing cliff of a judgment desk stood, turned, and walked toward the wings of the courtroom. One of them stopped, though, at the door, spoke for a moment with the others, then walked toward Hazzard.

"That," Admiral Dalim cy-Koenin said softly, "was one of the *stupidest* battles I've ever seen played on an after-action report."

Hazzard stiffened. "Yes, sir."

"You should have run as soon as you saw how badly you were outgunned. You know that, don't you?"

"Yes, sir."

"If Lieutenant Lasely hadn't had the bright idea of expending nearly all of *Uriel*'s water reserves in a last-ditch attempt to boost to *c* using his maneuvering thrusters, it would have been another hour or more before *Victor* reached you, and you all would have been dead or prisoners by then."

"I only wanted to save those ships and men, sir. I knew *Uriel* would win clear to the squadron. I thought I might be able to slow the P'aaseni enough to let some of our ships get clear."

"Risking your ship and crew that way was misguided at best, stupid at worst."

Which was no more than Hazzard had been telling himself since the battle's end. "Yes, sir. I have no excuse, sir."

"Uh. It was also one of the more brilliant pieces of military ship handling I've ever seen. You saved Bellemew's tail, that's sure. You single-handedly brought the Anarchate into the Union camp and without firing on them, though there'll be some hair-splitting over whether what you did constituted an attack or not. You fought a ship of the line to a battered hulk and were responsible for the capture of three out of six enemy sail and the repulse of the rest. You'll probably be getting a decoration for this one."

"Lieutenant Lasely deserves the medal, Admiral. He's the one that saved *all* our tails."

"He'll get it. Don't worry." Cy-Koenin placed his hands on his hips and shook his head. "Damn it, Dad. Sometimes I despair of you. But . . . well done!"

Hazzard released the breath he'd been holding in his lungs. His son extended a hand, and Hazzard took it.

Then they embraced.

It was one of the costs of a naval service that depended on near-*c* velocities for each jump to highspace or for riding the light barrier endlessly on blockade or patrol off the shoals of enemy systems. Greydon Hazzard had ten portwives on various worlds and, at last count, at any rate, had seven children, four girls, three boys, by different mothers. All but three were older biologically than Hazzard now, because most of·their lives had been spent groundside . . . and one, also a Navy captain, was sometimes older, sometimes younger when they met, depending on how much tau-minus each had accumulated in the intervening subjective since their last meeting.

Hazzard had racked up a hell of a lot of tau-minus over the objective years. His portwife on Groller, nearly seventy objective years ago, had been one Lauri cy-Koenin.

She was long dead, but their son, Dalim, had gone to the Union Naval Academy at Napola, risen through the ranks, commanded half a dozen ships in his illustrious career, and finally been promoted to admiral. With far less tau-minus on the books than Hazzard, he was now fifty-eight standard-objective years old and twenty-two years older than his father.

"You know, don't you, that cy-Dennever was right to bring you up on charges."

A pause. "Yes, sir." Reluctantly.

"The Anarchate was *this* close to declaring war after your little stunt with their PDBs. You're just damned lucky their military council decided to switch sides."

That was news to Hazzard. "I hadn't heard that, sir."

"Just came through on the last dispatch boat from Kaden. Turns out there was a faction of the Anarchate military that had decided to side with the Alliance because they were strongest and, sooner or later, when the Alliance beat us, the Anarchate would be wiped out by the Alliance's human-onlies. They figured that if they joined the Alliance, helped them, the Irdikad might be able to find a place in the new regime, even if only as second-class citizens."

"Huh. Maybe their decision wasn't so crazy after all." It made sense, after a fashion, according to Irdikad psychology.

"Yes, well, it seems that our winning that battle against those odds convinced them that *we* were the strongest, and therefore the ones to side with. Although . . ."

"Sir?"

"What they *said* was, 'Anyone crazy enough to pull a stunt like *that* is worthy of respect.' A rough translation, of course." He shook his head. "First time a Fleet officer has won a battle and a new ally by being insane."

"I prefer the word *lucky*."

"Someday, Dad," cy-Koenin said with a grin, "when you're as old as I am, you'll know that relying on luck just doesn't always pay off the way you expect."

"We make our own luck, son. Sometimes, it's just a bit harder and more expensive than other times." He didn't add that often the price was a little piece of your soul. *Poor cy-Tomlin.* . . .

"You in the mood for a bite to eat, Admiral? Courts of inquiry make me hungry."

"Thought you'd never ask."

Together, father and son, they strode from the chamber.

BLINDFOLD

by Robin Wayne Bailey

Robin Wayne Bailey is the author of a dozen novels, including the Brothers of the Dragon series, *Shadowdance*, and the new Fafhrd and the Grey Mouser novel *Swords Against the Shadowland*. His short fiction has appeared in numerous science fiction and fantasy anthologies and magazines, including *Far Frontiers* and *Spell Fantastic*. An avid book collector and old-time radio enthusiast, he lives in North Kansas City, Missouri.

Chilson Dawes stumbled out of the doorway of Madam Satterfield's brothel and into the dark Martian night. He stank of alcohol and sex. He didn't care. He still had money in his pockets, and pale dawn was hours away. He rubbed a hand over his stubbled chin, drew his cloak about his shoulders, and smacked his lips, thirsty for another drink.

A burly bear of a man in a worn leather spacer's jacket leaned near the door. He stubbed out a cigarette with a booted toe. "You're killin' yourself, you know." A note of weariness softened the gruff voice. "Why don't you call it a night."

Dawes heard the limping scrape of boot soles on the pavement. He groped for an offered arm and clutched it. "Mister Donovan," he said with a cheerful slur, "when I want a medical opinion, I'll call a doctor, not a broken-down washed-out wreck of an Irish freighter pilot like yourself." He patted the hand at the end of the arm. "You're a lousy friend, but like a good old dog always there when I call."

"We are a pair, aren't we?" Donovan said. "So—brothel, bar, or casino?"

That was the problem with a city like Tharsis. Too damn much to offer. All the sins and vices a man couldn't get on civilized Earth anymore, pleasures undreamed of for someone with too much money and too much time. Chilson Dawes had both.

"Just walk," he said with a sudden, self-pitying melancholy.

Donovan obeyed. Dawes, with a secure grip on the Irishman's arm, listened to the sounds around him as they wandered. The streets were alive tonight: music gushing from the open doorways of taverns; a woman's coarse laugh; a pair of boastful spacers drunk as Dawes himself; the rattle of what might have been a blowing newspaper; the soft rustle of his own cloak. A harlot called his name and an offer as Donovan led him on. Strong whiff of perfume. He waved a hand and grinned, wondered who she was.

"The moons," he said quietly, feeling the Martian wind in his hair. "Are they up yet?"

Donovan slowed his pace only a little. Chilson Dawes imagined the big man staring upward. "Deimos is, swollen and full, like a ripe tangerine."

"Bastard," Dawes muttered.

"Something else is up, too," Donovan whispered. His hand closed over Dawes' as he subtly increased the pace. "We're being followed."

Dawes frowned, his heart quickening. This was a rough part of Tharsis, but he was known here. The locals protected him and left him alone. Still, he trusted Donovan; he did his best to keep up. He had enough money on him to make robbery tempting. Maybe someone had followed him from Madam Satterfield's.

Donovan led the way quickly through the streets, around corners, down winding alleys into new streets. Carnival sounds swirled; cotton candy smells and body stink, urine, trash can noises, conversation, laughter. Another turn, and a quieter street.

Donovan stopped suddenly. A rush of footsteps. Donovan pushed Dawes' hand away and turned. A grunt, harsh intake of breath, sound of body falling.

A rough hand grabbed Dawes' shoulder. Not Donovan's—he knew that familiar touch too well. Angry, concerned for his friend, Dawes leaned sideways, twisting even as he thrust out a foot. Someone went flying over his leg. Someone else caught his wrist. He heard his name; so they knew him! With his free hand he snatched the attacker's wrist, twisted hard, heard bone snap as he dropped to one knee. A sharp, deep-throated scream of pain, another flying body.

His name again, then an energy whine, heat-sizzle past his ear, and an explosion of stone and brick behind him. "Dawes!"

An ozone reek filled the air, and he rose cautiously. He knew a warning shot from a laser pistol. He groped for the still-warm wall, leaned against it, fingered the catch of his cloak nervously, and huddled inside its folds as he waited.

"Damn you, you've injured two of my best men."

From either side new pairs of hands gripped his arms. A loud electric crackle, and anguished gasps. "Four," Dawes corrected with a horrible grin, as two more bodies fell groaning. He relaxed a little; he recognized the voice that had addressed him. "Next time you want to see me, Colonel, make an appointment—like everybody else." He paused. No one else tried to grab him, so he touched the catch of his cloak again, deactivating the microcircuitry hidden in its weave.

"You've been inventing again."

There was a certain pitying sympathy in Samuel Straf's voice that irritated Dawes. "A stun-cloak," he said. "What the hell did you do to Donovan, and what the hell do you want with me? I've got nothing to do with your damned Stellar Guard anymore."

"I'm okay, Chil." Donovan's voice said he was a little less than okay, but alive at least. "Just too slow on this bum leg. I turned into a left hook."

"He threw the first punch," Straf said. "Understandable, I guess, since we're not in uniform, but you don't wear those in this part of the city. You haunt a bad neighborhood, Chilson."

As if Chilson Dawes gave a starman's damn what Samuel Straf thought. The Guard had dismissed him and shit-canned his last civilian research project on Straf's recommendation. "Stuff it, Colonel." He held out his arm for Donovan, instructing his friend, "Get me out of here before this skunk stinks up the place."

"I've got a job for you," Straf said stiffly. "You're still drawing a Guard paycheck. Technically, you never retired."

Dawes gripped Donovan's arm. "You fired me when you canceled the *Sabre*."

"I put you on medical leave," Straf shot back. "You're blind, Chil."

Chilson Dawes felt his heart freeze. "Stay away from me, Sam," he said through clenched teeth. "Just stay away!"

"I'll give you back the *Sabre*," Straf said. A controlled but unmistakable urgency filled in his voice. "I'm authorized. It's fueled and ready."

"You're full of it," Dawes answered. But he listened. And shortly, he found himself sober on an atomic-powered tram from Tharsis City to the Guard starport at Valles Marinaris.

In two hundred years of starfaring, humans had discovered no other intelligent races. Recently, that had changed. Only a year after Dawes had lost his sight, the first exploratory ships had ventured past Vega into a sector named Burnham space after the astronomer who had mapped it. It was in Burnham space that the earthship *Lancelot*, under the command of Captain James Murray, first encountered the Kaxfen.

"Murray barely got his ship back to our outpost on Orth," Colonel Straf explained to Dawes over cups of steaming coffee. "The Kaxfen weapons weren't necessarily superior, but their numbers were. They swarmed over the *Lancelot* like insects."

Donovan spoke from the window that overlooked the starport. "If you've got a name to call them by, you must have established some kind of communication."

"Nothing face-to-face," Straf answered. "Only voice communications. They've warned us out of Burnham space. They're claiming it as their exclusive backyard, and they're quite territorial about it. They promise to destroy any ship that ventures near it."

Dawes sipped from his cup. "So humans have finally found neighbors in space, and managed to make enemies of them in our first meeting. I guess some things never change." He leaned forward, felt for the edge of Straf's desk, and set his cup down. "What do you expect me to do about it?"

There was a brief silence. Straf cleared his throat. "You brought the *Sabre* home like a sighted man, Chil," he said. "Even with your optic nerves burned out. Nobody knows that ship's systems, controls, or capabilities better than you. Nobody's touched her since you. No one dared."

"You can't be asking what I'm thinking," Donovan interrupted, his voice turning angry.

Straf's boots scuffed as he came around the desk closer to Dawes. "I'm asking if you think you can pilot the *Sabre*."

Donovan exploded. "Goddamn you, he's! . . ."

"Shut up, Donovan!" Dawes yelled. His thoughts whirled. When Straf had mentioned giving him back the *Sabre*, Dawes had assumed the colonel had meant in an advisory or research capacity. Could he pilot her? Did Straf realize what he was offering? He answered, "Hell, yes!" Then he settled back in his chair, suspicious. "But you haven't told me everything, Sam. The *Sabre*'s only a prototype, not a warship."

"I wasn't exactly truthful when I said no one had touched her," Straf admitted. "I've had her outfitted with the new Kleinowski planet-killer lasers. She's not totally defenseless."

"Or without offense either," Dawes said. "But what's this all about?"

Sound of paper rattling, and a light breeze fanned over Dawes' face. He envisioned Straf shaking a sheaf of pages as if Dawes could see them. It stopped suddenly, and Straf cleared his throat again. "We've got a cryo-ship. . . ."

"An ice-wagon?" Donovan said from the window. "Who the? . . ."

"Don't be crude," Straf said, then he continued. "A cryo-ship. Yes, they're antiquated, but certain religious groups prefer them to translight travel."

Dawes nodded. "Because they think the laws of nature and God don't apply to hypespace, they refuse to go there. They'd rather travel like a tray of ice cubes."

Straf cleared his throat again. "They're entitled to their

beliefs. But we've got a problem. The *Via Dolorosa* launched from Earth fifteen years ago, well before we knew about the Kaxfen. It's carrying a complement of five thousand New Hope congregationalists all in deep sleep to a new m-class planet in System 2X-185. Their course skirts right across the edge of Burnham space."

Dawes frowned as he leaped ahead of Straf's slow explanations. "Like most ice-wagons, the *Via Dolorosa* is operating only on computers. It's also totally defenseless. You want me to save some fundamentalist butt."

There was more than a hint of indignation in Straf's response. "My parents are on the *Via Dolorosa*," he answered. "I've pulled strings to give you back the *Sabre*, Chil. And if that's not enough incentive, I've got another trick up my sleeve."

A brittle click as Straf thumbed an intercom switch on his desk. A moment later the door opened. By the whiff of lavender perfume and a soft tread, Dawes guessed that a young woman had entered the room. Donovan gave a low, appreciative whistle. "You'd like the look of her, Chil," he said.

A tiny scrape of metal; a barely audible creak as of a lid opening. A stronger whiff of lavender as the woman bent close. A soft weight settled on Chilson Dawes' shoulder. For a moment, he sat tense, expectant. Then, he felt a creepy scuttling sensation near his neck. He gave a startled cry and lunged from his chair to encounter cool glass—the window—under his palms. "What are you! . . ."

Whatever the thing was, it clung to him. Scores of small caterpillar feet clutched his collar, prickled over his bare neck.

He shot out a hand for Donovan. "Get it off! Get it—" Gripping the Irishman's arm, he caught his breath suddenly and froze.

Like a black mist, the darkness that had filled his eyes
for three years dissolved. Through the reflected glare of his
own face in the glass, he saw the freighters and gleaming
starships in the port yards, beyond those the dark Martian
mountains and escarpments, and above the glimmering stars
in the night sky with Phobos high as Deimos sank in the
west.

Chilson Dawes forgot where he was, forgot the others
in the room, the creature on his shoulder. He covered his
eyes with his fists, then looked again. Tears began to stream
on his cheeks; he wept like a child, confused, shaking. Donovan had hold of him on one side, and Straf on the other.
He was barely aware of them as he stared outward at that
awesome vista.

Unexpectedly, the room seemed to rotate. Without turning, he saw Straf's worried face, older than he'd remembered, then another face, very feminine and quite amused.
The creature on his shoulder began to purr softly.

Dawes regained a measure of self-control. Donovan
hadn't lied. The woman was indeed something to see, even
in her shapeless lab coat. The creature seemed to like her,
too, though Dawes wasn't sure quite how he knew that. He
reached cautiously up to touch the thing on his shoulder.
His first impression had been right; it was much like a caterpillar, lightly furred, but nearly twelve inches long.

"I don't understand," Dawes said, half afraid the miracle would end. He stroked the creature with a forefinger; it
nuzzled against his ear, and its purring increased.

The woman laughed lightly. "Neither do we," she said.
"A team of explorers found it and its kin on a little mud-
ball planet in the Mintaka system. They don't seem to be
intelligent, but we're not sure. They do have a weird form
of tactile telepathy—a defense mechanism, we think, against
the numerous predators on their world. As long as you're

in physical contact, you can share sight, hearing, sensation. It doesn't seem to have a sense of smell, though. And when you feed it . . ." She laughed again. "I'd put it down if I were you and put up with a few moments of blindness."

Dawes looked at Donovan, then back to the woman. "I only have black-and-white vision."

She nodded. "You're seeing through its eyes, Mister Dawes, not your own. Those are still quite useless."

"I had this flown in for you," Straf said. "There are only a couple in the entire Sol system. I need you, Chil. Not only for my parents' sakes. We can't let five thousand people just be slaughtered in their sleep. Even at translight, our nearest ships can't reach the *Via Dolorosa* before she enters Burnham space. Only the *Sabre* can."

"Why Chilson, Colonel?" Donovan demanded. "You've had nearly two years to locate and divert this ice—this cryoship."

Straf frowned and seated himself on the edge of his desk. His voice turned harsh. "Frankly, we screwed up. Because the *Via Dolorosa* launched so long ago and is moving so slowly, the bureaucrats in Tracking Control forgot about her. On top of that, the Guard's been distracted with a lot of pirate activity lately." He paused and rubbed his chin. When he spoke again, the harshness was gone from his voice, replaced with an obvious fatigue. "Last week would have been my parents' wedding anniversary. I'm older now than they were when they launched with the other congregationalists. I'd just entered the Guard back then. Maybe I'm getting sentimental, Chil, because on a whim, I pulled out an old star chart my father left me outlining their course. I hadn't looked at it since I was a punk. When I saw the danger, I started pulling strings and bending a lot of rules to arm the *Sabre*, then trace you down, to . . ."

Dawes' mind raced as he considered all the angles. An

excitement he hadn't known in three years filled him. "What do you call this thing?" he interrupted, continuing to stroke the creature. It had a strangely soothing effect.

"We call it a Mintakan mind-worm," Straf answered.

Dawes scoffed. "You would. God, that's unimaginative." He thought for a moment, then addressed the caterpillar. "Okay, little fella, from now on, your name's 'Hookah.'" The woman in her lab coat still filled his vision; he wondered what his chances would be of getting a date with her, and muttered, "Because if this whole thing isn't right through the looking glass, nothing is." He wiped the last traces of tears from his cheeks and turned his shoulder so that Straf's face came into view. "And you're tossing in one hell of a fat cash bonus."

Even at translight, our nearest ships can't reach the Via Dolorosa *before she enters Burnham space. Only the* Sabre *can.*

God, how it must have killed Straf to make that admission. From the beginning he'd been skeptical of Dawes' project. Once a translight pilot himself, the colonel had done his best to delay funding and make himself an obstacle around which Dawes and his research team had had to dance—because, if successful, Project *Sabre* meant a total retooling, perhaps even a dismantling, of the Stellar Guard as it existed.

Project *Sabre* represented that kind of a revolution.

Translight vessels were the fastest ships ever developed by mankind. They had given humans the stars, allowed them to explore, to settle new colony worlds, given man frontiers undreamed. Yet, even translight vessels, traversing hyperspace, required time to journey from one point to another. Sometimes that time factor was a matter of weeks, sometimes a matter of months. Sooner or later, as mankind kept pushing out, it would be years, until even translight travel would become insufficient.

Project *Sabre* was the answer to that—the next step. With massive engines built into the body of a Foss Starfish, the largest ship in the Guard fleet, the *Sabre* not only folded space, it creased it. This *fold-space* drive system, Dawes' brainchild, made translight travel slow by comparison, obsolete. Practically instantaneous, in Dawes' opinion it was as close as man was likely to come to teleportation.

There were only two drawbacks. The field generated by the fold-space drive was, as Dawes liked to describe it, *gravitationally sensitive*. The ship had to be in deep space beyond the range of any stellar object before it was activated. That meant the ship had to carry a translight drive as well as the fold-space drive. This required a big vessel like the Foss Starfish. Nor could any other ship be within a parsec's distance because of the destructive distortion ripple caused by the field.

It was the second drawback, however, that had caused the *Sabre*'s cancellation after only a single experimental flight, a flight Dawes himself had piloted. Something about the drive system, or about that brief moment in fold-space itself, destroyed a human's optic nerve, leaving a person blind.

Now alone, speeding between the orbits of Uranus and Neptune, Dawes sat once more at the controls of his one-of-a-kind vessel. He trembled as his thoughts returned to that first flight. Out beyond the range of Pluto he'd sat, the same point toward which he was heading now. Then, his thoughts had been on far Proxima Centauri. He'd triggered the *Sabre*, experienced a moment of blinding whiteness such as he'd never known, followed by congratulatory voices from his communications console. Voices rising out of darkness.

He'd barely kept it together long enough to make the return flight home. After that—his shot glass had never been empty.

Through Hookah's eyes, he stared at the trigger control. The little creature stirred restlessly on his shoulder as if it sensed his nervousness. It wriggled, and the view shifted from the control to his own ear, then to the back of the cabin.

It didn't matter if his new pet looked around a little. He didn't need eyes to fly this ship. He tried to settle more comfortably into his seat as he considered his mission and the New Hope congregationalists frozen in sleep in their antiquated vessel. The *Via Dolorosa*, they had named their ship, *the Road of Sorrows*. An agnostic himself, the symbolism wasn't lost on him. At the end of their journey they hoped for resurrection and a new life on a new world.

He ran a finger along Hookah's back; the creature began to purr.

Dawes, too, had unexpected hope for a new life. "Port Authority," he said, activating the communications console. "Redesignate *Sabre*." That had only ever been the project's name anyway. "Record new designation, *Archangel*. Register." He waited, pleased with himself. The archangels were heaven's warrior class.

A voice that sounded like Straf's came back over communications. "*Archangel*—authorized and registered. "Now get your butt moving, civilian." Yep, the old man himself.

At seven-tenths the speed of light, he streaked by Pluto. Beyond the orbit of the Oort Cloud he pushed his vessel into translight.

He continued to pet Hookah, drawing reassurance, even courage, from the contact, and the creature rewarded him by watching the view screen where stars blazed like fiery beacons. Each one called his name; he'd thought he'd never see them again.

His hand hovered over the fold-drive trigger. He was far enough beyond Sol now, and the computer had his destination coordinates. Still he hesitated. Fold-space had blinded him before. What if it hurt him some other way this time?

And what about Hookah? Doctor Halama—the woman in Straf's office—theorized that nothing would happen to the mind-worm, that the creature's biology was too different. Still, it was only theory. What if he lost this second set of eyes? Hookah shivered on his shoulder, picking up on his fear.

Five thousand lives.

Another trip through fold-space, or another trip to the bottom of a bottle.

He knew which one he couldn't face again.

He hit the trigger.

With eyes or without, a burning white light swallowed him, a tiny instant spark that went supernova in his brain and expanded to engulf the stars in the viewscreen, the control console, the ship. Everything vanished into whiteness. He fell, fell, blinded by that light. And he screamed.

Then, he was looking at himself screaming, his mouth wide open, jaw straining. Sweat beaded on his pale face. The muscles in his neck stood out tight as cords, veins bulged.

He looked foolish. Ridiculous. Hookah scuttled to his other shoulder and nuzzled his ear. Dawes thought he looked just as silly from that side and shut his mouth. Hookah began to purr again.

"I think you're laughing at me," Dawes said, drawing a finger along the creature's furry back.

His trembling slowly ebbed as did the adrenaline fear-rush. He marveled that, even blind, he had experienced the white light phenomenon, and he wondered again if it was even light at all, or some property of fold-space itself. It suggested a new direction for his research.

Archangel's computer voice reported their position in Burnham space.

"Scan for the *Via Dolorosa*," he instructed.

The computer answered: Two point four parsecs to starboard. Just crossing the border into Kaxfen-claimed territory.

Through Hookah's curious eyes, Dawes watched himself scowl. While he congratulated himself for the pinpoint accuracy of the fold-space jump, he cursed Straf, who had assured him the New Hope congregationalists were two days from Burnham space. Dawes had hoped for time to turn around, reach the *Via Dolorosa*, and reprogram its course computers to skirt the region.

"*Archangel*," he addressed the computer, "scan for approaching vessels, known or unknown."

A pause. *Archangel* answered: Five vessels of unknown configuration approaching at maximum translight.

Kaxfen ships. It took only a moment more to determine that they were heading straight for the defenseless *Via Dolorosa*. Dawes considered that he might do the Stellar Guard a favor while he was out here and instructed the computer to backtrack probable trajectories for those ships. If they were flying a straight course for the congregationalists, perhaps he could discover the location of their home world, or at least one of their bases.

Meanwhile, he ran some hasty calculations and weighed his options. Six ships, and no idea of the arsenal he faced. But then, the Kaxfen knew nothing about him either. They had to be wondering where the *Archangel* had come from. Better, he decided to engage the Kaxfen out here as far away from the congregationalists as possible.

"*Archangel*." The computer answered Dawes promptly.

"See if the *Via Dolorosa*'s computers will respond to a hailing signal."

The computer responded: Affirmative. Contact established.

Dawes relaxed a little. Hookah, growing restive, crawled down the front of his shirt and gave him a glimpse of his own knees. He picked the little creature up and returned him to his shoulder. He gave his attention back to the computer.

"*Archangel*," he called again. "Transmit a continuous recognition signal to the *Via Dolorosa*." Dawes' mind raced. He had to assume that since some form of contact had been established with the Kaxfen, the aliens could read his transmissions. "But piggyback an encoded Stellar Guard priority override command with that signal. If the *Via Dolorosa*'s computers acknowledge, seize control of that ship. Then reprogram its course computers so that it exits Burnham space as quickly as possible. Determine a new course to its destination, and inform me the instant the ship begins to turn."

That left Dawes to deal with the aliens. At sublight speed, there was no chance the *Via Dolorosa* could exit Burnham space before the faster Kaxfen reached it. His fingers danced over control panels. Even blind he could have piloted this vessel; he'd designed every circuit, programmed every data crystal.

He directed *Archangel* straight for the approaching Kaxfen.

Five of the alien ships turned to meet him. One broke formation with the others. Dawes cursed; he didn't need a computer to guess that lone ship's intent. In the view screen, through Hookah's eyes, he watched its energy wake, sizzling like a burning lance across the dark of space.

The remaining five also changed formation. One took

point and came straight for him; two moved to attack from the port side; two more from starboard.

Archangel's computer addressed him. The *Via Dolorosa* had accepted the encoded priority override. *Archangel* now controlled the ice-wagon, and the lumbering vessel was turning.

"Get it the hell out of here!" Dawes muttered as much to himself as to his computer. He thought of the five thousand people whose lives depended on him, of Straf's sleeping parents, all unaware of the danger unfolding.

He drew a deep breath, and stroked a finger along Hookah's back. "Okay, little fella," he said, "it's you and me." And, he added silently, the finest ship ever designed. He resisted a laugh. For the first time in three years he felt alive!

He raced toward the aliens' point-ship. It fired on him, but from a distance beyond the effective range of its weaponry. On the *Archangel*'s instrument panel, an energy spike registered, then dropped off sharply. *Archangel* was untouched.

"My turn." He brought the Kleinowskis on-line and counted down ten seconds. Ever closer he drew to the alien point-ship. Then, "*Archangel*, fire!"

The Kleinowski planet-killers drew on the translight engines for their power. That had no effect on the vessel's present velocity, however. Across space twin beams of searing light stabbed. The Kaxfen ship exploded in a titanic fireball. *Archangel* sailed through the heart of its vaporizing debris. Dawes watched it all in grim black-and-white.

He placed his palm on the communications console. "Attention, Kaxfen ships," he said with a calm he didn't feel. "Break off your attack. The sublight vessel you came for is under my protection. Break off now!" He grinned suddenly as Hookah gave him an exploratory view of the inside of his left ear. He took the creature in one hand and pointed it at the view screen.

Archangel's computer informed him—the four alien ships continued to close. One of them fired, still too far away to effectively harm him. He touched the communications console again.

"Final warning," he said. "Break off. Or I will seriously fuck you where it hurts the most." He shrugged, wondering where that might be on alien anatomy.

Though he kept the communications channel open, no response came from the Kaxfen ships. They plunged toward him, drawing their squeeze play tight. An energy beam lanced across the bow.

A clean miss. However, *Archangel* estimated the aliens were now within weapons range to inflict damage.

"Looks like they need another demonstration," Dawes instructed the computer. "Target the vessel that just fired on us and destroy it."

A second time the Kleinowski planet-killers lanced outward. To starboard, a Kaxfen ship went nova in a horribly beautiful twinkling of disintegrating debris. But unlike the first time, the *Archangel* shuddered as its lasers fired.

"What was that?" Dawes demanded. His vision reeled suddenly with rapid views of the console, the view screen, the back of the cabin, his own nervous face. Hookah squirmed in Dawes' too-tight grip. He forced himself to relax; he returned Hookah to his shoulder and stroked the creature to calm it. "Sorry," he apologized.

Archangel was speaking. The planet-killers were offline—cause undetermined.

Dawes slammed his fist down on the instrument console. At the same instant, another energy spike registered there. Laser beams danced just beyond the view screen as the

Archangel took automatic evasive action. He couldn't dodge them forever, though, he knew that.

"Computer," he called, "where's the *Via Dolorosa* now?"

Just exiting Burnham space, it answered.

"And the pursuing alien ship?"

Still in pursuit.

"Try the planet-killers again!" he ordered. He cursed Straf and himself; so confident had they been in the big guns they hadn't installed any secondary armaments. With the Kleinowskis off-line, he was as defenseless as the ice-wagon he'd come to save.

The *Archangel* rocked under a glancing laser blast. On his shoulder, Hookah quivered. Through the creature's anxious eyes, Dawes did his best to watch the view screen. The Kaxfen ships drew near. He could almost feel the heat of their beams on his face.

Unexpectedly, two of the enemy ships slowed and hung back, covering him. The remaining ship came on. An electronically distorted voice crackled across his communications console. "You have invaded our territory," it stated coldly. "Surrender your vessel, human, and prepare to be boarded."

Chilson Dawes experienced a moment of dread and an almost overwhelming sense of failure. He saw himself reflected in a bottle of despair as five thousand corpses tumbled through space amid the ruptured ruins of their cryo-ship, never to achieve their sought-after miracle of a new life in a new world. Through it all came Donovan's condescending cluck and Straf's accusing eyes burning in his brain.

He shook himself and forced himself to think. Planet-killers be damned—his brain was his best weapon. He couldn't let the *Archangel* be boarded, couldn't let its revolutionary technology fall into the hands of hostile aliens.

Abruptly calm, he sat back down in his chair and placed his hand on the communications console. "I warned you," he said angrily. "Our two species might have been friends, but you forced this debacle. The result is on your heads, you bloody bastards."

He triggered the *Sabre* drive system. In the split-instant before the white light blinded him, he saw the resulting fold-space ripple, strike, and shatter the three Kaxfen vessels.

When the white light subsided, he took a moment to assure himself that he was all right, and that Hookah was all right, too. Then, by touch alone, he examined the controls. *Archangel*'s computer spoke up to tell him what he already knew.

He was back where he'd started from, beyond the Oort Cloud, just at the edge of Sol's diminishing gravitational influence. He'd programmed the ship to bring him home in case of an emergency, or as close to home as the *Sabre* drive system allowed. He turned Hookah toward the view screen. Sol winked in the center of it, only a little brighter than the surrounding stars.

Home. How good that sounded now that he knew there were wolves in the outer reaches.

He wasn't ready, though, to return home. His job wasn't finished.

"*Archangel*." He waited for the computer to acknowledge. "Calculate another jump. Estimate the *Via Dolorosa*'s current position and program coordinates for a fold-space exit just outside the minimum parsec's distance with an added five-percent safety zone."

He waited impatiently. Placing Hookah on his lap, he stroked and stroked the creature until it purred loudly. "Good baby," he murmured softly. "Good baby."

The computer finished its assignment. Dawes reached out for the trigger.

Yet again he fell through fold-space, seemingly alone without walls or ship to surround him. Yet, strangely in his mind this time he felt a presence, that purring, and knew his isolation was false, that he had a companion.

The stars resolved themselves once more in the view screen. As if anticipating him, Hookah stared outward and relayed the magnificent vision into his brain. Dawes caught his breath.

The *Archangel* had emerged into normal space near the Spider Nebula. Looming gigantic off the ship's port bow, its great glare lit the abysmal darkness. Staring into its heart was like staring into a furnace. Around that blazing heart clouds of dust swirled in constant motion. Particles collided, exploding in twinkling bursts. At its edges, great tenuous columns of stars rose up in weblike strands, light-years thick, to stretch and shimmer across the black firmament.

Even with only the muted shades of Hookah's vision, Dawes gaped in silent awe. Another man might have missed his own eyes more acutely in that moment; instead, he gave thanks for those borrowed ones he had.

"We've seen the Temple of God," he whispered to his pet. Oddly, he thought of Donovan and wished his friend was with him.

The *Archangel*'s computer spoke his name. They were now within one parsec of the congregationalists' cryo-ship, it informed him, and speeding straight for it. It detected no sign of the remaining Kaxfen vessel.

"Keep searching," Dawes instructed. "And resume control of the cryo-ship's computers. We may have to move fast." He realized with a mixture of irritation and amusement that he was addressing the computer as if it were a teammate. In a very real sense, it was.

In only a little time, the *Archangel* came abreast of the *Via Dolorosa*. The vessel glimmered dully in the reflected light from the Spider Nebula, an immense metal ball with conventional fusion drives jutting from its rear. Compared with the sleek designs of translight vehicles and with his own ship, it was an ugly monster without grace or beauty, a relic from another age.

And yet, though it crawled across the star trails like a slug in its shell, there was nobility in its ugliness, for it carried within it men and women who were explorers, adventurers, and world-builders, the seed of mankind, the carriers of Humanity's torch. For all that he disdained their means of transportation, Chilson Dawes admired the people within. As if possessed of a sense of pride, the *Via Dolorosa* slowly rotated, showing itself off.

Then with a start, Chilson Dawes discovered where the Kaxfen ship had been hiding. It hung in docking position attached to the cryo-ship's hull. Through Hookah's eyes, he saw it clearly.

And the Kaxfen saw him. Trailing a tangle of umbilicals, it ripped itself from the hull and turned.

Still without weapons, Dawes swallowed hard before settling himself in his chair. He couldn't destroy this alien ship with a fold-space ripple without destroying the *Via Dolorosa* as well. What to do?

He ran a bluff.

Placing one palm on the communications console, he hailed his foe. "Kaxfen ship," he said calmly. "I've destroyed your five companion ships. Don't force me to make it six. This ancient vessel and my own are now outside your claimed territory. Go home."

He waited, either for an attack or for an acknowledging voice on his console. Neither came. The Kaxfen ship took no action at all. It seemed to hang in space, watching him, waiting as he waited. Dawes wondered what went through the alien mind of an uncertain star captain.

The answer was an anticlimax. The Kaxfen ship banked away and sped back toward Burnham space.

Dawes breathed a sigh of relief. "Well, Hookah," he said to his pet, "I guess we know the color of their stripes, eh?"

With the little Mintakan creature purring in his ear, he maneuvered the *Archangel* toward the port where the Kaxfen had docked to discover any damage caused by their sudden departure. Laser burns on the hull revealed how they had blasted their way through cargo air lock doors. Through the rent, he could see drums and crates floating, prevented from escape into space by networks of secure webbing that bespoke an admirable foresight on the part of the ship's occupants.

But why hadn't the Kaxfen simply destroyed the *Via Dolorosa*? Their lasers were powerful enough. What had they sought within?

He decided to find out.

There was too much damage at the cargo air lock, so he searched for another. Hookah wiggled on his perch while Dawes worked the controls. A gentle thump shivered through the hull as docking clamps took hold. Dawes rose from his seat and moved through a series of corridors, pausing at a weapons locker to select a pistol and a communications link that would keep him in contact with *Archangel*. This he slipped onto his wrist like a wristwatch.

With Hookah's eyes showing the way, he moved into the air lock and crossed an umbilical bridge into the *Via Dolorosa*. Hookah seemed to sense what Dawes needed, and kept its attention focused forward. Indeed, without speaking or giving instruction, Dawes seemed able to direct the creature's eyes as if they were his own. It took but a little concentration—as long as Hookah felt calm.

The air was stale. His bootheels rang in a passageway that had not known sound in twelve years. Inside the *Via Dolorosa*'s air lock, a dozen pressure suits hung limp and empty on their racks, ghostly in the darkness. They seemed to watch him, and Dawes felt suddenly bleak and lonely in their presence, like an invader walking where he didn't belong. He found himself stroking Hookah, and was somewhat gladdened when it purred and rubbed his jaw.

Fluorescent lighting panels shone dimly and illumined what seemed to be miles of dull gray corridors. The ship's engines were silent; the *Via Dolorosa* sped toward its destination on inertia; its passengers slept without even the throb of machinery for their lullaby.

He had entered at an air lock near those engines. Seven levels above, and for seven levels above that, five thousand men, women, and children slept in liquid nitrogen coffins. Another deck above those were sperm and egg banks, frozen genetic legacies from another five million donors who would never know their offspring.

Did they dream, Dawes wondered, thinking of those people, of their god or their resurrection in a new world? Or were their dreams smaller ones, of blue skies and grass, of birds at dawn, of friends left behind? This he knew: they had a faith beyond his understanding, and he who believed in little envied them.

He had to see them.

A core-shaft elevator ran the length of the ship from bow to stern. He found it and ascended. When the doors opened, he nearly didn't get off. He hesitated, considered closing them again, then stepped forward.

He'd never seen the inside of a beehive, but he knew it was something like this. The central chamber was vast, overwhelming, deep. It curved around the core-shaft, blurring into gloom, reappearing again, Armor-glass coffins lined the walls, side by side and stacked one on top of the other. Through the misty shimmering ice that clung to the containers, he could make out pale outlines of naked bodies, their arms outstretched as if crucified.

A chill shivered down Dawes' spine, and he found himself gasping. He hurried, stumbling, back to the elevator. He'd never considered himself a coward; hell, here he was, a blind man fighting to defend these people. Yet, what they were attempting was so far beyond his definition of courage that it left him beggared. No, he'd never understand these people. They were as alien to him as the Kaxfen, and standing in their presence, he felt an unfillable emptiness.

He stepped back into the elevator and ascended to the command deck. Nothing there but empty chairs at empty stations, and computers, their lights winking in the yellowish gloom. He spoke to *Archangel* through his com-link. "How much extra time did we add by rerouting the *Via Dolorosa?*"

Their journey would take an additional twelve years. Total time to their new paradise—one hundred thirty-three years. Through fold-space he could get them there in the twinkling of an eye.

And blind them in the process.

He checked each of the stations on the command deck, then all of the computers, assuring himself everything was operational. Then stepping back into the elevator, he descended, intent on making his way back to his ship and heading for home.

When the elevator doors opened once more, he stepped out. Then he paused. The fluorescent lighting panels, dim as they were—why were they on at all? He'd been too creeped out to notice before. But with everyone asleep, the *Via Dolorosa* should have been tomb-dark.

Pistol in hand, Dawes softened his tread and headed for

the air lock. Maybe his presence had activated the lights. Maybe the Kaxfen had done so. Hookah's many feet dug into the fabric of his shirt as he hurried back the way he had come.

From ahead, the metal barrel of a pistol glinted. Barely in time, Dawes flung himself aside. An energy beam whined past his head. Deep in his brain, he felt a shock of pain, and the lights went out. Stretched on the floor, he fired his own weapon wildly.

He didn't see the beam.

In sudden terror, he grabbed at his shoulder. The little creature wasn't there! The lights hadn't gone out at all—he was blind!

"*Archangel!*" he shouted into his com-link. *Archangel* had control of the cryo-ship's computers. Maybe his foe couldn't see in darkness any better than he could. "Turn off the lights! On every deck!" Through his fear, he tried to think. The Kaxfen ship had left one of their crew aboard. With no other way to get home, the alien had made its way to where the *Archangel* was docked. In a more controlled voice, he whispered into his com-link. "Withdraw the umbilical and move away to a distance of one mile."

A moment later, he felt a vibration through the deck as the *Archangel* withdrew its docking clamps.

He was alone with the alien then, but his thoughts turned to Hookah. He groped on the deck, aware of his vulnerable position, but unwilling to retreat without his pet. At last, he found the furry body; it didn't stir when he poked it, nor move when he picked it up. Tears stung his blind eyes. Angry tears, he told himself.

He fired a shot up the corridor, then rolled to the opposite wall. The alien returned fire, aiming for his old position. Even without sight, the whine of the pistol told Dawes what he'd hoped for. He spoke into his com-link again. "*Archangel*, seal the interior air-lock door!"

The soft, sliding scrape of metal within a metal track made him smile. He sat up in his private darkness and hugged Hookah against his body. His exploring fingers found scorched fur. The little creature wasn't moving, hanging limply from his hand.

His anger grew. He hadn't gotten a look at all at the Kaxfen. His first contact with an alien species, and it was trapped beyond an air-lock door not a hundred feet away. His curiosity should have been eating him up—but it was anger that consumed him. He raised the com-link once again.

"*Archangel*." His voice was hard, cold as space. "Open the outer air-lock door."

He waited. And waited. He slipped Hookah's body inside his shirt, feeling its fur against his skin, hoping for some sense of life from it as he waited.

At last, there was no point in waiting any longer. Rising, he steadied himself with one hand on the wall as he moved toward the air lock. He summoned *Archangel*, and felt the impact of its docking clamps, the vibration of the umbilical bridge attaching itself. He tried to remember the layout of the air lock's interior; he'd have to make his way across it. He waited again while *Archangel* repressurized the chamber. Then, he opened the door and cautiously began his way across.

Something struck his wrist and he dropped his pistol. Thickly gloved hands seized him. He felt himself lifted and tossed through the air to strike the deck clumsily, painfully.

The pressure suits! The alien had taken refuge in one and saved himself.

He felt those thick hands on him again, felt himself lifted to his feet. But this time he reacted, catching one of those hands, twisting hard as he swept with one foot at the suit's ankles. The alien fell, metal helmet slamming on the deck.

Dropping to his knees, Dawes groped desperately for his pistol. He spied it suddenly, just inches beyond his fingers. Snatching it up, he fired as the Kaxfen, on its feet again, lurched toward him.

He burned a precise hole through the center of its chest and watched as it staggered and collapsed.

Chilson Dawes sat back panting. Then, with a surge of joy he realized he'd seen! He'd seen the pistol, seen the Kaxfen die! He felt for Hookah. His shirt had been ripped open; the little mind-worm's head poked out curiously.

Dawes rocked back and forth as he stroked the creature. "You had to be alive," he murmured. "I knew it; I felt it!" He held the creature up and nuzzled its fur with his nose. What he saw, though, was his own face close up, beaded with sweat, but strangely joyful. He laughed softly.

"*Archangel*," he said into his com-link, "we're going home."

As he climbed to his feet, he paused over the fallen Kaxfen. He couldn't leave without a look under that helmet. Odds were very good he'd started a war. He had to know the face of his foe.

With Hookah's eyes to guide him, he bent and removed the helmet. For a long time, he stood there looking. He knew why it hadn't fired its laser pistol; the gloved fingers wouldn't fit inside the trigger guard. Disappointment mingled with relief as he turned away and crossed the umbilical to the *Archangel*.

"It wasn't alien at all," he explained to Colonel Straf when he was home again on Mars. "The Kaxfen were a hoax perpetrated by pirates to keep the Guard away from their strongholds." He shook his head, still filled with a certain disappointment. An alien species! Surely somewhere among the stars. . . . But where?

He was glad he hadn't started a war.

Straf poured two more cups of coffee and set one in front of Dawes. "For my parents and myself, I thank you, Chil. Given everything, it's a miracle you saved those people."

Chilson Dawes groped for his cup with one hand. With the other he stroked Hookah, who was curled purring on his lap. He had an amusing view of the underside of Straf's desk, numerous secret wads of chewing gum, and his own crossed legs.

"I never believed in miracles," he said after a thoughtful silence, "but the blind were made to see."

WIPING OUT

by Robert J. Sawyer

Robert J. Sawyer's novels *The Terminal Experiment*, *Starplex, Frameshift*, and *Factoring Humanity* were all finalists for the Hugo Award, and *The Terminal Experiment* won the Nebula Award for Best Novel of the Year. His latest novel is *Calculating God*. He lives near Toronto; visit his Web site at www.sfwriter.com.

They say flashbacks are normal. Five hundred years ago, soldiers who'd come home from Vietnam experienced them for the rest of their lives. Gulf War vets, Colombian War vets, Utopia Planitia vets—they all relived their battle experiences, over and over again.

And now I was reliving mine, too.

But this would be different, thank God. Oh, I would indeed relive it all, in precise detail, but it would only happen just this once.

And for that, I was grateful.

In war, you're always taught to hate the enemy—and we had been at war my whole life. As a boy, I'd played with action figures. My favorite was Rod Roderick, Trisystems Interstellar Guard. He was the perfect twenty-fifth-century male specimen: tall, muscular, with coffee-colored skin; brown, almond-shaped eyes; and straight brown hair cropped short. Now that I was a Star Guard myself, I don't think I looked quite so dashing, but I was still proud to wear the teal-and-black uniform.

I'd had an Altairian action figure, too: dark green, naked—like the animal it was—with horns on its head, spikes down its back, and teeth that stuck out even when its great gash of a mouth was sealed. Back then, I'd thought it was a male—I'd always referred to it as "he"—but now, of course, I knew that there were three Altairian sexes, and none of them corresponded precisely to our two.

But, regardless of the appropriate pronoun, I hated that toy Altairian—just as I hated every member of its evil species.

The Altairian action figure could explode, its six limbs and forked tail flying out of its body (little sensors in the toy making sure they never headed toward my eyes, of course). My Rod Roderick action figure frequently blew up the Altairian, aiming his blaster right at the center of the thing's torso, at that hideous concavity where its heart should have been, and opening fire.

And now I was going to open fire on real Altairians. Not with a blaster sidearm—there was no one-on-one combat in a real interstellar war—but with something far more devastating.

I still had my Rod Roderick action figure; it sat on the dresser in my cabin here, aboard the *Pteranodon*. But the Altairian figure was long gone—when I was fifteen, I'd decided to really blow it up, with explosives I'd concocted with a chemistry set. I'd watched in giddy wonder as it burst into a thousand plastic shards.

The *Pteranodon* was one of a trio of Star Guard vessels now approaching Altair III: the others were the *Quetzal-coatlus* and the *Rhamphorhynchus*. Each had a bridge shaped like an arrowhead, with the captain—me in the *Pteranodon*'s case—at the center of the wide base, and two rows of consoles converging at a point in front. But, of course, you couldn't see the walls; the consoles floated freely in an all-encompassing exterior hologram.

"We're about to cross the orbit of their innermost moon," said Kalsi, my navigator. "The Alties should detect us soon."

I steepled my fingers in front of my face and stared at the planet, which was showing a gibbous phase. The harsh white light from its sun reflected off the wide oceans. The planet was more like Earth than any I'd ever seen; even Tau Ceti IV looks less similar. Of course, TC4 had had no intelligent life when we got to it; only dumb brutes. But Altair III did indeed have intelligent life forms: it was perhaps unfortunate that first contact, light-years from here, had gone so badly, all those decades ago. We never knew who had fired first—our survey ship, the *Harmony*, or their vessel, whatever it had been named. But, regardless, both ships were wrecked in the encounter, both crews killed, bloated bodies tumbling against the night—human ones and Altairians, too. When the rescue ships arrived, those emerald-dark corpses were our first glimpse of the toothy face of the enemy.

When we encountered Altairians again, they said we'd started it. And, of course, we said they'd started it. Attempts had been made by both sides to halt the conflict, but it had continued to escalate. And now—

Now, victory was at hand. That was the only thing I could think about today.

The captains of the *Rhamphorhynchus* and *Quetzalcoatlus* were both good soldiers, too, but only one of our names would be immortalized by history—the one of us who actually got through the defenses surrounding the Altairian home world, and—

And that one was going to be me, Ambrose Donner, Star Guard. A thousand years from now, nay, ten thousand years hence, humans would know who their savior had been. They would—

"Incoming ships," said Kalsi. "Three—no, four— *Nidichar*-class attack cruisers."

I didn't have to look where Kalsi was pointing; the holographic sphere instantly changed orientation, the ships appearing directly in front of me. "Force screens to maximum," I said.

"Done," said Nguyen, my tactical officer.

In addition to my six bridge officers, I could see two other faces: small holograms floating in front of me. One was Heidi Davinski, captain of the *Quetzalcoatlus*; the other, Peter Chin, captain of the *Rhamphorhynchus*. "I'll take the nearest ship," Heidi said.

Peter looked like he was going to object; his ship was closer to the nearest *Nidichar* than Heidi's was. But then he seemed to realize the same thing I did: there would be plenty to go around. Heidi had lost her husband Craig in an Altairian attack on Epsilon Indi II; she was itching for a kill.

The *Quetzalcoatlus* surged ahead. All three of our ships had the same design: a lens-shaped central hull with three spherical engine pods spaced evenly around the perimeter. But the holoprojector colorized the visual display for each one to make it easy for us to tell them apart: Heidi's ship appeared bright red.

"The *Q* is powering up its TPC," said Nguyen. I smiled, remembering the day I blew up my Altairian toy. Normally, a tachyon-pulse cannon was only used during hyperspace battles; it would be overkill in orbital maneuvering. Our Heidi *really* wanted to make her point.

Seconds later, a black circle appeared directly in front of me: the explosion of the first *Nidichar* had been so bright, the scanners had censored the information rather than blind my crew.

Like Peter Chin, I had been content to let Heidi have the first kill; that was no big deal. But it was time the *Pteranodon* got in the game.

"I'll take the ship at 124 by 17," I said to the other two captains. "Peter, why don't—"

Suddenly my ship rocked. I pitched forward in my chair, but the restraining straps held me in place.

"Direct hit amidships—minimal damage," said Champlain, my ship-status officer, turning to face me. "Apparently they can now shield their torpedoes against our sensors."

Peter Chin aboard the *Rhamphorhynchus* smiled. "I guess we're not the only ones with some new technology."

I ignored him and spoke to Nguyen. "Make them pay for it."

The closer ship was presumably the one that had fired the torpedo. Nguyen let loose a blast from our main laser; it took a tenth of a second to reach the alien ship, but when it did, that ship cracked in two under the onslaught, a cloud of expelled atmosphere spilling out into space. A lucky shot; it shouldn't have been that easy. Still: "Two down," I said, "two to go."

"Afraid not, Ambrose," said the Heidi hologram. "We've picked up a flotilla of additional Altairian singleships leaving the outer moon and heading this way. We're reading a hundred and twelve distinct sublight-thruster signatures."

I nodded at my colleagues. "Let's teach them what it means to mess with the Trisystems Interstellar Guard."

The *Rhamphorhynchus* and the *Quetzalcoatlus* headed off to meet the incoming flotilla. Meanwhile, I had the *Pteranodon* fly directly toward the two remaining *Nidichar*s, much bigger than the singleships the others were going up

against. The nearer of the *Nidichar*s grew bigger and bigger in our holographic display. I smiled as the details resolved themselves. *Nidichar*-class vessels were a common
Altairian type, consisting of three tubular bodies, parallel
to each other, linked by connecting struts. Two of the tubes
were engine pods; the third was the habitat module. On the
*Nidichar*s I'd seen before, it was easy to distinguish the living quarters from the other two. But this one had the habitat disguised to look just like another propulsion unit. Earlier
in the war, the Star Guard had made a habit of shooting
out the engine pods, humanely leaving the crew compartment intact. I guess with this latest subterfuge, the Alties
thought we'd be reluctant to disable their ships at all.

They were wrong.

I didn't want to use our tachyon-pulse cannon; it de-
pleted the hyperdrive and I wanted to keep that in full reserve for later. "Shove some photons down their throats," I
said.

Nguyen nodded, and our lasers—thoughtfully animated
in the holo display so we could see them—lanced out toward first one and then the other Altairian cruiser.

They responded in kind. Our force screens shimmered
with auroral colors as they deflected the onslaught.

We jousted back and forth for several seconds, then my
ship rocked again. Another stealth torpedo had made its way
past our sensors.

"That one did some damage," said Champlain. "Emergency bulkheads are in place on decks seven and eight. Casualty reports are coming in."

The Altairians weren't the only ones with a few tricks
at their disposal. "Vent our reserve air tanks," I said. "It'll
form a fog around us, and—"

"And we'll see the disturbance created by an incoming
torpedo," said Nguyen. "Brilliant."

"That's why they pay me the colossal credits," I said. "Meanwhile, aim for the struts joining the parts of their ships together; let's see if we can perform some amputations."

More animated laserfire crisscrossed the holobubble. Ours was colored blue; the aliens', an appropriately sickly green.

"We've got the casualty reports from that last torpedo hit," said Champlain. "Eleven dead; twenty-two injured."

I couldn't take the time to ask who had died—but I'd be damned if any more of my crew were going to be lost during this battle.

The computer had numbered the two remaining *Nidichar*s with big sans-serif digits. "Concentrate all our fire on number two," I said. The crisscrossing lasers, shooting from the eleven beam emitters deployed around the rim of our hull, converged on the same spot on the same ship, severing one of the three connecting struts. As soon as it was cut, the beams converged on another strut, slicing through it, as well. One of the cylindrical modules fell away from the rest of the ship. Given the plasma streamers trailing from the stumps of the connecting struts, it must have been an engine pod. "Continue the surgery," I said to Nguyen. The beams settled on a third strut.

I took a moment to glance back at the *Rhamphorhynchus* and *Quetzalcoatlus*. The Altairian singleships were swarming around the *Rhamphorhynchus* (colored blue in the display). Peter Chin's lasers were sweeping through the swarm, and every few seconds I saw a singleship explode. But he was still overwhelmed.

Heidi, aboard the *Quetzalcoatlus*, was trying to draw the swarm's fire, but with little success. And if she fired into the cloud of ships, either her beams or debris from her kills might strike the *Rhamphorhynchus*.

I swung to look at the hologram of Peter's head. "Do you need help?" I asked.

"No, I'm okay. We'll just—"

The fireball must have roared through his bridge from stern to bow; the holocamera stayed on-line long enough to show me the wall of flame behind Pete, then the flesh burning off his skull, and then—

And then nothing; just an ovoid of static where Peter Chin's head had been. After a few seconds, even that disappeared.

I turned to the holo of Heidi, and I recognized her expression: it was the same one I myself was now forcing onto my face. She knew, as I did, that the eyes of her bridge crew were on her. She couldn't show revulsion. She especially couldn't show fear—not while we were still in battle. Instead, she was displaying steel-eyed determination. "Let's get them," she said quietly.

I nodded, and—

And then my ship reeled again. We'd all been too distracted by what had happened to the *Rhamphorhynchus* to notice the wake moving through the cloud of expelled gas around our ship. Another stealth torpedo had exploded against our hull.

"Casualty reports coming in—" began Champlain.

"Belay that," I said. The young man looked startled, but there was nothing I could do about the dead and injured now. "What's the status of our cargo?"

Champlain recovered his wits; he understood the priorities, too. "Green lights across the board," he said.

I nodded, and the computer issued an affirming *ding* so that those crew members who were no longer looking at me would know I'd acknowledged the report. "Leave the *Nidichar*s; let's get rid of those singleships before they take out the *Quetzalcoatlus*."

The starfield wheeled around us as the *Pteranodon* changed direction.

"Fire at will," I said.

Our lasers lanced forward, taking out dozens of the singleships. The *Quetzalcoatlus* was eliminating its share of them, too. The two remaining *Nidichar*s were now barreling toward us. Kalsi used the ACS thrusters to spin us like a top, lasers shooting off in all directions.

Suddenly, a black circle appeared in front of my eyes again: there had been an explosion on the *Quetzalcoatlus*. A stealth torpedo had connected directly with one of the *Q*'s three engine spheres, and, as I saw once the censor disengaged, the explosion had utterly destroyed the sphere and taken a big, ragged chunk out of the lens-shaped main hull.

We'd cut the singleship swarm in half by now, according to the status displays. Heidi powered up her tachyon-pulse cannon again; it was risky, with her down to just two engines, but we needed to level the playing field. The discharge from her TCP destroyed one of the two remaining *Nidichar*s: there was now only one big Altairian ship to deal with, and forty-seven single-occupant craft.

I left Heidi to finish mopping up the singleships; we were going to take out the final *Nidichar*. I really didn't want to use our TCP—the energy drain was too great. But we couldn't risk being hit by another stealth torpedo; we'd left our cloud of expelled atmosphere far behind when we'd gone after the swarm, and—

And the *Pteranodon* rocked again. A structural member dropped from the ceiling, appearing as if by magic as it passed through the holobubble; it crashed to the deck next to my chair.

"Evasive maneuvers!" I shouted.

"Not possible, Captain," said Kalsi. "That came from the

planet's surface; its rotation must have finally given a ground-based disruptor bank a line of sight at us."

"Cargo status?"

"Still green, according to the board," said Champlain.

"Send someone down there," I said. "I want an eyeball inspection."

Heidi had already moved the *Quetzalcoatlus* so that the remaining singleships were between her and the planet; the ground-based cannon couldn't get her without going through its own people.

The remaining *Nidichar* fired at us again, but—

Way to go, Nguyen!

A good, clean blast severed the habitat module from the two engines—a lucky guess about which was which had paid off. The habitat went pinwheeling away into the night, atmosphere puffing out of the connecting struts.

We swung around again, carving into the remaining singleships. Heidi was doing the same; there were only fifteen of them left.

"Incom—" shouted Kalsi, but he didn't get the whole word out before the disruptor beam from the planet's surface shook us again. An empty gray square appeared in the holobubble to my right; the cameras along the starboard side of the ship had been destroyed.

"We won't survive another blast from the planet's surface," Champlain said.

"It must take them a while to recharge that cannon, or they'd have blown both of us out of the sky by now," Heidi's hologram said. "It's probably a meteor deflector, never intended for battle."

While we talked, Nguyen took out four more singleships, and the *Quetzalcoatlus* blasted another five into oblivion.

"If it weren't for that ground-based cannon . . ." I said.

Heidi nodded once, decisively. "We all know what we

came here to do—and that's more important than any of us." The holographic head swiveled; she was talking to her own bridge crew now. "Mr. Rabinovitch, take us down."

If there was a protest, I never heard it. But I doubt there was. I didn't know Rabinovitch—but he was a Star Guard, too.

Heidi turned back to me. "This is for Peter Chin," she said. And then, perhaps more for her ears than my own, "And for Craig."

The *Quetzalcoatlus* dived toward Altair III, its sublight thrusters going full blast. Its force screens had no trouble getting it through the atmosphere, and apparently the ground-based cannon wasn't yet recharged: her ship crashed right into the facility housing it on the southern continent. We could see the shock wave moving across the planet's surface, a ridge of compressed air expanding outward from where the *Quetzalcoatlus* had hit.

Nguyen made short work of the remaining singleships, their explosions a series of pinpoint novas against the night.

And Altair III spun below us, defenseless.

Humanity had just barely survived five hundred years living with the nuclear bomb. It had been used eleven times on Earth and Mars, and over one hundred million had died—but the human race had gone on.

But our special cargo, the Annihilator, was more—much more. It was a planet killer, a destroyer of whole worlds. We'd said when Garo Alexanian invented the technology that we'd never, ever use it.

But, of course, we were going to. We were going to use it right now.

It could have gone either way. Humans certainly weren't more clever than Altairians; the technology we'd recovered from wrecked ships proved that. But sometimes you get a lucky break.

Our scientists were always working to develop new weapons; there was no reason to think that Altairian scientists weren't doing the same thing. Atomic nuclei are held together by the strong nuclear force; without it, the positively charged protons would repel each other, preventing atoms from forming. The Annihilator translates the strong nuclear force into electromagnetism for a fraction of a second, causing atoms to instantly fling apart.

It was a brilliant invention from a species that really wasn't all that good at inventing. With the countless isolated communities that had existed in Earth's past, you'd expect the same fundamental inventions to have been made repeatedly—but they weren't. Things we now consider intuitively obvious were invented only once: the water wheel, gears, the magnetic compass, the windmill, the printing press, and the camera obscura arose only a single time in all of human history; it was only trade that brought them to the rest of humanity. Even that seemingly most obvious of inventions, the wheel, was created just twice: first, in Mesopotamia, six thousand years ago, then again, much later, in Mexico. Out of the hundred billion human beings who have existed since the dawn of time, precisely two came up with the idea of the wheel. All the rest of us simply copied it from them.

So it was probably a fluke that Alexanian conceived of the Annihilator. If it hadn't occurred to him, it might never have occurred to anyone else in the Trisystems; certainly, it wouldn't have occurred to anybody any time soon. Five hundred years ago, they used to say that string theory was twenty-first-century science accidentally discovered in the twentieth century; the Annihilator was perhaps thirtieth-century science that we'd been lucky enough to stumble upon in the twenty-fifth.

And that luck could have just as easily befallen an Altairian physicist instead of a human one. In which case, it would be Earth and Tau Ceti IV and Epsilon Indi II that would have been about to feel its effects, instead of Altair III.

We released the Annihilator—a great cylindrical contraption, more than three hundred meters long—from our cargo bay; the *Quetzalcoatlus* and the *Rhamphorhynchus* had had Annihilators, too, each costing over a trillion credits. Only one was left.

But one was all it would take.

Of course, we'd have to engage our hyperdrive as soon as the annihilation field connected with Altair III. The explosion would be unbelievably powerful, releasing more joules than anyone could even count—but none of it would be superluminal. We would be able to outrun it, and, by the time the expanding shell reached Earth, sixteen years from now, planetary shielding would be in place.

The kill would go to the *Pteranodon*; the name history would remember would be mine.

They teach you to hate the enemy—they teach you that from childhood.

But when the enemy is gone, you finally have time to reflect.

And I did a lot of that. We all did.

About three-quarters of Altair III was utterly destroyed by the annihilation field, and the rest of it, a misshapen chunk with its glowing iron core exposed, broke up rapidly.

The war was over.

But we were not at peace.

*   *   *

The sphere was an unusual sort of war memorial. It wasn't in Washington or Hiroshima or Dachau or Bogotá, sites of Earth's great monuments to the horrors of armed conflict. It wasn't at Elysium on Mars, or New Vancouver on Epsilon Indi II, or Pax City on Tau Ceti IV. Indeed it had no permanent home, and, once it faded from view, a short time from now, no human would ever see it again.

A waste of money? Not at all. We had to do *something*— people understood that. We had to commemorate, somehow, the race that we'd obliterated and the planet we'd destroyed, the fragment left of it turning into rubble, a spreading arc now, a full asteroid belt later, girdling Altair.

The memorial had been designed by Anwar Kanawatty, one of the greatest artists in the Trisystems: a sphere five meters across, made of transparent diamond. Representations of the continents and islands of the planet that had been Altair III (a world farther out from that star now had that designation) were laser-etched into the diamond surface, making it frostily opaque in those places. But at the gaps between—representing the four large oceans of that planet, and the thousands of lakes—the diamond was absolutely clear, and the rest of the sculpture was visible within. Floating in the center of the sphere were perfect renderings of three proud Altairian faces, one for each gender, a reminder of the race that had existed once but did no more.

Moments ago, the sphere had been launched into space, propelled for the start of its journey by invisible force beams. It was heading in the general direction of the Andromeda galaxy, never to be seen again. Kanawatty's plans had already been destroyed; not even a photograph or holoscan of the sphere was retained. Humans would never again look upon the memorial, but still, for billions of years, far out in space, it would exist.

No markings were put on it to indicate where it had come from, and, for the only time in his life, Kanawatty had not signed one of his works; if by some chance it was ever recovered, nothing could possibly connect it with humanity. But, of course, it probably would never be found by humans or anyone else. Rather, it would drift silently through the darkness, remembering for those who had to forget.

The flashback was necessary, they said. It was part of the process required to isolate the memories that were to be overwritten.

Memory revision will let us put the Annihilator genie back in the bottle. And, unlike so many soldiers of the past, unlike all those who had slaughtered in the name of king and country before me, I will never again have a flashback.

What if we need the Annihilator again?

What if we find ourselves in conflict with another race, as we had with the people of Altair? Isn't it a mistake to wipe out knowledge of such a powerful weapon?

I look at the war memorial one last time, as it drifts farther and farther out into space, a crystal ball against the velvet firmament. It's funny, of course: there's no air in space, and so it should appear rock-steady in my field of view. But it's blurring.

I blink my eyes.

And I have my answer.

The answer is no. It is not a mistake.

SMART WEAPON

by Paul Levinson

Paul Levinson, Ph.D., is the author of *The Silk Code*, which won the Locus Award for Best First Novel of 1999, and non-fiction books *Mind at Large*, *The Soft Edge*, and *Digital McLuhan*, as well as more than 150 articles on the philosophy of technology. His science fiction has appeared in *Analog*, *Amazing*, and the anthology *Xanadu III*. He is Professor of Communication and Media Studies at Fordham University.

The driving sleet lashed Treena's face like a whip. She showed no sign of it as she surveyed what was left of the planet we were about to abandon.

"Time for the weapon," I said through the cold. I beckoned her to take the seat beside me in the hopper.

"No." She shook her head slowly, eyes still fixed on the terrain. "We can't risk it."

"Let's continue this conversation upship," I said, and motioned her again to join me.

She took one last look at the sleet on Eridani II. "It's not even snow," she said. "Snow would have at least had the decency to cover the dead."

The thirty-six-hour trip back to Mu Cassiopeaie was no joy. Our latest stardrive made a light-year an hour. But it was still too long when your only companion didn't feel like talking.

"The scenario you outlined is still valid," I tried again

over breakfast on the last day of our voyage. "And we're running out of other options."

"I know that!" She smashed her fist on the table. Two cups of tea, one mug of juice, and one glass of water from the fourth planet of Chi Ceti all shimmered precariously. "I know that," she said a bit more calmly. "What about the cc-20s?"

Good. The cc-20s were marginal in this, and we both knew it. "They're having trouble with the light bursts. Throws off their highsight. Best estimates now are that they'll be little if any help to us."

She frowned. She was pretty in a blonde sort of way, but that meant nothing to me. "It's not only a question of winning the war," she said slowly. "It's a question of what kind of universe we'll have after that. We've respected the ban for so long—both sides. To break it now could be worse than losing."

"Losing means death," I replied. "Like those bodies on Eridani II. More than that. The death of our culture. Our way of life. What could be worse than that?"

She looked at me with her deep brown eyes. "Don't you see that breaking the ban would also kill our culture? It's the one thing that keeps us—and them—human." She shuddered. "No. We're not at that point yet. Inspect the troops after we dock, and give me a full report tomorrow morning."

"As you wish, General."

I had to admit that the troops looked sharp in the G5V sunlight of Mu Cassiopeaie. They gleamed brightly as they marched in formation on the fourth planet of this yellow sun, not only bigger but richer than Sol in its light. But appearances weren't everything.

Colonel Boden briefed me on their readiness. "So you

see, Adjutant, that they're superior to the enemy on every count."

"I'm afraid I can't share your optimism."

Boden's beefy face creased in surprise. "But the numbers are on our side. Surely—"

"Numbers aren't everything," I interrupted. "Besides, we've got to look at the entire picture on this. Sometimes winning a battle can lose you the war."

"At this point, losing any major battle could lose us the war," Boden countered.

"Not if losing the battle got us to change our tactics," I replied.

"So you're suggesting, what?" Boden asked, struggling in vain to fathom what I was getting at.

"That I could use a second opinion on your troop assessment," I said, and leveled the new brain scrambler that I'd acquired on Eridani II at the earnest colonel.

"Medic!" I shouted. Sudden cessation of brain function still happened from time to time—much like the cerebral hemorrhages of the ancients—especially to officers who labored under the colonel's burden. He'd be irrevocably dead before any medical attention arrived.

Tsung-Yung, Boden's replacement, was supposed to be more cautious than the late colonel. I certainly hoped the reports on her were right.

I told her, "I agree with you and the colonel that our force here is more than equal to the enemy." The cardinal rule in convincing opponents was to first show them how well you understood their position. "But that's precisely why I think we need to be careful, and not risk everything on this one battle."

Tsung-Yung considered. Rain clouds caused the triple moonlight to flutter on her face as we walked along the shore in the cool evening. It made her look even more anxious than she was. "I need more time to think about this," she said.

"We don't have more time," I said. "The Supreme General expects a final report from me in the morning. Boden— Colonel Boden—agreed with me completely. I have to get the assessment from you now."

"It's all happening too quickly," she protested. "I never expected Colonel Boden to die like this—we're *assessment officers*, not battle leaders. Why didn't he record his assessment?"

"We don't make records of such assessments. You know why. Too many eyes and ears of the enemy among us."

Treena reluctantly embraced Tsung-Yung's recommendation and sent out only three quarters of the force from Mu Cassiopeaie. "I'm not happy about sending out a weakened force," she said to me, "but I guess it's always good to leave a little in reserve."

"I'm not happy about sending any force in these circumstances," I responded. "We need to think in radically different directions."

Treena waved me off. "We've been through that already. Forget it."

No chance of that. In fact, all was going according to plan—even if the plan was last-minute and desperate.

But I didn't foresee the next step at all. "I want you at the battle scene—I don't trust anyone else," Treena said. "I've got a zip-ship ready to take you. You'll join the main force at our staging area around Iota Persei in sixteen hours."

"Iota Persei?" Another surprise—we had decided to change the staging area because word might have leaked out to the enemy—

"Yes," Treena replied. "Undoing a change meant to confuse the enemy can sometimes be the best confusion. Can you leave right now?"

"Of course." What choice did I have?

Iota Persei was a strange star system—actually, not a star system at all, because it had no planets. But it looked and was much like Sol, which raised questions. Why no planets? Why was bright Persei without family? Could its planets have been destroyed in some earlier war between foolish intelligences?

The lack of planets, at least, made the star ideal as a military staging area—no earthly distractions.

I joined I. M. Max on the bridge of the command ship. "An impressive force," he said, and gestured to the gleaming multitude in space. "Persei has a million children now."

"Impressive indeed, Commander," I agreed. The war ships shone whiter than stars on the wide view screen. "My compliments."

"Yes, but impressive for what? Most of those vessels will be worthless rubble after the battle," Max said.

"The price of war," I replied.

Max scoffed. He pointed again to the view screen. "We have our armadas of light, the enemy has theirs. We move them around like pieces in a chess game. What's the point? Why not just play a game of chess itself and be done with it?"

I said nothing. A philosopher in a uniform was a dangerous combination.

"Chess pieces," Max continued. "Pawns and knights and rooks. We move them from here to there. They move theirs. We knock some down. Vice versa. We both put some more on the board, and knock them down again."

"Civilians get destroyed too," I said. "You've seen the

pictures from Eridani II. You've seen the bodies. Believe me, they were worse in person."

The commander swore. "I was too far away, if only—"

"No," I interrupted. "You couldn't have made much of a difference, even if you'd been right there on the damn planet. The enemy was too strong."

"Will they be too strong for us tomorrow?"

"I don't know," I replied. "The General thinks not. But— maybe the time has come to think about other means."

The Commander of the Combined Fleets whirled around from the screen and stared at me. "You mean the weapon— the General's doomsday plan?"

"Yes."

Max shook his head. "She no longer believes in it."

"She might again, given the right inducements."

Max shook his head even more. "I'm not sure I would want to risk it either. We could well get outsmarted by our own weapon."

I fingered the brain scrambler, tucked inside my inner pocket. No, two brain cessations in such close proximity would never pass as coincidence. I'd have to play this out the hard way.

The battle—the meeting of the flying pawns, as Max liked to call it—was supposed to take place literally in the middle of nowhere, twenty-three light-years out from Iota Persei, with nothing else closer than twenty-eight light-years away.

The enemy, seen to be approaching from even farther away, suddenly disappeared as we were four hours—four light-years—from our expected intersection.

"How could that be?" I stared at the screen in disbelief.

Max scowled. "Any one of several reasons. My guess is that they have some form of travel blindingly faster than ours. Once the speed of light is surpassed, any speed is in principle possible—there are no real barriers beyond 186,000 miles per second."

"Why haven't *we* developed something like that?"

Max shrugged. "Technological progress is uneven. We develop one thing, they develop something else. In the end, it usually balances out. Assuming that both sides survive long enough."

I looked out at the emptiness on the view screen. For the first time, I felt a mixture of something akin to fear and regret. Maybe I was wrong to try to sabotage this battle on behalf of a larger good. . . .

Max was glaring at me. No, maybe just looking. "I know what you're thinking," he said. "Don't even bother to say it. That smart weapon you're thinking of isn't a step forward. It's a big step backward."

"I wasn't really thinking about that now," I said, truthfully. "I was thinking: so what do we do now to get out of here?"

"We turn around, head back to Iota, keep our eyes open, our lasers white, and hope for the best."

They were waiting for us back near Iota Persei. Max had apparently been right: they'd doubled back behind us at a speed so fast our instruments had missed them. The only good thing about the enemy formation that now lay straight ahead of us was that it seemed smaller than we had expected.

"Probably means they're holding back a few waves to attack us from behind once the battle is underway. Check, but not yet checkmate," Max said, then shrugged. I was beginning to see this was one of his favorite gestures. "We have no choice but to engage them now. We don't have enough energy to go hurtling back out into deep space. And we can't chance the enemy attacking us as we refuel."

At this distance, the enemy ships looked no different from ours. I wondered what we and they might look like to a primitive, solar-bound intelligence staring out at us from its first off-planet telescopes far away. Two swarms of light inevitably converging, some splendid form of stellar reproduction—the aftermath of cosmic love—except the aftermath of our engagement would be lots of death.

We began to see differences in the enemy vessels as we got closer. "Look at that, and that." Max pointed to two close-ups from different angles on the big screen. The focus zoomed in. "Those changes in design are consistent with what we might expect of ships that could move twice as fast as ours."

"How come our scouts missed that?" I asked.

Max shrugged again. "Camouflaging a new design in the shell of an old design is an ancient strategy. This is apparently the first time the enemy has tried this."

"Could they use that speed to come at us at closer quarters? Show up right in front of us out of nowhere?"

"Let's hope not," Max said. "My guess is if they could have, they already would have. Most long-range transport is awkward and even unworkable at short range."

Max was right again.

Still, the battle once joined was close and increasingly desperate. Not in the sense that I'd seen those civilians slaughtered on Eridani II. This was somehow more abstract, more universal, and maybe even more frightening. Huge storms of light winking in and out of existence. A bizarre ballet in which the dancing diamonds grew fewer and fewer, vessels evaporating like teardrops under lasers—"we're eyes that cannot cry," Max muttered at one juncture—directors of a throbbing light show that seemed to point to the end of light itself.

It lasted five continuous days.

Max kept a constant watch out beyond Iota Persei for a second enemy attack from space. But none materialized.

The enemy ships were apparently a little less effective in close combat than they'd been in the past. Max thought that their new design for speed twice as fast as ours at long distance—two light-years an hour, he'd calculated—somehow slowed them down a bit at short range. "Let's hope they learn that lesson too late."

I thought of dispatching Max with my brain scrambler many times. Losing this battle was the only way that Treena would be moved to implement the smart weapon, I was sure. Yet in the heat of battle—in the sway of those swirling strands of keen white lights on the big view screen—I didn't really want to lose this one. Despite all of my careful planning, I just couldn't bring myself to do this to our side. To I. M. Max.

At the beginning of the sixth day, the enemy withdrew what was left of their fleet. A few flickering flashlights limped back out into space.

Our side was scarcely better off, but we'd held our ground on Iota Persei.

"We didn't give them one iota," Max said.

I grimaced at his pun, but was not unhappy.

"They were not only a little slower in close combat than we'd figured," Max continued, "but I think their number was also less than we'd first projected."

I frowned more deeply at the implication of that. "So there's a bigger part of their fleet—bigger than what we first estimated—still out there somewhere."

Max nodded. "I doubt we can handle them, if they come at us now in our present condition."

His comm chimed, as if on cue.

"Word from Treena," he said, a minute later. He looked tired, grave. "An enemy force a third bigger than what you left on Mu Cassiopeaie just materialized beyond that solar system. Treena's struggling to get a workable strategy going, but she'll be badly outnumbered."

Not what I wanted. Treena's defeat would be the end of it for our side. If only she'd consider the smart weapon . . .

"Not much that we can do to help, I'd assume," I said.

The commander shook his head, grimly. "Not much at all. What we have left of our force here would take far too long to get there."

I looked at the variety of vessels, mostly ours, a few captured from the enemy, in various glistening angles and close-ups on the screen.

"Let's say at least *you* got there," I said. "You're the master strategist. Would that help?"

"Sure, but—"

"Any chance we could prevail upon one of the enemy to tell us how to fly one of their faster ships?"

The enemy wasn't stupid. They had programmed their new speed drives to self-destruct the instant the hull had been breached enough to prevent travel. As an extra precaution against their new technology coming into our possession, the drives were also programmed to burn out any time the ship was motionless for more than five minutes, and an override wasn't manually entered to stop the self-destruct. This apparently was designed to prevent us from getting the speed drive in the event of any enemy surrender.

Seven of the enemy ships we'd captured were thus useless.

We got lucky on the eighth.

"Look at this," one of Max's technical aides traced a path with an index finger, indicating where one of our laser beams had hit an enemy mirror on the edge, and splintered into at least a dozen tight beams. "We hit paydirt here." One of the razor-thin beams had sheared the node that held the self-destruct programming circuits. They had been knocked out of service well before the hull breach that had stopped the enemy ship.

"So this one should move at two lights an hour?" Max asked.

"Well, all I can certify is that the drive that enables that speed wasn't destroyed on this one," the aide replied, carefully.

Max thanked her, gave her an immediate promotion in rank, and turned to the task of finding an enemy pilot to talk to us.

The first three died under questioning. Not that we tortured them. They just died as soon as we asked certain questions.

"Waste of time," Max replied when asked if a fourth pilot should be brought to us. "They must have been rigged with something in the brain."

"So what now?" I asked.

"I was a pilot before I was a commander," Max said. "I'll figure out how to fly the damn thing myself."

We were on our way an hour later.

Space looked different at two lights an hour—more of a paisley pattern than at one light.

"Good thing you talked Tsung-Yung into recommending that a fourth of the force be left back at Mu Cassio," Max observed, "otherwise the General would be stark naked before the enemy now."

"Yeah." I turned from the paisley to the commander's

even more complex eyes. Could he know what I'd done to Boden? What I'd considered doing to him? My plan had been to field a weaker force, so we'd lose at Iota Persei or wherever we fought the enemy. That was to have pushed Treena into bringing the smart weapon into play with her remaining force, with enough time to meet the enemy on our terms. Instead, we'd beaten the enemy at Iota Persei. But it was a weakened enemy, because it had sent part of its unexpectedly superfast fleet to attack Treena at Mu Cassiopeaie—a surprise attack that likely would leave her with not enough time to do anything. Or precisely the opposite of what I'd intended. . . .

"I don't know if we'll arrive in time to do any good," Max said, as if reading my thoughts. "I don't know what I can do if we do arrive before the enemy attacks."

"We know about their new drives," I said. "We know that they're a bit clumsy at close range." I had to do what I could to keep Max from surrendering to that internal despair which could be more corrosive than an enemy's laser.

"True," Max said, not very heartened. "Have you heard anything more from Treena about her situation? Has she engaged the enemy as yet?" One of our communication teams had quickly installed our encodeline before we'd left.

"I don't know," I replied. "There's been no communication from her in the last hour. It's all a hash of noise now. I hope our comms aren't breaking down on this ship."

"Let's just pray that Perseus can save Cassiopeia again."

"Again?"

"An ancient myth," Max said. "Let's hope we can make it true in the present."

The first evidence we saw upon coming out of paisley space was bad.

Dozens of our ships drifting numbly in the void beyond

Mu Cassiopeaie's stony twelfth planet, spent shells like glittering chrysalides moving vacantly away from the death-blows that had dispatched them. . . .

"All of them are ours," I barely managed to say. "Where are theirs?"

"I don't know," Max said, in a voice no louder than mine.

He tried to reach Treena again on our encodeline. There was no reply.

"That looks like less than half of Treena's force out there," Max said, straining to make some sense out of what we saw. "A strange sort of rout to have just a portion of one side's force destroyed, and none at all of the other's. There's something more going on here."

"You think the General may have *sacrificed* this part of her limited forces?" I asked. I wasn't sure why that would have occurred to me.

Maybe because just a day or two earlier I had been contemplating the sacrifice of a far larger part of our fleet, out near Iota Persei, for what seemed a justifiably greater good to me. All of that seemed very far away now.

I thought of this small part of Treena's fleet coming out here, well beyond the twelfth planet of Mu Cassiopeaie, to be massacred by the enemy. That would account for why all the lead vessels were ours.

"But why would she do that?" I continued.

Max shook his head, half in response to me, half in response to another view he had called up on the big screen.

The space around Mu Cassiopeaie's sixth planet—a ringed thing, like Sol's Saturn—came sharply into focus.

"Oh, no," I said.

The enemy fleet, huge in comparison to ours, was feasting on our vessels.

"What the hell's going on?" Max demanded of our ships,

though none could hear him. "We're not even putting up a fight!"

I tried to count the number of our vessels on the screen. I asked Max to change the angles of the views. "There really aren't too many of ours there," I said. "Maybe a fifth to a fourth of what's out here."

Max sighed. He shook his head in anger, confusion, frustration. "So she still has almost half the force back in reserve to defend the fourth planet." He fiddled with the screen controls. He pounded the console. "The alignment of planets is blocking our view. We can wait eighty-five minutes, or we can move in for a better look."

"Let's move."

Max nodded. "But why sacrifice so much of her force?" he asked, picking up my question. "Whatever Treena has planned, surely she'd be better off with more on her side."

We finally caught a brief sight of what remained of Treena's fleet, hovering around Mu Cassiopeaie's fourth planet—the sylvan capital of our realm.

"No wonder we couldn't see her before," Max said. The huge enemy fleet was swooping in toward Treena and our planet, in a double, undulating formation that made each of its segments look like the wings of a single, horrendous creature. "When the planet alignment wasn't blocking our view, that monstrosity of a fleet was."

One of its wings flapped, and Treena's force was again obscured. Max tried again to reach her encodeline, again in vain.

The enemy wings seemed to swell and advance, now seeming to loom over the fourth planet itself. I thought of people eating breakfast, children laughing, couples strolling, all under that enemy shadow. It was an agonizing scene.

"Strange," Max said, focusing not on the view screen

but the encodeline. "At this range, it almost seems as if Treena is deliberately not answering us, not that her transmitter is engulfed in noise."

"How so?" I asked, eyes still on the view screen. "Like an eagle about to swallow a sparrow back on Earth. She doesn't have a chance," I said about the awful view.

"Well, her transmitter is indicating that it's receiving our message," Max answered about the communication. He shook his head, and then joined me at the view screen.

Something peculiar was beginning to occur upon it. Little pieces of the enemy fleet seemed to be burning up—little tears in the cavernous wings. They were soon repaired as enemy vessels shifted subtly in formation, but holes seemed to be appearing faster than they were fixed.

"Do you see that?" I asked Max.

He nodded. His face looked puzzled—and almost a little frightened, in a way I hadn't seen before. "Let's go for extreme magnification," he said to me, and the view screen took it as a command.

The tears became gaping holes on close-up, and the cause of them became clear. Treena's vessels were engaging the enemy's, one by one, and winning every time.

I took a quick look at Max. His mouth was open.

It wasn't that our ships were moving much faster than the enemy's. That wasn't it.

It was rather that our ships were moving in totally unfamiliar ways—darting in and out, changing speeds seemingly at random, hot needles rending the wings of the massive enemy eagle in ways it apparently could neither predict nor fathom.

I was frightened, too. But I think I was also smiling.

The huge wings were more than wounded now. The enemy tried repeatedly to re-form, but there were too many holes, too many dead cells, to fill. The wings began to crumble, shrivel, like old paper under myriad points of fire—the fire of our proud vessels. Soon all that was left of the enemy fleet around Mu Cassiopeaie were ashes. . . .

Treena's image-appeared on our view screen. Max commanded it to send ours back to hers.

She acknowledged Max, then looked right past him at me. "Congratulations," she said. "You got what you wanted."

The three of us walked along the shore, not far from where I had walked with Tsung-Yung in what felt like a millennium but was less than two weeks ago.

"There were two reasons I had to sacrifice so many of our vessels," Treena said to Max and me. "One, of course, was to lure the enemy in."

"Of course," Max agreed. "But why sacrifice so many?"

"There wasn't time to reprogram the robots in those ships to work with the humans piloting mine. Nor was there time to train my human pilots in how to work with totally robotic vessels. I had all I could do to get them up to speed on how to kill enemy vessels. Good thing human piloting has remained a form of pageantry sport on some of our worlds—I called every last one of those performers in for this. Their training is remarkably much the same as that prescribed in the ancient war manuals."

"Good thing?" Max asked, unable to mask his sarcasm.

Treena looked at him. "I like it no better than you. I resisted as long as I could."

Max was unconvinced. "We've kept the unpredictable fury of the human soul out of direct combat for nearly as long as humans have traversed the stars. It's the only thing that has enabled this civilization to progress, to move on, despite our sick penchant for war."

"We can control it," Treena insisted. "I was there. I commanded my own ship, and took out six enemy vessels. It was *invigorating*—like nothing else I've ever felt. But I can control it."

She had a wild look in her eyes that made me wonder.

Max, however, was sure. "No, you can't. You won't be able to. It's too intoxicating for you. For thousands of years we've had the sense to keep humans away from this—that's why, for the most part, civilians have been spared. If human brains, human angers, become the payload of our weapons, you'll get death for everyone." Max was shaking. "No, it was wrong of you to break the ban against the smart weapon—"

"Commander, calm down—" Treena began.

"No, I won't," Max was shouting. "You're wrong." And he raised a gun to Treena.

He started to say something, but I had my scrambler out and pointed at Max before he could finish. I couldn't take any chances. He was brain dead a split second later.

Treena stared at me and then Max on the ground, in horror.

"It's all right," I said, with more surety in my voice than my circuitry. "You did the right thing."

As had I.

After all, Max and I were only robots—like all military in this realm of ours until now, other than the Supreme General. And robots would be more expendable than ever in this new regime of the human weapon Treena had just brought into being.

PROCESSION TO VAR

by Andre Norton

Andre Norton has written and collaborated on over one hundred novels in her sixty years as a writer, working with such authors as Robert Bloch, Marion Zimmer Bradley, Mercedes Lackey, and Julian May. Her best known creation is the Witch World, which has been the subject of several novels and anthologies. She has received the Nebula Grand Master Award, the Fritz Leiber Award, and the Daedalus Award. She lives in Murfreesboro, Tennessee, where she oversees High Hallack, a genre-writers' library.

The Guardian lay belly down on the sun-heated rocks, as flat as if his yellow-furred skin held no body. In the wide canyon below, the intruder crawled at an even pace, seemingly undeterred by the rough ground. There were no signs of any legs below its oval bulk, no other signs of propulsion. It might be a Fos beetle swollen to an unbelievable size.

Almost directly below the Guardian's perch, it halted. Sound carried easily as a portion of the nearer side swung up. Movement there, then first one and a second creature emerged to stand beside the crawler, pointing to the rock wall and uttering loud noises.

The Guardian froze. It could not be true! For all the generations his breed had kept watch, there had been no such coming. Still, on the wall below were carved, painted, set so deeply that time had not erased, representations of figures akin to these invaders.

One of them ran back to the beetle, returning with a box. Holding that up with forepaws, the creature made a slow passage before the wall from one end of the procession to the other.

The Guardian's muscles tightened as he gathered his feet under him, rumbling a growl deep in his throat. What did they do? Was this offering a threat to the Far Time? Might they even be trying to wipe away this message of the Great Ones?

He edged backward. Now he could no longer watch them, but it was time he followed orders. These intruders looked so much like the pictures he had seen from cubhood.

Following a trail worn by countless generations of his kind, he pushed between two spurs into the opening behind. His claws were well extended, searching for holds as he passed into darkness.

It had been four seasons since the last inspection, but there had seldom been trouble with rockfalls. He dropped into a long chamber. Though the right-hand wall seemed intact, there were concealed openings that emitted enough light to serve a race with well-developed night sight. In turn, those offered spy holes.

He could hear sounds, meaningless to any pattern he understood, and sensed rising excitement. Two strides brought him to the nearest spy hole.

The invaders were just below him, and he studied them carefully for the report he must make. Like the Great Ones, they walked on their hind legs and were tailless. Their forepaws easily handled objects. But they were not altogether alike—the fur on the head of one was grayish while the other had a fire-red patch.

He began to understand that the constant sound was their form of communication. They would not—or could not—touch mind patterns in the proper manner. But perhaps—

One could contact a spas, though the winged ones of the heights were certainly not People, and those of the waterways also used mind touch. Dared he try such with these?

He centered his full attention on the one with the red fur and tried to channel. It was the only way he knew to understand who—or what—they were, or from where they had come.

The thought pattern he touched was alien—like a fastflowing stream ready to swallow up any mind thrust. Red Fur stopped his spray of sound, swayed back and forth, his paws holding his head. His companion caught his shoulder to steady him, uttering louder noises.

Instantly the Guardian threw up a screen. Even if he had not been able to truly contact the others, there was no reason to believe that they did not have power or powers like enough to his own to strike back.

Instead he sent a warning back to the Caves, addressing the duty officer. Only seconds later he was locked to Yinko and giving a report.

"They are somewhat like the Great Ones in appearance. And they are studying the Procession to VAR."

"Have they sought out the Gate of Retrieval?"

"Not so. They have only viewed the carvings. But could it be"—it might be blasphemy to send that thought—"some far kin to the Great Ones have returned after these tens of tens of seasons?"

Yinko did not immediately reply, but when he mind touched again, it was an order.

"Keep watch, report if they do more than look. We shall come."

Red Fur was on the ground leaning against a rock. His companion reentered the beetle. The Guardian studied that carrier as much as his angle of sight allowed.

It was well known that the Great Ones had had servants

not of their own species. Once, before they had left, they
had chosen to instruct the People in many strange things.
For a while after they had left, the People still controlled
things of metal which could eat out new caves and make
life easier in many ways. In time, those had died, though
some were kept in memory of those days.

The second intruder was returning with a container he
placed on the ground by Red Fur. He pushed something
into the mouth of the younger one who then drank from
the container. But he still sat with his head supported by
his hands, hunched in upon himself.

The Guardian was bemused. It was evident that Red Fur's
plight had been brought about by the attempt at mind touch.
So—these could not be any far kin of the Great Ones. They
had been masters at such contact.

Thus the People had a defense without having to de-
scend to claw and tooth. If his mild attempt had so brought
down Red Fur, what would an all-out thrust by the Elders
do? He relaxed as curiosity overcame wariness. What did
the beetle riders want here? They had appeared greatly excited by the wall paintings, one of the last rock messages
remaining. But it was not those faded carvings which had
stationed Guardians here so long.

Those only pointed the way to what the Great Ones had
put in keeping for a return which had never come. They
had stored secrets beyond secrets. This was the outer shell
of a storehouse and the warning had been impressed upon
the People that only the Great Ones should ever seek its
inner heart.

"—sun—"

Galan, Histechneer, Second Class, steadied his head with
both hands and somehow managed to answer Narco.

"Not sun—" With an effort he raised his head. His sight

was misted at first, but after a few moments he could see the anxiety in the other's face.

Galan drew a deep breath and tried to make sense of what had happened—not only for Narco but for himself. There was no reasonable explanation.

"In my head—something—from outside—"

Narco sat back on his heels. "An attack? But what—how?" He continued to survey the younger man closely. "All right—the old rule holds—to each world its powers and secrets. A mental invasion?" He slewed around to look at the wall. "A protection? But this is very old. Could any security device last so long?"

Not waiting for an answer, he went back to the crawler and returned wearing a shock helmet and carrying a second one for Galan.

The eye screen cut out some of the punishing rays of the sun. Wearing it did give a sense of security though Galan still felt shaky.

Narco had gone to stand before the wall at midpoint, his eyes sweeping from right to left and back again.

Perhaps it did conceal some secret, but the pictures were plainly meant to represent a journey. Only nowhere else during trips out from the survey camp had they found any indication of such a civilization as these pictures suggested.

There were a number of platforms apparently hovering above the ground unsupported in any way, each carrying heaped-up cargo. Scattered among these floating platforms were people: humanoids.

To have carved and painted this wall would have taken a long time, yet in their own sweeps of exploration they had not found any trace of settlement on this world. Of course the Zacathan head of their expedition might have information he had not yet shared.

"Who—what were they?" Galan staggered up.

Narco shrugged. "Guess. It always comes in the end to guessing. But this is a major find—will surprise some people." He grinned.

That was true. There had been grumbling in the camp lately, though Galan was sure no one yet had said they were wasting time—at least not when the Zacathan was within hearing distance.

Narco retrieved the recorder and was reciting into it a careful description of each section of the wall.

Yes, the time-blurred figures in that Procession were certainly humanoid. They walked erect. Unlike the floating platforms, they needed the support of the ground beneath their feet.

But no matter how hard he tried, Galan could not clearly distinguish any features. Their elaborate headdresses were as secretive as masks.

As Narco went to signal their find to base camp, Galan began to pace along the line of carvings. He noted now that the parade was led by a single figure several lengths ahead of the rest. All of them were wearing tight-fitting garments, each having a belt from which dangled a number of unidentifiable objects, The leader, however, carried a round ball breast high, resting on the palms of both hands. And that ball appeared to be of some substance not native to the cliff, dark gray in color.

The Procession ended just before a fault in the cliff wall itself. Instead of a smooth surface, there was a fissure, triangular in shape, one angle pointing skyward. This was packed tightly with rubble, thoroughly corked.

Tomb? Treasure chamber? Temple? Galan approached that matting of stones cautiously. There had always been a pattern in Forerunner finds on other worlds. Those had varied from the remains of cities to what might only have been temporary encampments. And there were many different races, so these finds had varied to a striking degree.

If something did lie behind that packing of rubble— Every seeker of the past longed to make the GREAT discovery. The Forerunners had spread through the galaxy, ruled a mighty stellar empire, only to vanish in a sea of time where his own people could not hope to venture beyond the shallows.

Stepping back several feet, he continued to survey that triangular mass from bottom to top. But, as Galan's glance reached the tip, he stiffened. Crowning that point very near the lip of the canyon was—

A carving? But one far more clear-etched,—it could have been finished this very day. A head! But not that of any humanoid. The features were almost hidden in a full bearding of red-gold hair or fur. While the broad nose and jaw appeared to resemble a beast's muzzle, the eyes were very large and a startling green, making one think of sun-touched gems.

Galan could not remember sighting that image during their previous close study. Suddenly, there was a grating sound and, from a point not far below that head, a detached stone fell. Galan's hand went to the stunner at his belt.

As his fingers closed on the weapon, they seemed to freeze in a rock-hard position. He struggled to call Narco, only to discover that he was not only held by invisible bonds but also unable to speak.

The green eyes continued to study him impassively for a long moment and then the head withdrew, leaving a dark hole behind. As it disappeared, he found himself free of the strange paralysis that had gripped him.

"Narco!" He felt he dared not turn his back on that hole, and his stunner was out and ready.

"What?" His companion stopped short when he saw the weapon.

"Up there—" Galan used the stunner to indicate the hole as he told what he had seen and how he had been helpless when he thought of trying to defend himself.

Yinko slipped back to where the Guardian and his own escort of scouts waited.

"Weapons they do carry, but against the Power those can not act. They are certainly not of this world." He paused and looked to the Guardian. "Since touch sent one into helplessness, it may be necessary for us to unite and open their minds, to discover what they would do here."

What he suggested was against the First Law and they all knew it. But there was also the oath by which the People had been bound. That which they guarded must not fall into the hands of invaders.

"Upon me," Yinko continued, "the debt of such an action shall fall."

Yinko's words were interrupted by an odd sound which none had ever heard before, a sound that seemed to come from out of the air. A "thing" crossed the pale green of the sky. Not a spas—infinitely larger and moving without any bending of wings.

Instinctively, the party on the cliff flattened themselves down on the rock. The sky thing coasted along above the canyon to where it widened at the northern end. There, the object dropped until it settled near the beetle and sand sprayed out.

As had happened with the beetle, a side opening appeared and more invaders disembarked. However, these did not resemble those from the beetle. The first was humanoid, the body covered with a form-fitting garment not unlike the hue of the rocks. A tight black cap covered all but the hu-

manoid's facial features. High on its shoulders the newcomer wore a bag; from this projected a second head, much
smaller and furred.

This first comer moved a short distance away, in a
manner which suggested wariness to the watchers above
though there was no weapon to be seen. Another figure
emerged from the flyer. This one was taller and not of
the same species, for all its visible skin was scaled. The
hairless head was backed by a fan of skin which rose like
a bristling mane, the forepart lying about throat and breast
like a collar.

There was an added oddity to this stranger. The left arm
was shorter, ending in a hand far too small for the size of
the rest of the body, and the appendage on the right was
hardly larger.

The scaled one raised that stub of a right hand and started
to join the earlier invaders. However, his companion swung
around suddenly, as if his body must shield the other from
the carved wall, while he also signaled.

Black Cap faced the cliff squarely while the creature he
carried in the backpack rested its chin on his shoulder to
stare at the carved wall.

On his way to join the newcomers, Galan halted also—
half expecting to see a furred head appear aloft.

Naturally, the Histechneer Zurzal had come at the first
report of their find. Ranking very high among the Zacathans,
he had supplied the backing to assemble this expedition.
This planet, for some reason of his own, had been his first
choice for investigation.

Black Cap was a Shadow, a professional guard, the Zac-
athan's constant companion, formally oathed to his service.
It was well known that Zurzal was on the Black List of the
Thieves Guild, having ruined one of their long prepared

missions, and it was well he did travel with one of the formidable Shadows.

The small creature was a Jat. No one had ever been able
to discover their full intelligence. However, when one
bonded with a human it supplied an ever-present awareness
of trouble—an alarm system of flesh, blood, and bone.

His guard's warning had halted the Zacathan. He folded
his long legs in a sitting position facing the wall. The Jat,
freeing itself from the bag, dropped to join him. But the
guard remained standing, positioning himself so he could
view both his employer and the cliff.

With the arrival of Zurzal, authority passed to him.
Galan's hand went to the strap of his helmet, half expecting another bolt to strike at any moment. It did, but this
time the thrust did not find him defenseless. The pain and
disorientation were less, heard through the helmet's warning signal.

Blinking his eyes, he saw that the Shadow had wavered
a step or two from his position but otherwise did not seem
much affected by the attack. The Jat and the Zacathan
showed no signs of discomfort.

Jofre, Oathed Shadow, swallowed and swallowed again.
As much as he had been trained in the inner Power, he had
had to meet that pressure with full strength, which aroused
the fear of deep brainwash, a rumored weapon of the Guild.
Zurzal continued to stare at the carvings, seemingly at ease.
Yan, the Jat, had laid a hand-paw on one of the Zacathan's
mutilated arms as if in protection.

"The scaled one," Yinko thought-linked. "That one has
power—as does the small, furred thing. Not our power, but
like to it."

"Great Ones?" The question expressed doubt. These were
too alien to People memory.

"Like—unlike," Yinko shook his maned head. "But I

doubt we can control these." Once more he looked down at the three who seemed to be waiting—perhaps hoping to discover what defenses the People had.

"We wait," Yinko decided.

Time no longer had any meaning; neither party made a move. At last, the two from the beetle joined the others.

Galan saluted. "There is—" He paused, wanting to explain with care. "It must be some security device. But where? We have not been here long enough for a full search." He glanced at that dull globe carried by the leader of the procession.

"Mind touch," the Zacathan returned calmly. "Hit you hard, did it?" He indicated the helmet.

"But—how? It's all just stone and paint!" He had heard of mind touch, mind speech. However, as far as he knew, he had never encountered it before. That had not been a touch but a stab, one he felt had been delivered with intended malice.

"That is what we see, yes," Zurzal nodded at the wall. "But no, there is no instrument set on guard here. Only living minds can reach so."

"What is to be done?" Narco joined them.

"It lies with who or what watches here." The Zacathan was scratching behind the Jat's large ears. "Wait for a space—"

But time was against them, for again the whine of a flitter echoed arrogantly from the heights. A flitter? But the only one known here was just behind them.

This was larger, and Jofre, well trained, caught sight of those threatening tubes pointing fore and aft. It was armed! And there was no Patrol Star to be seen on the dirty brown of the cabin side. That paint was meant to fade against the mountain lands and desert around them.

The warning came from the Zacathan. "Down—! This is—"

His hissed speech was drowned out by a roaring voice from above.

"Halt! Stand! See and fear!"

A lash of fire flicked out of one of the fore tubes, striking the cliff face. The tip crossed the rubble in the triangle to touch the globe carried by the leader of the procession.

Galan reeled, saw Narco fall, curling up like an insect touched by flame. The Shadow was on his knees, his head shaking from side to side. The Jat plastered itself tightly against the Zacathan's body, its mouth open as if it were screaming, though Galan could not hear through the roaring that filled his head.

Where that flash had fallen was dark—black—as if the very substance of the rock had been consumed. But the globe was alive—vivid ripples of blue, purple, and green were circling out from it. Galan found himself unable to raise his hands to push the helmet closer over his tortured ears. He was locked in place and unable to turn his head.

And now—

There was other movements beside those ripples. Not among the party in the canyon. Nor had anyone descended from the rogue flitter. Long, flattish bodies, the same color as the rocks, were slipping down from the crown of the cliff, hard to see except by their movement.

They avoided the curling streamers of color given forth by the globe, coming to ground to crouch in a defensive line before the Procession.

The black spots were spreading outward in patches as if the entrances to a number of caves were being revealed. In spite of his streaming eyes and painfully roaring head, Galan could not look away. Was this indeed the opening of some treasure-house?

There was a second ray from the enemy flitter—aimed now at that furred line waiting in what seemed to be a pitiful gesture of defense. The thrust did not touch, rather it turned in midair, flashing back toward its source.

The Zacathan and the Jat did not move, only stared ahead. Now the Shadow had crawled to them and raised a hand, though no weapon, so he also might grasp one of the mutilated arms Zurzal held out to him.

Before that deflected blast touched the flitter, it was gone. But the flyer itself bounced upward, steadying well above the cliff top as a hovering warning.

"This is surely of the Great Ones!" The Guardian broke the united mind hold. "Those—they gave to us Power—" He stared at the invaders, still quivering from that strange inflow of force he knew originated with the scaled one and his two companions.

Yinko mind sent in a way that commanded an answer. "Who are you?"

"Seekers of knowledge."

"And those above who would destroy?"

"Those who fear true knowledge. But do not hold them lightly. They are a part of a great evil which has spread from world to world—"

Yinko interrupted: "They turn what they find to their own use?"

"It is so— On guard!"

The flitter had been moving away, only now to circle back. There was an opening in its belly, though if these jackers had come for wealth or knowledge of the past and used even a gas bomb, the effects of which might last long in this canyon, they could defeat their own purposes.

Yinko looked to the Guardian. The order he gave was one which had not been used for a thousand years or more. With a burst of speed that seemed incredible to the watch-

ing invaders the Guardian threw himself as if to crash
against the wall. That wall which Galan saw was cracking
as the circling light of the globe appeared to bring destruction farther and farther out.

Into one of those enlarging cracks the Guardian plunged
headfirst. He was now back in the gallery from which he
had earlier spied on the strangers. Speeding across it, he
slammed his metal-sheathed claws into a spot on the inner
wall and exerted all his strength.

The door he attacked gave reluctantly. Those without
would buy him time if they could, but how strong was the
power of the others? Could their weapons be held for a second time by the united effort of the People and those who
had voluntarily aided at the first attack?

He was looking down, not into some dimly lit cavern
but rather into a very large space where at intervals along
the walls were set rods emitting light. Nearly all the floor
was covered with large, topless bins, packed in turn with
containers of all sizes and shapes. The Guardian turned left,
finding footing on a narrow ledge.

Outside, the jackers seemed in no hurry to press an attack. They must know that the offworlders below knew very
well the threat of that open hatch.

"You gave power—"

Zurzal still held the Jat and had drawn the Shadow closer.
"*We* gave power," he corrected

"Why? Are those not of your kind?" Yinko pointed upward.

"Not so," Zurzal's denial was quick. "They are enemies
who seek the destruction of many. My people came here
to learn of the Forerunners, those Great Ones of the past.
That is the work of my life. For knowledge is the greatest
weapon and defense that any life-form may have."

"Are you of the Great Ones? They had, we know, many forms." Yinko watched the Zacathan closely.

"We cannot be sure that long ago they did not give us life. But they were long gone before we rode the starways."

"Still you seek—for what—new weapons—treasure?" persisted Yinko.

"For knowledge such as you have guarded here."

"Much has long been forgotten. Those who come know not even what they seek. Unless—" he glanced overhead, "it is for gain, for death. Surely, these deal in death."

"I have said they are enemies of ours as well as of your people. Yes, they are death dealers."

"Yet they came not until you did. Therefore, perhaps you were their guide."

"Not knowingly. You have met us mind to mind. These have not mind speech," he indicated Galan and Narco. "But they are allied in our searching. Those," he glanced up, "may have followed, yes, but we knew it not."

Galan wondered why the jack flitter did not move in. They must be well aware that those in the canyon—at least seemingly—had no visible weapons of defense.

His answer came from the sky like the growl of some great predator.

"Down on your bellies, all of you! Or be crisped!"

The flitter was again on the move, slowly and with visible precision, as if those on board had a task needing great care.

Yinko's head jerked up as did those of his following.

"Though it has been forbidden, it must be done. We must use the great blanking—and from it there is no escape." His thought was as sharp as a knife thrust.

In the depths of the cracking cliff the Guardian had reached his goal. Never had this action been carried out, but all those who had held this duty during the years had been well drilled in what was to be done. He dropped from the ledge to land in front of a large screen. Staring at it, he flexed his claws.

"Galan! Narco!" They had guessed that the Zacathan had been in contact with the creatures by the cliff, but now he used normal speech. "There is only one chance for us now. These are about to draw upon mind power. You have not had the training, nor perhaps the inborn talent, but—there remains one small hope. Discard your helmets, open your minds. Think of yourselves as channels and welcome what comes. I cannot promise you survival, but this I know. We have no other hope against what the Guild will do."

Galan fumbled with the clasp of the helmet. This— It was beyond all reason, but one could only trust. If Zurzal thought they had a chance, he would try it. He closed his eyes as the helmet thudded to the ground beside him, not even looking to see if Narco had made the same choice.

The Guardian felt as if the whole of the mountain had come, shivering, to life. He jerked under the power of the order which came, bringing his claws down to depressions not made for the fingers of his kind but into which he could force them. He was no longer—no longer anything. Color, light, waves of darkness closed about him. He was—not!

Galan cried out as that which he could not see, only feel as a growing torment, filled his head. Then—then there was nothing at all.

From the cracks in the wall of the Procession came something. It could not be seen with blinded eyes, it could not be heard by deafened ears, nor answer to any touch. But the strength of it was beyond belief.

The jack flitter had released an oval object, yet it did not fall as it was meant to. Rather, it hung just below the opening through which it had come. None of those below saw; all of them had been woven into a single purpose.

With a jerk, as if it had been seized by a giant hand, the flitter spun and then was released. With the weapon still dangling below, it headed westward on out over the wasteland. And, as it went, it sped far faster then its designers had ever intended. Then, there came sound, sound which broke through the concentration of the defenders. Near the far horizon arose a fiery cloud.

For those in the canyon it was as if they fell helplessly from a great distance. Pain—such pain—Galan could not see! He felt as if there was terrible pressure trapped within his skull battering a way out.

He never knew how long he was encased in that hell of torment. On opening his eyes he noticed there was still a web of mist about him. There came a touch on his head. It did not add to the pain; rather, the torment began to fade. He cared only for that touch and the ease it brought. At last, he could make out the Zacathan bending over him. There were no stones or sand under him. But as the pain lessened, he became aware he rested on something soft—fur? The—beast things. As he turned his head slightly, still fearing a return of pain, he could see the furry face, closer to him than the Zacathan. The alien must be holding him.

"Rest," he was ordered and, even as he slid into waiting darkness, he was faintly aware that the order had reached him in a strange new way.

Morning brought full sight of what their defense had cost. Great cracks, slices of fallen stone lay against the wall. There was nothing left of the Procession to Var. But it was before the site of that irreparable loss that most of the People held conference with the offworlders.

"This shall be promised and sworn to by the First Law," Zurzal's thoughts came slowly as if he found it difficult to shape them.

Galan's hands were at his head again. There was pain;

there would be for some time, the Zacathan had told him. But he had awakened something he longed ardently to use— that he must learn.

"Sworn to," Zurzal was repeating. "Our report to those who sent us shall be that there is no evidence of any Fore-runner remains here. And that is now true."

"True," Yinko echoed. "Knowledge is worth much, but life is worth more. You have not asked what may lie within," he gestured to the riven cliff. "By your aid you have bought the right to know."

"No. There is this. I am a marked one. Those who at-tacked us here are my enemies. In some fashion they dis-covered that we were coming to your world to search. It is not my right to uncover secrets which should only be known by those left to guard them.

"This I promise you. There will be no report of what has happened. We shall destroy what records we have al-ready made. Nor shall we speak of the People. This shall be an aborted mission and a forgotten world."

He got to his feet, the Jat moving from the crook of his misshapen arm to lean against his shoulder. The Shadow was also on his feet, but he wavered a little until he raised his head with a look of grim determination on his drawn face.

The battle was not over for those three, Galan knew. Would it ever be?

Yinko lingered for a moment. "You serve the Power well. Truly the Great Ones must once have touched your people. Our People will guard until the stars change and those who once were shall come again."

The furred ones were already climbing the battered cliff. Galan searched for sight of a single figure, a carved curve of stone or a faded sweep of paint. It was gone, all gone. Suddenly, fiercely he longed to see it again.

This had been a major find. Yet, with the mind touch still with him, he knew that the Zacathan was right.

He could not guess what had been here, but he felt that it was something his species should not find. And if, by trying to discover more, they would again bring in the Guild— No. Let them raise ship and go.

"Galan," the mind touch could still startle him. "There are many worlds and many finds to be made. And a greater one may be waiting."

Zurzal started for the flitter, and Galan entered the crawler where Narco was already at the controls.

On the cliff top Yinko and the others watched them go, one set flying, one crawling. Then he turned and saluted with both forepaws.

"To you, Guardian, rest well in the place of peace. You have fulfilled the duty set upon you."

THE GEMINI TWINS

by Paul Dellinger

Paul Dellinger is a longtime reporter for the *Roanoke Times* (Virginia), which is the only place where he's worked with computers (the newspaper was upgrading from manual to electric typewriters when he started there). He still manages to crank out an occasional high-tech science fiction story, despite being cyber-impaired. Other stories by him appear in *Wheel of Fortune*, *The Williamson Effect*, *Lord of the Fantastic*, and *Future Net*.

Besides these gods of the earth, there was a very famous and very popular pair of brothers, Castor and Pollux (Polydeuces), who, in most of the accounts, were said to live half their time on earth and half in heaven.

They were the sons of Leda, and are usually represented as being gods, the special protectors of sailors, saviors of swift-going ships when the storm winds rage over the ruthless sea.

They were also powerful to save in battle . . .
　　　　　　　　　　—from *Mythology* by Edith Hamilton.

At first, it was only a pinpoint of light, lost among the others dimly visible through the Marsglow in the sky over Phobos—but it was different. Its light came not from any burning starfires within itself, but from that reflected from the butterscotch-colored dayside of Mars. And it moved, growing infinitesimally larger until it resolved itself into a helmeted head and suit-encased arms and legs.

It was a human, out here where no human could possibly be.

"Elb! Dino!" called the Marsman in command of Phobos Base, nestled in a crater of the little moon zipping around the main planet in less than eight hours, only some four thousand miles above its surface—a natural outpost. His shout echoed through all six chambers of the pressurized fortification. Two pairs of military boots, their adhesive soles tearing free of the treated floor with each running step, answered him.

Then they saw it, too.

The figure had moved close enough for the flickers of its jetpack to show, as it began its descent toward the pitted surface of the Martian moon. Descending—here!

"He handles that pack like one of those belters," Elb said in a voice that was almost a whisper. "You know?"

"Couldn't be!" said Dino. "We got them all. And occupied their asteroid mining hutches without Earth even knowing. The Earthworms still don't know. And if a lone belter did manage to survive, there's no way he could make it all the way here in just a spacesuit and jetpack!"

"Then you tell me who it is."

The intruder had drifted to the cratered surface now, and began a half-walking, half-sliding movement toward the Martian station. To the three armed men inside, the approach of the clearly-weaponless newcomer still seemed menacing, although none of them could say why—perhaps because no planet-reared human should have been able to compensate for the negligible gravity of Phobos so easily.

The first Marsman, the one in charge of the three-man squad, broke the silence. "Suit up, both of you. Let's bring him in."

The newcomer offered no resistance when they closed in on him a few minutes later. Twice, he even paused to

wait patiently as one or another of the less acclimated Marsmen bounced around awkwardly. Once back inside, they
shed their vacuum suits so their boots adhered to the artificial flooring once more.

Their prisoner did the same without being told, and
seemed oblivious to the angry buzzing of the hummers that
two of the Marsmen pointed at him. It took a few seconds
for those sidearms, powered by the rare Martian crystals in
their handles, to power up. That was why Martian troops
also carried the deadly short swords that had become their
symbol, to be able to fight instantly if necessary. But once
a hummer was ready, it could cut through the hardest metal
like a laser—or better, since those native crystals had proved
more efficient at stimulating coherent light than Earth ru-
bies had ever been. They might be slow to start, but—once
ready—they were frighteningly effective.

The man gazed calmly at his captors. His face seemed
young, beneath tousled blond hair, but there was a coldness
like that of space itself in his blue eyes. He was tall and
slender, but had a hardness about him, too, even while standing with his open hands held calmly at his sides.

Elb gripped his hummer more tightly. "Gemini," he
breathed.

"You know him?"

"Yes. He *is* from the belt."

"The belters are dead!"

"But I remember him. I was part of the honor guard,
back when Roderick was negotiating with the belters to supply us with minerals, the way they do Earth—or did. I saw
him out there, when Roderick and Vaida made their visit. . . ."

At the mention of Valda, Elb thought he saw the ice
thaw slightly in the prisoner's eyes. "He was the kid who
took on Bardo, in a free-fall fight. Watch him, he's quick."

As though the warning had been a signal, the figure

sprang past the two armed Marsmen and pushed the third aside. He seemed to fly to the dome's highest point and hung there like some silent bird of prey, glaring down at the three.

"Get back here!" ordered the ranking Marsman. The prisoner continued floating across the roof over their heads. "All right, then. Dino—Elb. Nail him. Very carefully."

The two hummers lined up on their youthful target. Whoever he was, the Marsman thought, he must be counting on a reluctance to fire inside the pressurized outpost. Obviously he had no idea how precisely a Marsman could gauge his hummer fire.

The buzzing rose in volume as two incandescent beams of light shot from the sidearms. But another sound came first—a faint, explosive pop, and the man called Gemini was simply not there anymore.

It was too late for the two Marsmen to stop the commands their brains had sent to their fingers. In seconds, both beams seared through the roof. Air erupted through the breach before any of them could even scream, much less grab a helmet or vacuum suit.

Soon, a deathly silence enveloped the interior. It was still silent hours later, when a new pinpoint of light appeared among the stars above the ruptured dome, gradually taking the form of a space-suited man. This time, there was no one on the dark little moon to see him coming. . . .

It had been a belter named John Egan who first realized the secret that would one day give rise to the legend of Gemini.

Egan had been one of the few belters who did not return to Earth, and the accumulated pay that would make him wealthy for life, after completing a work tour in the asteroids. Earth no longer held any attraction for the grizzled veteran belter and, out here, the loss of his legs in an accident preparing metallic rocks for transit to refining facilities in Earth orbit was no real disadvantage.

Now another of those all-too-frequent accidents had claimed Pol, his ward—not his ward in a legal sense, but in every sense that mattered. Pol had worked scores of asteroids, as had his brother, Cass, when Egan was not keeping them at their studies. He had been determined that, although they were growing up in the belt, they would not lack the education that planet-bound youngsters got. Cass seemed the only one to take those studies seriously, but whenever Egan tested the two of them, their scores were identical. And by now they both knew their way around an asteroid better than any longtime belters. They had survived a pirate attack that had wiped out an entire cruise ship, and now Pol had been lost to a freakish collapsing drill shaft. Of course, by rights, neither of the boys should ever have survived the destruction of the cruise ship *Gemini*, the first— and now, probably, the last—built by entrepreneurs back on Earth for very expensive and extended vacation tours in outer space.

Egan's fingers in their mini-servo-powered gloves played over the jetpack controls at his belt, shamelessly wasting propellant as he circled the potato-shaped rock. Four other belters orbited farther back, knowing they could do nothing but also knowing how Egan felt about the kid, ever since he pulled the twins out of a lifeboat more than twelve Earth-years ago.

Egan was remembering, too, the pink, puckered faces of the newborn infants through the window of the capsule, with their mother who was more dead than alive—and who did die a few hours later, despite all that Doc Stroude and the medical team could do. The hospital units placed out here within the belt were state of the art, by necessity, but they couldn't always perform miracles—at least, not for the mother. They did, however, for the babies.

Egan had never seen Siamese twins before. Their births during the *Gemini*'s three-year jaunt couldn't have been planned; the pregnancy must have happened after the trip had gotten underway. There had been no other survivors among some two hundred passengers. No other lifeboats had been launched, from what the belters later determined in examining what little remained of the wreckage.

As best they could guess as to what happened, the prospective parents would have been in the ship's sick bay near its center when the attack occurred. That would explain why their air supply lasted a little longer than in the outer hull, spinning to simulate gravity. The medical team may have gotten called away by the ship's alarm, which would have left the parents with their newborn infants on their own when the compartment doors reacted to dropping air pressure by sealing them off. But someone, perhaps the father, got them launched somehow. And a couple of belters had picked up the lifeboat's signal.

Egan had persuaded old Doc Stroude to operate, and at least save one of the twins. To his own surprise, Stroude saved them both, but there was no way to send them to Earth until the next ship brought replacement workers for those whose tours were up—and there was no surviving record of who their families had been, anyway. Egan became their caretaker by default. It was he who named them Pollux and Castor, after the Gemini Twins of mythology.

Only Doc Stroude knew that Egan had left a couple of sons Earthside, with a wife who had not been patient enough to wait after he'd signed on for the belt to try and earn them a better life. As it turned out, Egan always had plenty of help in raising the twins. Belters volunteered to spend off-shifts tending the babies. Nobody squawked at the extra cleaning cycles necessary when diapers ran short. The shop workers never quibbled over fabricating additional under-sized vacuum suits as the youngsters outgrew their earlier ones. Belters came and went, but all came to regard the boys as something like good luck charms.

Besides using his accumulated earnings to bring out ed-ucation modules and the latest bone-building exercise de-vices on the rare supply ships, Egan saw that the boys got their calcium and other supplements from the start. When they were old enough, he began a constant workout regi-men to make sure they would be fit for gravity if they ever decided to migrate to Earth. Again, it was Cass who worked hardest, while Pol sloughed off, arguing that he'd never want to live planetside, anyway.

And now he never would.

The asteroid had been a good one—high in iron ore, the usual concentrations of nickel and cobalt, and exception-ally high percentages of the more valuable trace minerals. The metallurgical stations outside the orbit of Earth's moon would boil off its components with mirrored solar beams and collect them for the space factories closer in.

All that was necessary was to move it from the belt to Earth orbit, which was the job of the belters. It was they who fitted the small fusion rockets into each chosen aster-oid, computed the course to bring it to a Lagrangian point where it would be gravitationally trapped between the Earth and moon, and sent it to join the procession of mineral chunks that made up the cornerstone of Earth's technology in the age of space.

But first you had to drill shafts to anchor the rockets, a dirty job and a ticklish one because each rock was a dif-ferent little world, with its own idiosyncrasies and dangers. Even the metallic ones often lacked complete solidity. This one had seemed relatively tame, until Pol was deep inside the first shaft spraying it with the quick-forming lining to hold the rocket in place. The walls had given way and Pol was trapped inside, stuck until his air ran out if he hadn't already been crushed. The rock had become a monstrous tombstone.

For the first time, Egan blamed himself for keeping the boys out here all these years. They might have been crowded and orphaned back on Earth, but at least they both would have been alive. Frustrated at his helplessness, he almost collided with the small, suited figure who jetted past him toward the asteroid. For a second, he'd thought it was Pol, that somehow the lad had dug himself free. Then he realized it had to be Cass—but hadn't Cass been working a repair shift at the current home base for this sector? How could he have known what was going on here?

"What are you waiting for?" Cass' voice crackled through the receiver in Egan's helmet. "Can't you hear him?" Cass touched down on the asteroid and anchored himself with a tool from his belt. Only later did it occur to Egan that he'd landed exactly where the shaft had been drilled, even though its closure made the spot indistinguishable from the rest of the rock.

"There's nothing we can do," Egan said in a tight voice. "Even if he's alive . . ."

"He *is* alive. He's in a pocket down there. If we drill along the edge of it, he can climb right out."

"Cass, it's no good hoping . . ."

"What the hell, Egan?" came another voice he recognized as Joe Nieminski. "Let him try. What's the difference?"

Three of the belters got the long white-coated drilling tube into position, aiming at a spot Cass marked. "Go in at thirty degrees," the boy directed. "Twelve feet—no, he says ten. Ten feet."

Egan shook his head. If Pol's radio was still working,

they would all have heard him. But nobody else said anything, so he didn't either. He squinted at the bright beam that began eating into the rock, vaporizing as it went. "Stop! That's close enough," Cass said, stomping his boots onto the surface to anchor them at the edge of the circular opening. He started to remind Cass that the shaft would be too hot to enter at once, when he realized he was seeing not one but two small vacuum suits on its perimeter. The gasps on his receiver from the others told him he wasn't hallucinating.

"Pol?" he whispered. *"Pol?"*

The Marsmen looked out of place within the hollowed-out asteroid, with their tight-fitting uniforms, shiny boots, and swords of all things. Even the supremely-confident Roderick, ruler of an entire planet, had to move gingerly in the negligible gravity. The belters, by contrast, lounged easily—some might have said insolently—on both sides and even above the line of visitors, and their functional garb seemed plain and worn compared to the crispness of the military-style clothing.

But it was Roderick's daughter, Valda, who drew the appreciation of this mostly-male bastion. Pol, perched next to Egan on the front rank, and Cass, who had arrived late from a job and ended up farther back, only just managed to keep from gaping openly. None of the few female belters they had known had prepared them for this. She was tall and slim, with long auburn hair that trailed behind her in the negligible gravity like the blazing tail of a comet. She wore garb as formal as the dozen Marsmen in the delegation, but its severity stood no chance at all against the stunning form it covered.

You were right, Cass, his brother's thought tickled his mind. *She's beautiful!*

As always, Cass had done the archival research on Martian history out of curiosity about the coming visit—studying old news accounts preserved in one of their educational modules on how Earth governments had used the original colonies to get rid of criminals and malcontents, figuring isolation would work at a time when the death penalty was in decline; how Roderick (and Cass could find no further name or additional background on him) somehow managed to form the growing number of misfits into a militaristic society, but how it was hampered by a lack of raw materials like those Earth got from the belt. Even without many basic ores, the Martians had quickly achieved limited space travel, and the boys knew many who thought that a few renegade Marsmen lay behind the occasional piracies against Earth ships coming out this far. Of course, a pirate base in the form of a space habitat was possible, but none had ever been located. And only parts of missing ships were ever found, giving rise to the thought that the pirates had a use for the materials that went into building them.

According to what Egan told the boys, there had likewise been little left of the *Gemini*. He did not suggest that Mars ships were the cause of its destruction, but Cass had reviewed enough news archives over the years to be suspicious. And so, of course, was Pol. After all, as only Egan had figured out, they thought with one mind, not two. Even now, Cass was experiencing the double vision that he once assumed was normal for everyone, seeing Valda from his distant perch among the belters and also seeing her up close through Pol's eyes.

Severing the physical link between the twins had not severed their mind-link. Who knew what kind of radiations might have affected their genetic formation before their births, either from the awesome energies of the pirate weapons or the environment of space itself? For whatever

reason, Pol and Cass eventually realized that a sharing of
senses was not normal for anyone else—a discovery that
they instinctively kept to themselves, until Egan guessed
following the accident in which Pol was almost lost.

Cass found himself responding to the sight of Roderick's sole heir, by a mother never publicly named. He imagined what it might be like to take her in his arms, to clasp
her tightly, to touch her lips . . .

As was Pol. For the first time in his life, Cass actually
resented sharing his brother's thoughts, and felt the same
unaccustomed wish for privacy emanating from his brother.

It took Pol a moment to realize that the man beside Valda
was Roderick himself, and another moment to care. But neither brother could resist looking more closely at this man
on whom the fate of worlds might depend—and certainly
the future of the belters. Egan had already told them what
Roderick's earlier emissaries were going to propose. If successful, it could change the way the belters lived forever.

Roderick had a receding hairline, a paunch, and a weak
chin. But when he began to speak, both boys forgot all that.
Later, when Cass transcribed the recording he had made
and analyzed the actual words, he found them flowery but
empty although they had certainly not seemed that way at
the time. "Mars greets you, people of the asteroids," Roderick began. "We salute this beginning of a friendship between your people and mine."

Before he had finished talking, Roderick had convinced
practically every listener in the chamber that Martian engineering was up to the task of creating an artificial planetoid out here in the belt, complete with gravity and
atmosphere, where the belters could live between work shifts
without suits, in habitations as open as those on Earth itself. Martian engineers would maintain this New Eden, as
he called it, in return for a tiny fraction of the ores being

furnished to Earth. A contingent of Marsmen would join the belters and learn the procedures to handle any extra work involved. And what the bureaucrats back on Earth didn't know wouldn't hurt them.

What did the belters have to lose? No ores would be launched to Mars orbit until New Eden had been created, and every worker in the belt had sampled it. "The orbiting factories around Earth aren't that far removed from such a worldlet," Roderick concluded. "Earth could have done this for you. Mars will do it."

Pol was surprised to hear spontaneous cheers from some of the entranced belters. He might have joined in, but his own reaction was muted by Cass' mental dissection of Roderick's speech. It had been a masterpiece, building to a climax that was bound to provoke a positive reaction—especially from people who felt themselves taken for granted by Earth to start with.

But they were both surprised when Egan's voice cut through the applause. "And when the powers that be on Earth find out we've made such a decision independently?" he asked. "It won't stay quiet forever, not with new workers replacing others going back to Earth to claim their rewards. And we're completely dependent on Earth for life support."

There was a stir among the Martian delegation, some even putting their hands on the hilts of their swords. "You need not be. Mars would be willing to supply your needs," Roderick said, smiling.

"And we'd be under your control instead of theirs," Egan replied, seemingly oblivious to the weapons. "Could that be what you're intending with all this largess?"

Murmurs echoed in the chamber from the belters, some agreeing with Egan's suggestion and others ridiculing it. Roderick raised his hands slightly and, such was his mas-

tery of the situation, the murmurs died out. "Earth could
not get along without the materials you supply," he said.
"They could not sever their relationship with the belt, whatever you did. But is it any of Earth's business if we have
a small contingent of scientists and engineers out here working on an artificial planetoid, which you and your succes-
sors can choose to utilize or not?"

*Not unless those scientists and engineers are not those
things at all, but an advance force for a military expedition into the belt,* Cass thought. And then he heard his
thoughts echoed aloud. Pol, he realized, had spoken them.

What had been a stir before became an uproar, with several Marsmen moving their hands to their sidearms, including a giant of a man who stood beside Valda. Several
pushed the studs in the handles to activate the weapons.
Cass had read about the hummers, developed on Mars when
there had been threats of open warfare among the underground cities, before Roderick managed to unify them
against a hostile environment instead of one another. But it
would take a few seconds for them to be ready for use.
Cass started to call out to the other belters, to disarm the
delegation before those fearsome weapons could be brought
into use.

Roderick reacted more quickly, ending the crisis with a
gesture. He waved his hand, and the Marsmen instantly
snapped off their weapons. The humming sound stopped.

And then Roderick's daughter spoke. "We came out of
friendship," she said in a rich, clear voice. "If we wanted
to take the belt militarily, we would have come in force.
With all due respect, I don't believe you could have
stopped us."

"Don't you?" Pol said with a reckless grin, directing his
reply at her. "We're in our element out here. We don't need
suction cups or whatever on our boots to get around. And

while you occupied one rock, we could be booby-trapping a dozen more."

Pol had become the focus of the entire Martian delegation, including Valda, which Cass knew was exactly what he'd had in mind. Cass found himself jealous of his brother getting the Martian girl's attention, yet another unaccustomed emotion for him, and there was no way he could hide it from Pol. He could not understand it. Never before had there been the slightest fracture in their thoughts.

"What's your name, boy?" asked Roderick, an amused smile on his face.

"Gemini," Pol responded. Again, Cass found himself irritated that his brother had usurped a name they had in common—especially when be saw that Valda was regarding Pol with what looked like genuine interest.

"Well, young Gemini, and you really believe you could stand up to one of my Marsmen in some type of combat?"

"Yes, sir. Not on Mars, but out here, certainly." Cass felt Pol's relief that his voice remained firm and did not crack embarrassingly.

"And would you care to demonstrate? In a contest with one of my men?"

"Well . . ."

"Excellent! It's good to see there are young men with sporting blood out here. Your people and mine will get along well, young Gemini." Roderick waved an arm around at the Marsmen around him. "And who in my little group would you like to try to best in a physical encounter?"

Pol nodded at the giant Marsman who stood next to Valda. "Why not him?"

"Now wait a minute . . ." Egan began.

Several other belters shouted him down. "Pol can take care of himself, Egan," Cass heard Nieminski say. In fact, Cass was not worried about that part either. He and Pol might be young compared to the other belters, but nobody could top their experience at handling themselves in this environment.

The Marsman glared down at Pol, his nose wrinkling in obvious distaste. "Very well, Bardo," Roderick said to him. "The boy may need a lesson, but try not to damage him badly."

"This is crazy!" Egan declared.

But Marsmen and belters had already cleared a space around Pol and Bardo. Bardo shook his head slowly, as though in disgust, and then made a feinting movement toward Pol. He looked chagrined when Pol failed to react with any defensive gesture at all. Then he reached out to grab his younger antagonist in all seriousness.

His fingers met empty air. Pol had leaped lightly from the rock floor and flipped over Bardo's head, just out of reach. He grabbed the arm of a belter in the audience, and used that leverage for enough impetus to land behind Bardo. Chuckles from the belters echoed within the chambers. The maneuver had been no real surprise to people used to living in relative free fall.

Bardo had spun almost in time to catch Pol coming down—but not quite. Pol landed with his back to the larger man and, without seeming to glance behind him, curled himself into a backward somersault that took him right between the giant's barrel-like legs.

Now, that maneuver was a surprise—to everyone but Cass, who knew Pol had seen his opponent's position through his brother's more-distant eyes.

Instinctively, Bardo, bent over to see where his adversary had rolled. Pol had spread his hands on either side to brace himself against the rock floor. He planted one foot against the Marsman's rump and pushed gently, sending the larger man pinwheeling into the air. He spilled, head over heels, into the ranks of those closest to the platform, as laughter rained down from the belters.

"Enough, Bardo, that will do," Roderick said as the Marsman scrambled into a crouch, a furious expression on his face. "I believe I see what the young man means. You really are in your element out here, aren't you?"

Cass could not help sharing Pol's feeling of triumph, not only at deflating some of the pomposity of the visitors but also at a minuscule payback for what both boys suspected other Marsmen had done to the ship on which they were born. Pol could not help glancing at Valda to see her reaction, but she was not looking at him. She was regarding Bardo with what seemed an infinite sadness on her face.

Far from scuttling Roderick's proposal, the friendly-seeming little contest seemed to cement it. Work would start as soon as the Martians could assemble the engineering equipment and bring it out. The Martian delegation left soon after, their squat little ship gradually moving clear of the habitat asteroid and disappearing into the blackness. Fifteen minutes later, Cass and Pol saw the silent flare of its rocket as it began its return trip.

The body would never have been found without the broadcast locator. Its beeps had been picked up by a team of belters working on a rock within sight of Roderick's departure trajectory. Pol and Cass got their first sight of it along with a couple dozen others when it was brought through the shelter air lock.

It was, or had been, a man. It was hardly recognizable as one, since it wore no pressure suit and many of its internal organs had ruptured in hard vacuum. But there was no mistaking that giant physique.

Cass felt his stomach turning but managed to hold it down. Pol didn't, causing a general rush for hand-vacs to suck up the contents of his last meal. Egan's only reaction was a grim tightening of his lips.

"I guess Roderick wanted us to know how he feels about failure," Egan said.

The project took nearly three Earth-years, as time was measured in the belt, but less than half of that by Martian time, as the Martian engineers and workers constantly observed. And this was Day One on New Eden, as Roderick had called it, fashioned mostly from materials in the belt itself. The Martians had proved to be as proficient at building a space habitat as Roderick had boasted.

In deference to the belters, the periods of light and dark were based on Earth-days on New Eden—or, rather, in the spherical habitat. Its globe was nearly three miles in diameter, with a spin that simulated Earth-like gravity along its inner equator. Its "sky" was at its center, complete with real clouds. Cass kept staring at them. He had seen reproductions on tape and in still pictures, of course, but never the real thing.

Day One also marked the first holiday in the belt since the start of mining operations. Even Roderick's visit three years ago had not prompted a total shutdown of work shifts. But this time, the belters had lifted a phrase from Roderick's speech: What Earth didn't know wouldn't hurt it.

Between five and six hundred belters—everyone in the belt, in fact, but one—had gathered on New Eden to bid farewell to the Martian workers and to spend an Earth-day walking on seemingly solid ground, lifting their unhelmeted faces to the sky, breathing in the air that was all around them.

Cass wondered what all the celebrating was about.

He felt naked, exposed, here in the open without even a pressure suit. He recognized how real the synthetic grass and trees looked, from the pictures held seen of Earth, but even they felt unnatural to him. The excited voices around him and Egan seemed strange, unfiltered as they were by helmet receivers. And the constant pull of gravity generated by the worldlet's spin seemed to him more uncomfortable than his and Pol's workouts in the centrifuge. Of course, he and Pol were the only belters who had never experienced continuous gravity before.

And here I am, three hundred miles away, came Pol's thought, tinged with disgust. Cass also picked up the thought that this had been the first time Pol had considered defying an order from Egan. Egan had two reasons for stationing Pol on a rock where be could observe the Martian fleet leaving the belt: one, to make sure it actually left, and, two, because Egan was not sure Pol could physically handle the stress of a constant one-G, since he had not kept up his conditioning over the years as had Cass. Pol had argued that he wouldn't have to stay at the equator; he could remain farther out from center, where the pull was weaker, and gradually work his way into stronger gravity. Besides, be had already tracked the three Martian ships past his observation post with its instruments, en route back to Mars. But Egan had been adamant, responding by radio—even though he and the boys knew he could have accomplished the same thing simply by using Cass as a human transmitter—that acclimation to gravity would require more preliminary work for Pol, and that the Mars ships were still close enough to change course and loop around for a return trip.

"Why should they do that?" Cass asked. "They've got what they want—assurance of a supply of minerals. And they've done their part of the bargain."

Egan, moving beside Cass in a motorized something he called a wheelchair, couldn't answer that one. It was simply that he didn't trust Roderick. Neither did Cass, for that matter. He still remembered being told what happened to the *Gemini*, and he'd seen firsthand what happened to Bardo.

Pol had some vivid thoughts about having to stay on his isolated rock, but Cass prudently decided not to relay those to Egan. Instead, he made some comment, more to Pol than to Egan, about preferring an absence of gravity to being pinned down by it.

"You'll probably end up enjoying it like everybody else," Egan said. "After all, your bodies were shaped for Earth, not the belt . . ."

A mild reverberation shook the walkway beneath them. Others noticed it, too, and the surrounding hum of conversation died out. A distant, hollow boom sounded from somewhere in the "sky," actually the hub of the worldlet.

Cass frowned. "Don't tell me Roderick is simulating thunderstorms for us, too?"

"If you'd ever heard real thunder, you'd know better," Egan said. "I don't like this. The hub controls access to and from this place. That's where all the suits and jetpacks are."

A second, closer explosion sent them sprawling. The silence around them turned to screams. Cass found himself on the ground, and pushed himself to his hands and knees. He glimpsed flames on the nearby horizon. He had seen fire once before, when a heating system in a shelter built into an asteroid had overheated. He and the other occupants of the shelter simply suited up, and opened all the air locks to hard vacuum which quickly extinguished it. But New Eden produced a continuous air supply, feeding the flames.

"Cass, get up!" said Egan, who lay beside his overturned chair. "You've got to salvage one of the suits and jetpacks. It's your only chance."

Cass was still half-stunned. "They may be burned up already. . . ."

"You've got to try! Lead the way for the others. Don't you see? All of us, in one place, for the first time in the history of the belt—*that* was Roderick's plan!"

"But you can't . . ."

"Never mind me. Go!" He shoved Cass away with one of his powerful hands. Cass found himself staggering, still unused to functioning in constant gravity. A third blast seemed to erupt under his feet, and he felt himself flung into the air.

The ringing was still in his ears an instant later, but all else around him was silent. The bright flames had given way to the darkness of a carved-out shelter within an asteroid. He and Pol regarded each other in amazement. And Cass realized, for the first time, that their link was able to convey more than mere thoughts between them.

Of course, the three Mars ships did come back. And so did others. Cass and Pol tracked each one as it took up its position in a different part of the belt.

The command ship made a slow pass through the area where New Eden had been constructed, its instruments making sure there was nothing left but debris. Its creators had only had to construct it to last for a single day; within an Earth-week, it would have become unstable and shaken itself to pieces, but any occupants would have had time to evacuate it before that happened. So it was made to self-destruct all at once, and take all its inhabitants with it.

All but one. Somehow, one of the belters had managed to get into a pressure suit and, through some freakish piece of luck, must have been blasted clear. The newcomers quickly zeroed in on the distress signal from his suit. Judging by its movement, its occupant was still alive. Colonel Noctis, Roderick's handpicked commander of the occupation force, considered leaving the belter where be was until his air ran out. On reflection, he decided the man might be able to provide his officers with information about the belters' operations, so he had the survivor brought aboard.

The Marsmen from the original three ships had pinpointed the equipment, supply caches, and working areas of the belters as best they could. Now they directed the occupation forces to pick up where the belters had left off, with Earth none the wiser—at least until the next supply ship showed up. But that was almost an Earth-year away.

Meanwhile, Noctis had two guards bring the surviving belter to his stateroom. The two Marsmen secured the man to an interrogation chair, complete with a polygraph attachment on one arm. The man floated about an inch above the seat, lacking the adhesive boots of his captors. He was secured only by the straps on his arms and around his middle.

Noctis stood over the lone belter, fixing him with the intimidating stare he'd practiced frequently in front of a mirror and used any number of times with other prisoners during Roderick's unification war back on Mars. "If you'd prefer a quick death like that of your fellows, you will answer all my questions completely and without hesitation."

The prisoner stared back for a moment, looked at the two guards on either side of his seat, the colonel's aide who had just handed the officer what looked like a tube of some liquid that could be water or wine, and the polygraph operator who looked only at the styluses drawing their fine lines along a piece of paper. Then he returned his gaze to Noctis and nodded.

"Wise," said Noctis, sucking delicately at the refreshment in the tube. "Were any of you able to transmit any information to Earth about what happened?"

The prisoner took a deep breath, then answered with a barely audible "No." Noctis glanced at the polygraph man, who nodded.

"Good. That means they will know nothing so long as we keep transporting the rocks on schedule—until we're ready to strike. Then the rocks will no longer be guided to Earth's orbital factories, but against targets on Earth itself."

"Yes, sir. Either they will become part of Roderick's unification movement, or go the way of the dinosaurs," the aide said.

Noctis nodded, then turned back to the prisoner. "Are there caches of oxygen, food, suits, and devices for moving the asteroids in places our Marsmen would not have seen, during their time out here?"

"The belt's full of them," murmured the man in the chair. Again, the operator nodded.

"You may have just bought yourself a reprieve, if you know where they are," said Noctis. He turned to the aide. "We can use those things, particularly the explosive materials and those fusion rockets for moving the asteroids. Although, once we occupy the key enclaves of Earth, there won't really be anyone left to fight us."

"Or to provide ships for us to prey on, sir," said the aide.

The prisoner turned toward the aide. "It's your people manning the pirate ships?" he asked.

"Who did you think it was?" the aide replied. "Did you really believe that tale we've been floating about pirates operating from some artificial habitat?"

"I'll ask the questions, belter," Noctis said. "Did you belters transmit communications regularly between yourselves and Earth?" The prisoner nodded. Noctis pursed his lips. "This may be another way you can prolong your life. We'll need someone who can keep those communications flow-ing seamlessly, so Earth doesn't suspect what's coming. Not that anyone is likely to suspect anything, as closely guarded as this operation has been."

"Only one security breach, in fact," said the aide. "But at least Roderick's daughter can't tell anyone, being under house arrest, as it were."

The prisoner looked up. "Valda wasn't part of what you did?" he asked.

The colonel swung the back of his hand against the prisoner's face, with a sharp crack. "I said I would ask the questions. You, on the other hand, will not demean the name of Roderick's daughter by mentioning it. She'll come to realize the brilliance of her father's program, in time— the unification of the solar system, humankind under a single directive, developing the resources of our own planets and then reaching for the stars. Another question: are you aware of any other survivors besides yourself?"

And to the surprise of everyone else in the ship's cabin, the prisoner smiled. "Yes."

"How many?" Noctis demanded, after glancing at the polygraph operator for confirmation.

"Just one. He and I have already fitted a small asteroid with life support and fusion rockets to head it toward Mars in a higher-speed trajectory than you could conceive. Asteroids can be moved at great speeds when the amount of available propellant is no object."

"You will give us the location of that asteroid," Noctis said.

"Sorry. No can do. It's already well on its way."

"Sir, we'll have to transmit a warning . . ." the aide began.

"We're not going to use it to impact your world," the prisoner interrupted. "It's merely transportation. From my studies of Mars, I understand you maintain a small installation to warn of approaching ships on your larger moon. We plan to replace your men on that moon, just as you've replaced ours out here. Its communications equipment should be more than sufficient to let Earth know what's happened, and give the home world time to send a military force out here to reoccupy the belt. Then we'll see what becomes of Roderick and the rest of you pirates, once the rest of the system knows about you and your crimes."

"You may yet talk yourself into an early death," Noctis warned.

"My brother once told Roderick of the mischief we could wreak on an occupation force here in the belt," the prisoner continued. "But that's nothing to what he and I can do on your home planet, once they send up replacements for us. You have no idea of the things we can get into and out of."

Noctis leaned forward, his face inches from the captive's. "Explain," he ordered in a low voice.

"I'll do better than that. I'll demonstrate. After all, that was the reason I came back to the vicinity of New Eden, so I'd get picked up by you people and learn what I've learned."

Noctis was beginning to look uneasy. "What's your name, belter?"

"Gemini." The word was followed immediately by a popping sound, like that of air rushing into a sudden void. The figure on the chair, his clothing, the straps that had been attached to him, vanished in an instant. A small, metallic object remained behind, on the seat above which the prisoner had floated.

The aide was the first to recover his voice, after the prisoner winked out of existence before all their eyes. "Say, that looks like one of the belter explosive devices we were talking about . . ."

No one in the occupation force was ever able to figure

out what caused the destruction of their flagship and the loss of their commanding officer.

The moving light over Phobos took on the form of a human, in a pressure suit, out here where no human could possibly be. . . .

THAT DOGGONE VNORPT

by Nathan Archer

Nathan Archer took to writing professionally when his "steady" government job ceased to exist in post-Cold War budget cuts, and has now authored half a dozen licensed novels based on *Star Trek*, *Predator*, *Spider-Man*, and *Mars Attacks*, as well as scripting a *Star Trek* comic book for Wildstorm/DC. Although the money to be made from spin-offs is nice, he is trying to get away from playing with other people's toys and is working on a novel about his own creation, Amelia Hand.

Amelia Hand didn't notice the first obvious sign that something was wrong at the Busted Fin. The fact that the huge service doors were standing open somehow didn't register; she was too concerned with getting inside, out of the blinding white Daedalus sunlight, and getting herself some decent beer and a look at the local talent. Seven weeks alone aboard her ship with nothing to drink but water and condensed fruit juice had left her desperate.

Once she set foot inside, though, she immediately knew there was a problem.

"What's that smell?" she demanded, before her eyes adjusted to the gloom of the interior. The usual odors of spilled beer and hot oil were overwhelmed by a stench she didn't recognize.

Then she saw the vnorpt and stopped dead in her tracks, her hand dangling near the butt of the blaster on her thigh.

It was standing at the bar—or rather, towering over the

bar, its crest stooped slightly to avoid scraping the ceiling—talking to Al, the bartender. Hand had never seen a vnorpt in the flesh before, but there was no mistaking it; no other sentient stood five meters tall and three meters wide.

And no other sentient smelled quite so awful either.

"He was a *pet!*" Al was shouting. "A companion!"

"Oops," the vnorpt said, in a bone-shaking rumble. It belched. "Sorry."

Hand looked around the room. Half a dozen humans cowered in the booths along one wall. The stools at the bar, and the other tables, were all deserted. A waitress stood cringing in one corner, staring at the vnorpt. She and Al were the only employees in sight, and the six in the booths, the vnorpt, and Hand herself the only customers.

There were at least six assorted freighters in port, a Patrol cruiser, and the starliner *Dreamship III*, as well as Hand's own *Tristan Jones*; the Busted Fin should have been jammed with people, some of them as eager for human companionship as Hand was.

"What's going on?" Hand demanded, her fingers lightly tapping the blaster.

Al looked past the vnorpt and said, "He ate Barnstable!"

Barnstable was Al's dog; Hand had never liked him much. She'd never had much patience with pets, and Barnstable, half bulldog, half basset hound, and half-witted, had been even less lovable than most.

"Was an accident," the vnorpt rumbled. "Thought it was snack. Pay for damages, yes." It dropped a credit chit on the bar with one of its feeding claws.

"You can't just . . ." Al began.

"*Said* was sorry," the vnorpt interrupted. "Now, beer, yes?"

"You ate my dog! You get out of here!" He pointed toward the service door.

"Uh-uh," the vnorpt said, lifting one of its hands off the floor and waving the stubby talons in Al's face warningly. "No racial incidents, yes? Treaty says vnorpt travel freely in public areas of human settlements, no refusal just for being vnorpt."

"I don't care if you're a vnorpt or a l'antar or a goddamn tree frog! You ate my dog!"

"Was *accident*," the vnorpt insisted. "*Very* sorry. Pay insurance value three times, yes? Now, beer."

"You ate my dog and chased away all my customers!"

"Not responsible for unfortunate prejudice of clientele. Beer, third time asked." This final sentence sounded very much like a warning.

Hand decided that it was time to intervene—and not by pulling a blaster. "Give him his beer, Al," she called, as she strode up to the relatively small section of bar not blocked by the vnorpt. "And file a protest about Barnstable later. You don't want to make this fellow angry."

Nobody *ever* wanted to be around an angry vnorpt.

Al glowered unhappily at her, but picked up the credit chit with one hand and a pitcher with the other, and opened a tap.

The vnorpt looked down at Hand. "Thanks," it said. It took in her size and general appearance, and said, "You little guy, yes? Kinda cute."

"Thanks," Hand said, not meaning it. She looked up at the vnorpt.

It was roughly egg-shaped, covered with bony brown armor. Four long, multiply-elbowed arms hung from its middle, and four feeding claws were arrayed below its gigantic maw, ready to shove in whatever got within reach. Four eyes on stubby stalks bracketed the immense mouth, all of them currently tilted toward her, and a greenish-yellow crest topped it off. Something yellowish was seeping between

plates of bone on one side of its head—if it *had* a head—
and Hand suspected that was the source of the worst of the
foul smell. Nothing corresponding to ears, nose, or other
human features was visible.

A typical vnorpt, in other words, completely nondescript
to anyone but another vnorpt. The only thing that made this
one unusual was its location, in a human-run bar in Daedalus
Port rather than out in vnorpt territory.

This character, Hand told herself, was clearly a problem
that had to be dealt with. The Busted Fin was the only
worthwhile bar in the entire port, as far as Hand was concerned. The others were all overpriced tourist traps that
would be full of the passengers off the *Dreamship III*. Hand
was eager to find a little action—a nice big freighter crew-
man would be very welcome—but she was not about to
waste her time on a bunch of overdressed twits who thought
tooling around on a starliner made them spacers.

And they probably wouldn't want to waste time on her
either, if the truth be told. She was no exotic offworld
beauty, just a stubby middle-aged woman with a blobby
nose that she kept meaning to get fixed but never had yet.

Freighter crews weren't so picky about details like that.
But freighter crews weren't going to set foot in the Busted
Fin so long as this mountain of alien meat was stinking up
the place; vnorpt were known to occasionally smash skulls
or break human legs "accidentally," just as this one had "accidentally" eaten Al's dog. They generally didn't actually eat
humans anymore, not since the treaty, but even that wasn't
impossible if a vnorpt got drunk enough. It would mean
apologies and reparations and warnings from the Patrol, but
that wouldn't do the vnorpt's dinner any good.

"What brings you to this part of town?" Hand asked.
She had hopes of convincing it to move on to a different

bar—the Stardust Lounge, maybe, where the tourists would probably be just *thrilled* to meet a real, live alien.

"Beer," the vnorpt replied. "Good beer here. Not like the others."

Al finished filling the pitcher and handed it to the vnorpt, which transferred it to a feeding claw, then tossed it down in a single gulp, like a human drinking a shot of whiskey.

"Can't argue with that," Hand said. "So you've tried the others? The Stardust?"

The empty pitcher dangled from the tip of the claw, swinging back and forth as the vnorpt said, "Tried Stardust. Beer there tastes like dirty water. Here is *real* beer." It reached up and dislodged the pitcher; Al dove forward in time to catch it as it fell. "More beer," it said.

"I'll have one, too," Hand said, as Al reached for the tap. "Just a half-liter, though, and make it a stout."

Al grumbled something and began refilling the pitcher.

"I didn't know that vnorpt like beer," Hand said, as she waited for her drink.

"Yes," the vnorpt said. "Tried some because humans talked about it so much. Good stuff. Got more respect for humans now. Anyone who invent beer is okay."

"Then you don't make your own? There's no vnorpt beer?"

"No vnorpt beer, because no vnorpt hops, no vnorpt yeast. Dumb question, little guy." A vnorpt hand lashed out in what was probably intended as a comradely gesture akin to a slap on the shoulder; the impact slammed Hand off her feet.

She reacted completely automatically. By the time she hit the floor, she had her blaster out of the sheath on her thigh and pointed at the vnorpt's head.

"Oops," the vnorpt said, but Hand wasn't looking at that—she was looking at Al, behind the bar, who had put

down the pitcher and was now nodding vigorously, drawing a finger across his throat.

"Self-defense," Al said. "I'm a witness."

Hand hesitated.

The vnorpt hadn't intended to hurt her, she was fairly
certain. Al was mad about his dog and what the vnorpt was
doing to his business, but the vnorpt was still a sentient
being and probably hadn't really meant any harm. Shooting it wasn't called for unless it actually attacked someone.

Besides, she was only carrying a standard-issue urban
blaster, where penetration was deliberately kept low so that
random shots wouldn't punch through entire blocks and take
out innocent bystanders. She wasn't sure what it would do
to vnorpt armor.

She lowered the weapon, but didn't return it to its holster.

"Sorry, sorry," the vnorpt said, and before Hand could
get back on her feet, one of those long arms had reached
out and grasped her shoulder. It picked her up, and two of
the vnorpt's other arms began brushing her off. "Very sorry,"
it said. "Low gravity tricky, yes?"

"I'm fine," Hand said. "Put me down." The gravity in
Daedalus Port was 1.08 gees—not low by human standards
at all, though Hand usually boosted her ship at higher acceleration than that, in the interest of saving flight time.

Vnorpt had apparently evolved under much higher gravity. Nobody really knew much about their origins, but that
much was widely believed.

"Just checking for broken bones, things like that," the
vnorpt said, as it stuck a hand in her crotch.

She really hadn't *intended* to fire, but that was too much.
The blaster bolt spattered glowing plasma across the brown
armored face.

The vnorpt dropped her, and she landed sitting on the

bar. The stench of vnorpt was now worse than ever—whatever that yellow stuff was, it smelled even ghastlier when it burned.

"Ouch!" the vnorpt complained, dabbing at a singed eye.

"Oops," Hand said, smiling broadly. "Sorry, sorry."

The other three eyes swung around to glare at her. It made a noise she had never heard before, and never wanted to hear again; she wasn't sure whether it was a laugh or a growl or what. "Beer," it said to Al. "And wet cloth."

Al was staring up at the vnorpt in astonishment, his mouth hanging open.

"Beer," it said again. "And wet cloth."

Al remembered himself, and handed up the refilled pitcher and a bar rag. When the vnorpt took them, he leaned over and said to Hand, "You *shot* it!"

She stared at him silently as she slid off the counter and landed standing at the bar.

"You shot it in the face at point-blank range, and it isn't even *hurt!*"

"I think it stung a little," Hand said.

"But you shot it in the face!"

Hand sighed. "Al," she said, "I have some buddies who fought the vnorpt in the Eridani campaign. They told me that the way they used to work was they would systematically cut the vnorpt ships to pieces, and then would go in and potshot the individual vnorpt as they drifted in vacuum. The vnorpt would shell up, to hold in their air as long as possible, and they could live a couple of hours like that, long enough for another vnorpt ship to rescue them, so our side didn't just let them alone, they went in and picked them off. It usually took a couple of shots to punch through the armor and let the air out, and that was with a ship's heavy plasma cannon, not some dinky urban sidearm. Sometimes even the cannon wouldn't do the job, and they'd knock 'em down into the nearest star, instead." She shook her head. "I used to wonder sometimes whether those guys were exaggerating, or whether the vnorpt crews wore extra armor, besides what nature provided. I guess not."

Al drew her a half-liter of stout while she made this speech; he passed it over and stared up at the vnorpt.

"Better," the vnorpt said, dropping the rag, which was now coated with yellow slime, onto the bar. "Yes, vnorpt pretty tough, compared to humans. Good side to that and bad side, yes?"

"Yes," Hand agreed. "No hard feelings?"

"No anger. Pet eaten, eye shot, bumps, thumps, pokes, no big deal. Tolerance required. Accidents and inappropriate things always happen when people from different cultures interact, yes?"

"Yes," Hand said again. In a way, she was almost beginning to like the vnorpt, clumsy and obnoxious though it might be.

But she didn't want it in the Busted Fin. There were too many of those inappropriate things happening. "Al," she said, "I bet our friend here would like to meet Mickey Finn—think he'll be in tonight?"

Al looked at her, then at the vnorpt. "He might be, at that," he said. He looked up at the vnorpt. "Want another beer?"

"Yes," the vnorpt said, handing down the pitcher.

Al started filling it, and glanced sideways at Hand. He needed her to distract the vnorpt so he could add something to the drink, of course.

"So," she said, "did you fight in the Eridani campaign?"

"Didn't fight," the vnorpt said. "Not a fighter."

"So you never saw a blaster before?" Hand asked, raising her weapon again.

"Saw lots of blasters, here and there. Never shot before,

though." The vnorpt's eyes were all focused on the blaster. Hand couldn't read its expression, but thought it was wary, worried that she'd shoot it again.

"Really? What'd it feel like?"

"Hot," the vnorpt said. "Stings. Like poke in eye with sharp stick. *Very* sharp stick. Very hard poke."

"Does it still hurt?" Al had a vial of something out, and was pouring the entire contents into the pitcher of beer.

"Some."

"So does my butt," Hand said.

The four stalked eyes all seemed to stretch toward her, and she could hear the creature's surprise. "Just from fall on floor? In this gravity?"

Hand nodded. "We aren't built anywhere *near* as tough as you." Al's vial was out of sight again. She put the blaster back in its holster.

"Sorry," the vnorpt said. "Was accident. Truly."

"Here's your beer," Al said.

He and Hand watched as the vnorpt downed the entire five or six liters of lager in a single gulp. Then Hand asked Al, "So when do you think Mickey will show up?"

Al shrugged. "Could be any minute now, Captain Hand. Ought to be here in ten minutes, fifteen at the outside."

"Then I'll wait," Hand said. She looked the vnorpt up and down and sipped her own beer. "Say, would you be interested in renting a cargo lifter, later tonight?"

"I might be, at that." He glanced up at the vnorpt.

The vnorpt dropped the pitcher on the bar, and smacked its lips. "Better and better!" it said.

Hand blinked, and asked the vnorpt, "So what brings you to Daedalus?"

She and the vnorpt made small talk for the next twenty minutes, while Al grew steadily more upset, glancing constantly at the clock on the wall. The sun set as they chatted, and the glaring white of a Daedalus day gave way to the multicolored glare of the port's neon-enhanced night.

The other human customers had all managed to slip out by the end of that time, and the waitress vanished into the back room and stayed there. Various potential customers and curiosity-seekers looked in, but once they saw the vnorpt they hesitated, then withdrew—no one but Al, Hand, and the vnorpt remained in the bar.

At last Hand said to Al, "Mickey's late. Got any way to give him another call, maybe?"

Al looked up at the vnorpt and shrugged hopelessly. "I used all I had last time," he said.

"Got something you can substitute?" She looked up at the vnorpt. "Maybe something appropriate for a toast in Barnstable's memory? After all, accidents happen. Even fatal ones."

Al looked at her. "You think so?"

"I think that vnorpt are big and tough enough that yeah, they do." She looked Al straight in the eye.

He knew what she was saying—she was advising him to go ahead and poison a paying customer, on the theory that it probably wouldn't kill something as monstrous as a vnorpt.

Of course, if she was wrong, they might be guilty of conspiracy to commit murder and treaty violations, but at this point Hand no longer cared. She wanted the vnorpt out of the bar. She wanted to be able to smell something again; her nose had long ago shut down in protest at the vnorpt's stench. She wanted other customers to come in here, so she could find some decent company to drink with and maybe take back to her ship.

"Let me see what's in the back room," Al said.

Hand kept the vnorpt occupied for the next several minutes; at last Al reemerged with a box. The vnorpt didn't notice.

"Want another beer?" Al asked.

"Yes!" the vnorpt said.

A moment later it gulped down another pitcher. Then it hesitated, and said, "Um."

"Is something wrong?" Hand asked.

"Didn't taste right that time."

"Maybe you've had enough, then," Hand suggested. "You wouldn't want to get really drunk, would you?"

"Wouldn't," the vnorpt agreed. It pulled in its eyestalks and folded its feeding claws, while dropping the pitcher to the bar. "Feel bad all of a sudden."

"You've just had too much to drink," Hand said. "It hits all of a sudden like that, sometimes. Get some fresh air, walk it off, and in an hour you'll be fine."

"Beer does this?"

"If you drink too much, yeah."

It started to say something, then belched instead. "Um," it said. "Oops."

"Fresh air helps a lot," Hand said cheerfully.

It dropped its four hands to the floor, then lifted itself up. "Fresh air," it rumbled. It picked its credit chit off the bar, then turned and staggered toward the big service door.

Hand watched it go, then turned and hissed at Al, "What did you give it?"

"The first mickey was chloral hydrate," he said. "A *lot* of chloral hydrate."

"Yeah, but it just shook that right off," Hand said. "What did you give it the *second* time?"

"Rat poison," Al said, holding up the empty box. "A full kilogram."

"A *kilo* of arsenic?"

"Hey, it worked, didn't it?"

"Al, that much might even kill a vnorpt!"

"Wouldn't bother me if it did," Al replied defensively. "It ate Barnstable, and chased away my entire clientele and most of my staff! It stank up the place—I'll have to put the recirculators on emergency overload to get the smell out. It was self-defense!"

Just then they heard a sound unlike anything either of them had ever heard before, coming from just outside the service door—a deep tearing gurgle, followed by splashing.

It seemed to go on forever, but Hand knew it wasn't really more than a minute or two.

After it ceased, there were several seconds of silence. Then the vnorpt called in, "Feel much better now. Go home, sleep it off."

Neither Al nor Hand replied; they were both overcome by the incredible new reek that had managed to penetrate even their overwhelmed noses. They stood, gagging, as the vnorpt staggered away down the street.

At last Hand managed to gasp, "Better get those recirculators pumping."

Al nodded, still unable to speak. A moment later the hum of the vent-fans climbed into audibility, and the air stirred.

Unfortunately, it stirred in the wrong direction, sucking air in through the service door, which meant it carried that unbelievable new stench.

"I didn't know anything *could* smell worse than vnorpt," Hand muttered. "But it figures that if anything could, it would be vnorpt vomit."

"I'm ruined," Al gasped. "The bar'll stink for weeks! They'll probably ticket me for a public health hazard."

"Drastic measures are called for," Hand said, pulling out her blaster.

"What are you . . ."

She ignored Al as she marched across the barroom floor and looked out the service door.

Sure enough, an immense puddle filled several square meters of the street there; only the raised threshold had kept the dozens of liters of yellowish fluid from spilling into the Busted Fin.

"I hope this works," Hand said, as she fired her blaster into the center of the pool.

And with that, Hand discovered an even worse smell, one that made her senses swim and the world fade away as she tottered on the verge of fainting—the scent of *burning* vnorpt vomit.

Hand didn't falter; she kept firing, waving the blaster back and forth.

And at last the smell faded, and she found herself firing an almost-discharged blaster at empty, entirely-harmless plastic pavement.

Slowly, as the fresh evening air began to clear her mind, she slipped the blaster back into its holster and looked around thoughtfully.

The quantity just a single vnorpt had consumed was truly astonishing. An entire planet of vnorpt would be a huge market.

"You know," she said to no one in particular, "I see an opportunity here for an enterprising trader. Like me."

Then she turned and went back inside, headed for a barstool.

Selling a few shiploads of beer to the vnorpt might make her rich, but it could wait. Right now, she wanted a drink. Whiskey, maybe, or gin.

But not beer.

THE SILVER FLAME

by *Josepha Sherman*

Josepha Sherman is a fantasy writer and folklorist whose latest novels are *Highlander*: *The Captive Soul* and *Son of Darkness*. Her most recent folklore volume is *Merlin's Kin*: *World Tales of the Hero Magicians*. Her short fiction has appeared in numerous anthologies, including *Battle Magic*, *Dinosaur Fantastic*, *Black Cats and Broken Mirrors*, and *The Shimmering Door*. She lives in Riverdale, New York.

As I brought *The Dart* out of hyperspace and into the Stataka system, I called up a visual on my ship's screen. I already knew details of the planet's gravity (a touch less than Human standard) and atmosphere (quite breathable). Now I could see what the computer had already told me: Stataka really did look absolutely . . . well . . . mundane, the standard classification of water-and-land planet supporting oxygen-breathing life. In this case, that life was a slender, gray-skinned biped race, vaguely like my own species, Human, in having two eyes, ears, and so on. So, locals plus whatever space travelers might have put into Stataka's one public port.

Ordinary? Maybe, but I didn't have any complaints about a lack of drama. The latest overhaul of *The Dart*'s hyerdrive engines hadn't been cheap, and incoming cash was going to be very welcome.

As *The Dart* sliced down through Stataka's atmosphere, I could see the gray buildings and bright lights of Kartaka, the city that sprawled around the spaceport. Kartaka had quite a reputation as a wide-open trading city. And yes, there was a quite a bit of illicit business taking place down there, if Alliance reports were accurate.

But from everything I'd been able to learn, Sei Sisar, the art dealer with whom I was dealing, had a reputation for honesty. The three-way contract to which I'd agreed, along with Sei Sisar and the Kuurae, was basic enough: Sharra Kinsarin—me—owner, captain, and one-woman crew of *The Dart*, to receive one religious artifact from art dealer Sei Sisar, and transport it back to its rightful homeworld of Kuuraet. Sei Sisar was footing half the bill to get the artifact home again, and the Kuurae were footing the other half.

Nothing unusual there: Reputable art dealers, once they realize they are holding stolen artifacts, do tend to return the things to their owners, since they want to keep their names clean. They return artifacts often enough for me to make a nice profit out of it.

Who am I? Nothing special to look at: Human, youngish, female, olive skin, and short dark hair. What I am is an art courier licensed in all one hundred and forty-three of the Alliance worlds and a few others—including provisional member worlds like Kuuraet—specializing in any objects too small and valuable to risk losing on one of the big ships. I'll add that I have another edge over the big guys: my little swept-winged *Dart* is swifter than most of them. I also, not incidentally in my line of work, have an implant that lets my brain adapt quickly to new languages.

Why me, though, and not a Kuurae emissary? Simple answer: The Kuurae are one of those races who don't like space travel. I mean, they really, *really* don't. The vastness terrifies them.

I brought my ship down through the layers of atmosphere, and a maze of other ships taking off or landing, to a waiting berth.

Sure enough, the ground crew insisted on bribes, but in such a good-natured way that I couldn't get angry. Besides, if things went according to contract, Sei Sisar would be covering this expense, too.

We settled on a price that included keeping *The Dart* ready for takeoff, and I set off to find my current employer. Daylight on this side of the planet, conveniently, which meant that I could get the artifact from Sei Sisar without any other delays. It would have made my life easier if someone had been waiting at the port with the object to be transported: signature, payment, refueling, and away. But Sei Sisar had insisted he was too busy for anything like that. Since I legally had to accept the artifact from him and only him, I was to meet him at his office, which he swore wasn't that far from the spaceport.

So be it. I fought my way through the crowds of embarking or disembarking travelers, fought my way into an empty groundcar, and gave it the proper coordinates, trying not to wince at the amount of credits it wanted for that relatively short ride. Should have walked—no, on second thought, this warehouse region wasn't exactly the place for a solitary stroll, even if I had included, as I always did when planning to carry art, my sidearm. Too bad Sei Sisar hadn't told me to meet him in his shop downtown; more people meant less of a chance of some would-be robber following me.

As the car made its efficient robotic way through row after row of dull gray warehouses and the occasional flurry of pallet-unloading activity, I glanced one more time at the little image I'd downloaded. The Kurrae artifact's name translated to the "Silver Flame," though there wasn't anything flamelike about the tranquil, cross-legged, beautifully carved statue. It was a female Kurrae, thin and delicate as all her kind, vaguely humanoid, assuming that Humans had knife-sharp cheekbones, huge eyes, and faint scaling, and worked from what looked like pure white stone. A saint figure? No one knew too much about Kuurae religious beliefs.

"We are .456 kilometers from the given coordinates," the flat AI voice told me suddenly. "I can proceed no closer."

I looked up in surprise—surprise that quickly turned to alarm. "Oh . . . damn."

What had been Sei Sisar's office was now a blackened ruin, still smoking faintly. Leaving the groundcar, I got as close as harried officials would let me. A fire, they told me unnecessarily. No survivors. No cause yet, though there were hints that it had been too hot to be natural, and maybe that there were some suspicious residues as well.

Well, as I've said, a lot of illicit business takes place in this city. Presumably someone had gotten annoyed at Sei Sisar for being too honest once too often.

No Sei Sisar. That meant no artifact. And no payment. Swearing under my breath and reminding myself that the late Sei Sisar had just had a rougher time of it, I turned back to the waiting groundcar—

Which was no longer waiting. Of course not, curse it! In my shock over the fire, I'd neglected to tell the thing to stay put. And I doubted I'd find another car so easily in this area.

All right. Start walking. You can find the spaceport again easily enough. Pretend you belong here, even though you don't look like a local.

Hell with trying to fit in. I'd just radiate my best "mess with me and die" expression and keep one hand on my sidearm. That worked on a good many worlds.

But as I strode defiantly along, a sudden whisper made me start.

"Captain Kinsarin! Please!"

I whirled, sidearm drawn. Who could possibly know my name—

The frantic hiss had come from a narrow space, not even a true alley, between two buildings. A slight figure huddled against one wall as though making a decision, then came toward me in a rush. I tightened my hand on the sidearm's haft, ready to fire—but he—she?—it?—stopped short just out of reach, almost completely shrouded in a cloak two or three sizes too big and charred at the edges. Looked as though there'd been a survivor of that fire, after all.

"Please, please, I am not harming you. Captain Kinsarin, you must be taking me off this world!"

I wasn't about to get involved in some gang's activities. Bad enough that this being, who or whatever, knew my name. "Sorry. I don't carry passengers."

"I am not that! You must know this: I am what you seek—I am the Silver Flame!"

"Ah . . . of course you are." *And how do you know what brought me to Stataka? . . .*

"No, wait!" A thin hand, six-fingered, not quite steady, and dead white, pushed back the shrouding hood just enough to let me see a dead-white face with enormous deep blue eyes and narrow, knife-sharp cheekbones.

She hadn't looked so weary in the image. Or so terrified.

The smallest pang of sympathy shot through me—along with a sense of downright "I've been had."

"Oh, hell," I said lamely.

The average Kuurae had tannish skin. This one wasn't an albino, not with those eyes. A mutation, then, and held sacred as a result. When you came right down to it, the contract had never actually specified a holy *statue* rather than a holy *living being*. And no one had ever actually agreed or denied that the artifact might be much more than merely stone.

But why the pretense of an artifact at all? To keep the matter private? Or . . . to make it more convenient. . . .

A cold suspicion settled at the back of my mind. It could well be.

Yes, but now that I had the "artifact," I also had a chance of getting paid by the Kuurae if not by Sei Sisar. Risky, if my suspicions were correct, but—if I wanted a safe, secure life, I would have joined one of the big corporations a long time ago. My ship could hold two as easily as one, so I added, "All right, let's get going."

"Yes, but—"

"You *do* want to get back to Kuuraet?"

"Yes! But *they* do not want it!"

They. I whirled to see four . . . beings. Definitely not from this world. Strongly muscled, tall as the average Human male, they stood on two legs, had a great deal of russet fur, gaudy jewelry, and sharp teeth—and they carried vicious-looking sidearms.

Great.

"Do you know them?" I whispered to the Silver Flame.

"They are of those who stole me!"

Even better. For a moment I thought of screaming and hoping that some of those officials going over the fire-charred ruins would come running.

Not a chance.

"Get behind me," I snapped. When the Silver Flame hesitated, I tried to push her.

"Don't touch me!" Her voice was suddenly that of an insulted aristocrat.

Oh, joy. "Just do it!" To the beings, I asked as coolly as though I wasn't looking at all those weapons, "You want her?"

Unfortunately, they didn't speak the local language. They also weren't giving my implant enough of a sample for me to understand theirs. But most kidnappers don't look so angry—that emotion, at least, I could understand on those furry faces—or so willing to shoot their own hostage.

I pointed my own weapon at the one who, judging from the glittery stuff about his (I assumed) neck, seemed to be their leader. Since they couldn't understand me either, I quoted from some ancient Human vid in the archaic Earth language and said, "Go ahead. Make my day."

The bluff worked. He held back the others, and in their moment of angry confusion I hissed to the Silver Flame, "Run!"

She avoided my shoving hand and darted away. Those ridiculously narrow alleys were almost too narrow for me. But as I squeezed my way through, following the slight figure of the Silver Flame, who had shed her bedraggled cloak to reveal a formfitting white sheath, I thought they at least served one purpose: They were too narrow for our hairy pursuers. One of those folks got off a blue-white shot of blazing force that sent stony splinters raining down on me, but I managed to return a shot of my own, and heard what was unmistakably a swear word from back there.

Yes, that smarted, didn't it? Too bad I don't have it set on killing force.

You didn't do that, not and risk killing a local by mistake.

The hairy guys weren't worried about public relations. They continued shooting blindly, bringing down more stones. Swearing, head down, stung by splinters and pelted by pebbles, I forced my way on.

Lunging out into the open again, I nearly crashed into the Silver Flame, who had stopped short.

"Don't *touch* me!" she insisted.

The being was beginning to get on my already tightly strung nerves. *Payment,* I reminded myself. *You've got the contract.*

We'd come onto a street fronted by closed warehouses. By sheer wild fortune, I commandeered a groundcar. Feeding it credits till it agreed to take us at top speed to the spaceport, I collapsed back on the thinly padded seat, struggling to catch my breath and staring at the seemingly self-possessed Silver Flame. "What the hell was that all about?"

She stared at me with those enormous blue eyes. "They wanted me back."

"Sure they did. That's why they were trying to kill us."

Her gaze never wavered. "That, I know not why."

"Of course not," I said dryly.

"I know not why," she repeated stubbornly, and turned away from me, falling resolutely silent, a white statue. And I, I thought, *Her people really are going to pay for this, they are, indeed.*

Still . . . maybe she was just scared? That wouldn't be surprising. Maybe she just didn't know how to—

"This car reeks," the Silver Flame said coldly, and killed my sympathy in that instant.

The car's AI couldn't be insulted, of course. "Kartaka, Spaceport," it announced.

No furry beings anywhere to be seen. Maybe we were going to get out of here in one piece. . . .

Yes, and surprise, surprise, the ground crew had been honorable in their bribe-taking. *The Dart* sat ready, looking sleek and narrow as its namesake, glinting in the sunlight. Beautiful, I thought with a surge of pride.

"Small," the Silver Flame summed up.

Oh, no, she wasn't going to anger me so easily! "After you, Your Saintliness," I said and ushered her inside without touching her. I didn't even attempt to help her strap herself in.

Our furry foes were still nowhere to be seen, but I asked for immediate takeoff clearance just in case. No problem there; another ship was already waiting for the berth. I sent *The Dart* soaring up through the atmosphere and the maze of air traffic, back out into the freedom of space.

Setting the ship's computer for Kuuraet's coordinates, I also sent off a quick, private, just-in-case message to the Alliance outpost nearest to that world. The Alliance is, of course, basically a trading organization, but it does have its defense branch. Granted, space is big and messages take time to arrive, but even so, I felt a little better for the sending—

And only then stopped to think that I had a Kuurae with me—a member of a race who couldn't endure space travel. If she went into shock—worse, I thought in sudden fastidious alarm, if she got spacesick in these close quarters—

But the Silver Flame . . . merely sat, her white face unreadable once more.

All right, so at least one Kuurae could manage space travel. I wasn't so sure about her reaction to hyperspace. I'm a rarity among Humans, one of the few who can travel through that nowhere noplace without needing to be drugged. But that utter lack of anything recognizable has been known to drive many beings insane.

Did I have anything that would safely drug a Kuurae? "What do your people take to get through hyperspace?"

Those great blue eyes gave me a sharp sideways glance. "My people do not go through hyperspace."

"Your, uh, kidnappers couldn't have come all this way by sublight speed."

"No. But I do not know what was done."

"Great." As I rummaged through my medkit, wishing I had just a little more medical data about her race in the computer than a standard "biped, warm-blooded," and the basics of pulse and respiration rates, I asked, "Are you going to tell me what was going on back there?"

"You do not question me." It was that autocratic tone again.

"Hell I don't. This is my ship, and that pretty much gives me sovereignty rights."

"You do not question me!"

"You know, I could really start not to like—" No. Wait. She really had been through a lot lately, enough to drive a weaker person into shock. I couldn't tell how old she was, either. For all I knew, the Silver Flame might have been nothing more than a child.

In a much gentler tone, I said, "It's all right. You don't have to be afraid. *The Dart*'s a swift ship, and I'll have you home before—"

"This is not a ship, but a *toy!* And I was not afraid."

"Have it your way. But I need to know if we're going to run into any more trouble."

"I am not a prophet."

No. You're a pain in the— "Who were they? At least tell me that!"

"You do not question me!"

"Look, I have no intention of meddling in Kuurae affairs—"

"You do not question me!"

A spark flared where her hand clenched the armrest, a wisp of smoke began to rise, and with it, the first hint of a flame—

I acted in pure instinct, practically tearing her from the seat, not even knowing how I'd unfastened the harness, and tossed her aside so hard that she went crashing to the cabin floor, stunned with shock. Of course I have a fire extinguisher in the cabin, and had the tiny flame out in about three seconds. But I lingered over the work for a few minutes more, trying to get my heartbeat back down to normal.

A pyrokinetic. The Silver Flame was a pyrokinetic. Rare, any type of psionic gifts, rarer still this sort.

I was still too angry and, yes, too scared, to care. Dragging her back up, I plopped her back into the seat, aware only now of how downright hot her skin felt.

"You *idiot!*" I shouted. "God of Worlds, you utter *idiot!* Starting a fire in a spaceship, a closed environment surrounded by space—what were you trying to do? Kill us both?"

She blinked up at me. "I did not think—"

"That seems pretty clear! Damn it, I could, by every law, throw you out of *The Dart* into space here and now!"

"Yes." It was the merest whisper.

A pyrokinetic.

God of Worlds, yes, I was on this ship with a—a psionic fire-starter.

Something clicked into place in my mind. "The fire," I said. "Sei Sisar's office . . . the whole building. That was your doing."

Her head drooped like that of a scolded child. "Was."

"But . . . why? And, damn it, don't give me that 'You must not question' nonsense!"

"It was not meant . . ." Her voice trembled. "I thought only of . . . escape. I had escaped. Sei Sisar . . . he has dealt with the Kuurae, so to him I fled. He helped. Sei Sisar contacted Kuuraet. And you."

She looked up at me. For the first time I saw genuine emotion clear in those big eyes, and was pretty sure it was sorrow. Of a sort, anyhow. And I thought, *I was right. Wasn't I?*

"How old are you?" I asked her suddenly. "By your people's standards, I mean."

Reluctantly, she confessed, "In years, not yet of the Grown. But I am the Silver Flame!"

An adolescent. No, an adolescent pyrokinetic. "No one's denying that. Please. What else happened, back on Stataka?"

"It was not a true escape, not for me. They are the Uwartai. And they found me. And I . . . they . . . I . . . did not mean to harm Sei Sisar. But I feared. So greatly I feared."

"And you panicked."

Her head drooped again. "Did."

Was she regretting what had happened? Or, I wondered uneasily, merely regretting her lack of control? I would almost have been willing to give her the proverbial benefit of the doubt . . . if only I hadn't seen that flame spark into life under her hand. What happened if she panicked again, here, aboard my ship?

But some more pieces were clicking into place. "They, the, uh, Uwar-tai kidnapped you to be a weapon, didn't they?"

"It was so. They wanted a storm of fire to sweep away their foes. But I—I cannot do that, not so wide a fire! They . . . they would not believe me."

"Hell," I said softly. "And they still don't."

A ship was forming on the view screen. From its coordinates, it could only have come from Stataka. And from its size and downright predatory shape, it could only be a warship.

Fight or flight? "First," I said, "let's see what they have to say."

"But you don't speak their language!"

I grinned. "Don't worry. I will."

"But—no! They are not truth-sayers! They will be false!"

Ignoring her, I opened a communications channel, standard Alliance frequency. Would they know it? Or were they really just the "shoot first" type?

Not quite.

The first words their glittery-necklaced leader said were, of course, unintelligible to me. Those were the most dangerous moments, when I didn't answer and they might lose patience.

Then the implant went to work, and after a dizzy moment, I was able to identify myself and my ship in reasonably smooth Uwar-taik. "Why do you follow us?"

"You know why! We are not at war with you—yet. Surrender that . . . thing and go your way."

I glanced at the Silver Flame, who had gone into her rigid statue-mode. "Sorry. Can't do that without a really good reason."

"She has killed!"

"So, I don't doubt, have you. So, for that matter, have I. In her case, it was self-defense."

"No!" That was a teeth-baring roar. "No! Never that! That *thing* you harbor is a foulness! She has *killed!*"

The full meaning of the word suddenly translated. With a shock, I realized that what he really meant was: Murder.

"Not!" the Silver Flame protested, but very softly. "Not."

"I don't deny she killed," I countered the Uwar-tai leader. "But only after you . . ." There didn't seem to be a word in Uwar-taik for "kidnapped." "After you stole her away from her, uh, pack."

"She murdered!" he roared. "Not honorably, not battled-red—she murdered my pack-brother!"

"Wait. Wait! I'm, uh, honor-tied to return her to her people. Then we can bring the whole matter before an Alliance court—"

"No courts! Blood!"

With that melodramatic howl, he broke contact.

"Hang on," I told the Silver Flame. "We'll shake them in hyper—"

But I didn't dare go into hyperspace! I hadn't a clue as to what would happen to a Kuurae—and the thought of a Kuurae pyrokinetic going berserk—

"Never mind," I amended. "*The Dart*'s fast enough in sublight."

Manual controls now . . . send *The Dart* zooming straight for a moon, slingshot around it and come back toward the enemy. Bank aside, slip past them, more agile than they. Damn, but their pilot turned almost at once, following me.

All right, my friend, try this!

I hurled my swift *Dart* around another moon, then onward through a maze of asteroids, banking this way, that, never quite in danger, never quite out of it. We were pulling away from the enemy, and I felt my lips peel back from my teeth in a sharp grin. We were going to—

"No!" the Silver Flame shrieked suddenly. "No, no, can't—can't stand—no!"

I gave her a quick, sideways glance and saw wild hysteria in her eyes. There was a limit to even this Kuurae space-endurance.

And where her hands clenched the armrests of her seat, smoke was beginning to rise. . . .

"Land," she screamed at me, "please, please! Land!"

Or go up in flames. Not exactly a choice. I did a quick, frantic scan: We were much too far from Stataka by now to return there, I didn't dare risk pushing the Silver Flame all the way over the edge by going into hyperspace, and nothing safe was near enough. . . .

Ha, yes. Maybe. That wasn't much of a planet, barely more than a moon, but it had rudimentary vegetation, atmosphere, and gravity. Enough to allow an emergency landing. Once the Silver Flame calmed down a little, I'd try whatever tranquilizers wouldn't kill her—

"Land!" she shrieked in my ear, and I jumped so violently I almost sent *The Dart* into a nose-dive.

"Shut up!" I shouted back at her, and won enough startled silence to let me concentrate on bringing my ship down safely. Popping the hatch, I said, "See? Solid land."

And then went into a coughing fit, because the air really wasn't thick enough to breathe.

That didn't seem to bother the Silver Flame. She was up and out of *The Dart* before I could unfasten my harness. By the time I caught up with her, she was dancing about easily in the light gravity, her face a white mask but her eyes blazing.

Let her play a little, I told myself. *Calm herself down.*

It was only play. Just a young thing letting off tension. Only play.

Then why was I suddenly so unnerved? Why was I thinking that very little I'd seen her do so far had been, when you came right down to it, rational?

Let her play, I amended, *then tranquilize the . . . fire out of her.*

I alternated between frantically checking the readings on my medkit and just as frantically scanning the nearly black sky, looking for a moving dot. Our pursuers, even if they caught up with us, couldn't land here, not with that big warship of theirs, but I prayed they didn't have something powerful enough to scorch this whole little planetoid.

Evidently not. Unfortunately, what they did have was a shuttle.

"Visitors," I snapped to the Silver Flame.

But she danced lightly out of my reach.

"Damn it," cough, "this isn't a time for," cough, "games! Don't you," cough, cough, "want to get home?"

The shuttle was landing. Cursing under my breath and fighting down further coughing, I drew my sidearm. If she wasn't going to come back, I was going to shoot her and pray the force only stunned her.

At this stage, I wasn't going to be praying too hard, either.

Damn! There was the enemy, ten . . . no, fifteen of them, led by that glittery-necklaced fellow. Suddenly the Silver Flame was back at my side, her eyes still bright.

"They shall die."

It was said so cheerfully that a cold shiver raced up my spine. "I thought you said you couldn't do that, not a fire that size!"

"I can. Will."

"But—no! Wait!"

God of Worlds, she meant it. And seeing that too-tranquil face and those wide, bright eyes, I knew the truth: The Silver Flame was nowhere near sanity.

The Uwar-tai had drawn their weapons, too, stalking warily forward. They didn't know; they weren't close enough to feel the heat radiating from the Silver Flame. In another second they were going to be a fireball, fifteen beings destroyed without a chance—

"Damn it, no!"

Maybe it wasn't the brightest thing I've done. I mean, I've never been the Willing Sacrifice. But the thought of watching fifteen murders—no! I threw myself between the Silver Flame and the Uwar-tai.

And she hurled fire at me. I dropped, rolled, and came up shooting. Yes, my weapon was still set only to stunning force, and for a moment I was sure that wouldn't be enough.

But with a sigh almost of disappointment, the Silver Flame crumpled.

The Uwar-tai came hurrying forward. *Now*, I thought, *I'm going to die.*

But what happened was that their leader beat out the flames in my clothing that I hadn't even felt.

Shaken, I looked up at him. "Thanks."

"I am Haimarg, pack-leader."

"I am Sharra Kinsarin, uh, of my own pack."

"Why do what you just did?" he asked, nose wrinkled in what I guessed was confusion. "Life-risking for an enemy?"

I got to my feet, standing between him and the Silver Flame just in case, not sure where this was going. "I don't like murder. Yes, and for the record," a phrase that didn't really work in his language, "I also don't like kidnapping."

That word didn't quite work in his language either, but it was close enough. Haimarg's lips drew back in a silent snarl. "You place honor-debt on me."

"Do I? Then tell me what this was all about, and call that a settlement."

He hissed at that, as did his fellows, and it took me an alarmed few seconds to realize the sound was an Uwar-tai laugh. "Courage as well as honor," Haimarg commented to the others. "Interesting." He turned back to me with the faintest lift of a lip. "It was not I who stole that creature."

Daringly, I suggested, "Your pack-brother."

"It is so. We are a warrior race; we fight with honor. But . . ."

"Killing from afar isn't honorable, is it? Your pack-brother wanted a weapon that would do just that."

Oh, smart move! He was at my side in a second, weapon against my neck, predator's breath hot on my cheek, and I froze, not even daring to breathe.

But then Haimarg released me with a grunt. "Courage,"

he repeated. "Yes. Muraik made that mistake, for the good of the people. That creature . . . killed him."

Time for another bout of courage. Or was that foolhardiness? "Seems to me the debts and wrongs are equaling out here. She wouldn't have had the chance to kill your pack-brother if he hadn't kidnapped her to use as a weapon."

Haimarg snarled, and his warriors echoed him. But in a flurry of motion, he was back among them, calling to me, "Get that creature back in your ship. We will follow, to be sure it reaches its home world."

Right. The Silver Flame was still breathing, and I think I was relieved at that. I tugged her back into *The Dart*, got her strapped in like a cocoon, just in case she did wake up before we reached Kuuraet. And off we went, with our . . . military escort.

It was a blessedly uneventful voyage until we actually reached Kuuraet. Then, all my instincts uneasy, I sent a message to Haimarg, "Stand ready."

"Understood."

His ship vanished into the planetary shadow.

Oh, my instincts weren't playing me false! As I'd suspected back on Stataka, when I'd first found myself facing a live being, not a stone artifact, I'd been set up. The Kuurae knew their holy being, their Silver Flame, wasn't exactly sane, and they didn't want the news publicized. Who would care if one small ship and one Human met with a tragic accident? Maybe the Kuurae didn't like deep space, but that didn't stop them from launching what might have been the only warship in their fleet.

That, of course, was when Haimarg brought his own ship out of hiding.

And joy of joys, there I was, caught between them.

I quickly opened channels to both ships. "Looks like I'm the translator here," I said in both languages. Switching to the Kuurae tongue, I told them, "You know who I've got here. And I know what you tried to do. Meet the Uwar-tai. Want to fight them?"

To the Uwar-tai, I said, "They're dishonorable, I agree. But I'm afraid they *are* members of the Alliance." Provisional only, but this wasn't the time to argue fine points. "That's one hundred and forty-two planets. Want a war with all them?"

"If we leave," Haimarg said, and a hiss of Uwar-tai laughter was in his voice, "then the Kuurae destroy you."

Yes. I'd thought of that problem. "Anyone out there?" I called over another channel, using Alliance Standard.

And to my utter relief, a voice answered, "Got your message. Here we are."

Three warships, three languages, and an awkward situation defused. Oh, and yes, I delivered the Silver Flame, through the Alliance, to the Kuurae, and the Kuurae delivered, through the Alliance, the total amount due me. The Uwar-tai, curious about the Alliance, agreed to preliminary discussions about membership.

Who knows? I might even get some new clients out of this. But right now, I'm heading for a brief vacation on Pentaiia. You may have heard of it. It's an all-water world.

No chance of . . . stray flames.

STARDUST

by Jean Rabe

When not writing, Jean Rabe feeds her goldfish, visits museums, and attends gaming conventions. A former newspaper reporter, she is the author of nine fantasy novels, including the *Dragonlance* Fifth Age Trilogy. Her latest novel is *Dhamon: The Downfall*. She has written numerous fantasy and science fiction short stories which appear in such anthologies as *Merlin* and *Tales from the Eternal Archives: Legends*, and she edits a BattleTech magazine for the FASA Corporation.

"In a lot of ways, they're just like us."

Luis gave her a curious look, clearly not understanding what she was talking about.

"The stars," Reah explained. "The stars're just like us." She was slender and dainty, not quite reaching five feet, her voice soft and seemingly appropriate.

Skinny, Luis had decided the day he met her in the spaceport, almost too skinny. She was wearing a tight chic outfit then, wrists and elbows and hipbones protruding, flesh taut against her jaw, teeth tiny and flawless. Her diminutive stature made it easy for her to curl up in the pilot's chair, despite her bulky flight suit, right leg tucked beneath her, left hugged to her body, the way a teenager might sit. She pointed at the view screen, her arm looking child-small despite the insulated fabric.

Luis' eyes followed her gloved finger. Displayed against the blackness of space was a glowing white ball the size of a plum. Haloed by red wisps, it looked eerily ghostlike, yet at the same time dramatic.

"They're born, they live, and they die. The stars." She pushed a strand of honey-colored hair from her eyes. Even her hair seemed thin, lying close to her head and cropped short like a cap, silky strands all in place and shimmering softly in the glow of the console lights. She released a sigh that sounded like fall leaves shushing together, cocked her head, and indicated the chair beside her. "They just happen to live ten billion or so years longer than we do."

Luis edged forward, groaning when he brushed his head against the ceiling of the cramped compartment. He wasn't a tall man. Indeed, he thought of himself as short at five-nine, but he had broad shoulders and a slight paunch, both of which were accentuated by the suit. He squeezed by Reah and sat in the only other chair on what passed for the bridge. It wasn't a good fit, knees pressed up against a control panel, shoulders rounded and shaved head making him look a bit like a crab scrunched up in a silvery shell. He pulled his head close to his chest and tilted it so he could see both the star and the pilot.

There was a hint of gentility to her heart-shaped face, which was smooth and unblemished and oh-so-pale. She'd seen plenty of suns, he knew that from the ship's flight log, but he suspected she rarely walked on some planet beneath one, never let its rays tan that perfect milky skin. Pity, he thought. She could do with some color. Still, the paleness seemed to suit her, making her look like an antique China doll, fragile and hiding her years. She appeared twenty, but he knew she was a little more than twice that, nearly his own age.

"N-G-C seven-oh-seven-eight," Reah stated, still pointing at the star. "What we came so damn far out here for."

"It's beautiful," he managed.

"Ah, and that's where stars're different from us," she continued, leaning forward and somehow looking graceful and catlike doing so. She nudged a lever, coaxing the ship in closer, but much slower now than it had been traveling. She flipped another switch. "Dad?"

There was a crackle of static.

"Dad, better get ready. It'll be another thirty-five, forty minutes and we'll be in position."

Another crackle.

"No. There's no sign of your pirates or any other company for that matter. We're blessedly all alone this time." She thumbed the switch off and reached down to her side, retrieving a helmet and balancing it on her knee.

"You were saying . . ." her visitor prompted.

Her turn to look confused.

"The difference . . ." Luis prompted.

"Oh. The difference between us an' them. When people get old, Luis, they shrivel. Stars do, too, in a sense. But people just dry up, fall ill. They get so . . . ugly. Their breath stinks, an' their teeth rot. Their flesh sags, an' they're shoved away in homes waiting for the day their hearts'll stop an' they'll quit being a burden to society. Not stars. Watch." Still balancing the helmet, Reah stretched to a panel on her right, arm intentionally brushing across Luis' leg. She pushed a series of buttons and the screen shimmered for an instant. She pushed several more and sat back.

"Beautiful," he repeated.

"The screen combines visible and infrared light, sorta like the lens of a telescope, showing you what your eyes can't otherwise see."

The red wisps were joined by a pink mist, slightly darker close to the sun, diaphanous and fading to nothing farther away, where it touched a glistening blue haze that seemed to swell and recede, as if the star was breathing.

"All the colors, they're layers of gas and dust, the red is the dissipating molecular shell of the star." Reah's voice was detached, clinical, sounding like a professor lecturing to an apt pupil. "There is a thin transition between the ionized region of the star and the otherwise invisible atmosphere. Most of the stars we've visited are more impressive. The butterfly of the bipolar planetary nebula M-two-nine, the Cats Eye, the Hourglass, the central stars of the Cotton Candy Nebula and the Silkworm Nebula, stellar pinwheels, globes within globes. This one is rather mundane. Once a star starts to die, it takes about thirty thousand years. And the closer a star is to death, the more amazing it becomes." The last was said with a tinge of reverence, the first real emotion Luis noted in her voice. "All their lives stars wage a war against gravity, the crushing weight of their outer layers struggling against the core. When they start to lose the war, the outer layers press against the inner ones, and in the process the stars exhaust their supply of hydrogen. Their cores contract, becoming denser and hotter, becoming first red giants, then white dwarfs. Then they go supernova, exploding with a light a million times brighter than they were in life. And in dying, they breathe life into space."

Reah fitted the helmet on her suit, but flipped up the faceplate so she could still regard Luis. "Decaying stars, the ones that go supernova, throw off iron and oxygen. The small ones spit out carbon, like this one is starting to do. So in essence, humans and animals, plants, much of what is on Earth and other habitable worlds is made of dying stars. We are stardust." She laughed lightly. "But then you already know all of that, don't you, Luis? That's what you're here for. That's why you paid so much for this ride."

"What we're all here for," he returned. Luis was sweating, not from the company or his ever-present nerves, but from the temperature. Despite the refrigeration of the ship and his flight suit, the heat was becoming more intense as they neared NGC7078. Space was cold, but not this close to a star, not in this ship, so large it had as much gravity as an asteroid. He extricated himself from the chair and squeezed by Reah as she flipped her faceplate down. He didn't see any sweat on her face.

"Dad's waiting for you," she said, her soft voice barely audible through the tinted mask.

Luis made his way through a narrow corridor, pressing his face against the walls every few yards. The walls were supercooled, and thus provided some relief. He tried to wipe the sweat away from his forehead, but it was a futile gesture. Should've railed against the Colonies' latest style, he thought, not shaved his head and let his graying hair soak up some of the water. Or perhaps he should've rethought this whole venture. He caught himself when the ship lurched, swinging around. A moment later and he was in one of the massive bays, a dozen suited men in front of him, all overshadowed by massive pieces of equipment they were inspecting and adjusting.

Luis purposefully strode toward the tallest man, the only one not wearing a helmet. "Sean . . ."

"Captain Melka," the figure corrected. The man was like his daughter only in that he moved gracefully. The captain towered over Luis. He was large, but not heavy, with long limbs, the thick muscles of which were hidden by the suit. His skin was dark, like oiled walnut. Caucasian, Luis knew the captain's skin had been darkened by his close exposure to dozens of dying stars. There were minute traces along his cheeks where sun blisters had been surgically removed, but for the most part his skin looked like smooth leather. His long black hair was tied at the base of his neck with a cord studded with tiny meteorite fragments. There were only sparse strands of silvery gray on the sides and peppering his short beard and bushy eyebrows.

He could have easily passed for fifty, Luis was certain, though he knew Captain Melka had recently celebrated his eightieth birthday. Perhaps living away from Earth, Mars, O'loth Four, and even the Dartmoth Colonies contributed to his and his daughter's youthfulness. Living away from the pollution and the press of people riddled with germs, away from planetary gravity and man-generated radiation. Luis envied the captain his longevity, but he wouldn't trade lifestyles to gain a few extra decades. Everyone eventually died.

Even the stars.

There were only a few wrinkles at the edges of the captain's unblinking eyes. Luis tried to look away, but found himself held by the old man's stare, as if he were caught in a vise. Those eyes were a milky blue, like Reah's, but where hers were placid and practically emotionless, the captain's were wide and wild. There was something dangerous and uncertain hiding behind them, madness perhaps, a keen intelligence. They filled Luis' vision and rooted him to the bay floor.

"Captain. Yes. Captain Melka. Sorry, sir," Luis finally managed "I am . . ."

"Late," Melka finished. "With my daughter again. No matter. We're not in as much of a hurry this go 'round. No sign of pirates."

"Pirates, Captain?"

The eyes narrowed and menace flickered behind them. "I've been plagued by them the past two years. I thought you knew. Mining companies trying to profit from my expertise."

Luis nodded. He remembered some mention of raiders in the bar at the spaceport, but he hadn't paid much attention. He was there only to talk Sean Melka into doing a little mining for him. Melka's fee was extraordinary, but Luis' family had the money—and would gain much, much more if this endeavor was successful. Luis explained he was looking for a certain type of star, and Melka knew how to find just what Luis wanted. But Captain Melka wouldn't tell him where they were going—not until moments before they left the port. And until Reah called it NGC7078, Luis didn't know the star's designation.

"I don't tell anyone where I'm going anymore," Melka had explained. "No flight plans. I don't even tell my crew. 'Sides, none of them have families. They don't need to be calling anybody." He pointed to his forehead. "Only I know the course up front. That way there're no leaks."

Luis learned during the voyage that while it takes a long while for a star to die, there are a few key and relatively brief points within that time frame when it releases the purest of substances, including high-grade neutrinos, bringing top dollar to those with the equipment and the courage to gather them. And at other precise stages, previously unknown elements were also belched out into space, these being the most sought after of substances. Miners could name their prices for these on Earth or the Dartmoth Colonies or sell them to the highest bidder at public or clandestine auctions. And Captain Melka, who had made a fortune several times over, and who had a few elements named for him and his daughter, was known for mining stars at just the right time. Apparently it was that knack and knowledge that caused the "pirates" to follow him rather than pursue their own planetary nebulae.

Lewis listened as Melka explained that they plundered his finds after he left a star to reach a port and drop his first load of cargo, raping the gases and particles so his return visit was like drilling for oil in a near-dry field. Once they were so close on his proverbial heels that he wasn't even able to fill his holds a first time. They chased him away with their lasers. Melka's ship was only lightly armed; weapons cut down on cargo space. The captain said he had been pestered thus only a handful of times. But it was apparent those times had birthed the suspicions and unease that now plagued the old man, perhaps contributing to that mad glint in his eyes. Melka's was not the only mining vessel so opportunized. Indeed, the larger operations were more frequent targets. But perhaps those few who had discovered Melka's routes, these "pirates" as the captain called them, profited more than the ones who chased other miners.

The old man knew more about dying stars and mining them than Earth's greatest physicists and astronomers. All that priceless knowledge stored away behind those wild, mad eyes.

"Pirates, yes," Luis said. "I understand your concern. But . . ."

"You should be wearing a helmet, DeBeers." Captain Melka put his own on, pushing his black hair up inside and locking the rim in place. The faceplate up, his eyes still held Luis.

"I misplaced it," Luis said. "Somewhere. When I was walking through the ship."

The captain made a gesture, and a spare helmet was brought for Luis.

"Are you certain you wish to join us, DeBeers?"

Luis nodded.

"Out there, *boy?*"

Another nod, more pronounced.

"The heat can be crippling." There was no trace of concern in the voice. The captain spoke evenly and matter-of-factly. "It has overcome veteran miners before. And you are certainly not a miner."

"You've been paid well. I want to be part of this. All of it."

A hint of a smile crept across Melka's face, then it was quickly banished. The faceplate was slapped down. Another gesture, and the dozen miners in the bay moved toward the great doors. They looked to Luis like squat, farcical land-birds in their bulky suits. Luis realized he looked the same, perhaps a little squatter because of his sedentary build.

When the doors opened, the chilling protection of the ship vanished and a wave of profound heat washed inside. Luis found himself gasping and reeling, struggling to stay on his feet as the miners trudged by him and out into space, tethered to the ship by umbilicals. A line had been attached to Luis, too, though he couldn't remember who'd done it. Couldn't for an instant remember why he was here. Could only think of the heat, which seemed to have a presence. It was a thing alive, threatening and smothering, a terrify-ing invisible monster that with each breath Luis took made him tremble. His lungs felt dry, and he couldn't swallow. Sweat streamed down his face and evaporated, only to be replaced by more sweat. His eyes burned and he blinked, but there were no tears to soothe them.

"Are you sure you're joining us, DeBeers?" This from Captain Melka, who stood poised by the door.

Luis heard him plainly, despite the suit and the meters that separated them.

"DeBeers?" The voice was coming from inside Luis' hel-met. He nodded and slowly moved forward, each step dif-ficult in the heat.

Then for a heartbeat the discomfort was disregarded, as Luis stood at the door and stared out at NGC7078. The plume had grown to fill space, blindingly breathtaking. The red-and-pink mist, the blue haze was gone, there being no filter on his faceplate to see the particles. There was only the immense brightness, which was repressed by the visor to prevent the miners from going blind. Luis gaped in utter amazement. The star had seemed so small on the view screen, and now he couldn't see it all. The miners were silhouetted against it, black drops of ink on white paper. One was motioning for him to move.

He considered retreating into the bowels of the ship. Luis DeBeers did not have to join the miners, could find some small window from which to watch them. It would be safer, the heat not so suffocating. And yet his family had paid well for him to be here, for the captain's services.

So bright.

He took a step out, expecting to fall as if he'd stepped off the roof of a tall building. Instead, he floated, away from the ship and into the oven of space. He remembered to use the controls on the suit, steering himself toward the largest figure, Captain Melka. Despite those unnerving eyes, Luis found comfort in being near the big man. He fumbled with the refrigeration panel, turning the cooling gauges as high as the suit allowed. The meter indicated a change in temperature, but he didn't notice it. There was only the monstrous heat.

Behind him, the equipment was guided out—by a dozen more miners who had come down into the bay. Fully half of Melka's crew was out of the ship now, all hovering around equipment that was being unfolded and positioned. It looked like huge, delicate insects, with net wings for collecting particles, cones and cubes that would draw in gases, spindly hollow legs capable of absorbing neutrinos. Few miners had the equipment to contain the latter.

Luis didn't understand precisely how the equipment worked, knew only that it did work, as evidenced by Captain Melka's impressive credentials. And he knew that it was more expensive than the ship that hauled it from dying sun to dying sun. The mining gear was able to withstand the heat-stress of a star for short periods, as were the suits. Luis was told he would hear a chime when it was time for him to return to the ship for a "cool down," which would help preserve the suit and himself.

There was more equipment on the ship that would store the collected elements, computers that would record amounts and purity, gather data on the star's death throes. Information was also marketable.

Drones were gliding about, aiding the miners in nudging the equipment closer to the sun, black against white, everything looking like hieroglyphics on a wall in front of Luis. He guided his suit closer, still staying out of the miners' way. That had been part of the agreement he'd made with Melka. Watch, but don't touch. Ask questions, but not too many. Pay your money up front and treat the captain with respect.

Distance was difficult for Luis to judge, so he pivoted about in search of the ship behind him, not wanting to travel too far from it.

Nothing. Only a solid sheet of black. The ship had vanished.

Fear hammered in Luis' chest and his breathing became even more ragged. Sweat streamed down his face and into his eyes, as he feverishly felt about on his control panel for the comm switch so he could notify Melka the ship was gone—fleeing from pirates, perhaps. It was gone and they were lost and would die, boiled so near NGC7078, and . . .

There. An angular grayness started to intrude in the black, and pinpricks of light emerged all around it. Luis swallowed his panic and took a few deep breaths, the calming act seeming to sear the depths of his lungs.

So hot.

He reminded himself that his suit's cooling capacity was

at its maximum, though it didn't feel like it. Rather, it felt like he was a lobster being cooked alive in a pot of water. A fat, squat lobster who could barely breathe. His chest ached.

The gray took on more features, became the ship he'd feared had vanished. Not lost, he thought after a moment more. A considerable measure of relief filled him. The light of NGC7078 had been so bright that when he looked away from it and toward the ship he had seen nothing at first. Only the black. Despite the visor it had taken his eyes a few moments to adjust. The ship was coming more into focus now, gunmetal gray against the ebony velvet of space, distant stars sparkling all around it. Luis forced himself to relax.

The ship looked massive and uninteresting, not at all like the others in port that had the vague and elegant forms of birds and turtles. But those had been passenger ships. Melka's ship, the *Mire*, was strictly a mining vessel, a series of huge, segmented boxes that gave it the appearance of an ancient Earth freight train. There were eight boxes, essentially cargo bays, all looking the same, no apparent engine or caboose. Only by inspecting it closely could Luis see a narrowing on one end, which he knew was the bridge. Was Reah watching them? Could she tell that he had panicked? He hoped that she instead considered him brave, a groundling with the guts to join the miners on this, his first real trip into deep space. Perhaps she would take a short leave with him after this expedition. She had brushed his leg on the bridge. He could ply her with beautiful, cut diamonds to tempt her. They could get away to someplace cold, someplace with mountains and snow. Would she like that?

Thrusting aside musings of what he'd come to think of as his pale China doll, Luis carefully maneuvered his suit around to face NGC7078 again, floated a few dozen meters closer, and did his best to endure the heat and the bright light as he watched the men hover about the equipment. Luis suspected drones could have managed all the work. But the miners claimed the robots were incapable of understanding the nuances of positioning some of the filter nets and reading if collection was truly functioning at one hundred percent.

Time blurred as Luis watched, uncertain if a few minutes or several hours had passed. He was breathing shallowly, finding it less hurtful, was concentrating on the scorpionlike piece of equipment that was gathering what he wanted in an effort to not think about the heat. He barely heard the chime in his helmet, and realized it had been sounding for a while, as the miners were all returning to the ship, one motioning for him to do the same. He maneuvered about, saw the blackness again, and waited until one of the miners passed him. Following that man toward the blackness where Reah waited, Luis found the bay doors and was tugged inside.

Several minutes later his helmet was off, and he and the other men were greedily swallowing water to replenish what their bodies had lost to sweat. Tubes were connected to the suits, refilling the cooling systems, drying out the sweat-soaked linings. Drones were inspecting the suits and equipment for heat damage. One miner was shrugging off a suit that had been sun-marred and was searching for another.

Captain Melka was watching Luis. "Congratulations, Mr. DeBeers."

Luis cocked his head.

"You basked in the sun without crumpling. I had expected to be hauling your unconscious carcass back here and tossing you in the medtent. For a land-bound, you have mettle." Then Melka was gone, disappeared behind the rest of the equipment that was being hauled in.

Luis had resolved that would be his only trip out of the ship. Once—just to have done it, to see the operation close-up, to have something to tell the family about. To impress Reah. But Melka's words had challenged him. He decided to see it through for the rest of the week, unless he succumbed before that—and he prayed that wouldn't happen. He rested his face against a cooled wall and waited. Four hours later they were cleared for another trip.

Time became unimportant, days and nights having no meaning next to the dying core of NGC7078. Luis worried at a sun blister on his cheek as he sat in the hold, inspecting some of the material the scorpion had retrieved for him. A hint of fragrant spice in the air caused him to look over his shoulder. Reah had entered the bay and was studying him.

"I wanted to see," she said, her voice sounding softer than usual in the cavernous hold.

"The diamonds your father mined for me?"

She nodded.

Luis happily gestured her closer. Spread out in bins in front of him was a collection of smoky crystals, ranging in size from that of a pea to a big man's fist.

She tugged off a glove and picked up a chunk. "I've seen diamonds. In the commons in spaceports."

"Those would have been cut."

"They were clear like ice. From Earth mines. I found them . . ." She poked out her bottom lip as she searched for a word. "Mesmerizing. I almost bought a diamond necklace once."

"What stopped you?" Luis wanted to say *What stopped you, since you have a fortune to spend?*

She shrugged her narrow shoulders. "Who would see it under this suit?"

Luis drew his lips into a thin line, decided to change the subject, but only just a bit. "They're mined on Earth mostly, but they're not from Earth. Not originally. Diamonds are from the stars, though a lot of geologists still argue that point."

She sat next to him on the cooled tile floor, her leg brushing against his. Reah was still examining the crystal.

"Black diamonds," Luis continued, "What you're holding are called carbonados, made of space carbon. Stardust. Dying stars release stars into the solar systems around them. Some of them release carbon that is embedded into meteorites, which strike planets and embed the chips there. It's the extreme heat and pressure that transforms that carbon into diamonds."

"The conditions that exist here," Reah said.

He nodded. "Geologists know that many diamonds on Earth are more than three and a half billion years old. That means the carbon in them predates animal and plant life by nearly three billion years. Proof, really, that diamonds weren't created on Earth. They really are stardust."

"And you have further proof here." Reah replaced the crystal and selected another.

"I don't care about the proof."

"Just the diamonds," she stated. "The stardust."

"There is nothing more brilliant in the universe than a cut diamond, especially black diamonds like these. Not even the stars come close. Not even the dying ones. The way the light hits their facets, bends and reflects, creating a rainbow. No other jewel has the luster of a polished diamond. So rare and precious."

"And so valuable."

He nodded. "Maybe as valuable as any new element your father might be discovering this trip."

"Your family . . ."

". . . has been involved with precious gemstones for centuries," he finished with a considerable amount of pride. "My great-grandfather is the one who suggested that diamonds came from space. He theorized that chondrites, that's a . . ."

"I know what a chondrite is. A class of meteorite." She set down the crystal and studied Luis' face instead. She saw excitement there, his breath coming faster as he explained his passion and heritage.

"A chondrite is filled with an incredible concentration of tiny diamonds. They're seeds, essentially. When they crashed into Earth in ancient times, the chondrites planted these seeds, and larger diamonds grew around them. The volcanoes thrust them close to the surface, where people discovered them. They discovered diamonds on Mars, too, though the deposits were mined out quickly."

"And now you've a new source and a new way to mine them."

"Exactly."

"And you'll be richer."

Luis' shoulders sagged. "Money's not what it's all about, even though it sounds that way. If it was just about money, my family would make synthetics. We did it late in the twentieth century. A machine, small—only thirty-five cubic meters. It squeezed a diamond shard, nearly a million pounds of pressure, and cooked it at about fifteen hundred degrees centigrade. Add a bit of graphite and some other catalysts to stimulate carbon grown around the shard. A couple of days later, you've got a diamond approaching two karats. You could tell the difference, of course, but not with your eyes. It takes a good jeweler's scope. People bought them, paid about as much as for a natural stone. So it's not money."

"What, then?" She had moved even closer, raised her small hand and wiped at the sweat on his forehead.

"Pursuit," he said after a moment. "Of the purest diamonds. The largest."

She drew her hand back and stood, attempted to smooth away the folds of her suit. "We're a bit alike, you and me. You into diamonds because of your family, just like I'm into sun-mining. Rich, and getting richer. And all in pursuit of the next, glorious find."

"Its not about the money." He didn't hear her leave, she was as quiet as a cat. However, he heard the chime echo through the bay telling him the cool-down period was over and it was time to venture into the oven again.

They'd mined NGC7078 for five days before the pirates came.

Reah was shining, displaying crack piloting skills as she guided the huge and bulky *Mire* away from the dying sun and the three fighter ships laying a line of laser-fire behind it. There was a big mining ship behind them, moving into the position vacated by Melka's ship.

"Damnation!" the captain hollered, as he paced back and forth in the tail cargo hold. His eyes were maniacally wild. "They weren't shadowing us!" One of the crewmen had suggested that, believing that one of the fighter ships had been in their last spaceport and followed them, radioing for support and the pirate mining ship.

"If they were shadowing us, they would've chased us off earlier. Wouldn't've let us get the choicest elements. They weren't shadowing us. Someone radioed out and notified them where we were going. It took them five days to reach our position."

He stormed from the bay, face red from NGC7078 and

his anger. He found Luis sorting through his uncut stones. Melka surprised him, dragged the smaller man up by the collar of his suit, holding him so only his toes touched the floor.

"So you paid me to mine for you. And the pirates paid you to reveal my stars. I ought to kill you. Toss you out the air lock and watch you explode." Spittle flew from Melka's lips, and his eyes held Luis', freezing the smaller man.

Luis couldn't speak, overcome by the madness and fury in Sean Melka's eyes. He tried to swallow, but found he couldn't manage that either. All he could do was sweat and listen to the pounding of his heart, the sound thunderous in his ears.

"Dad!" It was Reah's voice, and it was followed by a high-pitched whine.

The captain crumpled, stunned. Grateful and flabbergasted, Luis picked himself up off the floor and staggered back a few steps, thanking her. Captain Melka's chest rose and fell regularly, but his eyes were closed. He was unconscious.

"You stunned him good," Luis managed. The words were hoarse, and he worked to get some saliva in his mouth. "I owe you my life."

A generous smile was splayed across Reah's porcelain face. Her eyes were locked onto Luis'. Unblinking, they reminded him of her father's.

"I didn't notify any pirates," he began, wanting to explain his innocence to someone. "I don't know any pirates. He thought I did. He told me where we were going just before we left the port. And thought I . . . But I didn't. I wouldn't."

"I did."

He saw something else in her eyes at that moment, a wildness, a madness. He opened his mouth to say something else, but stopped himself and tried to put everything together. What could he say? Why was she doing this? What next?

"Its all about money, really." She answered his unspoken questions. Her voice was ice. "The raiders pay me well, money I don't have to share with my father. Still, I don't call for them until he's mined plenty—the cream from the dying sun. Money from them. Money from Dad's mining." She shrugged. "Besides, it makes his old age more interesting, running from pirates, looking over his shoulder. I'm helping him in a way, giving him a thrill, keeping him from getting complacent in his last years."

"Agitated like a dying star," Luis mused. "But he thinks I . . ."

"Of course he thinks you called them. And I'll tell him he was right. Tell him you were pulling a laser on him." She did that then, replaced the stungun and tugged a small laser pistol from her pocket, aimed it at her father and lanced him in the leg. His body quivered in response, but he remained unconscious. "I rushed in here trying to warn him, but you shot him before I could do anything. And so I retaliated." She turned the weapon on Luis, and he looked about for something to hide behind.

"Y–y–you're mad!" he stammered, backing up toward a tall crate.

"The stars do that to you." Her voice was still cold. She thumbed the trigger and a small white beam shot forward and stabbed at Luis' chest, burning through the suit and the skin beneath, finding his heart. She fired again and again, though he was dead before he hit the floor.

She turned to regard her father. "I'll get the men to carry you to the medtent," she said, knowing he couldn't hear her. "Tomorrow we'll find another dying star. One, I think, that has diamonds."

KEEPING SCORE

by Michael A. Stackpole

Michael A. Stackpole is an award-winning game and computer game designer who was born in 1957 and grew up in Burlington, Vermont. In 1979 he graduated from the University of Vermont with a B.A. in History. In his career as a game designer he has done work for Flying Buffalo, Inc., Interplay Productions, TSR, Inc., Hero Games, Wizards of the Coast, FASA Corp., and Steve Jackson Games. In recognition of his work in and for the game industry, he was inducted into the Academy of Gaming Arts and Design Hall of Fame in 1994. He's the author of *The New York Times* best-selling series of *Star Wars*™ X-wing novels, and the fantasy novels *Once a Hero* and *Talion: Revenant,* and *The Dark Glory War.*

The ambush seared scarlet light through the mauve jungle. Sara had felt it coming a heartbeat before beams flicked out—things had gotten too quiet for a second. The enemy fire manifested as full shafts of light instantly linking shooter and target, then snapping off, since light traveled far too fast for even the most augmented eyes to see it as tiny bolts. Ruby spears stabbed down from high branches, or slanted in from around the boles of trees, here and there, as the Zsytzii warriors shifted impossibly fast through the jungle.

Sara cut left and spun, slamming her back against the trunk of a tree. Her body armor absorbed most of the impact, and she continued to spin, then dropped to a knee on the far side of the tree and brought up her LNT-87 carbine. The green crosshairs on her combat glasses tracked along with the weapon's muzzle, showing her where it was pointed. The top barrel stabbed red back at the ambushers, burning little holes through broad leaves and striping trunks with carbonized scars. Fire gouted from the lower barrel as chemical explosives launched clouds of little flechettes at the unseen attackers.

Next to her, Captain Patrick Kelloch, the fire-team's leader, laid down a pattern of raking fire that covered their right flank while she concentrated on the left. Flechettes shredded leaves and vaporized plump, purple *lotla* fruit. She thought she saw a black shadow splashed with green, and hoped one fewer laser was targeted back at her, but the Zsytzii were harder to hit than she'd ever found in virtsims.

Bragb Bissik, the team's heavy-weapons specialist, stepped into the gap between the two human warriors. Underslung on his massive right forearm were the eight spinning rotary barrels of the gatling-style Bouganshi laser cannon. Into each barrel was fed a small lasing cell, consisting of a chemical reagent that released a lot of energy really fast. The cell converted that energy into coherent light of great power and intensity that blazed for almost a second once the reaction had been started. The cannon whined as the barrels spun. The red beams slashed in an arc, nipping branches from trees and burning fire into the jungle's upper reaches.

The weapon spat the smoking lasing cells out into a pile at the hulking Bouganshi's feet. The brilliant red beams bathed him in bloody highlights. Hulking and broad-shouldered, the Bouganshi could have been a demon from any number of human pantheons, and Sara hoped the Zeez would find him purely terrifying.

As Bragb's fire raked the higher branches, two beams

stabbed out from the ground to hit the Bouganshi's broad chest. Sara shifted her fire right, intersecting it with Kell's assault on the origin point of one of those beams. A purple wall of foliage disappeared in a cloud of smoke and mist. Something screamed, then something screeched, barely heard above the thunder of the fire-team's weapons. Red beams winked off from the Zsytzii line, then never appeared again.

Kell raised a hand. "Hold fire. They've run, I'm thinking."

Sara remained in her crouch as burned leaves fluttered down and smoldering twigs peppered the ground. "Makes no sense for them to run. They had us."

"Close." The Bouganshi slapped with a three-fingered hand at the smoking black scars on his purple-and-gray, camouflaged body armor. "Heat, no crust."

She checked her armor and saw a couple of dark furrows melted in it. "Likewise, toasted not burned."

"Better than I was expecting." His azure eyes bright, Kell gave her a nod. "Bit different than simming. It is, isn't it?"

Sara tucked a wisp of blonde hair back up under her helmet. "In sim they're relentless. They never break off like this."

"That's because, lass, you're using Qian simware. Much as they hate the Zeez, they grant them a bit more honor than in reality." Kell thumbed a clip free of his 87 and slapped a new one home. "For an honorable kill, you need an honorable foe. Only simZeez act that way."

Sara Mirke frowned. "I'm not clear on your meaning, Captain."

"Qian like order in their Commonwealth, hate mystery, and hate dishonor. They don't like to acknowledge it exists. Quirky, our masters." Kell rose and waved the others forward. "Let's see what we got."

Still covering the left flank, she moved out in Kell's

wake. Bragb came behind, watching their rear. They went up a slight slope and over the splintered remains of under-brush. on the other side of the crest the land sloped down into a tree-choked ravine, through which ran a small stream. Halfway down the hillside a body lay against a tree, twisted against itself, with a gray-green rope of intestines pointing back uphill.

Kell nodded. "One less to play with."

"Too bad it wasn't the Primary."

A gruff chuckle humphed from the Bouganshi's throat. "Too much Qian virtsim."

"Better to take the juniors first, Sara." Kell knelt by the body, emphasizing just how small the black-furred Zsytzii was. In life, it would have looked like a crossbreeding be-tween a chimp and a wildcat, with tufted ears rising high. It had a long black tail which Sara knew was not prehen-sile, though she checked herself on that assumption. *Most of the stuff I know comes from virtsim, so is subject to that Qian programmer bias.* The closed eyes should have been rather large, the closed mouth should have had nasty fangs, and the hands should have ended in savage claws, but as nearly as she could see they remained sheathed.

She shivered. The dead creature looked like nothing so much as a school child dressed up in some elaborate cos-tume. "It's like we're making war on children."

"More so than you know." Kell produced a knife from a boot sheath, turned the Zsytzii's head to the left, and cut up along the neck and behind the ear. He exposed the skull and dug out a small, cylindrical device that had been in-serted into a hole behind the right ear. The thing trailed two wires. "The Primary will be severing the link, but intel will want it."

Sara looked away from the body and busied herself

plucking a stray flechette from a tree. "We continue on the patrol, or head back?"

"We push on." Kell smiled over at Bragb, who reciprocated, exposing a mouth full of serrated white teeth. "We're ahead in the game, and they need to know that."

"I'm not sure I understand."

"I know, lass, which is why you're out here with us." Kell waved the Bouganshi forward. "Take point, I'll get the rear. We'll let Lieutenant Mirke continue her learning experience."

"Point." The Bouganshi hefted his weapon and marched along the ridgeline, then down into the game trail they'd been following before the Zsytzii had hit them. Bragb moved off at a pace that Sara thought was less than prudent and when she turned back to complain to Kell, she saw he'd slung his LNT by the strap over his right shoulder.

"This has got to be a game because you two are playing by rules I don't understand."

"War's not really a game, at least, not from the Qian point of view. Same can't be said of the Zeez, which is why the Qian hate them so much." Kell tipped his helmet back, exposing a lock of brown hair pasted to his forehead. "You know the Zeez only allow males to act as warriors, and that males come in two flavors. Juniors are born five or so to a litter, along with a Primary. They're augmented these days so the Primary can give them direct orders but, for all intents and purposes, the little hoppers are the mental equivalents of five-year-olds. The juniors can remember a command or two and carry them out, but without the Primary, they're very limited."

"I know, which is why killing the Primary is so important."

"That depends, Sara. If you're killing the Primary right after he's given his brothers an order to get some sleep, well then, well done and more of it. If, instead, he's just told them it's time to kill the enemy, and he's been a bit vague on defining enemy, you have little homicidal beasties roaming about."

"Omni-cidal, Kell." The Bouganshi glanced back, flashing a white curve of grin. "If understanding of Terran is correct."

"I'm corrected, Bragb." The team's leader smiled easily. "The Zsytzii seem to have a view about this conflict with the Qian Commonwealth that isn't quite clear to the Qian. Being as how the Zeez are augmented, fight differently, and have an annoying habit of being hard to kill, the Qian really want little to do with them."

"Which is why we're here." Sara sighed. The Qian Commonwealth had approached Mankind at a period when Men had only moved to a few of the other planets in the solar system. The Qian took humans in through something of a protectorate program, giving them faster-than-light travel— which they suggested humanity would eventually discover— and integrated them into their galaxies-spanning empire. Humanity contributed what it could, and some of the better exports were soldiers. A few were even seconded to the elite Qian Star Guards, with all of them serving in the Blackstar company.

As Kell had explained as they were inbound to the world Lyrptod, the *Zmnyl-grar qert-dra*, as the Blackstars were known in Qian, had a name that could be read two ways. The black star emblazoned on the shoulders of their armor was an emblem feared in the Commonwealth, but in Qian the name could also be read to mean *black hole*. Recruits for that unit came mostly from Ward worlds, and while the Qian used them to show the worlds that they valued their contributions, there was little doubt that the Blackstars were held in contempt by their Qian commanders.

Qian pride concerning their warrior tradition contributed heavily to this view, and was the source of Sara's being tossed into a mission before she even had time to unpack her belongings from the trip to join her unit. While Qian workers and the female leaders were all heavily augmented, Qian warriors were not. They were bred true and quite formidable, with those belonging to the Guards being of the highest caliber.

Sara, on the other hand, was what was colloquially referred to on Terra as a "graft." Genetic engineering on Terra had eliminated genetic disease, but environmental factors and spontaneous mutations meant children were still born with defects. These children were sold to corporations who then treated them and trained them, selling their contracts to companies or governments who needed their skills. Nastoyashii Corporation had used her in its Rota program, making her into a warrior. Test scores short-listed her for liaison with the Commonwealth and landed her the place in the Blackstars.

"Well, we're here, lass, because we're expected to handle this problem with some delicacy." Kell laughed lightly, a sound which seemed natural within the violet jungle.

Lyrptod, when surveyed initially, had fallen into the Ward world class. The humanoid indigs had a tech level equivalent to the settlers who formed the United States, though explosives development had not occurred. They lived in a theocracy that preached pacifism and salvation from the stars, so when the Qian came down, they were welcomed. The Commonwealth quarantined the world, which was located back a bit from the Zsytzii frontier, leaving it open only to scientific teams studying the flora and fauna.

No one was quite certain when the Zeez inserted a team, but scattered sightings were reported back to the Commonwealth. Kell and his team were dispatched to Lyrptod to figure out why the Zeez were there while their insertion ship, the *Chzrin*, orbited the planet. They'd established a base camp in the vicinity of a number of sightings and engaged on patrols for a week without incident.

Given the nature of the world, and its location, the Zsytzii presence posed little threat to the Commonwealth, but the nature of interstellar warfare demanded some sort of response. Because space had few natural features that barred hyperspace travel, frontiers didn't really exist. The only way you could hit an enemy was to land on a world where you knew he had a presence. Learning why the Zeez were in Lyrptod could help determine other potential targets, or if they would be coming back in force. If so, scattered forces could be gathered to hurt them.

"Delicacy, yes, sir." She resisted the temptation to sling her weapon over her shoulder. "I know it's a natural preserve. I'm surprised you didn't have us collect up our shells."

"Saw you getting that flechette, lass. Good enough for me, though the skulls and their think-team would probably like more policing of the battlefield." He stretched his arms out to the sides and let his gloved fingers play over velvety ferns. "The point about the Zeez and war being a game for them is this: a lot of their objectives don't seem to make a lot of sense for the Qian. For example, why they would send a team here is baffling, so we get to deal with it. I'm not thinking we're going to be finding out what they are up to, and the Qian wouldn't understand it if we did. We get rid of them and we'll have done our job."

Sara rolled the flechette needle between her fingers and thumb. "You're not expecting another ambush right now because of why, then?"

"It's the focus thing: the juniors handle a couple orders at a time. Shifting them between attack and run modes takes a bit of transition, which is why they tend not to retreat."

He jerked a thumb back toward the ambush site. "In past incidents they've fired upon indigs in the jungle, driving them off. I'm thinking their current orders are such that they engage briefly and scarper. There may be one out there watching us, but they're not going to hit us, not right now. We killed one of them, so that will take a new plan, and the Primary will be wanting to think on it a while."

"I understand the logic, but is that a safe assumption to make?"

"I hope so, lass." Kell winked at her. "Since I'm last in line here, likely I'll be the one they fry first."

Up ahead, the Bouganshi crouched at a point about ten meters back from where the trail opened onto a meadow. The stream which had been running through the ravine to their right bled down and out into a marshy area on the edge of a lake. The grasses in the meadow rose to hip height and had gone from a lavender to a bright golden color, contrasting beautifully with the lush purple jungle and violet-tinged waters of the lake.

Sara took that whole vista in with a glance, then focused on a tree near the lake edge. She felt fairly certain, based on its dark gray trunk, that it was dead, but the branches were not bare, clawing at the sky. Instead they were covered with blue foliage, iridescent in nature, that fluttered with a breeze that neither rippled the water nor rustled the grasses.

She smiled. "That tree is covered with butterflies."

"Or the nearest evolutionary equivalent, yes."

Bragb cast a glance back at Kell. "Not fair. To you, if it lives in water, it is a 'trout.' "

The team leader sniffed and raised his chin. "Fish are noble creatures, not bugs. Evolution being what it is, there are plenty of fish around. Probably some in that lake."

Sara chuckled lightly. "Can we go down there?"

The Bouganshi nodded. "Seems safe."

"Sure. If they're watching us, give them something to watch." Kell came up and sidled around Bragb, then led the way down the trail. It wound its way down a steep hillside, then along a high patch of ground that bordered the swamp. Nearing the lake he slowed and looked for a dry path toward the shore.

"Bragb, you watch our backtrail. Lieutenant, if you want, you can recon the bugtree."

"And you will survey the trout population?" Sara shook her head as she pushed the flechette through the strap on her LNT-87, keeping the steel needle in place. "And then come back here fishing sometime?"

Kell crouched at the shore and peered into the murky water for a moment, then turned to look at her. "Lieutenant, if you'd done the study of Lyrptod . . ."

"If I'd had the time to study the data . . ."

". . . you'd know there is nothing of commercial value to exploit here, and you'd know that taking wildlife without a study-permit is quite illegal." He shrugged. "Of course, an informal scientific survey, well, now, that couldn't be consi . . ."

The water boiled in a rush of bubbles as a huge, mottled gray-and-purple creature lunged up and out at Kell. Its leathery flesh, though glistening with water, had the same armor plates grown into it as the Bouganshi's skin did. The beast's mouth flashed open, white peg teeth contrasting with light blue flesh, then snapped down. The creature caught Kell by surprise, closing its mouth over him, leaving his legs kicking and arms waving as it raised its maw and tried to choke him down.

Sara's carbine came up instantly and she emptied a clip at the beast. She sprayed her fire over the water, aiming at its midsection, churning the water into froth, but not stopping the monster from sliding back beneath the surface. Her empty clip hit the ground and another had been slapped home in an eye blink, which was just enough time for her to realize gunfire wasn't going to stop the thing.

Before she could cast her weapon aside, Bragb came on a sprint and hurled himself into the lake. With a glittering silver, crook-bladed knife in one hand and freed of his cannon and its bulky ammo pack, the hulking alien splashed down noisily, spraying water everywhere. He sank from sight for a second, then his right hand rose with the dagger and fell. Once, twice, then too many times for her to count. A black stain filled the water. The creature's flat tail lashed, breaking the surface, then Bragb came up, gasping. Water cascaded from him, then he went down again.

A heartbeat later he came up and coughed, once, hard, then struggled to the shore. He had the creature's tail in one hand and dragged the thing from the lake. Ragged gashes had been opened along its twelve-meter-long spine—not all of them made by the knife—and the rhythmic little gnashing of its teeth indicated it wasn't quite dead yet.

That didn't stop the Bouganshi, who contemptuously spat out a hunk of green meat. Bragb flipped the creature onto its back, then stabbed his knife in near the hindmost of the three pairs of legs and cut along up toward the middle. The wound gaped and verdant guts came pouring out, along with the distended gray sack that was the monster's stomach. Another slash opened it. The Bouganshi reached in and dragged Kell from the stomach, sliding his slime-covered body onto the golden grasses.

Sara dropped to her knees and swiped a hand across Kell's lips, then opened his mouth, cleared it with a finger, and lifted up on his neck to open his airway. She pinched his nose shut, then covered his mouth with hers and breathed.

One breath, two, and a third. She shook off a glove and felt his throat for a pulse.

He had one, good and strong. She started to breathe for him again, but he pushed her away, rolled onto his side and puked. He sucked in a loud noisy breath, then coughed and vomited again. He tried to come up on all fours, but abandoned the effort and stayed down on his right side.

"You okay, sir? Anything broken? Bragb?"

Kell weakly waved a hand.

The Bouganshi, sitting with his knees drawn up against his chest, shook his head. "Fine." He stared at the dark stains on his knife, then glanced at the dead monster, and nodded to himself. "Tastes foul."

Sara swallowed a comment about how she would have thought it would have tasted like chicken, uncertain if Bragb's command of Terran would have let him follow the joke. She retreated to her carbine, picked it up and turned to face back toward the woods. "Nothing from the jungle."

"Good. Last thing I'm wanting to be hearing is Zsytzii laughter." Kell rolled onto his belly and came up on his elbows. "My helmet must still be in there. Be a good lad and fetch it for me, will you, Bragb?"

"Fetched you. On your own for equipment."

Kell sighed. "Guess I won't smell any worse for digging around in there, eh?" He heaved himself up and knelt for a moment, swaying slightly. "And thanks to the both of you for saving me. When it bit, it crushed my armor down, costing me my wind. Not that there was much to breathe in there anyway."

He crawled over to the creature and reached a hand into the slit through which he had emerged. He felt around, then smiled and pulled out a thirty-centimeter-long, finned thing. "See, they do have trout here."

Bragb snorted a laugh, then leaned away as Kell flung

the fish out into the lake. "Bolts food whole, lets it digest. Such creatures exist on Bougan."

"On Terra they're known as crocodiles." Sara smiled as one of the butterflies landed by the barrel of her weapon. "Stories tell of their stomachs being full of undigested junk."

"I'm thinking I'll ignore that insult, thank you." Kell winked at her, then pulled his helmet free with a wet sucking sound. He turned it over and a slime soup of fish, his combat glasses, and a tangled clump of fibers drained down into a puddle. He looked down at it and his smile abruptly died. "This isn't good, not at all."

She frowned. "What's the matter?"

"I'll be able to tell for sure, back at camp, but I'm thinking this knot of wires here, it's Zsytzii in nature." He spat to the side. "Seems I wasn't the only Xeno this beastie welcomed to Lyrptod. Unless I miss my guess, the last was the Primary leading our little team of Zeez."

The hike back to their base camp was remarkable in only one way. While Bragb and Sara were both quite content to have Kell at the back of their formation because of his stench, the butterflies must have thought the crocslime was pure ambrosia. They fluttered and flickered at him, trailing in his wake like ion exhaust from a fighter. With each fern frond that brushed him, a few of the insects would stop and feast on the transferred slime. Kell wiped off as much of it as he could, casting leaves aside to distract them. Even so, by the time they had reached the camp, two dozen still orbited him like little moons.

Their base camp was nothing worthy of holoing home about. They'd established it on a little wooded knoll, stringing a tarp between trees to make a shelter. They'd set up a couple of small camp tables, their perimeter warning gear, a radio and some simple scientific gear. All of it was very compact, and any serious analysis would require liaising with the scientific teams to the north. Still, the camp was dry and had access to a nearby stream for water, so it suited their needs very well.

While Kell stripped naked and cleaned himself up as best he could, Bragb studied the wire harness taken from the beast, as well as the device sliced from the Zsytzii junior they'd killed. As best he could determine, the two devices seemed to be of similar manufacture, apparently confirming Kell's guess as to the source of the wire from the monster's gullet.

Sara established contact with the xenobiological survey team to see if they'd had any more Zsytzii sightings in their area. She passed on the story of their encounter with the lake croc, as well as the attraction of the butterflies to the slime. The person at the other end of the radio link seemed less than impressed with the reportage, noted they'd seen no Zeez, and that they'd taken enough samples of the lake monsters and butterflies to last scholars several lifetimes.

Sara switched off the radio as Kell emerged from the camp shower they'd set up. "The Nobel Committee says it didn't see anything z-ish today, They weren't interested by our adventures either."

He shrugged and pulled a dark jumpsuit from his rucksack, then tossed his towel at the flock of butterflies on his armor. "I'm thinking it's a pity the Primary didn't make it out of the belly of the beast. We'd just have to follow the butterflies to the Zeez lair."

"Yeah, well, about that, to hear the scientists talk, the 'bluewings' are not true butterflies, but just gaudy maggotflies. If we go back to the Zee body or the lake monster, it'll be flyblown and alive with larvae." Sitting back, she wove a flechette end over end from index finger to pinkie and back again easily. "I could hear the disgust pouring through the airwaves when I called them butterflies. They have to think we're just ambulatory laser-artillery."

"They're assuming ignorance because of our calling."

"I know, and I don't like it. Don't like being judged because of what folks assume I am."

"Being a graft, you get a fair amount of that, do you?" Kell pulled on the fresh jumpsuit, then batted at one persistent bluewing. "Look at this one, would you? Go on with you, I'm not dead."

With a fluid economy Sara came up and out of the chair. She stabbed out with the flechette, piercing the bluewing through the thorax. The insect's wings flapped a couple more times, slowing down, then froze in place. Its feet clutched at the needle and its antennae curled in.

Kell had jerked back, but well after she'd stabbed the bug. "Damn, you are fast."

"Part of being a graft." She smiled slightly and returned to her seat, holding the bluewing up to study. "When I was a little girl, I used to collect bugs. Always dreamed about discovering some new species or something and having it named after me. All of us in the Rota program knew what we were being made into, but we all had other interests. The company tolerated it and even encouraged it in case war wasn't a 'growth market sector.' "

Kell laughed and the Bouganshi smiled. "Little chance of that, I'm thinking. If you're wanting to add that one to your collection, we might be able to smuggle it off-world for you."

She frowned. "If I still had the collection, it would be very tempting. It would be interesting to have something unique in my collection. Problem is I'd have to Mona Lisa it."

Bragb scratched the side of his domed head. "That expression is unknown."

Kell raked fingers back through his brown hair. "Famous painting on Earth. It was stolen back a century ago, never recovered. It's assumed to be in the hands of a private collector. He can't be showing it to anyone, or letting anyone know he has it, since the reward for its recovery is huge now."

Sara nodded. "Worse yet, and you know it will happen since the skulls are pulling samples from here, a black market for these things will grow among collectors. There will be bluewing poachers coming down. Next time we come back, we'll be fighting folks who did what I just did."

"Reflexes like yours applied to the problem, and I'm thinking Bragb and I will just sit back and keep score."

The Bouganshi smiled coldly. "Might hunt lake monsters. Know the bait they like."

Kell arched an eyebrow at him. "And I'd be thinking, were I you, about what eat them beasts, since you're just a pair of legs shy of being taken as one."

Bragb paled slightly. He frowned and narrowed his dark eyes. "Worth consideration."

"It is, but I'm thinking we'd all be better served if we turn our minds loose on the problem of finding the Zeez." Kell folded his arms across his chest. "We did okay today, but they could get lucky in a series of running ambushes."

The Bouganshi pressed fingers together deliberately. "They are not protecting the Primary. What else do they need to hide? Their camp? A recovery craft?"

"Could be one and the same, it could." Kell smiled slowly. "And recovering one of them would put us in possession of something as unique as your bluewing. I think, tomorrow, we head out on the same patrol, starting at the lake and working backward. See where we run into them, and see if our contact points can let us triangulate back to their base."

"Sounds like a plan, sir." Sara stabbed the flechette into the tree to which they'd tied the tarp. "Plots on the other sightings don't have a pattern, but the Primary probably saw to that. If they'll come out and play, we can probably follow them home."

"Good enough." Kell picked up his towel again and shooed bluewings away from his armor. "I'll take first watch so I can clean up this armor and patch it. Bragb, you'll go next, and you're the anchor, Sara. We'll see sunrise over that lake."

The Bouganshi smiled. "You just wish to see if trout will be hitting at insects."

"She has her hobby, I have mine." The man laughed. "Rack out now, morning will come much too soon."

Dawn broke over the lake, and Kell's trout were hitting the surface hard. Bluewings, in swiftly diminishing numbers, lay on the water and were scattered around in the marsh. Sara knelt on one knee to get a closer look and found dozens of them mashed into the mud by little feet. A few discarded flechettes likewise had been worked into the mud. Of the lake croc there was no clear sign, though lots of crushed grasses and more footprints suggested it had been dragged off into the jungle.

Sara frowned. "Wonder what the bluewings did to offend the juniors?"

Kell, crouched well away from the shore, shook his head as he scanned the Zsytzii backtrail. "No lasers used. Wasn't war against them, I'm thinking. Something else."

"Captain, take a look at this." Bragb stood next to the dead tree and pointed at a splash of blue. Sara and Kell both approached. Two bluewings had been stabbed through the thorax, one on top of the other, then pinned to the tree with a flechette. "The junior had to be moving that needle very fast."

Kell tipped his helmet back on his head. "Faster than even Sara here. Don't be jealous, lass."

She glanced over at him, but before she could snap off a retort, a throbbing pulsed from the rain forest. The three of them came around, weapons raised, and watched a small, disk-shaped ship rise from the jungle. The rate of climb could best be described as slow, but the ship remained stable in flight and moved upward at a steady pace.

Kell immediately keyed his radio. "Ground Lead to *Chzrin*, we have a Zsytzii craft coming up."

"*Chzrin* copies ground report. Zsytzii warship has just appeared in the solar system, headed this way. Tschai Mriap says we can burn your upcoming ship, but then will be destroyed by the warship." The Qian communications officer delivered the information flatly, with no inflection and no indication of personal involvement in the unfolding events. "He says five minutes go/no-go on the burn. Your mission, your choice."

Kell closed his eyes. "Stand by, *Chzrin*." He pointed his carbine at the Zeez ship and triggered the laser. The red beam tagged the ship, but did nothing to it. "They're leaving, so do we assume they are retreating and let them go, saving the Qian ship, or have they accomplished their mission, in which case we can't let them go? Input?"

The Bouganshi growled for a second or two. "Have to assume they accomplished their mission, whatever it was. The Zeez will burn *Chzrin*, then come down. Has to be done."

"Sara?"

Something odd here. She glanced at the bluewings pinned to the tree. *This is the key, I know it.*

"Sara?"

. A smile blossomed on her face. "Of course, yes, they accomplished their mission."

"That's what I'm thinking, too." Kell shrugged uneasily. "Gotta burn them."

"No, no, no, you don't. Let them go." Sara turned away from the tree. "Let them go. It will do more harm than good."

Kell frowned. "You've got two minutes to explain."

"It's all right here, the dead bluewings, the flechettes, the two pinned to the tree." She opened her arms. "You're thinking about stuff from an adult point of view, but the juniors, they aren't adults. They are treating this like a game, and they've won. Think about it. They scouted our scientific teams. They saw them taking samples, but the Primary probably recognized what was going on and was able to put those things in proper perspective.

"The juniors, though, once he died, only had orders to avoid detection and to study us. The Zsytzii mission here was the same as ours, to see what the enemy was doing on this planet. Face it, it has no obvious value, yet is quarantined. They suspect we're hiding something here."

Kell narrowed his blue eyes. "You're saying they think we're here to harvest bluewings?"

"Makes no sense to an adult, but to a child? We killed one of them, *then* killed the monster that killed their Primary. That got their attention, made us important in their eyes." She pointed at the two bluewings pinned together. "One saw me stab *one* out of the air. They got *two*, just to show who was better. The other needles here show other attempts. It was a kid's game, and just as we scored against them yesterday, getting two with one needle, that beats us today."

Bragb squatted on his heels. "So juniors are carrying a lake monster and bluewings. They think we came for them."

Kell smiled. "And the Zeez will spend time and resources trying to figure out why we want them."

"And when they can't, they'll be back with another survey team, or something more, and we'll know they're coming." Sara smiled. "The Zeez may not be trout, but chances are they'll be swallowing that bait whole, and be back to be caught."

"Ground lead to *Chzrin*. You'll be wanting to move our ride home out of the way. Let the warship get its little craft."

"Copy ground." The barest hint of relief threaded through the Qian's voice. "Running now. We will return, with help."

"Copy, *Chzrin*." Kell slowly smiled. "We'll have to check the Zeez camp, see what they left, then wait for our lift home."

"If taskforce comes back, could take days to organize." The Bouganshi squatted, resting a hand on the hilt of his knife. "Perhaps the Zeez will land more teams and give us something to do."

"I think I'd prefer they didn't." Sara smiled at Bragb. "Not that I'd want to ruin your fun."

"I'm agreeing with Sara there." Kell dropped to one knee and fingered a bluewing out of the muck. "Having been swallowed by a monster, I'd be content with some peace. And given as how them trout seem to be liking these bluewings, we won't be lacking for something to do."

"Fishing never struck me as the sort of thing Qian Star Guards would do." Sara arched an eyebrow at Kell. "Won't our commander take a dim view of our spending our time that way?"

"He will indeed, lass." Kell laughed. "And that will make it even that much more fun."

ALLIANCES

by Kristine Kathryn Rusch

In 1999, Kristine Kathryn Rusch won three Reader's Choice Awards for three different stories in three different magazines in two different genres: mystery and science fiction. That same year, her short fiction was nominated for the Hugo, Nebula, and Locus Awards. Since she had just returned to writing short fiction after quitting her short fiction editing job at *The Magazine of Fantasy and Science Fiction*, she was quite encouraged by this welcome back to writing. She never quit writing novels, and has sold more than forty-five of them, some under pseudonyms, in mystery, science fiction, fantasy, horror, and romance. Her most recent mystery novel is *Hitler's Angel*. Her most recent fantasy novel is *The Black King*.

"Forgive me, sir." Captain Roz Sheehan could barely hide her disgust, even if she was speaking to a superior officer. "I don't believe we should trust the word of a Crativ'n, two Dulacs, and a Hacrim."

Admiral Allen Galland reached across his wide oak desk and handed her an information pad. She did not look at it, instead studying the office around her.

Roz had been here a dozen times—and each time Galland had proposed some half-assed scheme. Most of them she'd been able to get out of, but lately that had gotten harder and harder.

She had a reputation for being the most creative captain in the fleet, and that had brought her to Galland's attention.

That, and the loss of her ship in the Cactus Corridor. She kept her command—after all, her crew got back alive and she had managed to defeat an entire squadron of Bá-am-ás—but Galaxy Patrol rules were hard and fast. Any captain who lost her ship had to go through retraining and reassignment.

Galland had prevented that, but he hadn't let her forget that favor. And so far, it had cost her eleven unsavory missions. Eleven missions that had fattened Galland's private purse and had left her with the feeling that she should never have taken his deal, even though it helped her retain her command.

The office wasn't making things any better. Oak desk, real Earth plants—spiders (which were hardy) and violets (which were not)—paintings older than the Galactic Alliance, and leather furniture that had antique stamped all over it. Every time she came here, she saw some new treasure, and she wondered how much of her sweat had gone into paying for it.

Not to mention the fact that Galland kept his office too damn hot. Hot and humid, filled with "real" sunlight. Good for the plants, he said.

Bad for her. Especially when she was trying to look cool and calm, unruffled by his latest stupid plan.

If only the Alliance had stricter rules for its base commanders. But they were military governors who operated without much oversight—and were as good, or as bad, as they chose to be. And Galland certainly wasn't choosing to be good.

"I could download the information to your personal account," Galland said, capturing her attention just like he wanted.

She sighed and looked at the information pad he had given her. A highlighted route appeared, running through the Cactus Corridor and beyond, well into uncharted space.

A small blue planet pulsed, begging her to touch the screen and enlarge the image.

She didn't. Instead, she handed the pad back to Galland.

"A treasure map," she said. "How delightful. Am I acting as a member of the Patrol now or as part of a newly created piracy force? Should I wear an eye patch, get a peg leg, and start calling you matey?"

"You forget, Captain, that you are talking to your superior."

She let out a large sigh and let her shoulders relax. "No, I haven't, sir. But frankly, you're not acting like my superior here. You're acting like a little boy who just found out that there's gold at the end of the rainbow."

"And you, Captain, should take this assignment more seriously."

"I would," she said, "if you had a reliable source. And if you were pursuing something that was possible. They're sending you—me, actually—on some kind of wild goose chase."

"I've heard enough about this universal translator to believe it's something we have to investigate."

"Then have someone bring it here," she said. "What's to stop someone from bringing the technology to us?"

"The Hacrim say that these creatures don't want to sell it."

This mission was getting worse and worse. "Then why would you want me to go to this place?"

"To see if the rumors are true," Galland said.

"They aren't," Roz said.

"Then find out."

"Through the Cactus Corridor. Into uncharted space. Breaking God knows how many regulations to track down a rumor?"

"You're an explorer, Captain."

"I'm a military officer, Admiral. I'm supposed to be patrolling a sector, not going on fantasy vacations in your stead."

"You're being insubordinate, Captain."

"And you're not acting like my superior officer, Admiral." Roz picked up the pad and looked at it one last time.

There was a lot of information missing from that route. The section of space after the Cactus Corridor was empty—completely black. Then there was the pulsating planet, and nothing else.

Space was never empty and it never had nothing there. Especially over distances that vast.

"Let me remind you, Captain, who saved your butt—"

"Yeah," Roz said. "In an incident that happened in the Cactus Corridor. No offense, Admiral, but I really don't want to take my ship back there."

"You won't be, Roz," Galland said, lowering his voice. "You'll be taking a prototype vessel. A small one. One that can handle the prickly nature of that nebula."

"And the Bá-am-ás?" she asked.

"You let me worry about the Bá-am-ás."

"No offense, sir, but I'm the one whose going to be taking a prototype ship through the Cactus Corridor, heavily mined and guarded by the Bá-am-ás, into space that isn't properly charted, in search of something that's *scientifically impossible*. I respectfully and forcefully decline."

Admiral Galland let out a small sigh. "Roz, I don't think you're in the position to argue—"

"Admiral," she said, putting her hands on his desk and leaning close. "Let me ask you a few questions."

He raised his dark eyes to hers. She thought she caught in them an expression of wary amusement. She didn't like that at all.

"Fire, Captain." Back to captain, then, were they? None of that too-familiar Roz crap any longer.

"Did the Dulacs speak English when they told you of this great find?"

"No," Galland started, but she didn't let him finish.

"Did the Hacrim? How about the Crativ'n?"

"No."

"Did they use one of these devices to communicate with you?"

"No," Galland said.

"So you had to speak to them through translators."

"Yes, but—"

"Human translators, trained at some university and hired by the Patrol, right?"

"Yes, but—"

"Don't you find that somewhat suspicious?"

"No," Galland said.

She couldn't believe he had just said that. "*No?*"

Galland nodded. "No."

She stood up. Now she was confused. "Why not?" And then she mentally kicked herself for asking the question.

"Because," he said, "they claim these creatures don't want the translator in anyone else's hands."

"So," she said, "on the off chance that this universal translator does exist, what am I supposed to do? Steal the technology?"

"That's your suggestion, Captain."

She let out a surprised laugh. "I was being sarcastic, Admiral."

"Really?" he said, "Somehow, I hadn't noticed."

She stared at him, shocked. "You can't be serious."

He grinned. "It was your suggestion."

She shook her head. How she hated the meetings with him. The thing was she knew she had little recourse. The

Alliance let a lot of things slide, particularly if the end re-sult benefited Alliance members.

And to think she had been idealistic when she joined up, believing that "for the good of all races" crap that had been in the recruiting ads. To think that she once believed she and her crew would fly all over the galaxy doing good.

How naïve was that?

Probably as naïve as letting Admiral Galland help her avoid reassignment.

"Admiral," she said, choosing her words carefully, "we couldn't invent a universal translator for human languages. Human beings—the same species—don't base our language on the same structure and concepts. How can there be a universal translator for humans and aliens? It's not possi-ble and you know it. You want me to risk my life and my crew's for someone's con."

"It's not a con," he said. "Three different kinds of aliens—"

"Yeah. They couldn't all have been bought off." She put up her hands as if to ward off his next remark. "That was sarcasm too, in case you didn't catch it."

"Look, Captain. You and I have both seen a lot of strange things in our careers. That's part of what space is about." Galland was being serious now. Somehow that disconcerted her even more. "What if this translator works for some alien races? If it works forty percent of the time, then it's better than anything we have."

"And if, in the remaining sixty percent, it mistranslates and we don't know it, aren't we setting ourselves up for something completely terrible?" she asked.

"Let's find out if it exists first, Roz. Then we'll worry about it."

"So I cross the Cactus Corridor, fight my way through

an uncharted section of space, find out the damn thing exists, come back, tell you, and you'll send me out again?"

"I'd rather take your first suggestion," Galland said.

"It wasn't a suggestion," she said. "And I won't steal for you or the Alliance. I'm not that dumb."

All the humor left Galland's face. "Really, Roz?" he asked. "Your record suggests otherwise."

"It does not. I've been one of the best officers in this fleet, and you know it."

"I know it," he said. "But it doesn't show in your record. In fact, the last eleven runs you did for me were off the books. Officially, Captain, you're grounded."

Her mouth went dry. "What?"

He shrugged. "We're pretty much an isolated outpost here, Roz. No one knows what happens out here unless we choose to tell them. For the past several years all your communications, all your assignments, and all of your command decisions have been run through me."

Of course it had. That was standard policy. She was feeling light-headed. He had manipulated standard policy to his own advantage? That was even lower than she had expected him to go.

"There aren't that many starships," she said. "Patrol Headquarters has to know that someone has been running the *Millennium*."

"Someone has," Galland said. "Just not you."

She licked her lips. They were dry, too. "What have I been doing then?"

"Penance, just like you were supposed to. Working dockside with me."

"You son of a bitch!" She started across the desk at him, but he caught her by her shoulders.

"Don't fly off, Roz," he said. "You don't dare. Or I'll report your usage of the *Millennium*. All of it illegal."

"That's not true. We've done surveys for the Patrol. We've gone on assignment—"

"True," he said. "All of it logged in under the new captain's name. The only runs that bear your signature are the eleven I asked for."

"All illegal," she said.

He shrugged. "All insurance."

She eased herself out of his grasp. "What about my crew?"

"Loyalty is a two-edged sword, Roz," Galland said. "They'll say anything for you."

"You'd ruin their careers, too?" she asked.

He smiled. "It seems that you already have."

She clenched her fists and had to walk around the office once to keep herself from flattening him. Asshole. She had been right. She should have trusted her instincts, should have believed in that feeling she had every time he gave her an assignment.

But she had wanted her ship back so badly, she had been willing to believe him. Willing to become his patsy.

Dammit, this was her fault. She willingly blinded herself so that she could have the command she felt she deserved.

Now she wished she could go back in time. She wouldn't refight the battle in the Cactus Corridor. She'd done that right. No. She'd report the entire thing to Headquarters when she got back to the base, just like she had planned.

But Admiral Galland had talked her out of it. He had said that he had taken care of the report, and he had told her to keep her information to herself because he thought he could save her command and maybe even give her the *Millennium*.

She remembered seeing the *Millennium*, brand new and sparkling, docked on the base's secure ring. She had wanted that ship. After the battles she fought, the risks she had taken, the way she had saved her crew and the mission, she felt she had deserved that ship.

And Galland had used those emotions. Used them all.

She made herself focus on the statue of a man on a horse on one of the bookshelves. It was a Remington, from Earth, twentieth century. She knew because Galland had told her. And she had looked it up one afternoon while lounging in her quarters. If the bronze statue was the original, it was priceless. It had once stood in the Oval Office of the White House, back when Ronald Reagan was president, centuries ago.

Had Galland stolen that, too? Or had he bought it?

She didn't know. Anyone could get rich out here, and still serve in the Patrol. Getting rich wasn't illegal. It seemed like very little was any more.

Damn him.

"So," she said, "you're even taking the *Millennium* away from me."

"Roz, you're the one who proved that full-sized vessels can't survive intact in the Cactus Corridor. That nebula would be dangerous without the Bá-am-ás and their mines. But the fact that the Bá-am-ás claim it and defend it, and the Corridor is filled with more debris than the average nebula, make it the most treacherous area of space out here."

"I've flown it," Roz said.

"And lost a ship doing so."

"If regulations hadn't insisted on one: successful completion of a mission and two: crew's lives above all else, I'd've gotten the damn ship out." She took a deep breath. "I want the *Millennium* on this mission."

"No."

"And since this mission's off the books, I'm not following regulations."

"Roz—"

"What are you going to do, Allen?" she said, being as disrespectful to him as he was to her. "Throw the book at me? You can do that already. If you want me to go, and it's clear you do, you do it my way."

"See the prototype first," he said.

"Has the prototype flown any farther than this base?"

"No."

"Have its weapon systems been tested in real battles, not simulations?"

"No."

"Has it ever flown in anything other than optimum conditions?"

"No."

"Then you give me the *Millennium*, or you find someone else to take this little joy ride of yours."

"I'll have your ass, Roz."

She smiled at him. "It seems that you already do, Allen. There's not a lot more that you can threaten me with. You do it my way, or it's not going to get done. Or did some other captain wrap a noose around her neck like I did?"

He stared at her for a long time. Then he sighed. "All right," he said. "You have the *Millennium*."

"Somehow," she said, "I'm not overjoyed."

Roz was even less overjoyed when the *Millennium* hit the Cactus Corridor. The Corridor was the name the Patrol had given one of the larger nebulas in this part of the galaxy and it was, as Galland had said, dangerous even without the mines placed in it by the Bá-am-ás.

The Bá-am-ás were a possessive race who claimed not only the space around their planet, but the space around their solar system as their territory. That they shared that space with at least seventy-five other sentient species didn't seem to bother them at all; that among the seventy-five were fourteen that were space-faring only bothered the Bá-am-ás in that they had to defend themselves.

And they did, against everyone.

To make matters worse, the Bá-am-ás were more technologically advanced than the Patrol. It meant that any space-faring ships that went into self-proclaimed Bá-am-ás territory had to be warships, and had to have a lot of maneuverability.

The *Millennium* had both, and normally, Roz would have felt all right going into Bá-am-ás turf with her ship, but things weren't normal, The *Millennium* was designed to run with a crew composite of three hundred. It could run well with anything down to two hundred and, theoretically, could function with a skeleton crew of one hundred.

Galland had allowed her the fifty crew members of her choice, promising to reassign all the others and rebuild their careers. She was happy for them—but the problem that she had was that to run the *Millennium* with half her minimal crew composite required her to use her best people—and those were the people she most wanted out of Galland's clutches.

Her only other choice was to take the prototype which she trusted as much as she trusted Galland. Better to run the Corridor with a tired overworked talented crew in the best ship in the fleet than run it with a new ship and an unfamiliar crew.

Or so she told herself.

If there had been a way to avoid the Corridor, she would have done it. But there wasn't, at least, not a quick way, according to the maps she had gotten from Galland. She would have interviewed his alien informants herself, but they had conveniently left the base just before she arrived.

She did watch the vids of the interviews and noted that all the pertinent information hadn't been filmed at all. Someone had shut off the vids at all the appropriate moments. That meant she couldn't even reconstruct the blacked-out vids. All she had was Galland's word, the crazy map, and supposition.

The interviews told her less than Galland had.

The fifth day into the nebula, the computer reported the first minefield.

The Bá-am-ás were clever. The mines were impossible to detect, at least with Patrol technology, but the Bá-am-ás always issued warnings in the parameter around the field. The warnings always ended with some Bá-am-ádian dignitary expressing its wish that no race get hurt in Bá-am-ádian territory.

So considerate.

Roz had the computer do a sweep anyway. She had learned, the last time she went through this nebula, that the Bá-am-ádian mines appeared on scans as bits of rock. Her plan was to avoid all rock as she went through.

If the Bá-am-ás had changed the configuration of the mines, however, the *Millennium* would get through the nebula by luck alone.

As soon as the announcement came through, Roz went to the bridge. She wasn't the best pilot on board, not anymore, but she was the most canny. She took the copilot's chair and served as backup as the ship crawled its way through the minefield.

Fifteen agonizing hours passed. Roz suspected they were nearly out of the field when the first Bá-am-ás ship appeared.

Bá-am-ás ships were slender and white, looking so light that they seemed to float in space. The Bá-am-ás never revealed themselves. Even their announcements came through as audio only, and all attempts to look at their planet were blocked.

Roz always imagined that they looked like their ships, white featherlike creatures without any substance to them at all.

"Message," said Ethan, her first on this mission.

"What language we got?"

"Bad English," said Ethan.

It annoyed her that the Bá-am-ás had learned the language of the Galactic Alliance, but the Alliance had never even heard the Bá-am-ádian language.

Maybe language was just annoying her all around these days.

"All right," she said. "Tell them to go ahead."

Although she could probably recite the announcement chapter and verse already. She still heard it in her dreams.

"Galactic Patrol Vessel," said the flat androgynous voice that was so obviously computer generated. "You are in Bá-am-ádian space. We request that you leave it immediately."

She had two ways of responding. She had tried the first the last time she had gone through and that had gone very badly. The Bá-am-ás seemed to have no patience with people who claimed that this part of space could not be owned.

She operated the communications array herself. "Bá-am-ádian vessel," she said. "We had no idea we were in your space. We've been called to an outpost on the other side of the nebula. We request safe passage to tend to our people."

There was a long silence before she got the response, "There are no Patrol outposts on the other side of the nebula."

"There is one," she said. She wondered how far she would have to take this bluff. "I can give you the coordinates if you like."

She hoped that the Bá-am-ás could not read her star

charts. If she had to send the information, she'd use the least informative way possible.

"You are already halfway through the nebula," the Bá-am-ás said. "You have guarantee of safe passage to the other side. But you must agree not to return through our space."

Great. All she was doing was putting off the inevitable. "That would require us to go several light-years out of our way."

"It is a small requirement to save your lives," said the metallic Bá-am-ádian voice.

Actually that was true. And it put a germ of an idea in her head, an idea she did not have to examine until she got back from Galland's mystery planet.

"We agree," she said.

Ethan swore behind her, and she waved him silent. The rest of the bridge crew was staring at her as if she had grown three heads.

"We accept your safe passage through the nebula and for it, we agree not to return this way."

There was a long silence on the other end. Then the computerized voice said, "We shall hold you and your people to this agreement. Now, follow us and we shall lead you out of the nebula."

"Thank you," Roz said and ended the communication.

Her bridge crew was still staring at her.

"That Bá-am-ás said 'your' people," Ethan said. "You don't have the right to negotiate something this big for the Alliance."

"I know," she said.

"Don't you know what kind of problems this will create?" Ivy, her pilot, asked.

"I know," Roz said.

"And you did it anyway?" Ivy asked. "Don't you know what's going to happen to you?"

"Nothing that hasn't happened already," Roz said. "I need a quick meeting of the senior staff. It's time you all know what's going on."

They frowned and returned to their posts.

She sat back and let Ivy do the hard piloting. But Roz made sure the computer was charting their course, and taking readings of the rocks and debris near the strange twists and turns. Maybe, just maybe, she'd be lucky enough to find a common material in all of that junk.

Maybe she'd discover how to locate a Bá-am-ádian mine.

"He's been tampering with all of our records?" Ethan asked, pacing around the conference desk.

The conference room in the *Millennium* was probably the prettiest room on the ship. On one wall, it had floor-to-ceiling windows open to space, on the others it had hand-painted maps of the known universe—maps which could be covered by screens if someone needed to make a large presentation.

Ethan was a burly man who'd made his way through the ranks on sheer brute force. It had taken her—and her crew—to show him that he had the intelligence to match that strength.

Now, however, she wished he was small and puny. He was using that strength to knock empty chairs and eventually, he'd knock them clear of their anchors in the floor.

Ivy was huddled beside Roz, looking as if she didn't want to be there. Three other staff members, petite Gina Fishel who headed security, no-nonsense Belle Curry who ran the medical team, and sturdy Tom O'Neal who led the engineering team, watched Ethan warily. He was expressing the anger all of them felt—Roz was smart enough to know that—but they still weren't comfortable with the edge of violence that was in all of his movements.

She was. She remembered having the same feeling in Galland's office.

"Yes," Roz said patiently. "He tampered with everything."

"And you trusted him?"

"He was my superior officer," she said. "We were following regulations."

Ethan growled and smacked another empty chair. "You should have double-checked on him."

"Why didn't you?" she asked, unable to control the impulse.

"Because that was your job."

"So, under your logic, you should have made sure that I did it properly." She folded her hands. "We'd all been on base since the loss of the *St. Petersburg*. We all had the opportunity to make sure that Galland was telling us the truth. We all chose to believe the system was working."

Ethan whirled, slapping his large hands on the table. "You can't blame this on us."

"I'm not," Roz said. "But I am pointing out that the mistake I made was somewhat logical. I've had a week to think about this. I screwed up, yes, and I allowed my desire to maintain a ship and a command compromise all of us. But we're here now—"

"We wouldn't be here if you'd told us that on base," Gina said softly.

Roz nodded. "I know that."

Gina's narrow face flushed. "You got us here under false pretenses."

"I need you to run this ship," Roz said.

"We could strike." That came from Belle. She crossed her arms over her chest and leaned back in her chair.

Roz looked at her with surprise. Belle, who had served

on more ships than the rest of them combined, never acted in an insubordinate manner. She accepted her work as easily as she accepted her silver hair and advancing years.

"You could," Roz said. "Then we drift. I can't run this ship alone."

"So your plan is to be Galland's lackey?" Tom asked.

Roz shrugged. "I figure we'll investigate this."

"Why?" Belle said. "You know it's not possible."

"I have a hunch Galland has sent us there for another reason," Roz said.

"And then how do you expect to get home?" Ivy asked, her voice soft. "You told the Bá-am-ás that we won't go through the Corridor. If we don't, we'll go so far out of our way that it'll take us two years to get back."

Roz nodded. Then she stood up and walked to the window. Through its protective coating and quadruple panes, all regulation thick, she saw dust particles floating like schools of fish. The *Millennium* could handle small particles of debris like that—it was built to withstand all sorts of space junk—but she knew that too many trips through a nebula would make microscopic fractures too small to measure, and eventually, something on the ship would buckle.

"It doesn't bother you that it'll take us forever to get back?" Ethan asked the question a bit too loudly.

"It bothers me," she said, "but I'm not going to worry about it right now."

"What are you worrying about?" Tom asked.

She rubbed her arms. "Getting to that planet. Finding the universal translator."

"I can't believe you're going to go through with the mission!" Ethan said.

She turned. The staff were all staring at her, waiting for her answer. "What do you want me to do?"

"We could contact the Bá-am-ás, and ask for passage out of the Corridor on the Alliance side," Ivy said.

"After the lie I told them?" Roz asked. "You think they'll buy that?"

No one answered her.

"And if we do return, then what? Do I put Galland on report?"

"Sarcasm doesn't help, Roz," Belle said softly.

"No, I suppose it doesn't," Roz said. "But you're not coming up with any solutions."

"Maybe we should turn ourselves in," Ivy said softly.

Ethan cursed and kicked the nearest chair. It shuddered on its post, and nearly toppled off.

"Don't go breaking the ship," Tom said to him. "We might have to live here for the next two years."

Ethan cursed again.

"Let's see what Galland wants so badly," Gina said. "I'm with the captain. We might have blackmail material here."

Roz looked at her sideways and smiled. "That's the kind of response I need from my staff. Blame me all you want, but let's come up with some creative solutions to get us out of this mess."

"Blackmail is creative?" Belle asked.

"It's the best thing I've heard so far," Roz said.

"Yeah. After we go to some stupid planet no one has ever seen before, and then take a route two years out of our way to get home." Ethan sat in the chair he had just kicked. The chair groaned under his weight. "By then, all this might not matter."

"It'll matter," Roz said softly.

"To whom?" Ethan asked. "For all we know, by then Galland could have retired."

"It'll matter to me." Roz shoved her hands in the pockets of her uniform. "It'll always matter to me."

*   *   *

They emerged from the nebula into a portion of space that Roz had only been to briefly, during her last encounter with the Bá-am-ás. This time, like last, she didn't have any time to explore. She had to fulfill her mission.

She couldn't articulate to her staff anymore why she felt she had to fulfill this bizarre quest. She had a hope, one she hardly expressed even to herself, that she would find something that would allow her to get some kind of revenge on Galland—or, at least, that would restore her good name.

Since the aliens who had informed Galland of the planet hadn't bothered to name it, and since it was uncharted—at least by the Alliance—Roz's crew had taken to calling it "Xanadu." They all giggled when they said it, and then looked at her sideways, as if afraid she would get the joke. She didn't, and she really didn't care.

The route they had been given took them into a new solar system. Most of the planets were not marked on the map. The exploration urge hit her again, but she ignored it.

She headed for Xanadu, hoping against hope she would find something she could use.

Xanadu turned out to be an Earth-type planet with oceans and six continents—three habitable to humans. The atmosphere had enough oxygen to sustain human life, which was not a surprise, given the makeup of the planet itself.

Roz had studied her chart enough to know that the creatures she was seeking lived on the small third continent. It reminded her of Australia, where she had been on her one trip to Earth at the age of fifteen. From space, it had looked like an island, but she knew that the land mass itself was vast.

She had her senior staff review the alien interviews—

with all the blackouts—hoping for a clue to what she was seeking. She also had the computer scan the surface, looking for signs of a space-faring civilization.

It found nothing on the surface so, in a moment of frustration, Ethan asked it to scan below the surface.

There the computer found catacombs that went on forever—all of them carved out of rock and supported by metal beams: not anything that would have occurred naturally.

It took three days to locate an entrance to the catacombs. Then Roz plotted the away missions, breaking protocol again and deciding to go herself. She wasn't going to orbit the damn planet waiting for news. If there was something below that she could use—or even if there wasn't—she wanted to see for herself.

The fact that her crew was even on this mission was her fault; the least she could do was shoulder all of the responsibility herself.

She went down in the first shuttle, along with ten crew members. Ethan stayed on board, protesting the entire time. Roz took Ivy, Gina, two other security officers, Tom and two of his most scientifically minded engineers, and a medical officer handpicked by Belle.

Despite the atmosphere readings, Roz insisted they all wear environmental suits. She hated the helmets and the clear faceplates as much as anyone else, but she wasn't going to lose a person on this mission. She wasn't going to take any unreasonable chances.

A second shuttle was supposed to disembark five hours later if hers didn't return. She never said it would be a rescue mission, but both she and Ethan knew it was.

Ivy piloted the shuttle down and balked when Roz ordered her to remain on board. But Roz didn't listen to Ivy's arguments; instead she hustled the rest of the team out of the shuttle and into the bright light on the planet's surface.

They had landed on a flat rocky area near the spot the computer had located as the entrance to the catacombs. The rocks were rust-colored, but the soil beneath, peaking out in various areas, was a dark brown. There were no plants here, but she hadn't expected any. The plants were two kilometers below them, in a valley that she could barely see from where she stood.

The environmental suit's cooling unit clicked on after informing her that the surface temperature was barely tolerable for human beings. The shuttle had read the ambient temperature of the air and had said it was cool enough to go without suits. But apparently the shuttle's equipment didn't measure how hot the surface got with the large sun overhead baking the strange red rocks.

Roz led her team to the coordinates for the opening to the catacombs. She had expected something elaborate carved into the rocks jutting up like cliffs. Instead, a metal box stood on the rock like a sign pointing toward the hiding place below the surface.

The box had a door on one side, and the door was open. Roz glanced at Gina, who shrugged.

"Might always be like that," Gina said. "No way of knowing."

Still, she motioned to the members of the security team, and they all went in first. Roz and the rest of the landing party waited until Gina gave an all clear.

Then Roz led the way inside.

Immediately, her suit's cooling unit shut off. The air was cooler in here and, her suit informed her, more oxygen rich. The ceiling glowed, creating a cool, unnatural light that illuminated the path before them. The floor sloped downward, a gradual slant so that even the most clumsy could keep their footing.

"This is weird," Tom said.

Roz nodded, but said nothing. She walked just behind the security team, noting the metal beams and the way the support structures disappeared into the rock.

The deeper the team went into the catacombs the wider the caverns got. Instead of getting darker, the path got lighter. The same material that had been on the ceiling above illuminated the floor below.

"Cautious creatures, aren't they?" Roz asked.

"If they were cautious," Gina said, "they'd've greeted us already."

"Says who?" asked Marek, one of Tom's scientists. "We have no idea how they operate."

"Or even if they exist at all," said Brock, the other scientist.

"Someone exists," Roz said. "Or existed. This didn't just appear by itself.

The catacombs opened even farther and up ahead, Gina whistled. It took Roz a moment to catch up to her. The path created a T where Gina had stopped. At the top of the T, someone had built a wall that came up to Roz's shoulders.

When Roz looked over the wall, she whistled, too. Above her, a carved ceiling glowed as bright as daylight—only this light was cool like the light that had illuminated their path— not red and furious like the planet's sun.

Beneath that domed ceiling was a cavern that seemed to extend for kilometers. And on every centimeter of that cavern floor were buildings and streets.

A city, made of white stone. The splotches of color came from paintings on the sides of buildings, from fabric spread on rooftops, and from the river that flowed through the city's center. She could smell the water up here, fresh and spicy and cool, and she could hear it as well as it churned its way past all the buildings.

Branches of the river flowed through the center part of the city like streets and it took Roz a moment to realize what she had taken as roads before weren't. They were calm branches of the river, their surface so flat that they shone.

"My God," Tom said. "I've never seen anything like this."

None of them had. It was stunning and unsettling at the same time.

Roz checked her system's clock. They'd been underground for two hours. She couldn't check in from this far below the surface. Which meant that she and the team had only an hour to interact with whatever lived below.

"Gina," she said, "send one of your team back to the surface. Tell Ethan to delay the second shuttle by five more hours."

"Yes, sir," Gina said. She relayed Roz's order, and one of the security members branched off, heading back the way they'd come.

Roz felt a slight pang, wondering if she should have sent a pair above, but so far she had seen nothing hostile.

"Does anyone see how to get to that city?" she asked.

"Either side will take us down," Tom said, pointing to the other side of the cavern. The paths followed the walls, slanting downward until they met directly across from where the team stood now, in what looked like a giant slide that led into the city.

Roz nodded. It would take them another half hour or more just to traverse the width of the cavern. But she saw no other choice.

This time, she led the team. The downward slope was much steeper here, and she had to hold onto the wall to keep her balance. So did the rest of the team. All the way down she watched for some form of alien life, and saw nothing. When they finally reached the far side of the cavern, Gina swore. Roz looked ahead.

What had looked like a giant slide from the other side looked more like a waterfall encased in stone on this side. The only way down it was to rappel or to slide down.

The stone waterfall ended in one of the pools that had branched off the river.

"Great," Tom said.

Strangers, a voice boomed.

Roz looked at the rest of her team. They looked as startled as she did.

State your business here.

Roz felt a shiver run through her. That was English—and, so far as she knew, the creatures in this place had never encountered any humans before, let alone those from the Patrol, those that spoke English almost exclusively.

"Um." She stepped forward. "We're from the Galactic Alliance, a loosely-based association of worlds on the other side of the nebula near here."

Tom was frowning at her. Did she sound as uncomfortable as she felt.

"We had heard that you had a universal translator. We were sent to check out the rumor."

The voice was silent.

Roz looked at her team. Gina shrugged. The other security members hung back as if the strangeness surprised them. The scientists were looking for the source of the voice, and the medical officer was frowning.

We do not allow strangers into the city, the voice said after a moment. *One of our representatives will meet you.*

Roz felt her shoulders relax, She really didn't want to face that frozen waterfall.

Then she heard a loud splash and a strange whirring. A

creature whirled out of the pool below them, and rose to their level. It landed, shaking water off as it did so.

It was small, mammalian in appearance, with forearms and webbed feet like a duck. It also had a beak. Its eyes were dark and had no whites. It seemed to be breathing the air, but it also had gills along the sides of its neck.

We have never heard of a Galactic Alliance. The little creature's mouth—or what Roz took to be a mouth—did not move.

"We've been around for nearly a hundred years," she said. "If you want, I could brief you on it."

Perhaps later. It folded its small forearms over its belly. It had what looked like six-fingered hands at the end of those forearms and it threaded the fingers together. *First we would like to hear of your universal translator.*

"Actually," Roz said, "we heard you had invented one."

We have no use for such a thing, the creature said.

"Yet you're speaking to us in our language."

The creature made a chittering sound. *I am not speaking.*

Telepathy. She had heard that there were creatures all over the galaxy that had it in one form or another. "How do you understand our language, then?"

I do not know. Only that we overheard your speech, then used what pieces of it we could find to create our own responses.

Roz glanced at Gina. Gina had pressed a small button on the side of her environmental suit. She was recording this. Although Roz figured it would do no good. If the creature was telepathic, the conversation would be distinctly one-sided.

How did you learn of us?

Roz told him of the Hicrum, the Crativ'n, and the Dulacs, and then she spoke of her assignment.

What good would a universal translator be to your peocle? the creature asked.

"We travel all over the galaxy," she said. "Our mission is to map the sectors we haven't seen before, and make diplomatic contact with peoples we haven't encountered before. We usually contact only space-faring races."

We were space-faring once.

"What happened?"

We chose not to be any longer. The creature shook some more water off its fur, then leaned over and groomed its shoulder with its tongue. It made a spitting sound, and shook again. *However, it is beginning to seem as if we will not be left in peace.*

"Because the Hacrim and the others are telling everyone about you?"

And you are all coming to investigate.

"We've been raised to believe that a universal translator is an impossibility," Tom said.

When you speak of this translator, you speak of a device, do you not? the creature asked.

"Yes," Roz said.

Then you have been raised correctly. So far as we know, anyway.

"But we're understanding each other."

The creature raised its dark eyes to hers then made that chittering sound again. She wondered if it was a sound of derision or disgust.

My people have the skill to understand most sentient beings. It is not a pleasant nor desirable trait, and it is the reason we have retreated here.

"The underground city?" Gina asked.

The river, the creature said. *It protects us. We have trouble absorbing through water.*

"What do your people call themselves?" Roz asked.

The creature made a sound that was something between a burp and a sneeze.

The creature studied them for a moment, then said, *If we had had the device you were looking for, what would you have done with it?*

"I would have reported to my superiors," Roz said, not sure that was what she would have done at all. "And they probably would have figured out a way to buy the technology from you."

Would they be willing to barter or trade?

"Of course," Roz said. "I'm sure a lot of races would."

I will speak to my people, the creature said. *You will return here after the next sunrise. You will then explain to us your hesitation at returning to your command and why you are both elated and disappointed to learn of our talents.*

Roz was startled. She had realized it was telepathic, but she hadn't realized its ability extended beyond the language skills. "All right," she said.

The creature tilted its head, which seemed like some sort of ritual movement (like a wave), then it raised its arms and laid itself on the stone waterfall. It slid down the fall and landed, with a splash, in the pool below.

Roz peered after it, but couldn't see anything in the murky depths. "Okay," she said after a moment, "that was weird."

"But promising," Gina said.

The pool below still rippled. Roz thought she saw movement. But she pulled herself away. "Let's head back to the shuttle before Ethan sends the next team down."

So they made the long trek back, radioed Ethan, and settled in for their first night on Xanadu.

Sunrise, it turned out, was two standard days later.

The wait was interminable. For the first time, Roz regretted leaving Ethan on board the ship. She wanted to hear his analysis. The others were reliable, but they weren't as blunt as Ethan.

She needed blunt right now.

The breaks in the recordings of the interviews bothered her more than ever. She had a hunch that Galland knew his universal translator wasn't a device, but a people. And she had an idea that he wanted her to bring just one member of that race back with her.

That was what she would have done if he hadn't threatened her, if he hadn't tried to manipulate her, and if he hadn't ruined her career.

She did speak to her team, and they all agreed that there was no way she would be able to convince the Xanadians— which was what they called the creatures, not being able to imitate that sneeze/burp sound—to continue to hide or even to move on. If three different alien races knew about them, it was only a matter of time before someone else did as well.

And their skills would be useful, whether on a voluntary or a coerced basis.

While she waited, she sent all the information she had back to the ship. Belle and her team examined it. Telepathy on a low level, Belle informed Roz, had been found in other races scattered among the galaxy, but nothing this sophisticated. Mostly telepaths were able to sense strong emotion among their own people. Belle had no records of any race that had telepathy with other races—and certainly not anything that included picking up a language in less than an hour.

"But," Belle had said, "as much as I don't want to admit that it's possible, I have to remind myself there's more to this universe than we can perceive. All I have to do is blow a dog whistle to know that."

It was her standard line when she encountered something

she didn't understand, and it bothered Roz. "Can't you at least make a guess at what they're doing?" she had asked.

"I can guess," Belle had said. "Not on the telepathy but on the language."

That got Roz's attention. She thought that was the impossible part, and she said so.

"Babies of all species which have language have a great ability to absorb and learn that language without formal training," Belle had said. "It's an ability most of us lose as humans by the time we're four. A handful retain it, like a talent. I'm guessing that this entire species had to learn language and telepathy as survival skills. I don't know enough about the ecosystem of the planet, but if we delve into it, maybe into the planet's history, we'll learn why these skills are so necessary."

Then Belle had grinned. "Or maybe they're just conning us like everyone else has managed to lately."

It was possible, Roz supposed, but she didn't know why there would be such an elaborate con. There were easier ways of trapping Galland, and the Galactic Patrol didn't even work this sector. So she was inclined to believe the Xanadians were real.

Her staff agreed. They thought the Xanadians were the real thing.

Now she just had to find out what the little gold mines wanted.

Instead of meeting her down by the city, the creature met her inside the door to the catacombs. Near the surface, it looked more molelike than she had expected, its dark eyes squinting at the light filtering in the open door.

Her own team waited just outside as the creature had asked them to do. It had pulled Roz far enough away that her voice couldn't be heard by her own people—and she wondered how it knew that or if it was just comfortable a distance away from the others—and then it said,

We are tiny race. We live in the—and again it made a sneezy burpy sound, which somehow she understood to mean the continent she was on—*and nowhere else. The other races on this planet leave us alone. They're frightened of our abilities. But now, creatures from space have come—several in the past year*—and by that she knew it meant its year, not her year—*and all of them seemed intrigued by our abilities to understand them. We get a sense of threat and we do not know why. You are the first to speak of trade, barter, buying, and we begin to understand. Our ability to communicate does not frighten you. You desire it, see it as a commodity, see it as something that will improve your lives.*

She nodded, then said, "Yes," just in case it didn't understand.

We sent the others away, telling them that we want to be left alone. And it seems, they all told your people. Why is that?

"Knowledge," she said. "It's a commodity, too, among my people."

The creature rubbed its handlike paws together, as if she had confirmed its thinking. *We had heard of your union. We were going to apply to it for its protection until you arrived. You have hesitations. It is as if you do not believe in the organization you represent.*

If she needed confirmation of the creatures' telepathic ability, then this was it. The creature had put into words the very thing that had been bothering her.

If she were to report back to Galland, he would come out here. Or he would send a force out here. He'd been far enough away to tamper with her records, hide the loss of a ship, and make himself rich enough to have expensive goods all over his office. If he made some kind of deal with these creatures outside Alliance guidelines—and any deal he made with them for his own gain would be—there would be no one to stop him.

At least not until it was too late.

She could, she supposed, let Headquarters know what was happening, but that would be difficult, especially considering how Galland had discredited her and her crew.

And, really, when she looked at it, what was the Alliance, anyway? A federation of planets with nothing more in common than their military unity. They claimed they were diplomats exploring the galaxy, but the races they found either joined the Alliance or became the Alliance's enemies.

She had no idea why the Bá-am-ás hated the Patrol, but she had a hunch the reasons she had been told weren't the ones the Bá-am-ás had.

She sighed. "I'm not the best representative for my people. I've been discredited and I allowed myself to be conned."

The creature turned toward her. Its dark eyes seemed to have grown even darker. *We know this.*

"Then you know that I no longer believe in the Alliance I represent."

It is why we talk with you. One of the creature's forearms fluttered like the wing of a grounded bird. *We believe you are the first alien we have encountered that might be able to help us.*

"Help you?" she asked. "How?"

It would require you to break several of your laws. The creature studied her as if it could see through her.

"It seems I've done that already."

And you would have to find new allegiances.

"I'm listening," she said.

So, with a wave of its little pawlike hands, the creature outlined its proposition.

She had to take the proposition back to her crew. The creatures were willing to wait while she returned to her ship. She held the meeting shortly after she arrived.

"We know nothing about these creatures," Ivy said. "If they want us to train them so that they can go back into space, how do we know they won't go out and conquer the galaxy?"

"All five hundred of them?" Belle asked.

The entire staff looked at her.

"I checked. We can scan below the surface, even if our communicators don't work there."

"Any way they could have fudged that?" Gina asked Tom.

"I suppose," he said. "If they have a great understanding of our technology and lots of time to prepare."

"I take that as a no," Roz said.

"Unless you're really paranoid," Tom said.

"Besides," Belle said, "they reproduce slowly. Even if all five hundred decide to conquer the galaxy, it'll be a while before they have the ability to do so."

"They say they reproduce slowly," Tom said.

"No," Belle said. "This one I could check. Gestation period of one of our years, two years in a pouch—they're more marsupials than mammals in some ways—and then nearly two decades to grow up."

"Okay," Ivy said. "So they can't conquer the known universe."

"Not in our lifetime," Belle said. "Besides, Roz said they're going to let us interview the other races on this planet about them."

"And how do you propose we do that?" Ethan asked.

"We don't speak any of the languages. And I don't exactly trust the only available translators."

"It boils down to trust," Roz said. "And I don't have any left, for anyone at least, except this crew."

No one spoke.

"Which brings up another problem," Roz said into the silence. "I mean, we're not going to limp back to Alliance space, not if we do this."

Everyone looked at her.

"You're proposing stealing the *Millennium?*" Ethan asked.

"On the books," Roz said, "we already have."

"And doing what with her?"

Roz sighed. She'd been thinking about this since she went through the Cactus Corridor. "She's our home, isn't she? None of us has family anywhere else."

The staff was silent.

"And we've been doing things we don't like for reasons that we all hated because we thought we were working for the Alliance. It turns out we weren't."

"So shouldn't we go back and get a court-martial for Galland?" Ivy asked.

"Maybe," Roz said. "If we can. If we believe it'll happen. Like I said, I don't believe in much anymore."

"What are you suggesting?" Ethan asked.

"They can't come after us," Roz said. "We've screwed up their passage through the Corridor. It'll take them a few tries before they realize that the Bá-am-ás believe there's an agreement, a few more tries before they anger the Bá-am-ás into believing the agreement's over, and then at least two years of flying before they make it here, our last known stop."

"We'd be fugitives for the rest of our lives," Gina said.

"Only in Alliance space."

The entire staff looked at her as if she had three heads. Roz was beginning to get used to that response.

She shrugged. "It's just an idea. I'm beginning to realize that I'm not the most subtle person in the world. Or the greatest brain. But I do have an ethical center. I'm not suggesting we go out and pillage this part of the galaxy."

"Then what are you suggesting?" Ethan asked.

"Doing what we were hired to do. Exploring. Helping when we feel it's right."

Belle rubbed her chin with her left hand. "You think helping the Xanadians is right."

"Not so that they relearn space travel," Roz said, "but so that they can defend themselves against anyone who wants to use their special abilities for the wrong reason."

"And what would you take in payment?"

"Nothing," Roz said.

"Nothing?" the crew asked in unison.

"Well, supplies," Roz said. "We're going to have to learn how to barter for those, if you follow my suggestion. And one other thing."

"What's that?" Ethan asked in a tone that suggested he hated the idea without hearing it.

"Adding a Xanadian to our crew. Provided we learn to like the creatures and feel we can trust them."

"Why?"

"A universal translator is a valuable thing," Roz said. "And the Xanadians want to learn what space flight is like. So we work together."

"Create a new alliance," Ethan said, sitting down hard, making the chair groan.

"Not a formal alliance," Roz said. "More like an association. A friendly interaction."

"It makes me uncomfortable. Any Xanadian on this ship will know everything about everyone."

"Unless it lives in some kind of water environment," Belle said. "Think you could jury-rig something like that over the next year, Tom?"

He nodded. "I even know the place to do it."

"It's not a sure thing," Roz said. "We wouldn't do it if we decide we don't like them or we can't trust them."

"Then what do we do?" Ethan asked.

Roz leaned forward. "We leave."

"Just like that?" Ethan asked.

She nodded. "What's holding us here? What's holding us anywhere?"

"Imagine what we'll see," Tom said. "Imagine what we'll do."

"It won't all be easy," Belle said.

"But it will be interesting," Gina said.

Ethan looked at Roz. "Is this what freedom feels like?"

She grinned. "I don't know," she said. "but I have a hunch it is."

The Xanadians agreed to the loose alliance. Roz made plans to interview some of the other species on the planet, and the *Millennium* orbited like a glorified guard ship while all of this was going on.

There was still a lot to work out. The entire crew had been notified, and she expected dissension in the ranks. Tom told her that one of the shuttles could be modified so that dissenters could try to fly back to Alliance space if they wanted.

So far, no one had volunteered.

Roz had a hunch no one would. The adventure out there was just too promising, the universe too vast.

Everyone on the crew had joined the Patrol for the same idealistic reasons she had, and the last eleven missions had whittled away that idealism. Since she made her decision to break off from the Alliance, though, she heard a lot more laughter on her ship.

The pressure was gone. It was as if they had worked for an evil master and were now free.

The key, of course, was to maintain their own idealism in the face of being alone on this side of the Corridor. She felt they could do it.

She felt like her life's adventure had just begun.

A TIME TO DREAM

by Dean Wesley Smith

Dean Wesley Smith has sold over twenty novels and around one hundred short stories to various magazines and anthologies. He's been a finalist for the Hugo and Nebula Awards, and has won a World Fantasy Award and a Locus Award. He was the editor and publisher of Pulphouse Publishing, and has just finished editing the *Star Trek* anthology *Strange New Worlds*.

Captain Brian Sable of the Earth Protection League could tell there would be a mission. Tonight was the night. The first mission in over a week. The border skirmish on the third moon of the Garland Star Cluster must have flared up again. Or something else threatened the security of Earth. The League was needed to stop the threat. He was needed, and he was ready.

Across the small nursing home room the old clock on the wooden dresser ticked, echoing in the small space and dim light, demanding his attention just as it did every night as he lay in his bed, awake, waiting. When he'd first arrived at the Shady Valley Nursing Home outside of Chicago six years earlier, that old clock had let him count down the seconds until he died. Long seconds, never-ending seconds that he had wished would go by faster.

Now the loud ticking of that old clock in the night counted the minutes until the next mission, until the time he could become young again. And the time waiting, getting older and closer to death went by too fast now.

Far too fast.

Now he wanted to stay alive, to stay with the missions and the Earth Protection League, to get the chance to be young enough to wear his Proton Stunners and fight the good fight against the enemies of Earth.

The clock ticked.

Time went by.

Down the dimly lit hall outside his room's door a nurse laughed at an unheard joke. Captain Brian Sable coughed, the sound weak and pitiful in the silence of the nursing home.

He glanced at the clock. He could barely see the hands in the light from the hall, but he could tell it was only a little after ten in the evening. It was still far too early for them to come for him.

He tried to roll his ninety-one-year-old body over on its side, but only succeeded in shifting the sheet slightly under him. He hadn't had the strength to pull himself out of bed for over two years, let alone roll over. And he couldn't remember the last time he'd walked across this small room on his own to the bathroom. A nurse's aide always had to carry him and plop him on the cold toilet, then carry him back to his bed or wheelchair.

He laughed, and the laugh again turned into a rough cough that sent his old heart pounding. He forced himself to calm down and to not think about how he was at the moment. He hated thinking about how old he was, how frail his body had become, how dependent on others he now was. He reminded himself that none of that mattered like it used to.

Now he had the missions for the Earth Protection League. The missions gave his old life purpose, his continued liv-

ing in this way station of the dying a valid reason. And
even though there hadn't been a mission for almost a week,
he knew tonight was the night.

He could tell.

It was all in the details. For example, the night nurse
had left the rail on his bed down. The nurse never did that,
except on mission nights.

They had also cleaned him up early and put him to bed.
They never did that either unless there was a mission to run.

Of course, when he had first talked to them about the
missions after his first one, they had all laughed at him.
They had said there was no such thing as the Earth Protection League. They claimed that he had just had a strange
dream.

But he knew better.

He'd gone on a mission, gotten young again. He had
helped Earth defend itself against the evil scum of the
galaxy. And since that night he'd gone on many, many more
missions.

Tonight he was ready again.

Hell, he was always ready. There was nothing else for
him to do.

The clock ticked the night away minute by minute, second by second. On the night of a mission, waiting was the
hardest. Sometimes he wished he couldn't tell when a mission was. It would make sleep easier.

So he forced himself to think about other things. First
he thought about his long-dead wife, Margaret. She would
have laughed at him if she knew what he was doing. But
she wouldn't have minded. She had always supported him
in everything he did, one of the many things he had loved
about her.

Their children, Strom and Claire, didn't have time for
him much anymore. They had their own lives, their own

jobs, their own kids to raise. He hadn't bothered to even hint to them about the missions. There would have been no point. They were part of his past, his life as a grocery store owner. None of that compared with his life now as a captain in the Earth Protection League.

He watched the clock as it ticked away the time.

At some point along the way, at least an hour after midnight, he dozed off.

"Captain Sable?" the young, male voice said.

Strong arms picked him up from the bed and moved quickly toward the sliding glass door that lead into the center court of the nursing home. "We need your help again, sir."

"Always ready to help," Sable said. His old vocal cords managed to barely choke out the words. Those were the same words he always said at the start of every mission.

He glanced at the old clock on the way out. Three-sixteen in the morning. He would be back shortly.

If he lived.

The sliding door to the outside was open and the Chicago night air was cold against his old skin. But the young soldier who carried him didn't even pause. He strode across to the center of the court and then tapped a badge on his wrist. A white beam of light from above lifted them quickly into the transport ship.

Sable knew that around the country the same thing had happened, or was happening, at least forty-one other times as his crew was gathered from their respective nursing homes and retirement apartments.

The young man with the strong arms quickly moved to a silver, coffin-shaped sleep chamber and laid Sable down slowly on the soft cushions.

"Any hints as to the fight?" Sable asked. "The nature of the mission?"

The young soldier smiled. "Couldn't tell you if I knew, sir," he said. "But they never tell us grunts what's happening on this end. I just wish I could be there with you."

Sable laughed. "I wish you could, too, son."

But both of them knew that wasn't possible. The reason the ninety-one-year-old Sable was going instead of the young soldier was because of the problems with Trans-Galactic flight. Simply put, it regressed a human body. If that kid had come along, he'd be nothing more than a baby, if that, when they dropped out of Trans-Galactic flight.

And so far no one could figure out why it did that, or so he was told. He had heard all the explanations of relativity, the curved nature of space, and the different fixed states of matter, but it still had made no sense to him.

All he knew was that he was old when the flight started and young again when it ended. The farther and faster the ship flew, the greater the distance from Earth, the younger he got. At times he wondered if the Earth Protection League had a group of middle-aged soldiers for shorter-range work, but he had never been in a position to ask anyone.

He was just glad space flight worked this way.

The young soldier patted his shoulder. "Have a good trip, sir." Then he closed the lid on the coffin and tapped it twice as a signal to Sable that it was secure. In this old body, it didn't matter. He wouldn't have been able to even push the lid open if he tried.

A moment later the rose-smelling gas filled the chamber and he drifted off into the sleep of the dead as the Trans-Galactic ship jumped out of Earth orbit and headed toward the center of the galaxy.

The top of the coffin snapped open with a hiss and cool oxygen bathed his face. Captain Brian Sable snapped his eyes open, then held his arms up to look at them. What he saw was the young skin and shapes of youth. He flexed his fingers and the muscles under the skin rippled.

It felt wonderful!

No pain, no aches. Just the sense of health and youth.

Yes! He had made it again.

With both hands he grabbed the sides of the sleep module and lifted himself out, kicking over the side without so much as a caught heel. The feeling of youth was simply wonderful.

He still wore his old man's nightgown, but he quickly pulled that off and tossed it back in the coffin. He'd need it for the return trip, if he lived through this coming fight. If not, they'd need it for his body. And tomorrow morning his kids would get a call that he had died peacefully in his sleep.

He flexed the muscles in his shoulders and neck. His body was one he barely remembered from his youth. Yet each time he went on a mission, this body returned, good as ever. Whatever the strange relative-matter-physics involved in Trans-Galactic travel, he loved this body.

Quickly he dressed in his uniform of the Earth Protection League. First the leather pants and high boots, then a silk blouse that flared under his arms and fit tight over his shoulders. Next he put on a leather vest over the blouse that had the EPL triangle symbol on the chest. Then he strapped on his twin Photon Stunners, one on each hip.

Brushing a hand through his full head of dark hair, he turned and glanced at the only mirror in the small room. The reflection that greeted him was one of his youth, control, and power. He couldn't be more than twenty-one or twenty-two. Only the knowledge and memories inside the young body were of a ninety-one-year-old man who had, seemingly moments before, been asleep in a nursing home room just outside of Chicago.

He patted the Stunners on his hips, then with one more quick look in the mirror, he turned and strode out of the room, turning right toward the command center of the Galactic-Transport ship. He knew this ship like the back of his young hand. He'd been on board it for dozens of missions now, had flown it through some of the toughest space in this sector of the galaxy. It felt like home, far more than his home back in Chicago had ever done.

Throughout the ship his men would be awaking, dressing, getting ready for whatever faced them tonight. He didn't wait for them, but instead strode directly to the empty command center and dropped down into the captain's chair.

His chair.

Around him there was only one other station on his left, with a high-backed chair like his and view screens above it showing the blackness of space.

In front of him a small screen on the panel flared to light and the smiling face of General Datson Meyers filled it. He had deep blue eyes, white hair, and more wrinkles than almost any human Sable had ever seen. Yet the face was one that seemed comfortable with command. "Glad you made it, Captain Sable."

"Glad to be here, sir," Sable said. "What's happening?"

The smile cleared from the face of the general, making some of the wrinkles vanish instantly. "The Dogs have broken through."

"What?" Sable said, stunned. The Dogs, as everyone in EPL called them, were a race of ugly aliens that occupied the territory along one of the EPL's borders. They looked like a bad cross between a huge slug and a ten-legged poodle. They were the meanest damn things Sable had ever fought, and he had fought them often along that border.

Unlike the dogs on Earth, humans and alien Dogs hated

each other with a passion that didn't allow any type of agreement beyond fighting.

The general went on. "They broke through our outer defenses yesterday. Our allies in the League and border patrols couldn't stop them."

"That bad, huh?" Sable asked. A feeling of dread was quickly replacing the wonderful feel of being young again.

The General nodded. "This morning we got data that leads us to believe that they are headed to Earth to destroy the center of the League once and for all."

Sable looked intently at the general, not letting the worry filling his chest show. "How many ships did they send?"

"Over five hundred got through the border and are headed for your position at a slow Trans-Galactic speed," the general said. "Your job is to try to slow them down even more, give us time behind you to form a second and third line of defense."

"Understood," Sable said. "We'll slow them down. Maybe knock their numbers down a few. You can count on that."

The general nodded. "I knew I could depend on you, Captain."

The screen went blank.

Sable sat there in the command chair, stunned. This would be the last mission. He would die young and in deep space, just as he had always hoped he would. Better than in his sleep in the nursing home back on Earth. He just hadn't expected this last mission to be so soon.

But Earth and the League needed him. He would not let them down!

He took a deep breath, shoved the fear aside, and got to work.

Quickly he ran his fingers over the controls in front of him. It showed that there were eleven other League ships in formation beside his. And each ship was manned with forty-two people like him and carried forty single-man fighters. One of the big transport ships might be a match for a single Dog Warcraft, but a single-man fighter wasn't. It would be like sending a mosquito after a real dog back on Earth.

"What are we up against this time, Captain?" a cheery voice asked behind him.

He glanced over his shoulder at his second-in-command, Carl Turner. Carl lived in a nursing home in northern California and was gaining on one hundred years of age. At the moment he was a brown-haired man who looked like he was in his middle twenties. He had a spring in his step and a smile that could light up a room, and often did. They had worked dozens of missions together before and had become best friends.

"The Dogs broke out of their fence," Sable said. "We're supposed to try to slow them down until the League can mount a decent defense behind us."

"Shit," Carl said as he dropped down into the chair beside Sable and stared at the screen. "How many?"

"Five hundred of their warships. Twelve of us."

"The League have any idea how we're supposed to do this?" Carl asked.

"Nope," Sable said, smiling at his friend. "They left it up to our ancient wisdom to come up with something."

"I hate it when they do that," Carl said.

"Yeah. Me, too," Sable said, laughing. "You work on finding out how much time we have until they get here, what speed they're moving, and so on, while I brief the rest of the crew."

He pushed himself easily to his feet and strode across the command center toward the crew area. He could have done this task from his command chair, but he wanted to feel young again, walk quickly again, just one more time.

It was halfway through the briefing with the forty members of his gathered crew that Captain Brian Sable came up with the plan that just might save them. And Earth.

He sprinted back to the command center of the ship and dropped back into his chair. "How long?"

"Five hundred Dog Warships will be on our front steps in exactly thirty-five minutes."

"Perfect," Sable said. "Have our ships get ready to match their Trans-Galactic speed."

Carl glanced over at him. "Perfect if you like getting your butt kicked by slug-looking poodles."

"How old are you, Carl?" Sable asked, his fingers working on the board as he talked.

"Six months short of the big one hundred," Carl said.

"And how long did it take us to get from Earth to this position?"

"From what measuring point?" Carl asked.

"Earth time?"

"Forty or so years," Carl said.

"Shipboard time?"

"Six days, ten hours, and a few odd minutes."

"And it will take us that long to get back?" Sable asked, "Right?" He finished the work on the command board and turned to Carl.

"Shipboard time," Carl said. "They'll speed up the ship slightly on the return voyage and we'll end up back in our beds less than thirty minutes after we left, Earth time that is. You know that."

"So how are the Dogs handling the same matter/relativity problem on their flight toward Earth?"

"How the hell would I—"

Suddenly Carl stopped and smiled at Sable. "I see where you're headed, Captain. Their life-spans are shorter than ours, right?"

"Exactly," Sable said. "Which is why they are moving at a slow Trans-Galactic speed, because they don't dare go any faster or they would end up Dog-pups by the time they reach Earth."

"Which means they have to be damn old Dogs right now," Carl said, "at the beginning of their flight."

"Exactly," Sable said. "And you and I both know how well old Dogs like us move."

Carl laughed. "We're young, they're old. You're right! Perfect!"

"I'd say it's time to kick some wrinkled butt, wouldn't you?" Sable asked. He punched the communications link to all his men and the other ships. Quickly he explained what he had figured out and how they were going to fight the Dogs.

"Keep the single-man fighters on full thrust and constantly turning, diving, retreating. We'll break into units of twenty fighters with each twenty ship unit attacking one Dog ship, then moving on. Keep moving as fast as you can, all the time. They're slow and old, just as we all were a few short hours ago. Remember that, and they won't stand a chance."

Twenty minutes later they launched the single-man fighters. Only Carl and Sable remained in the Command Ship, since it only took the two of them to run the ship. Everyone else was needed in the fighters.

A few minutes later the Dog Warships appeared on the view screens. They were ugly, sausage-looking ships, with slick-looking hulls and protruding weapons systems and thrusters. The fighters had been ordered to stay away from in front of the weapons and target the thrusters. Their mission was to slow them down and, as Carl said, there was no better way to do that than shoot a Dog Warship in the ass.

"You know how to override the autopilot on this ship?" Sable asked, turning to Carl as the fighters broke into groups and swarmed toward the oncoming Dog Warships.

"I think I could do it," Carl replied. "Why?"

"I'm just wondering," Saber said, "what would happen if we plowed right through the middle of that fleet at full Trans-Galactic speed?"

"Besides destroy us?"

"Won't hurt us," Sable said. "At full Trans-Galactic speed we're on complete screens, big enough to knock just about anything out of the way. Remember?"

Carl stared at Sable for a moment, then laughed. "Bowling for Dogs. I love it!"

Carl set to work on taking the autopilot off the Trans-Galactic controls.

On the screen the fighters were having some luck. The Dog Warships were firing, but not really hitting anything. The fighters were picking at the thrusters of the ships like a kid picked at a scab. Two Dog ships were already dead in space, left behind by the fleet. But there were already four single-man fighters destroyed. Four men who wouldn't be returning alive to their nursing home rooms tonight on Earth.

Sable wondered if any of them would be at this point.

"Got it!" Carl said.

Sable carefully set the Trans-Galactic drive for only a sixteen-second burst. That would take them through the Dog Warship fleet and some distance beyond, but not too far. Too far and they'd be too young to get the ship back into position.

Quickly he informed the other transport captains of what

he was going to try to do, then turned to Carl. "Ready to lose a little time?"

"And with luck, a few Dog Warships in the process," Carl said.

Sable eased the transport directly at a mass of the Dog Warships, then said, "Do it!"

Carl flicked the switch and for the first time in all the missions, Sable saw what space looked like at full Trans-Galactic speed.

It was a blur of black-and-white streaks.

Nothing more. Not even pretty.

Then, as quickly as it started, it ended and the stars were back, solid in space. There was no sign of the Dog War-ships, or the rest of the League transport fleet.

"We've gone almost to the Dog Border and we're four weeks younger than a few seconds ago," Carl said.

"I knew I felt better," Sable said. "Don't you just love how this relativity and mass stuff works?"

"Yeah," Carl said. "Just wish I understood it."

"I hear you there," Sable said.

Sable flipped the ship over and with a quick run of his fingers over the board reset the controls to return them to just a few seconds after they had left.

"Do it," he said.

"Firing for the return!" Carl said.

Again the view screens showed black-and-white streaks for a long six seconds, then normal space returned.

"Holy cow!" Carl said. "I think we got a strike."

"Maybe two," Sable said, staring at the damage they had done. They had punched not just one, but two holes in the fleet of Dog Warships, damaging and destroying at least thirty of them.

And the single-man fighters were taking advantage of the confusion to cause even more damage.

"Tell the other transport captains exactly what we did and then let's go again," Sable said.

"They're going to come up with a terrible name for this, you know," Carl said.

Sable had already reset the Trans-Galactic drive for another six second burst and aimed the nose of the ship at a mass of the Dog Warships. "And what would that be?"

"The Sable Yo-Yo Maneuver," Carl said.

"Sounds good to me," Sable said, laughing as he punched them back into full Trans-Galactic speed once again. And for a few seconds, he got even younger again.

The fresh-faced soldier carried the frail frame of Captain Brian Sable out of the cold of the Chicago night air and into the warmth of the small nursing home room, then laid him carefully on the bed.

Sable glanced at the clock. Three thirty-seven in the morning. He'd only been gone just a little over twenty minutes Earth time, yet for his memory it had been much, much longer.

It had taken him and the other eleven transport ships six more punches through the Dog Warship fleet before the Dogs finally gave up and turned back.

They had chased them, snapping at their tails the entire way.

He had lost seven fighters and seven very brave men in the fight. The entire casualty list for all twelve transports was just under sixty. The general was stunned at their success and extremely pleased, to say the least. He couldn't believe that twelve transport ships with single-man fighters could turn back a five-hundred-strong fleet of Dog Warships.

Actually, neither could Sable. But they had done it. They had saved Earth and the League.

For the next twenty-four hours, the general had let them all party in their young bodies. As the general said, *You men all deserve it.*

Sable couldn't have agreed more. He had relished every minute of it.

Sable looked around the dim, nursing home room. It was a room he hoped he would never die in. If he died, he wanted it to be in space, fighting for the League and Earth.

Then he laughed, not hard enough to task his old lungs, but enough to relax him a little.

Now he had one task. He had to stay alive until the next mission.

"Anything I can get for you, Captain?" the young soldier asked as he pulled the thin blanket up over Sable's frail body.

"No, thank you, son," Sable said, smiling.

"You did a great job out there, sir," the young man said. "It's an honor knowing you." He snapped to attention, saluted, and then turned for the door.

In a moment the night sounds were shut out and the small nursing home room was silent except for the ticking of the clock.

To the empty room and no one in particular Captain Brian Sable of the Earth Protection League said, "Thank you," very softly. "The honor was all mine."

ENDPOINT INSURANCE

by Jane Lindskold

In the course of watching old movie serials, Jane
Lindskold discovered the hidden powers of insurance
investigators. In this story, Captain "Allie" Ah Lee[1]
discovers that working for an insurance company can
mean taking real risks. Lindskold is the author of
over thirty-five short stories and several novels—
including *Changer* and *Legends Walking*. She lives
in Albuquerque, New Mexico with her husband,
archaeologist Jim Moore, and is currently at work on
another novel.

Spike was the one who told me that pirates were using
the Endpoint system to launder stolen goods.

Allen "Spike" West worked for AASU Insurance, a
sturdy, reliable company that had offices on any world or
space station with a population of five thousand or more.
As the Endpoint system had recently topped the fifteen thousand mark, AASU practically qualified as an old timer.

AASU insured both my ship—the *Mercury*—and my life,
so I guess I thought pretty highly of them.

Spike had visited the *Mercury* so that we could discuss
possible changes in the ship's policy. I'd thought his coming to me rather strange since we usually met in his office
and the *Mercury*'s cabin was pretty small—indeed, we were
practically sitting knee to knee. However, my own concerns

---

[1] Allie also appears in "Winner Takes Trouble" published in *Alien Pets*,
edited by Denise Little, DAW, 1998.

about my current financial woes kept me from pursuing these thoughts further.

I make my living as a freelance courier, carrying messages and small goods from system to system. The only reason I made a living at all was that I was willing to go out to fringe colonies with just a couple dozen inhabitants. I also knew more about the shady side of commerce than any proper courier would admit, but more about that later.

Knowing that Spike's gaze was safely locked in the middle space in front of his eyes while the computer jacked into a port beneath his right ear presented my account for his inspection, I studied him, trying to guess what his answer would be.

Spike wasn't a bad-looking fellow if you liked tall, lanky, dark-haired men with large noses, brilliant blue eyes, and goony expressions. When he wasn't staring vacantly into empty space, Spike had an appealing grin and enough intensity to power a stardrive. Most of the time I even liked him. Today, he had too much power over my financial future for me to feel at all relaxed in his presence.

In contrast to Spike's long leanness, I'm diminutive by modern standards—a result of growing up on a forgotten colony world where rations were limited for most of my childhood. My hair is glossy black and my eyes, beneath the epicanthic folds of my eyelids, are dark as well. Some have told me I look like a doll.

Happily, I'm more than a toy. When my birth colony's sponsors back in China settled their then most recent war, they'd sent out a belated supply ship. Help had come before permanent damage had been done to any of the colonists—except that most of the children remained rather small. I enjoyed being regularly misjudged—as if size and ability have anything to do with each other!

When Spike frowned slightly and blinked twice, prepara-

tory to banishing my files from his virtual screen, I straightened and studied the *Mercury*'s message reader, making a
few notes for future business. Spike might have even been
fooled. I have a great poker face.

"You could reduce the coverage, Allie," Spike began,
"but I wouldn't recommend it. Moreover, your lienholder
on the *Mercury* might not okay such minimal coverage."

"AASU," I reminded him, "is also the lienholder."

"Well, then," Spike said, a slight grin tugging the left
corner of his mouth, "I can say that your lienholder would
not permit such minimal coverage. We take enough risks
with you."

"Bosh!" I protested, knowing that he knew as well as I
did that I ran a tight ship.

Spike laughed loudly.

"I'd think," I said stiffly, "that AASU could make an ex-
ception for a faithful customer like myself. I've always paid
my premiums on time and my claims *have* been modest."

"True," Spike said, "but we are assigned certain guidelines for underwriting policies. I've already stretched the
limits for you. Now, if you worked for AASU . . ."

He let the sentence trail off, and if I wasn't a skilled
haggler and poker player, I might have missed his hint.

I glanced at him sharply. "What's on your mind? AASU
has its own courier fleet. You don't need to hire me."

"Not as a courier," Spike said, "but we could use your
help catching some pirates."

"Me?" I felt my expression turn suspicious and schooled
it into a comfortable neutrality. "Why me? I'm just a freelance courier."

"Bosh," Spike said, deliberately echoing my inflection
of a moment before. "Captain Ah-Lee, you have a good
many skills and lots of knowledge you don't advertise, but

before I puff up your ego, let me tell you about AASU's problem."

"Go ahead," I replied, settling back in my chair. "For all my much-vaunted knowledge, I haven't heard that pirates are using Endpoint."

"The local government," Spike admitted, "has tried to keep it quiet. Pirates aren't good for business. Up to a point, AASU is willing to support this view, but not when the local government's unwillingness to act means that the pirates have easy use of the system."

"I can see that," I agreed. "You're sure it's pirates, not smugglers? I don't have anything against smugglers."

"Pirates," Spike assured me. "A rather large consortium of pirates, if I don't miss my guess. Let me fill you in."

According to Spike, about a hundred standards ago, Endpoint took a large leap in population. Part of the increase was due to the arrival of refugees from the war between the Absolutes and the Loyalists in the Bath system, part to a successful advertising campaign.

Nearly five thousand new colonists registered for permanent taxpayer status. Fifteen thousand isn't many people by the standards of a world like Home Earth, where I hear even a small city can number in the millions, but by the time you add in visitors like myself, resident aliens, and nonpermanent residents, you have a large enough population that no one can know everyone else.

Right on the heels of this new influx came the pirates. Endpoint didn't provide enough traffic to be tempting for actual piracy—though I didn't doubt that this would follow in time. However, there was plenty of cover for illicit shipping

"Pirates are like epidemics and property taxes," I commented cynically when Spike paused, "they come with growth. Why are you so worried?"

Spike frowned. "Because AASU insures many of the ships and businesses the pirates prey on. Whether it's a cargo that doesn't get to its destination or a local business that gets undercut by black market competition, piracy hurts our clients. Most of the time we can't touch the pirates—AASU doesn't maintain a private military fleet . . ."

"But fences and money laundering are less violent crimes," I said, just to show him I was with him, "and you want me . . ."

"To help me trace this end of the pirate's operation," Spike replied promptly. "AASU would hire you and everything."

He grinned slyly. "We even can offer you a special insurance rate reserved for employees in good standing."

"That's right." I couldn't help laughing, though the problem was serious. "Twist my arm. Seriously, Spike, why me? AASU must have lots of people more qualified to take on this job."

"More people," Spike agreed. "More qualified? That's questionable. As much as I hate to admit it, the pirates could have spies inside AASU. I didn't go into the details before, but there has been a small but significant upturn in the number of valuable cargos being taken. One way the pirates could learn about these cargos is by having a mole inside AASU. That's why I wanted to meet you here rather than having you come to my office."

I frowned thoughtfully. Someone working with the pirates from inside an insurance company did make sense.

"How about working with the local militia?" I asked.

Spike looked disgusted. "Remember, Endpoint's system government is not yet acknowledging that there *is* local pirate activity."

"That seems impossible!" I protested.

"Not really," Spike shrugged. "Nonviolent crime is always easier to overlook."

"I see." I kept my tone noncommittal

Spike's voice took on a pleading note. "Allie, you know this system—everyone who counts, both in legitimate business and otherwise."

"Hardly," I demurred dryly, but Spike did have a point. I'd been coming to Endpoint since the original hundred settled. I knew the system pretty well.

Spike persisted. "You know the jump points the smugglers use, the likely places to cache fuel or supplies. You even know the surrounding systems. Besides, you and I get along."

"What," I asked frostily, "does that have to do with anything?"

"Why," Spike beamed, glancing around the crowded confines of the singleship's cabin, "I'll be coming with you. Certainly you don't think I'm going to let you have the fun of catching the pirates all by yourself!"

I gave in, of course. The salary AASU was offering was generous, especially when I factored in company insurance rates. Even after taking out a much more comprehensive policy, I was now making enough money to cover my expenses and to put a substantial amount aside for the future.

The data disk containing our contract was hand-carried to AASU headquarters by a private courier I personally selected for discretion and reliability. Thus, as far as regional AASU was concerned, Captain Ah-Lee remained nothing more than a freelance courier. Anyone on the inside of the company who might be working with the pirates shouldn't be able to discover my new involvement.

Next, my new partner went undercover. Allen "Spike" West took a liner out-system to investigate a claim on heavily populated Fyolyn. He would slip back in-system a few standards later on the ship of a smuggler who owed me more than a few favors.

While Spike was away, I hunted for signs of the pirates' operations. Since I'd carried a few cargoes of dubious legality in my time—mostly information rather than actual goods—folks would talk to me who would never talk to a more usual insurance investigator. I played poker with smugglers and black-marketeers, hung out in seedy spaceport bars. It didn't take long to learn that the local operators were feeling pressure from outside.

"It's them Batherite refugees, Allie," one smuggler told me. "It's not just displaced parents and sad-eyed kids who've come in on those ships. Somebody else has come in with 'em."

A dealer in slightly-used ship parts nodded.

"My business has dried up," she said, "just when things should be hot as a nuclear plant. I nosed around a bit and learned that somebody else is selling—and not just parts. I've seen ships come in that I could swear I'd seen listed as missing by the Watch."

"And the black ships don't interfere?" I asked, Normally the members of the Silent Watch couldn't wait to cause trouble for people.

"I guess they try," the black-marketeer shrugged, "but what can they do if the registration is all in order?"

Another smuggler, one who augmented a perfectly legitimate business carrying food supplies by transporting the occasional crate of high-duty luxury goods, added:

"I've been hit, too. You should see what's being sold in the market at the edge of the Bathtub. Oh, on the surface they're just poor folks trying to make do by selling home-made delicacies or whatever they salvaged before they got off planet, but if you keep your eyes open, you'll see that they're selling things that no refugee could have grabbed."

"Like?" I said, reaching for the deck of cards—it was my turn to deal.

"Like," the food merchant said, "cases of stabilized wines in the kind of packing that the luxury cruisers use. I swear I caught a glimpse of the Orion Lines logo on the side of one crate. It had been painted over, but you could still see the curves."

He didn't need to add more. The word "pirates," though unspoken, hung in the air. The suspicion of pirates also answered the question of why these normally feisty outlaws weren't going after the competition. No spacers in their right mind tangled with pirates. The pirates' reach was too long and their methods of retribution too ruthless.

I wondered what I'd let Spike get me into.

Obviously, the place for me to continue my hunt was the Batherite refugee section that the news services had dubbed—rather derisively—the Bathtub.

Early the next morning, I put the *Mercury* into a parking orbit, then hailed one of Endpoint's squat, in-system shuttles to take me down to the main planet's largest—and pretty much only—city.

Endpoint's major inhabited planet was named Gilbert, after the explorer who had organized the initial colony group. The capital city, with great originality, was called Gilbert City. It had started out as a couple of pressurized domes meant to protect the colonists from whatever secret horrors the planet might hold. The domes weren't bad. In fact, I'd grown up in similar structures.

Once the colonists confirmed that the worst hazards were weather-related, they tailored their architecture to combat these. It wasn't long before Gilbert City sprawled out around the original domes. These had eventually been torn down and recycled, leaving no trace of that historical first settlement other than the position of the main spaceport.

When the shuttle unloaded at the spaceport, I hopped a tube to the end of the line where the Bathtub had evolved into a small town of its own.

Clearly the residents of Gilbert City had tried to make the refugees welcome. From where I stood packed flank to flank in a crowded tube car, I could see that when the refugee camp had been initially designed the registration center had been positioned as a hub from which neat rows of prefab dwellings extended like spokes on a wheel.

As the war between the Absolutists and the Loyalists grew uglier and uglier, more refugees flooded out. To remain was to be forced to take sides—and the Absolutist fanatics didn't care if this was against your will. With the new influx, the tidy order of the camp had broken down. Now buildings were being put up any old way, the only criteria being access to water, sewage, and power.

Between the prefab units, huts like you might see on some primitive world had been erected, shelters where the spillover residents from the houses slept and perhaps dreamed of the day when they could return home.

Gilbert City had provided only one tube stop to serve all the inhabitants of the Bathtub. No one had anticipated that the camp might grow large enough to need more than one. I shuffled my way to the station exit, glancing at the tired faces of men and women burdened down with packages of goods dearly bought in the main city. Some were empty-handed, burdened only with sorrow and disappointment.

Fortunately, at least for now, there was plenty of work available throughout the Endpoint system—one of the reasons that it had become a popular choice for the refugees. As I walked briskly down the wide avenue leading toward the registration center, I had a feeling who one of the less reputable employers might be.

Pirates would find this refugee camp a good recruiting ground. As my smuggler friends had noted so acidly, it would serve even better as an outlet for black market goods and as a place from which the pirates' planetside spies could gather information.

From the pirates' point of view, the Bathtub would be all the more attractive because of the secondary spaceport that had been erected nearby. Theoretically, the port was solely for refugee ships—there having been complaints that refugee traffic was crowding the main spaceport. Realistically, other ships could get clearance to land and take off. Endpoint's orbital traffic control, like everything else, was strained these days.

Thinking thus, I bypassed the registration center and walked through the prefab sprawl to where a makeshift market had grown up on the fringes of the Bathtub. Here, if my contacts were correct, evidence of illicit commerce could be found.

Steeling myself to the task—for no spacer walks when she can ride—I trudged up and down rows marked out in a more or less orderly fashion. Sound-deadening barriers along the edge of the secondary port muted the noise, but intermittently I heard the rumble of a spaceship engine— mostly shuttles like the one that had brought me ground-side, but every so often the deeper roar of a larger vessel.

The thundering of these high-tech vessels provided an odd contrast to a market so simple that its like had existed anywhere humans had gathered. Many of the vendors merely spread a blanket or tarp on the ground and piled their wares on top. A handful had set up stalls cobbled together from packing crates or from less identifiable scavenged junk.

Along these tatty corridors of commerce, men and

women sold everything from household goods and old clothes to cheap luxury goods. A few of the more ambitious sold food or offered opportunities for entertainment.

After one quick tour through the surprisingly crowded lanes, I ducked into a stall selling puffy fried cakes seasoned with curry and onions—a Batherite treat. I traded some of my unassigned credit vouchers for a heaping platter and something pungent, iced, and cool to drink.

Seizing a seat on a plastic crate at a table that had begun life as a cable spool, I mulled over what to do next. Overall, everything was as innocent as could be. The vendors were Batherite refugees mixed with a few entrepreneurs from Gilbert City come to take advantage of the crowds. Most of their wares were just what you'd expect.

It had been among the shoppers, not the vendors, that I'd caught a glimpse of something that didn't fit the setting—a few men and women whose body language didn't match the pervading mood of exhaustion and pathetic hope. They were too confident, too eager to be interested in the sort of rag-trade, used goods, and craftwork ostensibly being sold in this marketplace.

After some cautious observation I thought I even recognized a couple of these shoppers. In the parlance of the underworld, we called them "shuttlers" because they made their money buying goods of dubious legality at low prices and reselling them with the registration stamps and such mysteriously in place.

Essentially, shuttlers were high-tech fences with operations that often spanned multiple star systems. As such, they were useful to both smugglers and planet-based fences. Since shuttlers could often locate what more usual channels could not, some even had a semi-legitimate status. My most recent contact with one had involved a perfectly legal request on the part of a well-known artist for an exotic hallucinogen.

Of course, most shuttlers were scum, buying low, selling high—often to the very people from whom the goods had been stolen in the first place. I didn't doubt that some shuttler had made a good profit returning Orion Lines their "misplaced" wine—and perhaps more importantly, the expensive stabilizing crates.

Licking the last of the curry-seasoned oil off my fingers, I decided to wander until I spotted one of the shuttlers, then follow him or her and see with whom my mark did business. Despite my aching feet, I set off in an optimistic mood. Three days later, I was less cheerful.

Perhaps the last of the black market goods had been sold the very morning I spotted the shuttlers in the market. Perhaps that was why enough shuttlers had been present for me to pick them out of the crowd. For whatever reason, the Bathtub market had descended into mundanity. I did find a copy of a hard-to-locate holo-documentary about one of my favorite musical performers, but as far as anything that would lead me to the pirates, I came up as cold as the interstellar void.

Spike was due back the next day and I wasn't looking forward to telling him I had nothing to offer, so I put in one more tour.

Now, I hadn't been such a rube as to roam around the market day after day without any disguise at all. The first day I'd gone pretty much as myself. It was reasonable that I'd want to look around a new part of town. The next several days I'd gone dressed in the general style of a system local, but as a different type of person each time. Usually, I'd changed my disguise more than once in a day.

It isn't hard to seem what you aren't—especially when you're small and slight to start with. Built-up shoes and padding make you seem larger. Very active body language makes you seem younger. Add in basic changes in hair or eye color or manner of dress and you're set, especially in a crowd where no one person is in your company for too long. Really, the only thing that gave me trouble were my aching feet, especially when I wore built-up shoes.

For my last tour before Spike's return, I went as myself. During earlier jaunts, I'd noticed a couple of gambling parlors and figured that I'd sit in on a poker game or two when my feet got too tired for wandering through the market. Since my skill at the game is well-known in some circles, I sometimes have trouble getting into a high-stakes game. If any of my local acquaintances recognized me, they'd figure I was looking for a hot game. If I was lucky, they'd even pretend not to see me.

Courtesy, you know.

I was deep into a game of seven card stud, the Fyolynese version that offers some real challenges when calculating the odds, when I heard the distant rumble of a large ship landing out in the field. I didn't think anything of it. Many large ships arrived after dark. It's all one and the same to the ship's pilots and eases things for system traffic control by decreasing the amount of competition from routine daytime air traffic.

Several hands later, I noticed an increase in the amount of activity outside the gaming parlor. "Parlor" was really a courtesy title. The place I was frequenting was little more than a tent. As the night was warm, the side-flaps were up to let in some fresh air.

"New visitors," grumbled one of the other players, a stately, plump young man who had introduced himself as Buck. "Wouldn't think there was anyone left on Bath to fight the war."

Buck's use of the euphemism "visitor" rather than the

blunter "refugee" labeled him a Batherite, as did his accent. As he had obviously gotten out of the system rather than fight, I thought his criticism less than fair, but didn't say anything. One of the other players—a weathered older woman—was more vocal.

"You sound like you *want* the war to continue," she said, her voice rusty with exhaustion. She had introduced herself as Cookie and carried with her the scent of curry, onions, and sugar.

"I don't!" Buck protested, glancing at Cookie, then back at his cards. "I was just making a comment."

"Are you in?" asked one of the other players, his eagerness betraying a good hand.

"I am," Buck said. Cookie nodded, pursing her lips into a thin, angry line.

Play went on for several hands without further comment. The Batherite War wasn't something the system's natives liked talking about. It wasn't just a political thing. Some of the weapons the Absolutist fanatics employed embarrassed even those who favored their cause.

The cards were with me, but the increased activity outside of the tent distracted me from my game. I misplayed what should have been a sure thing and pushed back from the table.

"I'll quit while I'm about even," I said. Actually, I was ahead, but they didn't need to know. Cookie grunted something that might have been good-bye. No one else seemed to notice my departure.

Outside, the market was busier than it had been for several days. It seemed as if all the Bathtub had turned out to see the new arrivals who, their arms filled with bundles or small children, hurried down the road toward the registration center. A few pulled small wagons, but such were rare.

Apparently, most of the refugees had been limited to what they could carry on their persons.

"No need to rush!" called someone from the market, following the comment with a good-humored laugh. "The center'll keep you waiting long enough."

The sense of this seemed to get through to some of the new arrivals. While the majority continued pushing their way toward the center, a few peeled off from the flow. Most of these headed for the food stalls, doubtless tired of ship's rations. Some drifted about asking after the location of friends and family. I noticed that the name "Kingsley" came up repeatedly, though matched with different surnames.

Admittedly, Kingsley is a popular Batherite personal name, in honor of Kingsley Moisan, the charismatic leader who founded the original colony. What caught my fancy was how often the request was made to a perfect stranger— and how often that stranger seemed to have directions or guidance to offer.

I trailed after one of these parties, noticing that the bundles they carried seemed particularly heavy. We worked our way through a maze of streets to where a row of prefabs from the earliest days of the camp stood. They were well-kept, with a minimum of tents and auxiliary buildings around them. I wondered if Gilbert City zoning was trying to maintain some standards.

Inside the buildings lights glowed and sounds of domestic activity drifted from the open windows. I heard a baby crying, the sizzle of something dropped into frying oil, running water, laughter. All well and normal, even pleasant.

The refugees were directed inside a building near the middle of the street. I slipped into the shadows between two buildings across the way, watching. While I lurked there, two other guided parties arrived. Then a few people departed. Although they had all the hallmarks of new arrivals, they were not the ones I had followed, so I continued my vigil.

After a time, my group came out. Their guide was not with them, but otherwise, they seemed much as before—even a bit more cheerful. They laughed and their steps were light as they hurried toward a cross street that would take them to the registration center.

Then it hit me. Their feet were light! Though they still carried their bundles, these were clearly no longer as heavy. No chat with folks from home, no matter how friendly, could have relieved the burden. Clearly an exchange had been made.

I pondered for a moment, wondering whether or not to follow the new arrivals. Then I decided. These were probably just mules carrying goods. The real action lay inside that building. I hunkered down in the shadows, preparing for a long wait.

A few more parties of bundle-bearing refugees came through, but not many. I decided that this must be only one of several places where smuggled items were being dropped off. To occupy myself, I tried to reconstruct the chain of events that had gotten the goods to this point and decided that whatever had been brought here wouldn't stay here long. Eventually, the houses grew quieter and lights were extinguished—all but a faint glimmer low on the wall to one side of the house I'd been observing.

It was an odd place for light to show. For speed of construction these prefabs had been erected without basements, but I was willing to bet that what I was seeing was light from just such a subterranean room. The opening was completely shielded by a neatly placed trash can. During the daytime, it would probably be invisible. Only the light gave it away now.

My curiosity grew as I estimated the chances of successfully satisfying it. After I'd staked the place out for quite a while longer and traffic on the street had diminished to nothing, I decided that I'd never forgive myself if I didn't take a look.

Padding across the street, I gained the side of the house. Fortunately, the wall of the structure on the other side of the narrow alley was windowless. If I stayed pressed close to the wall alongside the bit of light and no one on the street—should anyone pass at all—looked directly down the alley and noticed movement from behind the trash can, I should remain unseen.

The source of the light proved to be—as I had deduced— a makeshift window cut into the prefab material. The scrap had been skillfully shaped into a shutter that would cover the hole, but it was propped open now. I lowered myself slowly prone, both so I would be less visible and to get my ears closer to the opening.

Conversation, lazy and sporadic, accompanied by rather interesting thuds and clanks came to me. I lay there in the dirt, wishing I'd brought along some peepers, hoping that someone inside would speak up. I didn't dare sneak a look until I had a better sense of where the occupants were in relation to the hole.

Tired as I was from my long day, the ground seemed quite comfortable and the warm night air made my watch almost relaxing. I believe I was close to drowsing when a new voice, male and commanding, addressed the group in the basement.

"Almost done?"

"Almost, Your Absoluteness," replied one, bolder than the rest. These could only manage mutters of agreement. I could almost hear the bowing and scraping.

"Very good," the first voice replied. "We shall ship out in the morning. You may as well get some sleep. A mistake at this point would be fatal to our Cause—and we must be alert for our meeting with our new allies."

I could hear the capitalization in his tones. Nor was I in the least sleepy any longer. Adrenaline coursed through my veins, adrenaline with a chaser of pure terror.

The Absolute! Here, separated from me by just a few meters of prefab and dirt stood the monomaniacal, charismatic leader who had galvanized his followers into what had become the Bath War. Just a dozen standards or so past it had been reported that he had vanished following the bombing of his headquarters. His opposition claimed he was dead, but his followers proclaimed him alive and fought on as if he was still at their head.

Apparently, he was. Equally apparently, he didn't want anyone to know precisely where he was or he would have been enthroned in some public palace, defying anything short of a planet-splitter to kill him.

I remained outside the window while the Absolute took his leave. Then I dared a peek through the window. I glimpsed a small room, roughly dug out of the heavy, clay soil. There was no evidence that power tools had been used, so it must have been dug by hand—a considerable task.

Inside, by the light of battery-powered lights, four Batherites were stacking crates near the foot of a ladder that ended below a trapdoor—closed now, though it must have been through that square that the Absolute had addressed his followers. Even as I watched, the workers finished their task and began to ready themselves for rest.

They were sweaty from their labors, yet their only comforts were a plastic cooler of water, some ration bars, and a covered bucket that served as a chamber pot. When the four had finished their sparse meal and limited ablutions, they lay down on the floor, pillowed their heads on their arms and dropped off to sleep. The last to lay himself down extinguished the light.

Until the ragged note of an exhausted snore convinced me that they had settled in, I waited. Then, still shaken by what I had learned, I made my stealthy escape.

I wondered what Spike would think of my report.

I picked Spike up at our planned rendezvous several hours after my return from Gilbert City. I'd insisted on launching into my report as soon as he was aboard, talking as I inserted the *Mercury* into a parking orbit on the dark side of one of the lesser moons of Gilbert. In my excitement, I didn't give him a chance to get a word in edgewise or to tell me his own plans—something I'd regret later.

"I don't think we're dealing with pirates here," I said, concluding my tale, "or not just pirates. Those were Absolutist fanatics I saw."

Spike nodded. He looked particularly goony today, clad in coveralls like those worn by most shippers instead of his usual suit. As he listened, he kept his hands in his pockets, playing with some junk he'd stuffed into them.

"So," I concluded, "there's no way that this is just an insurance matter anymore. We need to notify the authorities. There's time before morning reaches Gilbert City. They might be able to catch the Absolute."

"Endpoint system," Spike said, quite mildly for someone who had been forced to endure a monologue, "is neutral regarding the Batherite conflict."

"But the Absolute is a mass murderer!" I said aghast.

"Technically, he is the leader of a political group—the legitimate elected ruler of a large portion of Bath."

"Technically," I snarled.

"Allie," Spike said, still mildly , "I didn't know you were so political."

"I'm not," I replied, more calmly, "but you and I both know that the Absolute is a fiend—that the votes of those who elected him were meaningless."

"So his opponents say."

"So the chemists say," I retorted. Then I calmed down, realizing that I was being unfair to Spike. "Chemists who have analyzed the blood of some of his deceased followers. The fanatics are so pumped up they'd shoot their own sweethearts if the Absolute gave the command."

"The Absolutists say that their soldiers are chemically enhanced to make them strong and faithful," Spike said, infuriatingly insisting on playing the devil's advocate. "And there seems to be some evidence to support that position."

"You're not," I growled stubbornly, "on his side, are you?"

"No," Spike assured me. "Personally, I can't stand the Absolute and what he advocates, but going after him isn't my job. That wouldn't stop me if I thought we could actually *do* anything about him, but without Endpoint's support, we can't touch him groundside. I'm more interested in the contents of those crates you saw. Those might fall within the range of my job."

"Stolen goods?" I asked.

"Maybe," Spike rubbed his chin. "Most of the ships carrying refugees don't carry just refugees. It wouldn't pay. Nor do they make a one system trip. It would be easy to make a trade for passage, to use some of the refugees as mules for stolen goods."

"The pirates would give them some identification code," I said, nodding, for Spike's picture matched the one I'd been working out while I staked out the building. "Then when the refugees get here, they hand over whatever they've been carrying. It's repacked and sold. The plan's a bit elaborate, though, and it doesn't account for larger shipments like crates of wine."

Spike shook his head. "I don't agree—you haven't been elaborate enough—and you haven't accounted for the presence of the Absolute. Absolutist holdings in the Bath system have suffered serious assaults. Their troops move constantly—buoyed, doubtless, by some of those chemical stimulants you mentioned earlier. Their ships gnaw, bite, and snap—winning battles but rarely holding ground. Even so, the Loyalists are hard pressed."

"That's what the news services say," I agreed. "Now, tell me, what elaboration am I missing?"

"Those very chemicals you mentioned," Spike said, "take time and high-tech facilities to synthesize. Their formulas are highly guarded secrets, known only to the Absolute and a few trusted minions. One of the first things the Loyalists did was pinpoint and destroy as many of the Absolutist factories as they could and so limit the supply."

"And you think," I cut in eagerly, "that what I saw in those crates were the Absolute's potions? Those, at least, we could get Endpoint's authorities to seize. The killer drug in particular has been outlawed universally—no one wants their local troublemakers both hopped up and suggestible."

Spike held up a hand. "No, Allie, I don't think it's killer drug—not exactly. I think what you saw were the ingredients for the drug, smuggled in piecemeal so that no one could trace them and suspect what's going on. I think that the Absolute plans to mix up a batch and get it to his troops."

"But he won't do it planetside," I mused, "because that would leave him open to local law."

"Right." Spike gestured into the star-flecked darkness outside the *Mercury*'s view ports. "Somewhere out there a factory is waiting—probably on a pirate ship since we know they're using this system and the Absolute mentioned allies. The Absolute will go there, do his voodoo, and return home. His greatest weapon will go with him, scattered among several ships so one or two lucky shots can't destroy it all."

"And with a new supply of the drug, the Absolutist fanatics will win," I said, "because with the drug, the Absolute can convert even the most unwilling Loyalists to his side."

Spike nodded, then he grinned his goofy grin.

"Unless, of course, you and I stop them."

I stared at him and started to laugh.

The ships carrying the crates—and the Absolute—left the surface of Gilbert at midmorning. In the meantime, I'd gotten some sleep, as had Spike. In between naps, I'd scanned the Endpoint system, mapping out every blip and crackle so that we could locate the factory ship when the time came. Every so often I'd come across something I'd flag for myself, not bothering Spike with that particular detail.

Making this map should have been an impossible task—would have been except for two things. One, the *Mercury* has some of the best communications and scanning equipment money can buy. Two, Spike and I had an idea what we would be looking for—and that there would be something out there for us to find.

We figured that the factory ship couldn't have been given an advance location where it had to wait. Too much could go wrong with that sort of plan—someone else in the area, a bit of unanticipated debris drifting through, a breakdown or delay.

Therefore, the factory ship would be sending out a signal of some sort to direct the Absolute and his supply ships to where it waited. "Would be" because it wouldn't start emitting the signal until the Absolute sent it a query signal first. If the factory ship had been delayed in getting to the rendezvous, there would be no response to the query signal. The supply ships would take a parking orbit and wait, signaling occasionally and scanning the appropriate bands.

Spike and I were sure we'd worked out the same chain of logic the pirates would have used, but even so I nearly jumped from my seat when a broad band scan announced a new signal. It came intermittently, but always from the same direction. If we hadn't been looking for it, we would have dismissed it as background noise.

"Checking Gilbert," I said aloud, my hands moving across the scanner bands. "Yes! A ship just left immediate orbit and is heading in the direction of the signal."

"Wait until we're sure, Allie, before starting to follow," Spike said. "If we're right, we have time. They won't be going anywhere for a while."

I nodded, listening to my comm unit's report. "Another ship just left orbit. It's going out on the same general vector—probably they were filed as a convoy."

"A good safety measure," Spike replied solemnly, "in these pirate-plagued reaches of the stars."

"Well," I said, feeling pretty satisfied with myself, "we've found them. What next?"

"The pirates won't have unloaded whatever goods they smuggled in," Spike said promptly, "not until their rendezvous with the Absolute is completed. Therefore, there's certainly something incriminating in the hold of the factory ship. When we get there, I'll go take a look."

I stared at him, unable for a moment even to speak.

"You're not planning on going aboard alone?" I finally managed. "Twenty trained spacers—twenty marines!—would consider that foolhardy. You don't know how many pirates are aboard, but I doubt that the Absolute is traveling without a bodyguard."

"Twenty marines," Spike mused aloud, his expression wry and mocking. "Would twenty-one be enough, then?"

"Don't be an idiot!" I shouted, then I went on more calmly. "Just how do you plan to get aboard, anyhow? I doubt they have time for traveling insurance salesmen right now."

"Those ships don't have just one entrance," Spike said, valiantly ignoring my sarcasm. "I plan to enter via a service port near the engine room. Once aboard, I'll shut down the ship's drive. Then, once the ship can't get away, you'll signal for the Silent Watch."

"And how will you get through the entry port?" I said. "They aren't usually left unlocked."

In reply, Spike produced a mag-key from one of his coverall's voluminous pockets, tossing the rather routine piece of equipment from hand to hand as if it were some great amulet.

"This one is set to decode a wide variety of locks," he explained, as if I wouldn't recognize the make.

"And the ship's engine?" I asked. "Do you think the engine crew will just sit by while you turn the engine off?"

Spike scowled at my doubt, but produced a packet of gas pellets from another pocket.

"I thought I'd put these in the ventilation," he explained. He brightened and reached in his coverall again. "I have a mask."

I sighed and rubbed my hands over my face. He probably had a weapon of some sort, too, and a coil of rope and who knows what else. The man had seen too many action vids.

"It's my fault for not asking in advance what you planned," I admitted, "but I never dreamed you planned on taking them on alone. Listen, I have another idea."

I told him. Spike looked interested, but slightly disappointed. I think he'd been looking forward to playing the hero and capturing a pirate vessel single-handedly.

When I finished, he only had one question for me.

"And if they won't come?"

"I think they will," I said with more certainty than I felt. "As you've noted, they've been hurt by the pirates, too, and here's a chance to get back something of their own. And if they don't show, well, we can always fall back on your plan."

The three ships we were tracking—a third had joined the convoy while we were arguing—headed in the direction of a large planetoid just beyond a broad asteroid belt.

The backside of this planetoid was a favorite place for smugglers to linger before bringing in a cargo, since it gave them a chance to scan the system and make certain that the black ships were patrolling elsewhere. Most successful smugglers carried legal goods as well as illegal, but who wanted to risk a search if one could be avoided?

So popular had this particular lurking spot become that the black ships checked it as a matter of routine. Still, the Absolutists might not know that. Once I was fairly certain where the convoy was headed, I took the *Mercury* out along a different route, one that took advantage of intervening asteroids and other bits of space debris to obscure our signal. I prided myself that the supply ship never knew we were closing on them.

Meanwhile, I sent out tight-beam comm squirts to a couple dozen locations I'd marked earlier—places where a faint signal hinted that a ship with damped identification beacon drifted, its power down—a typical smuggler's trick. My message was scrambled, just in case the wrong ship intercepted it, and pretty terse. In a few words it invited these outlaws of the solar lanes to join the *Mercury* in kicking some pirate butt.

Responses came rapidly, crammed with the same questions over and over: "Why are you doing this?" "Where's the pirate?" and, most often, "What's in it for me?"

I sent out the answers, offering each ship that joined me and Spike a share of the loot. Most of the outlaws agreed, tantalized by the promise of gain beyond a smuggler's dreams—and enticed further by the chance to get even with hated pirates, those big operators who made it almost impossible for a little ship to turn a slightly dishonest profit and who ruined a good market just when the smugglers had opened it up.

Not knowing how they'd respond to the political angle, I kept the news of the Absolute's presence to myself for now. I figured if we took the pirate, I could act as surprised as anybody, and if we didn't, it wouldn't matter.

We glided through the Endpoint system, our engines powered down as low as possible. The fact that we were approaching a smuggler's rest most of us had used at one time or another helped us to hide our presence. So did the fact that we were coming toward our target and the mass of our ships masked our engine signatures.

As we approached, I used the *Mercury*'s comm system to collect and relay information. I got each ship to give me her strengths and weaknesses. I knew from past experience—and a couple of devastating poker losses—that a couple of the other ships' captains were brilliant tacticians. They took the information I beamed to them and transformed it into a possible plan. Despite their input, the *Mercury* remained in command since only her comm system had the reach and power to blip out and retrieve information so swiftly that the pirates would have no chance of detecting our signals.

Even as we laid our plans, every ship in my outlaw fleet kept alert for the black ships. At this moment, we were doing nothing precisely illegal—though some might argue that we had turned pirate ourselves—but a delay would be bothersome and the presence of a black ship or two cruising these reaches might spook the pirates into deeper cover.

However, there was no trace of the Silent Watch in this vicinity. Doubtless they were being kept busy by the increased traffic in-system, but I did wonder if a Watcher or two—perhaps the officer who set the duty rosters—had been paid to keep the black ships out of this area. A solar system is vast beyond mortal comprehension; not even the black ships could be expected to patrol every bit of it.

Eventually, the *Mercury* closed on our target. Signaling my approaching allies to hold their various concealed positions, I set the *Mercury*'s scanners to a broad sweep that would be unlikely to trip even an alert comm tech. Thus, the picture that appeared on the *Mercury*'s screen had to be cleared and enhanced. It hardly mattered. We had found what we sought.

A hulking vessel large enough to dwarf the *Mercury*—though small in comparison to some war ships I'd seen—hung in the shadows behind the planetoid. Its orbit was set to avoid easy detection both from Gilbert and from the more or less inhabited reaches in the planet's vicinity. Tellingly, the identification beacon required by interstellar law had been pulled—even smugglers usually only damped theirs—as clear a sign of a pirate ship as a skull and crossbones had been millennia before.

The pirate vessel was not a pretty ship, her hull scarred and patched, her blocky shape constructed for deep space, not atmospheric entry. She had probably started life as an ore hauler. Such ships were often drafted into pirate service as general cargo carriers.

Ore haulers' massive bay doors permitted small vessels to be tucked inside the hold and their powerful engines—designed not only to maneuver a great deal of mass but often to fuel processing plants within the ship—gave the unattractive ships surprising speed for short bursts. Many a pirate-hunting expedition had been left gaping when a seemingly sluggish target had departed in a contemptuous burst of speed.

I told Spike all of this, cautioning him not to underestimate the vessel and adding that the three supply ships we had followed had probably been taken directly on board. As I saw it, we were lucky that there was only one ship waiting out here, but doubtless the pirates weren't wasting vessels.

One ship to the fourteen in our outlaw fleet. Victory looked easy enough in the abstract. The thing was, only half or so of our ships were armed. Most smugglers didn't bother with armament—it drew too much attention. Other recruits to our fleet were guilty of prospecting without a license; other ships held fugitives from the justice of one system or another. A few were simply the dwellings of interstellar hermits.

Armed and unarmed, sleek and beautiful, or battered bits of metal and machinery eking out a last few years before being scrapped for junk, the outlaw ships slipped through the chill void, taking heed of my cautions, tight-beaming their communications so that all the pirate ship could have heard were vague whispers that would have been dismissed as the hissing pops of a star's breathing.

In less than an eye blink the pirate hulk found herself surrounded by a sphere of some dozen plus ships, each carefully positioned to balance our various strengths and weaknesses. Since the *Mercury* was unarmed and unarmored, built for speed and communications rather than war, we were placed where the pirate's first shots should not be able to reach us.

Spike was disappointed, but I was rather glad. I would rather not risk my life—no matter how well insured.

When the glittering globe of lights on my board showed me that the outlaw fleet was all in place, I hailed the pirate ship:

"Beaconless ship, this is Captain Ah Lee of the *Mercury*. Identify yourself and open your ports to inspection or prepare for the consequences!"

I had deduced—perhaps "hoped" is a more honest term—that the pirate ship would not fire. No matter who had been paid off, no matter how far up the chain of command, none of Endpoint's guard ships could overlook a fire fight right in system and the pirates wouldn't want to attract notice.

To my dismay, the pirate ship fired almost immediately, a thin beam of eye-searingly brilliant light jolting out from forward energy batteries.

The blue-white light melted an ugly runnel through the heavy armor of the ship holding the dangerous post directly in front. Later I'd learn that an engineer had been killed. Even as the energy weapon did its worst, the nameless pirate's gunnery tubes belched forth slower, but more deadly missiles. Energy fire from our own side caught these before they could reach their destination, but I saw that the missiles had been meant merely as a distraction.

On one side of the pirate vessel the enormous bay doors began slowly sliding open. My tactical masters had been ready for something like this. As briefed, I thumbed a precoded message from the *Mercury*'s board, jamming the doors long enough for a barrage from a couple of the prospectors' digging lasers to ruin them beyond use.

Our unarmed ships were maintaining a jamming screen, making it impossible for the pirate ship to call on others of its ilk for help—if any others were near. Based on our pooled observations we thought this unlikely, but still the possibility could not be overlooked.

Having given the pirate a chance to surrender without a fight, now our side attacked. Only four of our outlaw fleet had proved to be heavily armed—all of these mining ships, which could conceal armaments as digging lasers or more domestic explosives. A few other of the outlaws' ships possessed light lasers, these meant more for meteor defense than for battle. Each ship had been assigned its target in advance—points plotted out and selected by tight-beam communication from the moment I sent out an image of our target.

Beneath our initial barrage, the pirate vessel seemed to rock. Burning air gouted forth from several breached compartments; scanner readings showed a loss of power from various systems.

Still, the pirate hulk held up remarkably well. None of the systems we had targeted had been completely destroyed. Engine power remained strong. Even as our ships danced in evasion of expected retaliation, the *Mercury*'s scanners reported that backup systems were coming on-line all over the pirate ship.

In this initial attack, it had been to our fleet's advantage that the *Mercury* had been able to scout ahead, to our advantage as well that none of our number believed we could take a pirate vessel without coordinated effort and planning. In that way, our small flotilla was wiser than marines and militia, for these often underestimated their opponents.

I bit my lip in growing desperation, speaking more to myself than to Spike:

"We can't keep this up for long. None of our ships has the power to keep firing and we don't have a warship's armory. If we don't take the pirate out soon, it will get away and leave us to do the explaining when the black ships arrive."

"The pirates don't know that," Spike said suddenly.

He'd been rather quiet since the real fighting had started, though he'd had plenty to say while the outlaw fleet assembled—some of it useful, too.

"What?" I asked.

"*The pirates* don't know that," Spike repeated with emphasis. "They might suspect our capacities are limited, but not those hop-headed Absolutist fanatics. They aren't going to want to see their treasured Absolute blown into oblivion. Can't you . . ."

"I'm right with you," I said, hands surging over my boards as I worked up something that would splice into the pirate ship's intercom system and override any other messages. "Spike, get on another channel and tell our fleet to prepare for another strike. Don't worry about being overheard. It might be better if we were."

Spike nodded, and moments later I could hear him snapping out orders to the others. We'd all hoped that we'd never need fire a shot, but not one of us had been so optimistic that we didn't plan for a fight. As we hadn't lost a ship—though there had been damage—our second strike could go ahead as programmed.

The most heavily armed of the miner ships—a ship I suspected of doing a bit of small-scale piracy itself when opportunity presented—took the front this time. A red-orange globule was forming on the tips of the forward energy weapons when I broke through the pirate's internal communications.

"This is the commander of the fleet surrounding you," I said, promoting myself shamelessly. "Surrender, else we will destroy you. You have been warned once. We will not be so gentle a second time. Since we want your cargo, not your persons, we will be targeting personnel compartments. No one can expect to survive our next attack."

It was all bluster and balderdash, but I was counting on what Spike had said, counting, too, that the pirates would not be quite certain just what armaments we might have hidden among our motley fleet. After all, their ship looked like nothing more than an ore carrier. What might we be?

"You have a five count to surrender—absolutely," I announced.

The last was a hint to the pirates. Surrender the Absolute, and we'd let the rest pass. Who knows, maybe the pirates would take us for Batherite Loyalists who'd tracked the Absolutist leader into hiding.

I wondered what the rest of the fleet would think.

"Absolutely!" I repeated as thunderously as possible. Then I started counting, "Five! Four! Three!"

On five, the globes of energy forming at the tips of our ships' energy weapons turned white hot. On four, missile tubes rotated, some preparing to vomit forth nothing more than junk—but the pirates didn't know that. On three, I added a bone shivering frequency beneath my vocal track. On two, a thin, panicked voice yelled over a broad band.

"Don't fire! Don't fire! It's over here. In control! We'll surrender! We have everything under control!"

It didn't sound like the speaker had even himself under control, but I heard Spike sonorously address our allies:

"Stand by, fleet. Don't power down. I repeat. Don't power down."

A crackle from another channel—from one of the hermits, I think—reported simultaneously:

"Scan shows no evidence that pirate vessel is powering up. We still hold the advantage."

I addressed the panicked voice. "Identify yourself."

"I'm . . . Jeremy, Jeremy Langthorp. I'm with this ore carrier, the *Deep Pockets,* it is."

"*Deep Pockets,*" I confirmed. "You seem to have pulled your ID beacon, Captain Langthorp."

"I'm not the captain." Langthorp shrilled a thread of near hysterical laughter. "They shot the captain, the fanatics did, shot her soon after they came aboard and she wouldn't drink their foul tea."

Over the next hour, the full story came out. It seemed that when the Absolute and his fanatics had boarded, the pirates found themselves the victims of piracy. Several of the crew had already been bought by the Absolute and these attacked their shipmates. It had been intended that the turncoats would handle the ship while the Absolute did his work in the on-board chemistry lab. Then richer by a ship and a hold full of drugs, the Absolute would have returned to his war.

However, the rest of the crew hadn't been as easily sub-dued as the Absolute had planned. The *Deep Pocket*'s cap-tain had died early on in the take-over, as had her first officer and several others, including over half of the turn-coats. At that point, the rest of the pirates had submitted philosophically, first pointing out to the Absolute that they couldn't run the ship with their brains turned to goo by one of his "teas."

Jeremy Langthorp had been the chief gunnery officer— and cook when there was no shooting to do—and although he had ordered the first volley against our fleet, he had de-layed a second strike, claiming that some of his systems had been damaged.

Then my announcement had thrown the fanatics into a panic—even the Absolute, who had not realized to that point what danger he'd put himself in.

While the fanatics were dithering, the remaining pirates had counterattacked. The fanatics had retreated into the chemistry lab where the pirates had imprisoned them—presumably with the Absolute.

"My shipmates and I are ready to surrender," Jeremy Langthorp said. "Ready and willing if you'll promise us safe delivery to Gilbert."

"Where, doubtless, they have some crooked lawyer ready to get them off," I grumbled to Spike. Then I asked Langthorp directly, "How many of you are left?"

"Four," Langthorp replied promptly, "not counting the fanatics in the chemistry lab."

Spike gave me one of his lopsided grins. "I guess it's time for me to take over, Captain Ah Lee. You've done your part."

Standing, Spike crowded the *Mercury*'s tiny cabin, but he managed to get his blaster—a showy metallic blue model with a chromed grip and holographic insets along the barrel—out of his coverall pocket.

"Coming with me, Captain?" he asked, holding the blaster at a jaunty angle.

I sighed. "Let me see who else can go over to *Deep Pockets* with you. I don't quite trust the pirates. We only have their word that there are just four left."

"I trust Langthorp," Spike said. "There was real fear in that man's voice, but I suppose I could use a few extra hands to help defeat the fanatics."

Rolling my eyes at his supreme overconfidence, I beamed a request to the other ships.

Remembering various conversations over poker in spaceport bars, I figured that while many of the smugglers might be apolitical regarding the Batherite question, there was enough resentment over how the pirates had used the refugees as cover for their own operations to attract a posse—especially now that we had taken *Deep Pockets* and the promise of loot was sweet and near.

With very little persuasion on my part, a volunteer from every ship agreed to go aboard *Deep Pockets*—as long as I went, too. Poor Spike's feelings were hurt, but I reassured him as I suited up.

"It isn't you, Spike. They trust you—remember, they came on your promise of payment. It's just that I got them into this and they're going to make sure I'm in as deep as they are."

"Code of the underworld?" Spike asked, checking his own suit's seals.

"Something like that," I muttered.

Jeremy Langthorp, a short, fairly heavyset man with curly hair the color of sunlit sand and washed-out blue eyes, met us at the entry port. He looked more like a well-fed cook than the popular action vid depiction of a pirate and I could tell that Spike was disappointed.

"Where are the fanatics holing up?" Spike asked as soon as routine introductions had been made and four members of our posse had peeled off to discretely cover the pirates.

"Chem lab," Langthorp said. He tapped up a schematic on a view screen. "When we took this job, we adapted part of the factory deck to a lab. It's the only thing down there except for our cargo."

"So we can't," I said quickly, just in case Spike was about to suggest it, "blow out that deck without damaging the cargo."

"That's about it," Langthorp agreed, his round face rueful. Clearly, the pirates had considered the idea and had decided that whatever punishment their own higher up doled out for losing a cargo were worse than being doped by the fanatics.

"The bulkheads?" asked Beatty, one of the prospectors.

"Armor grade," Langthorp said. "Goes back to when *Deep Pockets* was an ore carrier."

Beatty nodded sharply. "Then we can't hope to cut through with any speed. Can we just shut off life support to that deck?"

Langthorp didn't hesitate at this brutal suggestion, but I saw Spike wince.

"Could," Langthorp agreed, "but they have suits and the chem lab has both scrubbers and extra air. The Absolute ordered them 'cause he said he preferred to mix his potions on a big scale and didn't want to risk soaking up the stuff through his skin."

"Whether or not that's the case," I said, forestalling a debate as to the Absolute's real motives, "we can't get them that way, not before the black ships get here."

" And if we want to get paid quickly," Beatty said, "we don't wait."

"Right." I frowned and studied the diagram. "If I had time, I could try and override the bulkhead locks, but we don't have time for that. I only see one solution that's both fast and has a chance to work. The ducts."

Spike nodded. "I didn't want to suggest it, Allie. It's above and beyond the call of duty."

I shrugged. "But I'm the only one small enough to crawl through while wearing a suit. Spike, you still have those gas pellets?"

The insurance investigator produced them rather reluctantly.

"They won't work if the fanatics are suited," he warned.

"I know," I said, "but I'm betting that they won't all be sealed tight. A sealed suit gets pretty claustrophobic if you're not used to it, and those poor slobs I watched back in the Bathtub weren't spacers."

Beatty had been studying the diagram, his finger tracing the blue lines of the ductwork for the benefit of the rest.

"It's gonna get snug, Allie," he warned.

"When you've only got one ace," I said, glad that my deadpan expression didn't betray my pounding heart, "you've got to bet it or fold."

Crawling through those conduits is something I don't really want to remember, so I won't share the nightmare here. If it hadn't been for Spike keeping me on course through my suit radio, I'd have probably gotten disoriented, but eventually, I made it to the chem lab.

Through the filter grille, I looked down on the Absolute and his fanatics—twenty in all. Only a third—including the Absolute, I was sorry to see—were sealed in their suits.

After sending this information to Spike and the others—who were waiting outside both of the entries to the chem lab—I started dropping gas pellets.

With his sense for the dramatic, Spike had chosen pellets that sent up theatrical swirls of dark purple smoke. This brand did work faster than any other type on the market, so within a few moments the fanatics in the unsealed suits were puffing and wheezing. A few fumbled for faceplates and seals. Most of the rest just dropped, taken off into deep purple dreams.

"Gas!" shouted the Absolute. "Cover the entry ports!"

He was smaller than I'd guessed from news coverage, but his voice made him seem a giant. I wondered if he had some sort of hypnotics implant because I found myself relieved to realize I was already heading that way—though from behind the wall.

I radioed my guess to the others, suggesting they switch off any external sound reception.

A fanatic now covered the duct through which I'd dropped the pellets, but I was sliding toward an opening closer to the floor. It was a squeeze, but I made it, ending up flat on my stomach, but with my arms free and in front of me. From here I had a clear view of two sets of closed and locked doors. With another wriggle, I managed to get a slim, high-powered energy pistol out of my sleeve holster.

Without bothering to remove the duct cover, I squeezed off a beam targeting the lock mechanism. Beatty—confirming my guess that he did a little piracy in his spare time—had assured me that a direct hit would cause the door to unlock.

When I fired, the fanatics jumped back from the explosion of heat and light, spinning to see where the shot had come from. They didn't have time to come after me. My buddies were forcing the door open and giving them lots to think about.

As much as I wanted to watch, I shifted my attention to the second door and fired again. When that door was opened, I started kicking. With my cover blown, I was like a cork in a bottle and I didn't want to be stuck there if someone got a moment to give the cork a pull.

By the time I had struggled free, the fight was over. It hadn't been easy for all its speed. We'd lost two and several more were wounded—including Spike who had a nasty burn along one arm—but we had won.

Spike stood over the collapsed Absolute, blaster in hand, his triumphant pose balanced by an expression of wide-eyed shock as he looked at the carnage. Several of the fanatics had gone killer-crazy and now their internal organs were splattered on the bulkheads. The rest had been taken prisoner and were being herded to a makeshift brig.

My leg muscles still cramped, I staggered over to Spike. "Get to, man. See a medic," I said, taking the blaster from him. "We've still got work to do."

"Gotcha, Allie," he said. When he managed one of those funny grins, I knew he'd be all right.

While rapid repairs were made to those of our ships that

had taken damage during that first barrage, the *Deep Pockets* was stripped to the very dust in her hold. Spike, recovered somewhat now, stood by the exit port, taking pictures of the goods for later identification and research into the pirates' activities.

Spike claimed the *Deep Pockets* as AASU's cut and no one was complaining, not with the rich haul from her hold as compensation. Spike had declared that the booty—which if insured by AASU now legally belonged to the company— was being awarded as payment for services rendered.

Jeremy Langthorp and his surviving shipmates were offered the choice of waiting in the brig or parole to work the ship. Wisely, they offered their parole. They knew their chances of escape were nil. Already, several of the black ships were approaching and some out-system traffic was drifting in our direction. Cooperation would help their case.

Despite Spike's assurances that they were safe from arrest, the various members of our outlaw fleet chose to depart before the black ships arrived. I itched to join them, not liking the Silent Watch a bit, but I kept telling myself I had nothing to fear from them. This time I was an official insurance investigator.

Then I remembered. Spike had his own ship now. My job was done. My own ship's tiny hold was full of perfectly legal goods that I could sell elsewhere for a tidy profit. Why should I wait around?

I grinned, gunned the *Mercury*'s engines, and surged off into interstellar space, Endpoint's sun glowing over my shoulder.

Science Fiction Anthologies

☐ **STAR COLONIES**

    Martin H. Greenberg and John Helfers, editors 0-88677-894-1—$6.99
Let Jack Williamson, Alan Dean Foster, Mike Resnick, Pamela Sargent, Dana
Stabenow and others take you to distant worlds where humans seek to make
new homes—or to exotic places where aliens races thrive.

☐ **ALIEN ABDUCTIONS**

    Martin H. Greenberg and Larry Segriff, editors 0-88677-856-5—$6.99
Prepare yourself for a close encounter with these eleven original tales of
alien experiences and their aftermath. By authors such as Alan Dean
Foster, Michelle West, Ed Gorman, Peter Crowther, and Lawrence Watt-
Evans.

☐ **MOON SHOTS**

    Peter Crowther, editor   0-88677-848-4—$6.99
July 20, 1969: a date that will live in history! In honor of the destiny-
altering mission to the Moon, these original tales were created by some
of today's finest SF writers, such as Ben Bova, Gene Wolfe, Brian Aldiss,
Alan Dean Foster, and Stephen Baxter.

☐ **MY FAVORITE SCIENCE FICTION STORY**

    Martin H. Greenberg, editor   0-88677-830-1—$6.99
Here is a truly unique volume, comprised of seminal science fiction stories
specifically chosen by some of today's top science fiction names. With stories
by Sturgeon, Kornbluth, Waldrop, and Zelazny, among others, chosen by such
modern-day masters as Clarke, McCaffrey, Turtledove, Bujold, and Willis.